WEIRD TALES

Weird Tales

Best of the Early Years: 1926–1927

EDITED BY

Jonathan Maberry and Kaye Lynne Booth

Weird Tales
Best of the Early Years: 1926-1927

Edited by Jonathan Maberry and Kaye Lynne Booth

Foreword copyright © 2022 by Jonathan Maberry

Original publication information at end of book. These stories are in the public domain.

Weird Tales logo used with permission.

EBook ISBN: 978-1-68057-381-7
Trade Paperback ISBN: 978-1-68057-380-0
Hardcover ISBN: 978-1-68057-382-4

Cover design by Janet McDonald.

Published by WordFire Press, LLC
PO Box 1840
Monument CO 80132
Kevin J. Anderson & Rebecca Moesta, Publishers

WordFire Press Edition 2022

Printed in the USA

Join our WordFire Press Readers Group for new projects, and giveaways. Sign up at wordfirepress.com

Contents

Foreword: Writers Are Weird

Jonathan Maberry

Writers are weird.

Yes, I know, what a news flash. Who would ever have thought?

So, on one hand, anyone who sits alone in a room, making up outrageous lies in the hopes someone pays them to do so, and acts very much like the semi-benign god of their own universe is a bit odd.

On the other hand, some writers are on the "nice and safe" end of that spectrum, and others are way the hell over into the 'there's something wrong with that one' zone. Not that these more extreme writers are dangers to society or are antisocial misanthropes who should be on watch lists. It's not like that at all. In fact, except in a few notable cases, the writer is seldom an obvious champion of the genre in which he or she writes.

Stephen King, for example, is a pretty nice chap. I had a lovely conversation with him and his charming wife, Tabby, at the Edgar Awards banquet back in 2007. It was the year he was receiving the honor of Grandmaster. We talked writing, baseball, family, blues music, and cars. At no point did spurting blood, unspeakable horrors, or ghouls from beyond come up in that conversation. Same thing when I first met Peter Straub. I believed we talked 19th-century mystery literature. I talked about the evolution of the publishing industry in the post-digital world with Anne Rice; and on a very long call with George Romero, the writer-director of the landmark *Night of the Living Dead*, we talked about our favorite reality competition TV shows. He was a fan of *Project Runway*. And that, in itself, is weird.

Fans often think that the story and the storyteller are two sides of the same coin. If that's true, then I recommend that anyone who holds to that pull out a quarter and look at both sides. Different images, different themes, different design philosophies.

Writers are like that.

What we write comes from a lot of different sources. Usually, it begins with something we've read—a novel, short story, or comic book—or something we've seen on TV, a movie screen, or on stage.

For my part, to give an example, I had a creepy grandmother. Not bad creepy—she didn't lure children into her gingerbread house, though I would have nominated some jerks from my neighborhood— but was closer to, say, Luna Lovegood from the Harry Potter books. She believed in everything. Ghosts, vampires, werewolves, night haunts, demons, witches, crisis apparitions and all the rest. She was a child of the late 19th century (aged forty when my mother was born; and eighty-one when my mother had me in 1958) and was born in Alsace-Lorraine on the border of Germany and France, but with strong Scottish forebears. She was a rural kid in a world as unlike our contemporary one as the surface of Mars is to the Amazonian rain forest. Her house was filled with books in five languages, maps of exotic places, black cats, raptor birds she'd nursed back to health, countless decks of tarot cards, crystals for gazing, and abstract paintings that made no sense to anyone but her.

I loved her to pieces.

It was she who introduced me to what she called the "larger world." But she encouraged me to do more than just indulge in old tales of things that creep through the shadows. She pushed me to read the anthropology and psychology, so I understood why people believed what they believed. My older sisters were deeply creeped out by her. I was her biggest fan. Then, and now, even though she passed, at age 101, when I was still in my twenties.

I was exposed to the folkloric monsters before I even met the literary ones. The connective tissue there is that by considering why people believed in monsters—and what those beliefs meant to them— I was able to more clearly understand why writers were drawn to write about them. Since I always wanted to be a writer pretty much since I was an embryo, understanding the "why" of it mattered.

Roll forward to when I was an avid reader and as-yet unpublished writer, I would gobble up interviews with authors to try and get inside their heads. I wanted to know why they chose the genres they did, how they took that genre and bent it to their will, and how they managed to craft tales that were uniquely and compellingly their own. Funnily enough, the introductions to anthologies and short story collections were often a great source of insight into these writers. Nowadays up-and-coming writers get a lot of the same juice from panels at genre conventions, podcasts, interviews, TikTok and YouTube subscriptions, and social media posts. Same effect.

Along a similar line, the genre and/or thematic path some writers take are chosen because a doorway opens up and, if there is success in terms of a sale, money, good feedback, and the potential for more of the same, often the writer keeps driving in that lane. I, for example, never intended or wanted to write fiction for teens. But a novella I wrote for Christopher Golden's *New Dead* anthology—which was marketed exclusively to adult readers—somehow put me on the YA radar. My agent took that story out and suddenly I had a multi-book deal—the biggest of my career to that point—for post-apocalyptic zombie novels for kids. The first in that series, *Rot & Ruin,* is required reading in hundreds of schools and remains my biggest-selling book. And I wound up writing six sequels.

When opportunity knocks, sometimes you invite it for more than a cup of coffee. Sometimes it pulls a Gandalf and invites you along for quite a long and unexpected adventure.

And, sometimes a publisher, an editor, an agent, or a magazine becomes a kind of magnetic lighthouse, in that it shines so brightly you take notice, and it pulls you toward it.

Weird Tales was that for a lot of writers. A hell of lot of them. Some you've never heard of, some who were one-shot wonders, and some who not only yielded to that magnetic pull...but ran toward it like Olympic sprinters.

With the stories collected in this volume and its companion *(Weird Tales: Best of the Early Years 1923-25)*, we get a snapshot of young writers, largely or completely unknown at the time, who went on to become key figures in genre fiction.

The careers of some key contributors are inextricably tied to *Weird Tales.* The two that most quickly spring to mind are Robert E. Howard and H.P. Lovecraft.

Howard was a brash young man from Texas who created some of fictions most enduring, if brutish, heroes. Conan the Cimmerian is by far the most famous, and arguably the most famous character ever to emerge from our pages. Conan became a household name because of the enormous success of the Lancer Books reprints of the Conan stories—including many that were originally written about *other* characters but revised by L. Sprague de Camp and Lin Carter—and the box-office success of Arnold Schwarzenegger's films, *Conan the Barbarian* and *Conan the Destroyer.* Sadly, Howard was a troubled person and took his own life in the mid-1930s, but his legacy lives on. Various publishers hired a bevy of top writers to pen new Conan tales —including Andrew J. Offut, Karl Edward Wagner, John C. Hocking, Sean A. Moore, Poul Anderson, Leonard Carpenter, Steve Perry, John M. Roberts, Roland Green, Harry Turtledove (leading creator of the alt-history sub-genre) and Robert Jordan (author of the magnificent *Wheel of Time* novels, now on cable). And Marvel Comics established a long-running and wildly popular *Conan the Barbarian* comic book that ran for 275 issues, with Roy Thomas writing the first 115 issues.

Howard would go on to write fifty-four stories for *Weird Tales* before, sadly, he took his own life.

As for Lovecraft, he was a moody writer from Providence, Rhode

Island who took elements of cosmic horror first established by Robert W. Chambers in his disturbing 1895 book, *The King in Yellow,* and greatly expanded upon it. The sheer scale of Lovecraft's vision is incalculable. And he did something unique that echoes a century later—he invited other writers to take his story elements and use it for their own works. That opened a floodgate of new cosmic horror stories—variously known as "Lovecraftian" or the "Cthulhu Mythos" (if those writers borrowed certain specific characters). The list of writers then and since who have penned these kinds of stories would likely fill every single page of this book, front and back. And, no, that's not really an exaggeration.

Every year there are new anthologies of Lovecraftian stories, and the writers are a who's who of pop culture. To give you just a taste, here are some key players in no particular order: August Derleth, Robert Bloch, Clark Ashton Smith, Jorge Luis Borges, Michel Houellebecq, Brian Lumley, Thomas Ligotti, Frank Belknap Long, Fritz Leiber, T.E.D. Kelin, Colin Wilson, Joanna Russ, Mike Mignola, Christopher Golden, Richard A. Lupps, Roger Zelazny, George Alec Effinger, Phillip Jose Farmer, Ramsey Campbell, James Chambers, Gergory Frost, Basil Copper, David Conyers, Lindsay Ellis, Philip José Farmer, Sonia Greene, Lois Gresh, S.T. Joshi, Henry Kuttner, Graham Masterton, China Miéville, Joanna Russ, Carrie Cuinn, Brian Stableford, Akihiro Yamada, Victor LaValle, Matt Ruff, Jonathan L. Howard, Ruthanna Emrys, Nick Mamatas, Edward Lee, Khurt Have, L. Sprague de Camp, Lin Carter, John Langan, David Wong, Ted E, Grau, Ron Marz, Jeff VanDerMeer, Gemma Files, Alan Moore, Laird Barron, David Drake, Caitlín R. Kiernan, Junju Ito, Joe Hill, Josh Malerman, Brett Talley, John Hornor Jacobs, Algernon Blackwood, Ruthanna Emrys, Peter Clines, Jim Butcher, Nick Cutter, Joe R. Lansdale, Richard F. Searight, Hugh B. Cave, Gordon Linzner, J. G. Ballard, William S. Burroughs, F. Paul Wilson, Gene Wolfe, Harlan Ellison, Alan Dean Foster, Thomas F. Monteleone, Tim Lebbon, Richard Laymon, Yvonne Navarro, Poppy Z. Brite, Weston Ochse, Brian Hodge, Elizabeth Bear, Cherie Priest, Tim Pratt, Joh Shirley, David J. Schow, Molly Tanzer, Michael Chabon, Cody Goodfellow,

Tum Curran, Steve Rasnic Tem, Carrie Vaughn, Neil Gaiman, and Stephen King.

And again I say...that's just a snapshot.

Lovecraft's contributions to *Weird Tales* included forty-nine stories written on his own, but he also did another four in collaboration with friends and colleagues. There are a number of stories for which he did revisions and others he ghost-wrote, and even now that exact count is in debate.

Both Howard and Lovecraft made indelible marks on the magazine, and that, in turn impacted the whole of horror, science fiction, and fantasy fiction that is felt strongly to this day.

Countless authors graced *Weird Tales* with stories that were not tied to Lovecraft, however. One of the things that made *Weird Tales* so popular with writers as well as readers is the career building. The editors not only published stories by established "names," but went out of their way to find newer writers, and in many cases writers with new characters, and they would cultivate that. A lot of landmark characters and story set-ups were born in those pages. Swords & Sorcery fiction, which existed in an uncategorized way prior to *Weird Tales*, became a certified genre. The Conan tales of Robert E. Howard were a huge part of that, as well as his tales featuring other popular and enduring brawny heroes who first drew swords in those pages, such as Kull, King of Atlantis; the brooding puritan swordsman, Solomon Kane, and the wise and fearless Pict, Bran Mak Morn.

C.L. Moore created the sub-genre of female swords and sorcery with her Jirel of Joiry character. Seabury Quinn's crafted over ninety adventures of occult detective Jules de Grandin, many of which resulted in some of the more racy and lurid cover stories (often with artwork by the legendary Margaret Brundage). Two of his stories are included in this volume.

Other writers in those early issues made huge splashes with readers as well.

A. Merrit, one of several *Weird Tales* writers who was later inducted into the Science Fiction Museum and Hall of Fame, and his 1926 story, *The Woman in the Woods* (included here) was voted by readers as the most popular tale of that issue. He went on to write many excellent works of prose and poetry.

Robert Bloch, author of *Psycho,* made into a film by Alfred Hitchcock, is often credited with creating the slasher genre. He contributed fifty-four absolutely compelling stories for the magazine, many of which have been staples of reprint anthologies ever since.

August W. Derleth, who's "Bat's Belfry" was one of the first *Weird Tales* stories I ever read, and the tale that introduced me to his oeuvre, is included here. He was a friend and correspondent of Lovecraft's, and it was Derleth (not, as many people insist, Lovecraft) who coined the phrase "Cthulhu Mythos." And he was the first to collect Lovecraft's stories following that author's death. Derleth was a prolific writer and one of the earliest authors of popular pastiche fiction with his amusing and entertaining "Solar Pons" stories that had fun with and yet honored Sir Arthur Conan Doyle's legendary Sherlock Holmes. He is also the writer who sold the most stories to the magazine...a whopping 101!

Edmund Hamilton, best known for his Captain Future stories, was also a fan favorite who penned seventy-six tales, often with a strong science fiction bias. And one of his earliest tales, "The Atomic Conquerors," included here, is an alien invasion story with a real twist.

Poet and prose author, H. Warner Munn, was a meticulous craftsman of fiction who got his real start with a pair of stories that appeared in early issues of *Weird Tales.* "The Werewolf of Ponkert," which is in the companion volume to this one; and the creepy "A City of Spiders" in this book. He wrote for a number of pulps, including *Argosy, Air Wonder Stories, Astounding,* and *Amazing Stories,* but much of his most inspired work was for *Weird Tales.*

Manly Wade Wellman, remembered as the king of Appalachian horror and fantasy, wrote thirty-nine tales for the magazine, including this volume's "Back to the Beast," which takes a bit of inspiration from H.G. Wells' *Island of Doctor Moreau.* He would go on to write folkloric fantasy tales featuring Silver John, John Thunstone, and others, largely at the request of his literary agent, Oscar J. Friend, who was a partner in the Otis Kline Literary Agency. A pair of Kline's creepy tales are included in the companion volume out of the nine he wrote for the magazine. Wellman was also a popular writer in what is now called the "young adult" genre.

Interestingly, Otis Adelbert Kline and Oscar J. Friend—apart from being pulp writers and editors themselves—represented many of the authors who wrote for *Weird Tales*. And that list includes Ray Bradbury (who wrote four stories), Wellman, and Robert E. Howard.

E. Hoffman Price, who, alas, has mostly been forgotten today, wrote two dozen stories for *Weird Tales*. He was a fan, friend, and avid correspondent with Lovecraft, and their plans to create a kind of literary supergroup—since they were both high output writers—was never realized because of Lovecraft's death. It's rather delightful that this volume contains a pair of Price's stories, each showcasing different aspects of his considerable skill. Included in this volume are "The Peacocks Shadow" and "Saladin's Throng Rug".

And we can't forget Frank Belknap Long, a beloved, prolific, and versatile writer of short stories, novels, poetry, essays, nonfiction, and plays over his seventy-plus year career. He wrote twenty-eight stories for the magazine and got his start in the writing business in *Weird Tales*. One of his later works for the title, *The Hounds of Tindalos*, is regarded as a masterpiece, but there's a whole lot to love in the story we present here, *"The Dog-Eared God."*

As with the list of writers who penned Lovecraftian fiction, the list of amazing storytellers who graced the early pages of *Weird Tales* goes on and on. And that right there is part of the reason no one wants the magazine to fade into obscurity. It's why we've brought it back, why we worked out a deal with Blackstone to launch a new Weird Tales Presents novel imprint, and why the bright young creatives at Western Colorado University have worked with us at *Weird Tales* to curate these two volumes of stories from nearly a century ago. Too much literary history is tied to *Weird Tales* to let it be a footnote. Too many careers were launched or propelled forward in that magazine's pages. *Weird Tales* is one of the Great Wonders of the modern literary world. Without doubt or fear of contradiction.

So, settle back and turn the page and let the weirdness sweep over you and through you.

And...never be afraid to be weird.

—Jonathan Maberry
Editor of *Weird Tales Magazine*
San Diego, 2022

The PEACOCK'S SHADOW

By E. Hoffmann Price

M on Vieux, what do you say to a bit of housebreaking?"

This, from Pierre d'Artois, a gentleman of France and a master of the sword, seemed unusual, to say the least.

"Well, why not?" I agreed, not to be outdone by the d'Artois nonchalance. "But whose house do we invade? What the devil, do you fear I will become homesick if from time to time there is not something to remind me of my own native land of liberty?"

"*Mais non!* No, we are not going as prohibition agents. Not at all! And it is no ordinary house into which we are to break. We invade the château of Monsieur the Marquis de la Tour de Maracq," announced Pierre as he stepped on the accelerator of his favorite car, the Issotta roadster.

"But what of Monsieur the Marquis?" I suggested with what seemed to be a touch of reason.

"He is very busy at Biarritz at a fencing tournament."

Well, this solved one riddle: I now knew why d'Artois, that fierce old *ferrailleur*, had overlooked a chance to demonstrate his exquisite mastery of the sword.

"But, *mon Pierre*, what of the housebreaking? What loot are we after?" I ventured as we cleared Pont de Mousserole and left behind us the gray battlements of Bayonne.

"The truth of it is, I am playing what you call the hunch," he evaded, then continued: "But he is the good hunch. There has been an elopement, and it is for me to locate the lady."

Worse and worse yet! A quiet month in Bayonne.

"Who is the girl?" D'Artois laughed.

"A princess, and the daughter of a king."

"Not bad for a marquis. And young and beautiful?" I retorted to the mockery I saw in his keen old eyes.

"Beautiful, yes. If you like such beauty. But young, no. In fact, older than I am."

"The devil!"

"The truth! Thirty-seven hundred years old at least."

This was too much!

"Mais non. I do not jest," continued Pierre. "She was stolen from the Guimet museum of Lyons and carried all the way to the château of the marquis."

"Well, and that is a case for the police, is it not?"

"No. For one is not really certain; it is but strongly suspected that he accomplished the almost impossible feat of looting the museum and carrying the mummy to his château. Monsieur the Prefect of Police, not being any too sure of himself, has taken me into his confidence and asked me to investigate unofficially. A false move would ruin him, since Monsieur the Marquis is a man of influence."

"But why should anyone steal a mummy, especially de la Tour de Maracq, who is rich as an Indian prince, and of a house as old as Charlemagne?"

"A scholar, a soldier, a man of letters," enumerated d'Artois, continuing my thought, "and a fantastic madman, if this report is correct. He is too talented for sanity."

"Even as yourself," I hinted.

"Touché!" acknowledged d'Artois. "But I do not elope with ladies 3700 years old."

He fingered a pack of *Bastos*, but thinking better of so foul a deed, decided to light the Coronado I had given him.

"All very quaint. But let's get to facts," I urged. "What have you to work on in this love affair?"

"I have the good hunch. And it is more of a love affair than you realize."

Which was logical enough. Those whom gold could not tempt, might indeed steal objects of art, jewels over which to gloat in secret, a relic, an antique rug, but a shriveled mummy! Well, tastes vary.

And the case should be simple of solution, at least as regarded the marquis; for the missing lady could not be concealed with any degree of facility. A simple matter of walking or climbing into the château and leaving again with our princess; or else reporting that she was not to be found, and that Monsieur the Marquis was not her abductor. A jewel could be hidden; but a mummy ...

———

The château was perched upon a crest some hundred meters off the road. We parked the Issotta and proceeded on foot.

Instead of knocking at the door, as seemed to be his intent, despite his quip about housebreaking, d'Artois selected a key from his ring, tried it; selected another, picked at the lock, but to no avail. The third, however, was applied with more success; the heavy door yielded to his touch, admitting us into a vestibule, thence to a salon.

"Welcome to Tour de Maracq," murmured d'Artois with a courtly bow. "Quick about it, and we'll be out of here long before he has fought his last bout."

"But the servants?" I suggested.

"They are few in number. It seems the marquis has an aversion to women, so that there are no female domestics to contend with. Thus, it is that one of the *ménage* has gone to Bayonne to negotiate with a stranger who sought to buy some rare vintages which are to be pilfered from the master's cellars. Another is keeping a rendezvous with a demoiselle who hailed him a week ago and made an engagement for today. Each has some illicit engagement whereof he will not babble. Now it would have been inconvenient to arrange on short order for lovers for any female servants. Praise be to the eccentricity of Monsieur the Marquis!"

I noted the rich tapestries; the massive teakwood furniture; the floor of rare hardwoods partly masked by Chinese and Indian rugs. And on the walls were arms of infinite variety: wavy-bladed kresses, kampilans, simitars; halberds, assegai, lances; maces and battle-axes in endless number, all grouped in clusters. Some of these arms were burnished, but many bore dark, ominous stains.

And thus, we roamed through the house, from one apartment to another, I am wondering at the beauty, the grotesquerie, the oddness of the furnishings and adornments, d'Artois regarding all with an appraising glance that revealed nothing of whatever interest he might have felt.

Strange gods in bronze and onyx and basalt glared at us, brandished their distorted arms in futile rage, mouthed threats with their twisted lips; resented our presence in every way possible to inanimate things; inanimate, yes, but enlivened with the spiritual essence absorbed from their centuries of devotees. But no mummies. Nevertheless, d'Artois studied his surroundings. But nothing seemed to arouse his interest, until ...

"Ah...look!"

He indicated a tiny *darabukeh*, a small kettledrum whose body was of grotesque carven wood, its head of a strange hide–strange to me, at least.

"Curious, yes. But what has this to do with mummies?"

"Nothing at all. But I fancied that drumhead ..."

A smile concluded his remark. Now what the devil significance had that little tom-tom?

"But no mummies, Pierre."

"True. But one can picture a man's mind from the house he keeps. Fancy then the odd brain that twists in the skull of de la Tour de Maracq!"

And thus, room by room, we searched the château proper,

servants' quarters, basements, passages and all. Toward the end of our tour, we stumbled upon a stairway which led to an apartment which we had overlooked.

It was a large room of contradictory appearance: a study, if one judged from its desk, table, bookcases; a bedroom, surely, if gaged by the lordly canopied bed of antique workmanship; or a museum, if one drew conclusions from the ornaments.

As we had done in the salon, we found again a collection of arms, armor, polycephalous gods with contorted limbs and features. And this time, mummies, two of them: one in its sycamore case, the other, not only encased, but enshrined in its massive granite sarcophagus.

Naturally I was exultant.

"Useless!" exclaimed Pierre. "See how they fit their cases; and see also that none of the cases would fit the princess we seek."

With a tape he laid off the dimensions of the mummy we sought, showing clearly that those present were of greater stature.

"Not so good, Pierre, not so good. Apparently, we're stuck."

"Not entirely," muttered Pierre absent-mindedly.

I saw him examining an *épée*, a slim, three-edged dueling sword. The pommel, which was adorned with a tiny silver peacock, seemed to fascinate d'Artois. Which was natural enough, Pierre being a connoisseur of the sword, and its undisputed master. Still, business was business....

A dried, mummified human head, wrinkled and shrunken, a Patagonian relic, hung by its hair from a cluster of arrows. And this, attracting my eye to the library table over which that gruesome trophy hung, drew me to the table itself. I picked up from the inestimable Kurdish rug which covered its top a thick book, leatherbound, and emblazoned with a peacock.

"Hell's fire! It's bound in human skin!"

"So it is," agreed Pierre. "I wondered how long it would take you to recognize human hide when it was tanned. You passed up that little drum without noticing it."

And then Pierre thumbed the pages, began to read to himself. Glancing over his shoulder, I saw that he well spared himself the trouble of reading aloud. The book was either in Arabic or Persian, neither of which I could understand.

As Pierre read, and fumed, and muttered, apparently quite interested, I devoted myself to the one bright spot in that necrophagous apartment: a painting in oils, a portrait of a young woman, lovely beyond all description, with smoldering, Babylonic eyes, full, delicately sensuous lips; fine features whose every line and curve bespoke calm, aristocratic insolence. And this smiled from a cluster of swords and was enshrined in an atmosphere of death and doom, and gruesome relics! Whether or not the kidnapper of a mummy, this marquis was surely a freak.

Pierre's smile, as he laid down the book he had been reading, resembled that of a cat who has just had a pleasant *tête-à-tête* with the canary. Whether the worthy marquis had expressed his unusual humor by having a book of Arabic jests bound in human hide, I couldn't say, but Pierre seemed on the inside of something which had been evading him.

The portrait caught his eye.

"Very lovely. Yes, I met her, twenty years ago, shortly before her untimely death. His last mistress."

Death ... death ... even that loveliness enshrined by morbid trophies was itself a memento of death. I shuddered, chilled, despite the sun's slanting rays which warmed and illumined that necrophiliac room.

"And he sleeps here. Or is this but an antique, a decoration?"

I glanced again at the lordly bed, half expecting to find festoons of skulls about the canopy, fringes of scalp locks, strands of teeth. Then I noted an unnatural curvature of the drawn curtains, something which forced them forward, and out of their natural drape.

"*Que diable!* Another mummy! And no case to match."

D'Artois took from his vest pocket his tapeline, took measurements, compared them with his notebook; studied the wrappings, the markings.

"The very lady!"

I advanced to pick up the aged beauty. Simplicity, this quest. And this, after all Pierre's halo of mystery!

"*Jamais! Pas du tout!* We must locate the case; all or nothing. If we alarm him, who knows what may happen to the case? *Allons!*"

But before leaving, he paused to regard once more the portrait of the girl with the Babylonic eyes.

"That was a lovely little *épée*, that one with the peacock on its pommel. It seems strangely familiar ... well, and since the marquis has probably fought his last bout and is on his way back, we leave opportunely," remarked d'Artois, as the Issotta's long nose headed toward Bayonne.

———

At Place de Théâtre we parked, found a table on the paving, well within the shade of the awning. D'Artois called for a weird favorite of his, whose two ingredients he himself mixed, and then diluted with charged water: a milky, curiously flavored drink, Anis del Oso and Cordiale Gentiane, a suave, insipid madhouse in a slim, tall glass. The springs of the Isle of Patmos must have flowed with Anis del Oso!

As we sipped and smoked, I noted the great limousine of Monsieur the Marquis de la Tour de Maracq draw up to the curbing, returning from Biarritz. Lean, aquiline-featured, elegant and courtly in bearing, and haughty as Lucifer was the Marquis. Touching the brim of his high hat with the head of his stick, he acknowledged the salute of the footman, then handed from the limousine a woman whose features, to say the very least, startled me.

"What in—!"

"No, *mon cher*," murmured d'Artois, "she is no ghost, though she may be the reincarnation of the lady whose portrait we saw at Château Maracq. There is no telling what deviltry the marquis has worked in his day, but this is a flesh-and-blood woman. And now do you see a light?"

"A light? What in the world has she to do with this mummy?"

D'Artois laughed maliciously.

"I'll swear you have mummies on the brain! But just wait. Well, that is Mademoiselle Lili Allzaneau of 34 rue Lachepaillet. Like her scriptural counterpart, she lives on the city wall in an apartment overlooking the park."

Which last was of course superfluous: for the mention of her address was quite sufficient. Yet La Belle Allzaneau bore the stamp of the thoroughbred: the patrician insolence, the smoldering Babylonic eyes, long, narrow, veiled; the slim, gracious hands of a princess of the blood. And her dress, and her figure, and her bearing were all in accord. Behold the *grand dame* of the château, and her double, La Belle Allzaneau of rue Lachepaillet!

———

A few days elapsed, during which Pierre left me to my own devices. And then, emerging from his preoccupation, he sought relaxation in a stroll which took us along the Adour, around, and back to the ramparts of Lachepaillet.

To our right was the Gate of Spain, its drawbridge and guardhouse; far beneath us, at the foot of the city walls, on whose parapet we sat, was the bottom of the dry moat; while to our left front, across the moat and a hundred meters beyond its outer bank, was the Spring of St. Leon and the cluster of ancient trees that half concealed it. Though their crests almost met, their trunks were widely separated, so that the spring and its low, hemispherical cupola were in a small clearing.

The sun was setting. Long shadows marched slowly across the gently rolling ground beneath us, and to our front. Pierre d'Artois, as he took from his case and lit a villainous *Bastos*, stared at the Spring of St. Leon. And then he resumed the thread of his rambling discourse, continuing a tale he had so often before begun and abruptly abandoned.

"With that lunge I could have impaled the devil himself, for I had him swinging like a windmill, skillful swordsman though he was. Yes, and had it really been Monsieur the Devil himself, and not Santiago with whom I crossed swords, I still hold that someone must have struck me down from the rear to save his lord and master!"

He spoke of his secret duel by moonlight with Santiago the Spaniard, two years ago, in the small clearing by this very Spring of St. Leon, and of the outcome of the affair: how, as after hard, fierce fighting he had slipped through the Spaniard's guard to impale him with a thrust to the chest, there had been an awful flare of elemental flame, followed by blackness and oblivion; how Jannicot, his servant, had come in search of him, carried him back to the car; and how, on the return trip, they had found Don Santiago dead beneath his own car, wrecked on the way *from* Spain, hurrying, apparently, to keep his rendezvous with d'Artois.

"Since Santiago never reached Bayonne to meet me, then who? A double? For that stout wrist was not that of an apparition, nor do illusions or phantoms leave footprints, nor can they beat one's blade so that one's arm tingles up to the shoulder. Impossible!"

"But then what did hit you?"

"Who knows? Perhaps a confederate, despite our having agreed to meet without seconds. But by the time I recovered full possession of my wits, several days later, any bruise the blow might have left had subsided. Yet something must have struck me ..."

In the lengthening shadows, the Spring of St. Leon appeared less and less as a place for midnight trysts, either for love or war. And though listening to Pierre's dissertation, my thoughts were of Bayonne, this 'pet' city of mine which is still girdled by walls and moats and earthworks; whose ground is steeped with blood spilled in centuries of warfare, and undermined with casements, and passages, and dungeons. Some of the passages had been built by Vauban when he fortified the town; but there were many others, of much greater antiquity; vaults wherein Roman legionaries had worshiped Mithra, Saracen emirs practice necromancy, and medieval alchemists sought the immutable Azoth, and dabbled in thaumaturgy.

"A curious thing I noted," continued d'Artois, "was that a small silver peacock adorned the pommel of his *épée* ... strange how one notes such details before a duel.

Silver peacock ... why, we had seen a similar sword at Château de la Tour de Maracq the other day! I wondered ...

And out of that network of passages, what might not have emerged from a mining casemate to strike Pierre from the rear and save the day for Santiago, or Santiago's double, or the devil, or what it was that d'Artois had met?

Something had loosened the ordinarily well-shackled d'Artois tongue. I marveled and encouraged its wagging. And then he stopped short, pointing toward the Spring of St. Leon.

"By the—!" he exclaimed, quaintly distorting a selection from the American doughboy's lexicon, which he strove most valiantly to master. "What is *she* doing there?"

A girl stood at the spring; a slim girl whose white arms and shoulders and iridescent gown gleamed boldly against the shadows of the grove and the dark cupola of the spring.

"La Belle Allzaneau," explained Pierre, for I lacked that old man's keen vision.

As he spoke, she rounded the cupola of St. Leon, its low gray mass hiding her from sight.

"But how can you recognize anyone at that distance and in this light, Pierre?"

"Her general outline, the gown she wears ... which by the way is a trifle inappropriate for the locality ... I have often seen her at the Casino at Biarritz."

———

That evening, as Jannicot brought our coffee, d'Artois, after theorizing for a while about the duel at St. Leon, abruptly switched to the mummy, poor neglected lady whom he seemed to have entirely forgotten.

"Your imagination, *mon cher,* is entirely dead," he declared. "And in this quest of the mummy case (for we have the lady herself located) one needs much imagination. *Alors,* to you shall fall the duty of private soldier; that of sentry-go by night. Jannicot shall walk post during the day."

"What?"

"Yes. Sentry-go. You watch by night."

"Why pick on me?"

"You are too conspicuous in this small town. Jannicot, watching a cow staked on the city wall, would never be noted, for he will look like any other yokel similarly occupied. Whereas you ..."

I bowed elaborately in appreciation of the compliment.

"Whereas you, under cover of darkness—but that is obvious."

"But how will watching 34 rue Lachepaillet assist you?"

"It will prevent your disturbing my meditations."

"Still, what has that girl to do with mummies?"

"Imbecile! You have no imagination. So, take your post at sunset, watch until morning, and report to me all the exits, entries, and doings of La Belle Allzaneau, and her visitors as well. Though few but Monsieur the Marquis call at her apartment."

And thus, I spent a week, walking post by night. Not truly walking, but rather lounging on the parapet of the ancient battlements, always keeping an eye on the door of Lili Allzaneau, who lived on the city wall, who had ensnared a marquis; "a peer of France," as they used to put it.

And what was Pierre, *beau sabreur* and master of devices, doing as I frittered away my time, noting the princely cars which stopped at the door of Lili of the City Wall; listening to the sound of merriment subdued to a patrician pitch: an aristocratic reserve in keeping with the *lorette* who designed to accord only to the lords of the world the pleasure of her presence?

Each morning I rendered my report, usually with mocking formality, imitating the supposed manner of a private detective. I especially enjoyed the report of the fourth vigil: "Monsieur Pierre d'Artois, noted boulevardier and swordsman, was seen entering the apartment of Mademoiselle Allzaneau at about 11:30 p.m., apparently having returned with mademoiselle from the theater. When I quit my post at sunrise, he had not yet left."

"Idiot!" snapped Pierre, relishing the jest. "You slept on post."

"The devil I did. I watched most vigilantly."

"Well, since you must know it all, the apartment of Mademoiselle Allzaneau has an exit on 43 rue des Faures, the alley which parallels rue Lachepaillet. Now, are you ashamed of your base insinuations?"

I was properly squelched. Later, I checked up on rue des Faures and verified his claim. But what in all creation had Pierre been doing in the company of La Belle Allzaneau? A man of his age! Though I could well conceive that any lady of the world could take pride in being seen with Pierre d'Artois, that fine, courtly old master of the sword.

What a mess! Not a trace of connection between any of the diverse elements that danced before my eyes: a marquis, a mummy he had stolen, her still missing case; a duel, fought two years ago at St. Leon, and a *lorette* with Babylonic eyes ... yes, and the lady of the portrait at the château, the double, the deceased original whose reincarnation La Belle Allzaneau seemed to be. Too much for me!

But one does not question d'Artois to any purpose.

A week, as I said, had passed: uneventful espionage. And then, just as I was to leave Pierre's house to resume my vigil, he detained me.

"A moment, *mon vieux*. I have again the hunch. It will happen tonight."

"What, for the Lord's sake, will happen? The mummy seeks her ease, or you elope with Lili? Or challenge your rival the Marquis?"

"Anything is more than likely to happen tonight. I hear that Monsieur the Marquis has gone to Spain. And Mademoiselle Allzaneau will receive no visitors this evening, not even me. And so on ... I have the hunch, as you so elegantly put it, that hell will be popping tonight."

"Well, where do I come in?"

"You? You shall follow her should she leave her apartment; follow her, and see it to a finish, whatever it be. It may be to a strange place, *mon vieux;* therefore, take these with you."

He passed me a Luger automatic, a blackjack, and what appeared to be a left-handed, fingerless, mailed glove—strangely like a Roman cestus, at least as to its obvious purpose.

"Looks like trouble, Pierre," I remarked, as I strapped the Luger and its holster under my left arm. "But why this glove ...? And ... what the devil! A peacock decorating it!"

"Yes. It may serve you well. If you are accosted, exhibit the peacock, and you will be passed on without question."

"Lay off, Pierre, lay off! Have you a dime novel complex?"

"*Mais non*. Do not laugh. You may have no occasion to try it. But remember the peacock. A full moon will make your task easier, or more difficult ... that depends ... As for me ... we may meet unexpectedly. But if not, see it to a finish, and do not fail me."

With this command firmly impressed upon me, I took my post, wondering at the assortment of junk which he had forced upon me. A Luger ... well, that was sound judgment; a pistol is an excellent playmate. And a blackjack could conceivably come in handy. But that fingerless glove with its peacock!

———

Nearly midnight. Not a car in front of her apartment all evening. La Belle Allzaneau evidently was carrying on revery and not riot during the absence of her lover in Spain.

A copper kettle of a moon was rising.

"Do not fail me. Follow her and use your judgment."

Well, and into what sort of mess would Pierre be venturing in the meanwhile? Rich entertainment somewhere for someone!

Lord, what a sleepy night! Silence along rue Lachepaillet, and more silence in the park beneath me, beyond the dry moat that girdled the walls. The night before Christmas was fairly spiked to the mast for pure stillness.

Follow Lili ... where? Why the pistol, the blackjack, the ornamental brass knuckles? Brass, the devil! I'd have sworn they were gold ... or perhaps it was the moonlight.

A light in Lili's window, just for a moment. Then darkness again.

And then the door on the rez-de-chaussée opened. Lili herself, in a gown of star-dusted, metallic luster stepped into the street, crossed, paused within a meter of my lurking place.

In the entire world had I never seen a woman half as lovely, as perfectly formed, as faultlessly arrayed as she was, from her silver slippers to her dusky hair ... great Lord! A peacock tiara, all aflame with small rubies, and emeralds, and sapphires and diamonds glowed in the darkness of her coiffure! It began to seem as though I had but to step forth, show her my brass knuckles and their silver peacock, and claim her as a partner in whatever devil's dance was in store for us.

"Follow her and use your judgment."

No, better not accost her; else he'd have said, "Accompany her."

All this in an instant; then she turned to a low, narrow entrance directly beneath my position on the parapet, and vanished into its opening.

Now what on earth was that faultlessly gowned girl doing in an ancient powder magazine or storeroom which used to serve the garrison in days past? I'd prowled around in many of them; all were crowded with rubbish, and filth, and the dust of centuries.

Now when should I begin to trail her? If immediately, I should betray my presence; if I paused, I'd lose the trail. And then I became aware of the aura of perfume she had left behind her, a rich, heavy, arabesque fragrance. The very scent a sample of which Pierre had let me smell the other evening! Now, by the rood, I could trail that persistent, curious perfume anywhere.... So, after a pause of a few more moments, I leaped from the parapet and plunged into the magazine.

"Plunged" is the right word, though I didn't begin plunging until my third step into the darkness, when I stepped into vacancy. I came to a stop at a landing, ten steps down. With belated good judgment, I sized things up with my electric torch. More steps, steep, narrow, rubbish-laden, leading to abysmal blackness far below. And in darkness I edged my way down. The haunting, persistent fragrance of La Belle Allzaneau led me on.

I paused at the foot of the last flight. My feet were on sandy bottom. I listened but heard nothing save the breathing of that fierce silence. And from the subterranean mustiness came the perfume of Lili, reaching from the blackness to enfold me. She had been there and had not branched off into any lateral passages on her way down.

Luger in one hand, torch in the other, I stabbed the gloom. Vacancy. I was alone in that ancient vault, alone with the perfume of a girl who wore a jeweled peacock in her hair.

There were tiny footprints on the sand. And then I noted a low archway, an exit, which, being on the shadowed side of a bastion, had not had its presence betrayed by the entrance of outer moonlight. Lili had left the vault, whose bottom was on a level with the bottom of the dry moat; had left the enclosure of Bayonne, and was without the walls, somewhere.

Then I picked up the trail, tiny footprints in the sand. She had kept close to the wall, heading along toward Porte d'Espagne. But I knew she would not pass that point; for no woman would ruin her footgear in the slime and mud of the moat bottom past the Gate of Spain, the result of seepage from the locks of the Adour.

Beneath the drawbridge of Porte d'Espagne, I picked a lingering trace of perfume; and likewise, her footprints, which for several paces I had lost. She had edged away from the wall, crossed the moat, ascended the steep bank.

Her destination? Logically, any place; she had choice of the whole countryside. Nor could I trail her any farther. Tracking in sand is the limit of my skill!

I took stock of my surroundings. If she continued in a straight line ...

Hell's hinges! She was bound for the Spring of St. Leon, that unsavory spot where d'Artois, in his moment of victory over Santiago, had been struck from the rear.

Conceivably she might be keeping a rendezvous with the Marquis, or more likely, some other lover. And we had seen her there a week ago, at sunset.

Things seemed to be pulling together but leaving me still confused. The girl had some connection with this spot where Santiago, armed with a sword whose pommel was adorned with a peacock, had met d'Artois. The Marquis had a similar sword; and the Marquis was the girl's lover. And the girl was the living image of the former mistress of the Marquis. She wore a peacock in her coiffure, and I wore one on my left hand. Well, what of it? Something, yes; but what?

A sequin glistened on the ground. In the stillness of the clearing, the heavy air still bore a trace of her perfume. But she was nowhere in sight.

I sized up the ground near the spring. There, in that small, flat space, Pierre and Santiago had crossed swords. There was the rock on which he had laid his hat and coat. Here he had taken his position, sword in hand, on guard....

I whirled in my tracks. Pure nervousness—a reflex occasioned by the memory of that something which had struck d'Artois from the rear. There, in the shadow of a small knoll, was the entrance to a casemate, seemingly at least. Another sequin gleamed on the ground. On her way, she had severed a thread of her gown, and was now shedding sequins every few paces. With her short start, she could scarcely have left my range of vision, unless she were deliberately hiding. Then ... logically, she had entered the casemate; had at least paused at its entrance, as the sequin dropped from her gown indicated.

Without any excessive eagerness or exultation, I entered the casemate. Darkness, absolute. But a trace of her perfume! I smelled not only perfume, but trouble; here, for a fact, I was really getting into something.

A few steps, feeling my way in the dark. I dared not risk the torch. Ahead of me, apparently around a curve, was a faint glow, as of a dim light still farther beyond, a shadowy reflex of a half-concealed illuminant; so dim that I had not perceived it for a moment. Well ...

Halt!" snapped a voice.

The flare of an electric torch smote me full in the face, blinding me. But before I could draw the Luger ...

"You are late," continued the voice, "and I doubt that the master will receive you in that garb.

"Never mind my clothes," I temporized, catching my wits and also a glimpse of my accoster now that the ray had left my face. "Has the lady of the peacock—?"

I touched my forehead with my left hand, a more instinctive than deliberate gesture to indicate Lili's coiffure. As I lowered my hand, the watcher bowed low, kissing the peacock's figure.

That was an excellent little blackjack I wielded with my right, smacking neatly across the inclined head of the warder.

"Well, and if the master is particular about costumes, perhaps this will answer."

After stripping the hood and cape from the sentry, I bound and gagged him, arranged him snugly against and parallel to the wall, and continued my way down the passage; down, literally, as it inclined at a rather quick slope, curving ever to the right, so that it led back toward the citadel of Bayonne, and far beneath its foundations. At regular intervals, candles cast a dim light.

I had noted the swarthy, foreign features of the warder I had blackjacked, and wondered still more. Almost anything was likely to happen ... and where was Pierre?

Then came steps, winding, circular steps, leading to the very heart of the earth. Chilly dampness had displaced the outer warmth. To what strange festival was that girl bound? And what was that peacock which had such talismanic effect on the warder? Who the master? And why the costume?

At the foot of the winding stairs, I found a twisting passage, this time level. Turns ... more turns ... a murmur of voices, chanting sonorously ... and then ...

A heavy iron grillwork, a gate, barred my progress. I flattened myself close against the door jamb, peering through the bars at a unique sight. Before me, at the end of the passage, was a great vaulted chamber, illumined with a deep red glow. As much of the walls as I could see was covered with black arras, figured grotesquely in silver embroidery, monstrous designs of intertwining forms and unheard-of creatures alternating with medallions inscribed in characters resembling Arabic. At the far end of the vault was an altar, behind which stood the enshrined image of a great peacock, his painted fan fully spread, and enameled in naturalistic colors. A bronze railing rose waist-high before the altar; and from a cleft in the platform between the railing and altar, two great black hands, palms uplifted, reached forth.

Kneeling on the floor in crescent formation were a dozen robed and hooded figures, worshipers at the peacock's shrine. The chanting had ceased; and from the group rose one who advanced to the altar steps, facing the image, extended his arms, and began the recital of a ritual. At times he paused for the response of the communicants; resumed his chant, ceasing again to make gestures and genuflections. But not a word of it could I understand; neither of the priest, nor of the worshipers.

Well, and where was La Belle Allzaneau, she who wore on her forehead the unusual symbol which seemed to be the key to this secret place into which I had wandered? And Pierre? Certainly, he had not sent me on into this place and stayed off the scene himself; or had he miscalculated, sending me to real action instead of reserving it for himself ...? And thus, I wondered, wondered at the scene, at the rites, at the unholy tapestry of the walls, and the cornices which depicted in sculptured panorama the unsavory themes of Asian mysteries ... the predecessors of the peacock.

Pierre ...? No, Pierre could not have miscalculated so far as to send me into the midst of things and follow a false lead himself.... Great Lord, could it be Pierre who conducted the ritual? Absurd; but the audacity of the man knew no limits!

On and on rolled the rich, resonant voice of the priest. Acolytes marched about the crescent of kneeling communicants, swinging censers and chanting; retired, grouped themselves about the altar. And then ...

The priest turned to face the congregation. Not Pierre, but Etienne, Marquis de la Tour de Maracq! He who had stolen the mummy of a princess; he who lived surrounded by death's symbols, a servant of polycephalous idols, he who studied an obscure book bound in human hide, found time also to act as high priest of the silver peacock.

A sweeping gesture, another sonorous phrase and the assemblage rose, bowed, backed out of the vault, toward the iron grating through which I peered.

I shrank back against the wall, becoming a shadow among the shadows, and waited for the grill to swing open, and let the worshipers enter the passage so that, emerging from my angle, I could mingle with them, one of them, disguised in my hood and mask, and guarded by the peacock on my wrist. And once they had passed on, I could return.

And then I remembered the warder I had bound and gagged. Would they notice him lying in the shadows? Should I hasten on ahead of them, conceal the sentry outside the passage, and thus avoid the alarm caused by his discovery? Damn that sentry! Why had I left him where he dropped?

The door clicked. Too late to run on ahead to clear the way. The cloaked worshipers crowded even into my corner in that narrow passage, not even noticing me. One, however, seemed to mistake me for a comrade who had knelt beside him, and had left at his elbow.

"The master seemed hasty tonight, don't you think, Raoul?"

I shrugged my shoulders, mumbled a phrase in Tagalog. The ruse served well. Evidently men of all languages met there.

"Oh, pardon, Monsieur ... "

And he went on through the passage in search of his comrade.

I mingled with the dozen who were leaving, contriving to fall back unobtrusively, thus avoiding the appearance of lingering in a place from which all were departing. And as the tail of the file of hooded men rounded the first turn, I dropped back and resumed my post at one side of the grill, deep in the shadows, seeing, but unseen.

———

The Marquis descended from the altar steps, halted in the center of the vault; stroked his black mustache; frowned. Three swift steps to his left brought him to the heavy black arras, which he parted.

"They have gone, *chérie*."

And from behind the embroidered hangings came La Belle Allzaneau, white arms and shoulders and iridescent gown agleam under that deep, lurid light.

"Etienne, I'm somewhat disappointed. I had expected ..."

"To see something grotesque and awful, and outlandish? *Ma chere,* those whom you saw were neophytes, and the rites of the innermost shrine are not for their eyes," explained the Marquis as he again parted the arras and drew from behind it a low table laden with refreshments.

He then drew up a chaise lounge among whose cushions the girl enthroned herself. The Marquis took his place opposite her, and facing me, so that while I could look him full in the eye, I could see but the profile of La Belle Allzaneau, Lili of Lachepaillet, the *lorette* who had the manner of a queen.

"No, *petite,*" continued the Marquis, "those were neophytes. But to you I shall reveal—"

"Yet am I not even more of a neophyte?" interrupted the girl as she selected a wafer from the tray before her.

"Nevertheless, I shall reveal to you, as I promised, the innermost secrets; you shall enter the adytum, the awful holy of holies."

"But, Etienne, you must explain. Who is this peacock, and what is his significance?"

Who, indeed, was the peacock? I forgot, for the moment, that the bound and gagged sentry might be discovered by the departing communicants, thus betraying the fact that someone had intruded. Still, it had taken me ten minutes to enter; and they, going upgrade, up flights of steps, would require more time. And should they return, they would search each passageway, taking their time, in all thoroughness, probably twenty minutes or half an hour.

Well then, and what was that glittering bird whose image had caused the warder to bow and kiss my left hand?

"The peacock," explained the Marquis, answering the girl, as well as myself, "is the symbol of him we serve—Malik Taûs, which in the Persian signifies 'Lord Peacock.'"

"Which explains exactly nothing, Etienne!"

"Malik Taûs," he repeated, as one who humors a captivating but unruly child, "is none other than he whom they call Ahriman ... Lucifer, the Morning Star ... Satan, the outlaw, he whom we, the rebels, the battered but unvanquished ones serve. Now do you understand?"

Eavesdropping on devil-worship! What next?

And La Belle Allzaneau smiled her slow, enigmatic smile, unterrified at that which made me shudder.

Thus, as they ate and drank, the Marquis explained the monstrous scenes depicted on the cornices, Oriental perversions antedating Malik Taûs, the girl interrupting from time to time. I watched and wondered.

Very curious it was that their voices seemed to come from my right clearly, but as from a greater distance than the speakers seemed to be. It was as if I were watching some phantasmagoria. Her voice I heard as her lips parted; but it seemed to come not from her lips, but from my right.

And then it struck me as odd that they both were left-handed. Both ate left-handed, picked up their goblets with their left hands. The Marquis, striking a match, struck it with his left. Was this left-handedness another manifestation of the rites of Malik Taûs, or was it but coincidence that both the girl and her host were left-handed?

"This is an ancient shrine," continued the Marquis, his voice clear, but coming not from in front of me, down a long, narrow passage, but seemingly from my right. "This is an ancient shrine in which Mithra was worshiped by Roman legionaries; and renegade Moslems and those who followed the Moorish forces into Spain bowed here before Tanit, and Istar, Mylitta, and Anaïtis, all of whom are one, one goddess who came out of Egypt ... Isis, the Great Goddess."

I listened, fascinated by the rich voice of that strange, dark man; nor wondered that the girl was ensnared by his pagan chant, his intoned syllables which sang of monstrous rites and unheard-of lore. I forgot, remembered, and straightway dismissed the thought of the possible return of the departed neophytes. My Luger would serve me well, if necessary and for hand to hand, the brass knuckles.

As the Marquis smoked and drank, and expounded, I saw that his gaze went past the girl, seeming to seek me in my alcove of blackness. But no, surely he could not see me, where I crouched in darkness. He frowned passingly, shook his head, made a fleeting gesture of annoyance, as of one who is irritated by the buzzing of a mosquito. Then, continuing his speech, he reached again behind the arras.

I heard a click, and at the same time a faint, droning, humming sound. For a moment the lights dimmed. And then, suddenly, I awoke to the significance of that which had occurred. In the darkness I saw very distinctly a bluish violet glow, an aureole which surrounded each of the bars of the gates before me. That click had been the sound of a latch slipping into place; and that glow was the leakage into the air of a high tension electrical current?

Hell's bells! Had he seen me? Did he know of my presence? Or ... perhaps ... most likely it was that he suspected the presence of some loitering neophyte, some eavesdropper who had paused, and who would, as he leaned against the grillage, be seared and scorched lifeless by the flaming death that lurked in that ironwork. My advance was barred beyond all hope.

Well, I could watch; and in case of a pinch, a shot from my Luger would reach down the passage. For I felt sure that the Marquis designed some outlandish deed; not only the words of Pierre, but the atmosphere of the place, the very expression of the man himself so worked on my nerves that I sensed the presence of something hideous and unheard of. That lurid light, that glittering peacock, those black hands upraised toward the altar, and the hypnotic words and chanting tones of the Marquis ... I shuddered. It is not pleasant to consider shooting an unarmed man from ambush, but ... as these French put it, *que voulez-vous?*

"Without evil, there could be no good," continued the sonorous rhythm of the Marquis. "They are extremes of the same essence, even as heat and cold are of the same nature. And to serve the Lord of Evil (if evil indeed there is) is to pay a just tribute to him without whom there could be none of the so-called good, if good indeed there is. Thus in time to come, when Malik Taûs spreads his painted fan over all the earth, we who now serve him shall be princes and lords and shall inherit the world. Look!" he commanded, his voice rising imperiously as he pointed to the shrine; "look and see his thousand eyes that watch over us!"

The girl turned, following with her eyes his compelling gesture. And in that instant the Marquis, never pausing in his speech, dropped into her wine a tiny pellet.

The man was mad with a fearful, unspeakable madness. And here I was, barred from preventing what I now sensed to be impending, a sequel to the preliminary rites I had witnessed, a manifestation of demonaltry in which none but the high priest would officiate.

"Those black hands? They are the hands of Abbadon, the Dark Angel who serves Malik Taûs; and on them we lay that which we dedicate to the Lord Peacock," explained the Marquis.

I loosened the Luger in its holster. At times one must shoot from ambush ... but not yet.

"And so, you are the only adept, Etienne?" queried the girl, resuming her wine.

"There was another, but he is dead. Through my fault. Don Santiago de las Torres Negras."

Lord, what a revelation! Here, in this awful place, I was about to learn another side of that uncanny duel fought by Pierre d'Artois at midnight, at the Spring of St. Leon.

"He challenged one Pierre d'Artois," continued the Marquis, "to fight in secret, at midnight, at the Spring of St. Leon. And the Master forbade—"

"And why did you forbid, Etienne?"

"I didn't. No. The Master of Masters ..." The Marquis lowered his voice. "A stranger out of Kurdistan, one whom I recognized as a master of adepts, by the signs he gave ... *the Master,* I now believe ... Malik Taûs himself, the Lord Peacock incarnate as man! He forbade the duel. I feared for Santiago, and wished to prevent it, out of deference to the Master's wishes, and from fear of d'Artois, a swordsman without like or equal. So, I invited Santiago to a château across the border, in Spain, set back all the clocks, sought to divert him, deceive him until, when at last he did sense my device, it would be too late for him to keep his rendezvous. Rob him of his honor, yes; make him fail in his word, yes; but I sought to spare him that meeting with d'Artois, and from the vengeance of the Master."

"And did you succeed?"

"No. Santiago detected the trick before it was absolutely too late, leaped into his car, and drove fiercely into the night, with still a chance to keep his word inviolate. "

"So, he fell in the duel?"

The Marquis winced.

"No, *chérie*. He never reached the rendezvous. A storm arose; and he skidded on a dangerous turn, doubly dangerous on account of the rain. The wrecked car crushed the life out of him. Had I but let him go, he might have won; or at least died like a man ... thus I killed Santiago, my friend... And this stranger from Kurdistan may have been an impostor, a fraud...Imbecile! I believed him to be the Lord Peacock incarnate!"

Christ, what a tale! Was it then the Kurdish stranger whom d'Artois had met, and almost vanquished? The devil who had inspired the Marquis to meddle, and caused the death of Santiago on that lonely road from Spain? My brain reeled with the madness of it all....

And then I raised my eyes again to regard that marquis who chanted sonorously to that lovely girl, serene and calm, reclining among silken cushions in the Adytum of Darkness, in the very shrine of the Oriflamme of Iniquity, face to face with its high priest... and this without changing expression, save to shake her patrician head in pity ... what a woman!

Had they discovered the gagged warder? Were they returning? I was in a devilish mess, literally. Devils on all sides, and in an atmosphere of demonaltry.

———

The girl nodded ... sank back among the emblazoned cushions. Drugged. Inert. The tiny pill had done its work.

The Marquis rose, thrust the table behind the arras; listened to the breathing of the sleeping Madonna; straightened himself to his full height. Madness and despair flamed in his somber eyes; his lips drooped; his lean cheeks were drawn. The muscles at the point of his jaw were knotted and quivering. If not the devil, then was this marquis his double: Satan overcome with sorrow, but unrelenting.

What now? Madness was his. But what form would it assume?

With swift, sure fingers he removed the silver slippers of La Belle Allzaneau; stripped from her the glittering, iridescent gown; and then the tenuous silk which clung to her form.

Cristo del Grao! What had that madman in mind...?

And then he lifted her body from the chaise longue, strode up the cinnabar-strewn pathway toward the shrine, ascended the altar steps, and placed his burden upon the upraised, black palms of those great hands that reached for their prey.

Turning from the altar, he took a small mallet and struck a gong whose thin note shivered and hissed, with a rustling, lingering vibration, chilling, sighing, not full-throated as bronze should be. And from panels on either flank of the altar emerged those same hooded, sheeted figures that had passed me a short time ago, filed now to their places and knelt before the shrine, a vermilion crescent of demonaltors bowing before their chief and their god.

One of the number, after his salaam, arose and advanced to the altar steps, leaned over the brazen railing, and with a stick of rouge marked on the side of the unconscious girl, then a mark on her breast, and then on her forehead a mark. At the same time, coming from the right, just beyond my angle of vision, were four who pushed forward on rollers a massive stone trough, a trough over whose sides slopped some of the liquid it contained. Trough? No trough at all, but a sarcophagus, chiseled with Egyptian hieroglyphics! And is if by symmetry, there came from the left four others, each pair of whom bore a mummy case. These cases were placed on either side of the altar, standing upright. One, the mummy case of a man; the other, of a woman. This I knew from their sizes, and from the gilded masks which depicted the features of the deceased.

The case of the man seemed heavy. But those who carried the case of the woman bore it as though it were empty. And I wondered if indeed that could be the case we sought, Pierre and I.

The hooded figures, after putting their burdens into position, resumed their places in the crescent of devotees, leaving the Marquis alone on the altar steps, facing the shrine.

Well, and at least I need fear no attack; for those who had passed me at the gate had but doubled back and waited behind the scenes for their signal to reappear. It had all been stage-setting. And it all apparently amounted to nothing more than an initiation of the girl into the secret order of demonaltry. I relaxed and let the Luger sink into its holster.

And then I noticed what under normal circumstances I would have noted immediately; the solution of that which made both the marquis and the girl seem left-handed, and that which made the voices seem to come from my right, instead of from directly in front of me. I was looking into a mirror, into one, or three, or some odd number of mirrors which caused a reversal of left and right. Had I not shrunk back into my corner, against the doorjamb, I would have noted that those who filed past me had not come directly toward me, but rather from one side. I could now distinguish my image before me, very faint, almost imperceptible, yet there, nevertheless.

So! And here I was to witness an initiation into the inner circle of demonaltry. My fears for the girl had been panic, and nerves, almost hysteria. And the mummy case, the smaller one, was doubtless that which Pierre sought.

But where was Pierre? No matter. In the morning we would return and loot the place.

The Marquis, after bowing before the shrine of the peacock, extended his arms, chanted in a tongue unknown to me. Then, after tossing incense into the brazier on the altar, he began anew, this time in French.

"Malik Taûs, Standard-bearer of Iniquity, Lord of the Outer Marches, Prince of the Borderland, thee we revere, and before thee we bow! Hear then our prayer, Malik Taûs, Thousand-eyed Lord

Peacock, Sovereign Rebel, Dark Prince! To thee we consecrate this sacrifice on behalf of Santiago who defied thee; and for him we crave pardon and peace, for him across the Border we raise our prayer!"

"Amin!" intoned the congregation, bowing their heads to the floor. "So be it!"

A pause. And again, the Marquis raised his voice.

"Santiago, Santiago my friend, whose death I caused, concede to me your pardon, and accept from me our prayer! I who sent you to your death, and these my servants alike seek to make atonement!"

"Amin!"

"And this woman without like or equal, I offer to you, Santiago; and to you I consecrate her, to be yours until the end of time. Santiago, you whom I sent to your death, accept her who is the very image and likeness of her I loved very long ago; accept as my peace offering this wondrous one who is my lost one incarnate. Santiago, in the name of Thousand-eyed Malik Taûs, I offer to you this woman whom I shall embalm in rich spices and wind in linen and encase in sycamore and enshrine beside you to be yours for ever and ever!"

"Amin!"

Lord God! A poniard gleamed in his upraised hand. I drew and leveled the Luger ... remembered I looked into a mirror ... dropped my eyes, sick with horror ...

A blinding, awful incandescence flared about me, illuminating that vault with the blue-white flame of noonday sun ... a muffled, choked report ... the mirror before me was clouded. A dense mist fogged the air. Hooded figures rushed to and fro, confused, colliding with each other, clawing and rubbing their eyes, blinded by that devastating flame.

And among them strode one not hooded, who moved with sure, swift certitude. Pierre d'Artois, wielding a blackjack! Each swing brought down a hooded figure; down they went before those cool, deliberately placed strokes ... one stroke, one man ... the cruel precision of machinery ... the last man had taken the count. Pierre stepped to the wall, reached behind the arras, withdrew his hand, snatched from the wall an antique battle-ax, and dashed down the passage toward me.

"Don't touch that grill!" I shouted.

"The juice, he is turned off."

And to prove it, Pierre assaulted that grillwork with his massive ax, smiting fiercely, bending and deforming the sturdy bars. I crawled through, followed him back to the Adytum of Darkness.

"Take the girl," he commanded, as, true to his nature, and never forgetting his mission, he seized the mummy case, the one designed for a woman, and led the way to the exit.

As I leaped to the altar railing, lifted the still unconscious girl from the black hands, and wrapped her in my cape, I noted that the other mummy case was empty, and that its cover had been kicked aside.

One or two devil-worshipers stirred and twitched. Others groaned. Striding over that miniature battlefield, I followed in Pierre's trace. And we made good time, Pierre and I, for the devil, though down for the count of ten, still lurked in that awful vault.

———

No one accosted us as Pierre led the way across the park to his car. What a pair we were: a vermilion-robed figure embracing a mummy case, and I, likewise robed, bearing in my arms a girl whose hair streamed to the ground, whose limbs gleamed brightly in the moonlight.

Well, the madman's jubilee ended in Pierre's apartment.

Lili, quite calm and magnificent in Pierre's silken lounge robe, sipped a bit of cognac and took the entire affair as a matter of course, though she did have certain regrets.

"Those lovely shoes! Monsieur Landon, perhaps you would return for them?" she mocked.

And then, to Pierre, "Do tell me what it all was about."

"*Chère petite*, it is a very long story. The stolen mummy would not interest you, directly; but my search for Madame the Princess and—

what you call in English, her wooden negligee, *n'est-ce-pas*—? her sycamore case is what made me cross your trail. *Voyez!*"

Pierre showed us a photograph.

"This, Mademoiselle, does it not resemble you?"

"Quelle bêtise!" flared Lili. "What a notion!"

And then she admitted the resemblance, acknowledged, that that face of gilded sycamore, carved 3,700 years ago, might pass as an Egyptian-esque version of her own loveliness.

"So? It does resemble, yes? And the painting in the château, that of the mistress he adored twenty years ago, that could be your portrait of today, were not the lady's costume a shade out of date. Behold the succession of resemblances, partly real, partly fancied. That I noted, immediately. And moreover, I saw, as did you, *mon ami*, that book bound in human hide; but unlike you, I read therefrom, many strange things. Then those drums whose heads were of human hide, and the arms, and all the other trophies of death ... death ... death which has haunted Monsieur the Marquis, turned his brilliant mind, and made him do this madness which we witnessed.

"And the duel at St. Leon, two years ago. I knew that Don Santiago was the good friend of Monsieur the Marquis; and I knew also that there had been something very odd about that midnight meeting. Thus, when I saw you, Mademoiselle, all so lovely in the sunset, I added the two and the two by intuition. Very simple, *n'est-ce pas?*

"And this Santiago," continued the old man, "wore on the pommel of his sword a peacock; as also did Monsieur the Marquis on that sword at his château. None of which really proved anything; however, I began to think. Thus, it was but a matter of having you watched, Mademoiselle, until things happened.

"And while you watched, *mon vieux,* I prowled around, and found the plans of Vauban's fortifications and engineering works and saw that he had not built the passage leading to St. Leon. And as for last night, I attended the preliminary rites, having, as you so nicely put it, beaned one of the worshipers and assumed his costume."

"What the devil! You joined in their ceremonies?"

"Yes. It was I who spoke to you; but you did not take the tumble, so you missed some rare sport. I had but to put myself into the case which had contained the embalmed body of my ancient enemy, Santiago. And thus, they carried me into position at the altar. Then, at the crucial moment, I kicked off the cover, and fired a press photographer's flashlight gun. Dazzled by that fearful light, they could see nothing. As for me, I closed my eyes as I fired, and then, after the flash ..."

He affectionately caressed the blackjack.

"And with this wonderful little implement, I worked them over, as you might say it, while they still blinked and rubbed their eyes, utterly blinded by that sudden flare."

"He really was going to kill me?" queried the queen of Lachepaillet, who had scarcely grasped the entire sequence of events, and their significance.

"Exactly that, *chère petite.* In his way, he loved you, for yourself, and for the sake of his departed sweetheart; and therefore, he was to sacrifice you, and embalm you, and set you up in state, in the mummy case of a princess, thus performing the supreme penance, making his peace with the Lord Peacock, and with Santiago alike. An artistic soul, Monsieur the Marquis! He is leaving for Spain ... unless unhappily I struck him too hard! But he will not annoy you again."

"These uncanny resemblances, Monsieur d'Artois ... it is all so fantastic," suggested Lili. "I resemble his former mistress, and I resemble a mummy. Am I then a mere shadow?"

"That is really not so incredible. For you, Mademoiselle, are the niece of her whom Monsieur the Marquis loved twenty years ago; so that that resemblance is not at all a subject of wonder, even if extraordinary. This, however, he did not know, nor I either, until I investigated! Nor did you know. As for the mummy, well, coincidence ... and a stretch of fancy."

"But your duel, Pierre, at St. Leon?"

"Who knows? Illusion ... a stranger from Kurdistan ... I attempt no explanation. Santiago is dead, even as may be the Marquis and some of his followers; but the Stranger still lives, and the Peacock's shadow still hangs over us."

THE WHITE LADY OF THE ORPHANAGE

SEABURY QUINN

D r. Trowbridge? Dr. de Grandin?" Our visitor looked questioningly from one of us to the other.

"I'm Trowbridge," I answered, "and this is Dr. de Grandin. What can we do for you?"

The gentle-faced, white-haired little man bowed rather nervously to each of us in turn, acknowledging the introduction. "My name is Gervaise, Howard Gervaise," he replied. "I'm superintendent of the Springville Orphans' Home."

I indicated a chair at the end of the study table and awaited further information.

"I was advised to consult you gentlemen by Mr. Willis Richards, of your city," he continued. "Mr. Richards told me you accomplished some really remarkable results for him at the time his jewelry was stolen and suggested that you could do more to clear up our present trouble than anyone else. He is president of our board of trustees, you know," he added in explanation.

"U'm?" Jules de Grandin murmured noncommittally as he set fire to a fresh cigarette with the glowing butt of another. "I recall that Monsieur Richards. He figured in the affair of the disembodied hand, Friend Trowbridge, you remember. *Parbleu*, I also recall that he paid the reward for his jewels' return with very bad grace. You come poorly introduced, my friend"—he fixed his uncompromising cat-stare on our caller—"however, say on. We listen."

Mr. Gervaise seemed to shrink in upon himself more than ever. It took small imaginative powers to vision him utterly cowed before the domineering manner of Willis Richards, our local nabob. "The fact is, gentlemen," he began with a soft, deprecating cough, "we are greatly troubled at the orphanage. Something mysterious—most mysterious —is taking place there. Unless we can arrive at some solution, we shall be obliged to call in the police, and that would be most unfortunate. Publicity is to be dreaded in this case, yet we are at a total loss to explain the mystery."

"U'm," de Grandin inspected the tip of his cigarette carefully, as though it were something entirely novel, "most mysteries cease to be mysterious, once they are explained, *Monsieur*. You will be good enough to proceed?"

"Ah—" Mr. Gervaise glanced about the study as though to take inspiration from the surroundings, then coughed apologetically again. "Ah—the fact is, gentlemen, that several of our little charges have—ah —mysteriously disappeared. During the past six months we have missed no less than five of the home's inmates, two boys and three girls, and only day before yesterday a sixth one disappeared—vanished into air, if you can credit my statement."

"Ah?" Jules de Grandin sat forward a little in his chair, regarding the caller narrowly. "They have disappeared, vanished, you do say? Perhaps they have decamped?"

"No-o," Gervaise denied, "I don't think that's possible, sir. Our home is only a semi-public institution, you know, being supported entirely by voluntary gifts and benefits of wealthy patrons, and we do not open our doors to orphan children as a class. There are certain restrictions imposed. For this reason, we never entertain a greater number than we are able to care for in a fitting manner, and conditions at Springville are rather different from those obtaining in most institutions of a similar character. The children are well fed, well clothed and excellently housed, and—as far as anyone in their unfortunate situation can be—are perfectly contented and happy. During my tenure of office, more than ten years, we have never had a runaway; and that makes these disappearances all the harder to explain. In each case the surrounding facts have been essentially the same, too. The child was accounted for at night before the signal was given to extinguish the lights, and—and next morning he just wasn't there. That's all there is to say. There is nothing further I can tell you."

"You have searched?" de Grandin asked.

"Naturally. The most careful and painstaking investigations have been made in every case. It was not possible to pursue the little ones with hue and cry, of course, but the home has been to considerable expense in hiring private investigators to obtain some information of the missing children, all without result. There is no question of kidnapping, either, for, in every case, the child was known to be safely inside not only the grounds, but in the dormitories, on the night preceding the disappearance. Several reputable witnesses vouch for that in each instance."

"U'm?" de Grandin commented once more. "You say you have been at considerable expense in the matter, *Monsieur*?"

"Yes."

"Good. Very good. You will please be at some more considerable expense. Dr. Trowbridge and I are *gens d'affaires*—businessmen—as well as scientists, *Monsieur*, and while we shall esteem it an honor to serve the fatherless and motherless orphans of your home, we must receive an adequate consideration from Monsieur Richards. We shall undertake the matter of ascertaining the whereabouts of your missing charges at five hundred dollars apiece. Do you agree?"

"But that would be three thousand dollars—" the visitor began.

"Perfectly," de Grandin interrupted. "The police will undertake the case for nothing."

"But we cannot have the police, as I have just explained—"

"You cannot have us for less," the Frenchman cut in. "This Monsieur Richards, I know him of old. He desires not the publicity of a search by the gendarmes, and, though he loves me not, he has confidence in my ability, otherwise he would not have sent you. Go to him and say Jules de Grandin will act for him for no less fee than that I have mentioned. Meantime, will you smoke?"

He passed a box of my cigars to the caller, held a lighted match for him, and refused to listen to another word concerning the business which had brought Gervaise on the twenty-mile jaunt from Springville.

———

"Trowbridge, *mon vieux*," he informed me the following morning at breakfast, "I assure you it pays handsomely to be firm with these captains of industry, such as Monsieur Richards. Before you had arisen, my friend, that man of wealth was haggling with me over the telephone as though we were a pair of dealers in second-hand furniture. *Morbleu*, it was like an auction. Bid by bid he raised his offer for our services until he met my figure. Today his attorneys prepare a formal document, agreeing to pay us five hundred dollars for the explanation of the disappearance of each of those six little orphans. A good morning's business, *n'est-ce-pas?*"

"De Grandin," I told him, "you're wasting your talents in this work. You should have gone into Wall Street. "

"*Eh bien,*" he twisted the tips of his little blond mustache complacently, "I think I do very well as it is. When I return to *la belle* France next month, I shall take with me upward of fifty thousand dollars—more than a million francs—as a result of my work here. That sum is not to be sneezed upon, my friend. And what is of even more value to me, I take with me the gratitude of many of your countrymen whose burdens I have been able to lighten. *Mordieu*, yes, this trip has been of great use to me, my old one."

"And—" I began.

"And tomorrow we shall visit this home of the orphans where Monsieur Gervaise nurses his totally inexplicable mystery. *Parbleu*, that mystery shall be explained, or Jules de Grandin is seven thousand francs poorer!

———

"All arrangements have been made," he confided as we drove over to Springville the following morning. "It would never do for us to announce ourselves as investigators, my friend, so what surer disguise can we assume than that of being ourselves? You and I, are we not physicians? But certainly. Very well. As physicians we shall appear at the home, and as physicians we shall proceed to inspect all the little ones—separately and alone—for are we not to give them the Schick test for diphtheria immunity? Most assuredly."

"And then—?" I began, but he cut my question in two with a quick gesture and a smile.

"And then, my friend, we shall be guided by circumstances, and if there are no circumstances, *cordieu*, but we shall make them! *Allans*, there is much to do before we handle Monsieur Richards' cheek."

However dark the mystery overhanging the Springville Orphans' Home might have been, nothing indicating it was apparent as de Grandin and I drove through the imposing stone gateway to the spacious grounds. Wide, smoothly kept lawns, dotted here and there with beds of brightly blooming flowers, clean, tastefully arranged buildings of red brick in the Georgian style, and a general air of prosperity, happiness and peace greeted us as we brought our car to a halt before the main building of the home. Within, the youngsters were at chapel, and their clear young voices rose pure and sweet as birdsongs in springtime to the accompaniment of a mellow-toned organ:

> *"There's a home for little children*
> *Above the bright blue sky,*
> *Where Jesus reigns in glory,*
> *A home of peace and joy;*
> *No earthly home is like it,*
> *Nor can with it compare . . . "*

We tiptoed into the spacious assembly room, dimly lit through tall, painted windows, and waited at the rear of the hall till the morning exercises were concluded. Right and left de Grandin shot his keen, stocktaking glance, inspecting the rows of neatly clothed little ones in the pews, attractive young female attendants, and the mild-faced, gray-haired lady of matronly appearance who presided at the organ. "*Mordieu*, Friend Trowbridge," he muttered in my ear, "truly, this is mysterious. Why should any of the *pauvres orphelins* voluntarily quit such a place as this?"

"S-s-sh!" I cut him off. His habit of talking in and out of season, whether at a funeral, a wedding or other religious service, had annoyed me more than once. As usual, he took the rebuke in good part and favored me with an elfish grin, then fell to studying an elongated figure representing a female saint in one of the stained-glass windows, winking at the beatified lady in a highly irreverent manner.

"Good morning, gentlemen," Mr. Gervaise greeted us as the home's inmates filed past us, two by two. "Everything is arranged for your inspection. The children will be brought to you in my office as soon as you are ready for them. Mrs. Martin"—he turned with a smile to the white-haired organist who had joined us—"these are Dr. de Grandin and Dr. Trowbridge. They are going to inspect the children for diphtheria immunity this morning."

To us he added: "Mrs. Martin is our matron. Next to myself she has entire charge of the home. We call her 'Mother Martin,' and all our little ones love her as though she were really their own mother."

"How do you do?" the matron acknowledged the introduction, favoring us with a smile of singular sweetness and extending her hand to each of us in turn.

"*Madame*," de Grandin took her smooth, white hand in his, American fashion, then bowed above it, raising it to his lips, "your little charges are indeed more than fortunate to bask in the sunshine of your ministrations!" It seemed to me he held the lady's hand longer than necessity required, but like all his countrymen my little friend was more than ordinarily susceptible to the influence of a pretty woman, young or elderly.

"And now. *Monsieur*, if you please—" He resigned Mother

Martin's plump hand regretfully and turned to the superintendent, his slim, black brows arched expectantly.

"Of course," Gervaise replied. "This way, if you please."

"It would be better if we examined the little ones separately and without any of the attendants being present," de Grandin remarked in a businesslike tone, placing his medicine case on the desk and unfolding a white jacket.

"But surely you cannot hope to glean any information from the children!" the superintendent protested. "I thought you were simply going to make a pretense of examining them as a blind. Mrs. Martin and I have questioned every one of them most carefully, and I assure you there is absolutely nothing to be gained by going over that ground again. Besides, some of them have become rather nervous, and we don't want to have their little heads filled with disagreeable notions, you know. I think it would be much better if Mother Martin or I were present while the children are examined. It would give them greater confidence, you know—"

"*Monsieur*"—de Grandin spoke in the level, toneless voice he assumed before one of his wild outbursts of anger—"you will please do exactly as I command. Otherwise—" He paused significantly and began removing the clinical smock.

"Oh, by no means, my dear sir," the superintendent hastened to assure him. "No, no; I wouldn't for the world have you think I was trying to put difficulties in your way. Oh, no; I only thought—"

"*Monsieur*," the little Frenchman repeated, "from this time onward, until we dismiss the case, I shall do the thinking. You will kindly have the children brought to me, one at a time."

To see the spruce little scientist among the children was a revelation to me. Always tart of speech to the verge of bitterness, with a keen, mordant wit which cut like a razor or scratched like a briar, de Grandin seemed the last one to glean information from children naturally timid in the presence of a doctor. But his smile grew brighter and brighter and his humor better and better as child after child entered the office, answered a few seemingly idle questions and passed from the room. At length a little girl, some four or five years old, came in, the hem of her blue pinafore twisted between her plump baby fingers in embarrassment.

"Ah," de Grandin breathed, "here is one from whom we shall obtain something of value, my friend, or I much miss my guess.

"Holà, ma petite tête de chou!" he exclaimed, snapping his fingers at the tot. "Come hither and tell Dr. de Grandin all about it!"

His "little cabbage-head" gave him an answering smile, but one of somewhat doubtful quality. "Dr. Grandin not hurt Betsy?" she asked, half confidently, half fearsomely.

"Parbleu, not I, my pigeon," he replied as he lifted her to the desk. *"Regardez-vous!"* from the pocket of his jacket he produced a little box of bonbons and thrust them into her chubby hand. "Eat them, my little onion," he commanded. "*Tête du diable*, but they are an excellent medicine for loosening the tongue!"

Nothing loth, the little girl began munching the sweetmeats, regarding her new friend with wide, wondering eyes. "They said you would hurt me—cut my tongue out with a knife if I talked to you," she informed him, then paused to pop another chocolate button into her mouth.

"Mort d'un chat, did they, indeed?" he demanded. "And who was the vile, detestable one who so slandered Jules de Grandin? I shall—s-s-sh!" he interrupted himself, turning and crossing the office in three long, catlike leaps. At the entrance he paused a moment, then grasped the handle and jerked the door suddenly open.

On the sill, looking decidedly surprised, stood Mr. Gervaise.

"Ah, *Monsieur*," de Grandin's voice held an ugly, rasping note as he glared directly into the superintendent's eyes, "you are perhaps seeking for something? Yes?"

"Er—yes," Gervaise coughed softly, dropping his gaze before the Frenchman's blazing stare. "Er—that is—you see, I left my pencil here this morning, and I didn't think you'd mind if I came to get it. I was just going to rap when—"

"When I saved you the labor, *n'est-ce-pas?*" the other interrupted. "Very good, my friend. Here—" hastening to the desk he grabbed a handful of miscellaneous pencils, pens and other writing implements, including a stick of marking chalk "—take these, and get gone, in the name of the good God." He thrust the utensils into the astonished superintendent's hands, then turned to me, the gleam in his little blue eyes and the heightened color in his usually pale cheeks showing his barely suppressed rage. "Trowbridge, *mon vieux*," he almost hissed, "I fear I shall have to impress you into service as a guard. Stand at the outer door, my friend, and should anyone come seeking pens, pencils, paint brushes or printing presses, have the goodness to boot him away. Me, I do not relish having people looking for pencils through the keyhole of the door while I interrogate the children!"

Thereafter I remained on guard outside the office while child after child filed into the room, talked briefly with de Grandin, and left by the farther door.

———

"Well, did you find out anything worthwhile?" I asked when the examination was finally ended.

"U'm," he responded, stroking his mustache thoughtfully, "yes and no. With children of a tender age, as you know, the line of demarcation between recollection and imagination is none too clearly drawn. The older ones could tell me nothing; the younger ones relate a tale of a 'white lady' who visited the dormitory on each night a little one disappeared, but what does that mean? Some attendant making a nightly round? Perhaps a window curtain blown by the evening breeze? Maybe it had no surer foundation than some childish whim, seized and enlarged upon by the other little ones. There is little we can go on at this time, I fear.

"Meanwhile," his manner brightened, "I think I hear the sound of the dinner gong. *Parbleu*, I am as hungry as a carp and empty as a kettledrum. Let us hasten to the refectory."

Dinner was a silent meal. Superintendent Gervaise seemed ill at ease under de Grandin's sarcastic stare, and the other attendants who shared the table with us took their cue from their chief and conversation languished before the second course was served. Nevertheless, de

Grandin seemed to enjoy everything set before him to the uttermost, and made strenuous efforts to entertain Mrs. Martin, who sat immediately to his right.

"But *Madame*," he insisted when the lady refused a serving of the excellent beef which constituted the roast course, "surely you will not reject this so excellent roast! Remember, it is the best food possible for humanity, for not only does it contain the nourishment we need, but great quantities of iron are to be found in it, as well. Come, permit that I help you to that which is at once food and tonic!"

"No, thank you," the matron replied, looking at the juicy roast with a glance almost of repugnance. "I am a vegetarian."

"How terrible!" de Grandin commiserated, as though she had confessed some overwhelming calamity.

"Yes, Mother Martin's been subsisting entirely on vegetables for the last six months," one of the nurses, a plump, red-cheeked girl, volunteered. "She used to eat as much meat as any of us, but all of a sudden she turned against it, and—oh, Mrs. Martin!"

The matron had risen from her chair, leaning halfway across the table, and the expression on her countenance was enough to justify the girl's exclamation. Her face had gone pale—absolutely livid—her lips were drawn back against her teeth like those of a snarling animal, and her eyes seemed to protrude from their sockets as they blazed into the startled girl's. It seemed to me that not only rage, but something like loathing and fear were expressed in her blazing orbs as she spoke in a low, passionate voice: "Miss Bosworth, what I used to do and what I do now are entirely my own business. Please do not meddle with my affairs!"

For a moment silence reigned at the table, but the Frenchman saved the situation by remarking, "*Tiens, Madame,* the fervor of the convert is ever greater than that of those to the manner born. The Buddhist, who eats no meat from his birth, is not half so strong in defense of his diet as the lately converted European vegetarian!"

To me, as we left the dining hall, he confided, "A charming meal, most interesting and instructive. Now, my friend, I would that you drive me home at once, immediately. I wish to borrow a dog from Sergeant Costello."

"What?" I responded incredulously. "You want to borrow a—"

"Perfectly. A dog. A police dog if you please. I think we shall have use for the animal this night."

"Oh, all right," I agreed. The workings of his agile mind were beyond me, and I knew it would be useless to question him.

Shortly after sundown we returned to the Springville home, a large and by no means amiable police dog, lent us by the local constabulary, sharing the car with us.

"You will engage Monsieur Gervaise in conversation, if you please," my companion commanded as we stopped before the younger children's dormitory. "While you do so, I shall assist this so excellent brute into the hall where the little ones sleep and tether him in such manner that he cannot reach any of his little roommates, yet can easily dispute passage with anyone attempting to enter the apartment. Tomorrow morning, we shall be here early enough to remove him before any of the attendants who may enter the dormitory on legitimate business can be bitten. As for others—" He shrugged his shoulders and prepared to lead the lumbering brute into the sleeping quarters.

His program worked perfectly. Mr. Gervaise was nothing loth to talk with me about the case, and I gathered that he had taken de Grandin's evident dislike much to heart. Again and again he assured me, almost with tears in his eyes, that he had not the least intention of eavesdropping when he was discovered at the office door, but that he had really come in search of a pencil. It seemed he used a special indelible lead in making out his reports and had discovered that the only one he possessed was in the office after we had taken possession. His protestations were so earnest that I left him convinced de Grandin had done him an injustice.

Next morning, I was at a loss what to think. Arriving at the orphanage well before daylight, de Grandin and I let ourselves into the little children's dormitory, mounted the stairs to the second floor where the youngsters slept, and released the vicious dog which the

Frenchman had tethered by a stout nail driven into the floor and a ten-foot length of stout steel chain. Inquiry among the building's attendants elicited the information that no one had visited the sleeping apartment after we left, as there had been no occasion for anyone connected with the home to do so. Yet on the floor beside the dog there lay a ragged square of white linen, such as might have been ripped from a nightrobe or a suit of pajamas, reduced almost to a pulp by the savage brute's worrying, and—when Superintendent Gervaise entered the office to greet us, he was wearing his right arm in a sling.

"You are injured, Monsieur?" de Grandin asked with mock solicitude, noting the superintendent's bandaged hand with dancing eyes.

"Yes," the other replied, coughing apologetically, "yes, sir. I—I cut myself rather badly last night on a pane of broken glass in my quarters. The window must have been broken by a shutter being blown against it, and—"

"Quite so," the Frenchman agreed amiably. "They bite terrifically, these broken window-panes, is it not so?"

"Bite?" Gervaise echoed, regarding the other with a surprised, somewhat frightened expression. "I hardly understand you—oh, yes, I see," he smiled rather feebly. "You mean cut."

"*Monsieur*," de Grandin assured him solemnly as he rose to leave, "I did mean exactly what I said; no more, and certainly no less."

"Now what?" I queried as we left the office and the gaping superintendent behind us.

"*Non, non,*" he responded irritably. "I know not what to think, my friend. One thing, he points this way, another, he points elsewhere. Me, I am like a mariner in the midst of a fog. Go you to the car, Friend Trowbridge, and chaperone our so estimable ally. I shall pay a visit to the laundry, meantime."

None too pleased with my assignment, I re-entered my car and made myself as agreeable as possible to the dog, devoutly hoping that the hearty breakfast de Grandin had provided him had taken the edge off his appetite. I had no wish to have him stay his hunger on one of my limbs. The animal proved docile enough, however, and besides opening his mouth once or twice in prodigious yawns which gave me an unpleasantly close view of his excellent dentition, did nothing to cause me alarm.

When de Grandin returned, he was fuming with impatience and anger. *"Sacré nom d'un grillon!"* he swore. "It is beyond me. Undoubtedly this Monsieur Gervaise is a liar, it was surely no glass which caused the wound in his arm last night yet there is no suit of torn pajamas belonging to him in the laundry."

"Perhaps he didn't send them to be washed," I ventured with a grin. "If I'd been somewhere I was not supposed to be last night and found someone had posted a man-eating dog in my path, I'd not be in a hurry to send my torn clothing to the laundry where it might betray me."

"Tiens, you reason excellently, my friend," he complimented, "but can you explain how it is that there is no torn night-clothing of Monsieur Gervaise at the washrooms today, yet two ladies' night-robes —one of Mere Martin's, one of Mademoiselle Bosworth's—display exactly such rents as might have been made by having this bit of cloth torn from them?" He exhibited the relic we had found beside the dog that morning and stared gloomily at it.

"H'm, it looks as if you hadn't any facts which will stand the acid test just yet," I replied flippantly; but the seriousness with which he received my commonplace rejoinder startled me.

"Morbleu, the acid test, do you say?" he exclaimed. *"Dieu de Dieu de Dieu de Dieu,* it may easily be so! Why did I not think of it before? Perhaps. Possibly. Who knows? It may be so!"

"What in the world—" I began, but he cut me short with a frantic gesture.

"Non, non, my friend, not now," he implored. "Me, I must think. I must make this empty head of mine do the work for which it is so poorly adapted. Let us see, let us consider, let us ratiocinate!

"Parbleu, I have it!" He drew his hands downward from his forehead with a quick, impatient motion and turned to me. "Drive me to the nearest pharmacy, my friend. If we do not find what we wish there, we must search elsewhere, and elsewhere, until we discover it. *Mordieu,* Trowbridge, my friend, I thank you for mentioning that

acid test! Many a wholesome truth is contained in words of idle jest; I do assure you."

———

Five miles out of Springville a gang of workmen were resurfacing the highway, and we were forced to detour over a back road. Half an hour's slow driving along this brought us to a tiny Italian settlement where a number of laborers originally engaged on the Lackawanna's right of way had bought up the swampy, low-lying lands along the creek and converted them into model truck gardens. At the head of the single street composing the hamlet was a neatly whitewashed plank building bearing the sign *Farmacia Italiana*, together with a crudely painted representation of the Italian royal coat of arms.

"Here, my friend," de Grandin commanded, plucking me by the sleeve. "Let us stop here a moment and inquire of the estimable gentleman who conducts this establishment that which we would know."

"But what—?" I began, then stopped, noting the futility of my question. Jules de Grandin had already leaped from the car and entered the little drug store.

Without preamble he addressed a flood of fluent Italian to the druggist, receiving monosyllabic replies which gradually expanded both in verbosity and volume, accompanied by much waving of hands and lifting of shoulders and eyebrows. What they said I had no means of knowing, since I understood no word of Italian, but I heard the word *acido* repeated several times by each of them during the three minutes' heated conversation.

When de Grandin finally turned to leave the store, with a grateful bow to the proprietor, he wore an expression as near complete mystification and surprise as I had ever seen him display. His little eyes were rounded with mingled thought and amazement, and his narrow red lips were pursed beneath the line of his slim blond mustache as though he were about to emit a low, soundless whistle.

"Well?" I demanded as we regained the car. "Did you find out what you were after?"

"Eh?" he answered absently. "Did I find—Trowbridge, my friend, I know not what I found out, but this I know: those who lighted the witch-fires in olden days were not such fools as we believe them. *Parbleu*, at this moment they are grinning at us from their graves, or I am much mistaken. Tonight, my friend, be ready to accompany me back to that orphans' home where the devil nods approval to those who perform his business so skillfully."

———

That evening he was like one in a muse, eating sparingly and seemingly without realizing what food he took, answering my questions absent-mindedly or not at all, even forgetting to light his customary cigarette between dinner and dessert. *"Nom, d'un champignon,"* he muttered, staring abstractedly into his coffee cup, "it must be that it is so; but who would believe it?"

I sighed in vexation. His habit of musing aloud but refusing to tell the trend of his thoughts while he arranged the factors of a case upon his mental chess board was one which always annoyed me, but nothing I had been able to do had swerved him from his custom of withholding all information until he reached the climax of the mystery. *"Non, non,"* he replied when I pressed him to take me into his confidence, "the less I speak, the less danger I run of showing myself to be one great fool, my friend. Let me reason this business in my own way, I beseech you." And there the matter rested.

Toward midnight he rose impatiently and motioned toward the door. "Let us go," he suggested. "It will be an hour or more before we reach our destination, and that should be the proper time for us to see what I fear we shall behold, Friend Trowbridge."

We drove across country to Springville through the early autumn night in silence, turned in at the orphanage gates, and parked before the administration building, where Superintendent Gervaise maintained his living quarters.

"*Monsieur*," de Grandin called softly as he rapped gently on the superintendent's door, "it is I, Jules de Grandin. For all the wrong I have done you I humbly apologize, and now I would that you give me assistance."

Blinking with mingled sleep and surprise, the little, gray-haired official let us into his rooms and smiled rather fatuously at us. "What is it you'd like me to do for you, Dr. de Grandin?" he asked.

"I would that you guide us to the sleeping apartments of Mère Martin. Are they in this building?"

"No," Gervaise replied wonderingly. "Mother Martin has a cottage of her own over at the south end of the grounds. She likes the privacy of a separate house, and we—"

"*Précisément*," the Frenchman agreed, nodding vigorously. "I well understand her love of privacy, I fear. Come, let us go. You will show us the way?"

Mother Martin's cottage stood by the southern wall of the orphanage compound. It was a neat little building of the semi-bungalow type, constructed of red brick, and furnished with a low, wide porch of white-painted wood. Only the chirping of a cricket in the long grass and the long-drawn, melancholy call of a crow in the nearby poplars broke the silence of the starlit night as we walked noiselessly up the brick path leading to the cottage door. Gervaise was about to raise the polished brass knocker which adorned the white panels when de Grandin grasped his arm, enjoining silence.

Quietly as a shadow the little Frenchman crept from one of the wide, shutterless front windows to the other, looking intently into the darkened interior of the house, then, with upraised finger warning us to caution, he tiptoed from the porch and began making a circuit of the house, pausing to peer through each window as he passed it.

At the rear of the cottage was a one-story addition which evidently housed the kitchen, and here the blinds were tightly drawn, though beneath their lower edges there crept a faint, narrow band of lamplight.

"*Ah—bien!*" the Frenchman breathed, flattening his aquiline nose against the windowpane as though he would look through the shrouding curtain by virtue of the very intensity of his gaze.

A moment we stood there in the darkness, de Grandin's little waxed mustache twitching at the ends like the whiskers of an alert tomcat, Gervaise and I in total bewilderment, when the Frenchman's next move filled us with mingled astonishment and alarm. Reaching into an inner pocket, he produced a small, diamond-set glasscutter, moistened it with the tip of his tongue and applied it to the window, drawing it slowly downward, then horizontally, then upward again to meet the commencement of the first downstroke, thus describing an equilateral triangle on the pane. Before the cutter's circuit was entirely completed, he drew what appeared to be a square of thick paper from another pocket, hastily tore it apart and placed it face downward against the glass. It was only when the operation was complete that I realized how it was accomplished. The "plaster" he applied to the window was nothing more nor less than a square of flypaper, and its sticky surface prevented any telltale tinkle from sounding as he finished cutting the triangle from the windowpane and carefully lifted it out by means of the gummed paper.

Once he had completed his opening, he drew forth a small, sharp-bladed penknife, and working very deliberately, lest the slightest sound betray him proceeded to slit a peephole through the opaque window-blind.

For a moment he stood there, gazing through his spyhole, the expression on his narrow face changing from one of concentrated interest to almost incredulous horror, finally to fierce, implacable rage.

"*À moi*, Trowbridge, *à moi*, Gervaise!" he shouted in a voice which was almost a shriek as he thrust his shoulder unceremoniously against the pane, bursting it into a dozen pieces, and leaped into the lighted room beyond.

I scrambled after him as best I could, and the astounded superintendent followed me, mouthing mild protests against our burglarious entry of Mrs. Martin's house.

One glance at the scene before me took all thought of our trespass from my mind.

Wheeled about to face us, her back to a fiercely glowing coal-burning kitchen range, stood the once placid Mother Martin, enveloped from throat to knees in a commodious apron. But all semblance of her placidity was gone as she regarded the trembling little Frenchman who extended an accusing finger at her. Across her florid, smooth-skinned face had come such a look of fiendish rage as no flight of my imagination could have painted. Her lips, seemingly shrunk to half their natural thickness, were drawn back in animal fury against her teeth, and her blue eyes seemed forced forward from her face with the pressure of hatred within her. At the corners of her twisting mouth were little flecks of white foam, and her jaw thrust forward like that of an infuriated ape. Never in my life, on any face, either bestial or human, had I seen such an expression. It was a revolting parody of humanity on which I looked, a thing so horrible, so incomparably cruel and devilish, I would have looked away if I could, yet felt my eyes compelled to turn again to the evil visage as a fascinated bird's gaze may be held by the glitter in the serpent's film-covered eye.

But horrid as the sight of the woman's transfigured features was, a greater horror showed behind her, for, protruding half its length from the fire-grate of the blazing range was something no medical man could mistake after even a split-second's inspection. It was the unfleshed radius and ulna bones of a child's forearm, the wrist process still intact where the flesh and periosteum had not been entirely removed in dissection. On the tile-topped kitchen table beside the stove stood a wide-mouthed glass bowl filled with some liquid about the shade of new vinegar, and in this there lay a score of small, glittering white objects—a child's teeth. Neatly dressed, wound with cord like a roast, and, like a roast, placed in a wide, shallow pan, ready for cooking, was a piece of pale, veal-like meat

The horror of it fairly nauseated me. The thing in woman's form before us was a cannibal, and the meat she had been preparing to bake was—my mind refused to form the words, even in the silence of my inner consciousness.

"You—you," the woman cried in a queer, throaty voice, so low it was scarcely audible, yet so intense in its vibrations that I was reminded of the rumbling of an infuriated cat's cry. "How—did—you —find?"

"*Eh bien, Madame,*" de Grandin returned, struggling to speak with his customary cynical flippancy, but failing in the attempt, "how I did find out is of small moment. What I found, I think you will agree, is of the great import."

For an instant I thought the she-fiend would launch herself at him, but her intention lay elsewhere. Before any of us was aware of her move she had seized the glass vessel from the table, lifted it to her lips and all but emptied its contents down her throat in two frantic swallows. Next instant, frothing, writhing, contorting herself horribly, she lay on the tiled floor at our feet, her lips thickening and swelling with brownish blisters as the poison she had drunk regurgitated from her esophagus and welled up between her tightly set teeth.

"Good heavens?" I cried, bending forward instinctively to aid her, but the Frenchman drew me back. "Let be, Friend Trowbridge," he remarked. "It is useless. She has taken enough hydrochloric acid to kill three men, and those movements of hers are only mechanical. Already she is unconscious, and in another five minutes she will have opportunity to explain her so strange life to One far wiser than we.

"Meantime," he assumed the cold, matter-of-fact manner of a morgue attendant performing his duties, "let us gather up these relics of the poor one"—he indicated the partially cremated arm-bones and the meat in the shining aluminum pan—"and preserve them for decent interment. I—"

A choking, gasping sound behind us turned our attention to the orphanage superintendent. Following more slowly through the window in de Grandin's wake, he had not at first grasped the significance of the horrors we had seen. The spectacle of the woman's suicide had unnerved him, but when de Grandin pointed to the relics in the stove and on the table, the full meaning of our discovery had fallen on him. With an inarticulate cry he had dropped to the floor in a dead faint.

"*Pardieu,*" the Frenchman exclaimed, crossing to the water-tap and filling a tumbler, "I think we had best bestow our services on the living before we undertake the care of the dead, Friend Trowbridge."

As he recrossed the kitchen to minister to the unconscious superintendent there came an odd, muffled noise from the room beyond. *"Qui vive?"* he challenged sharply, placing the glass of water on the dresser and darting through the door, his right hand dropping into his jacket pocket where the ready pistol lay. I followed at his heels, and, as he stood hesitating at the threshold, felt along the wall, found the electric switch and pressed it, flooding the room with light. On the couch beneath the window, bound hand and foot with strips torn from a silk scarf and gagged with another length of silk wound about her face, lay little Betsy, the child who had informed us she feared being hurt when we made our pretended inspection of the home's inmates the previous day.

"Morbleu," Grandin muttered as he liberated the little one from her bonds, "another?"

"Mother Martin came for Betsy and tied her up," the child informed us as she raised herself to a sitting posture. "She told Betsy she would send her to heaven with her papa and mamma, but Betsy must be good and not make a fuss when her hands and feet were tied."

She smiled vaguely at de Grandin. "Why doesn't Mother Martin come for Betsy?" she demanded. "She said she would come and send me to heaven in a few minutes, but I waited and waited, and she didn't come, and the cloth over my face kept tickling my nose, and—"

"Mother Martin has gone away on business, *ma petite,*" the Frenchman interrupted. "She said she could not send you to your papa and *maman,* but if you are a very good little girl you may go to them some day. Meantime"—he fished in his jacket pocket, finally produced a packet of chocolates—"here is the best substitute I can find for heaven at this time, *chérie.*"

———

"Well, old chap, I'll certainly have to admit you went right to the heart of the matter," I congratulated as we drove homeward through the paling dawn, "but I can't for the life of me figure out how you did it."

His answering smile was a trifle wan. The horrors we had witnessed at the matron's cottage had been almost too great a strain for even his iron nerve. "Partly it was luck," he confessed wearily, "and partly it was thought.

"When first we arrived at the home for orphans, I had nothing to guide me, but I was convinced that the little ones had not wandered off voluntarily. The environment seemed too good to make any such hypothesis possible. Everywhere I looked I saw evidences of loving care and faces which could be trusted. But somewhere, I felt, as an old wound feels the coming changes of the weather, there was something evil, some evil force working against the welfare of those poor ones. Where could it be, and by whom was it exerted? 'This is for us to find out,' I tell me as I look over the attendants who were visible in the chapel.

"Gervaise, he is an old woman in trousers. Never would he hurt a living thing, no, not even a fly, unless it bit him first.

"Mère Martin, she was of a saintly appearance, but when I was presented to her, I learn something which sets my brain to thinking. On the softness of her white hands are stains and callouses. Why? I hold her hand longer than convention required, and all the time I ask me, 'What have she done to put these hardnesses on her hands?'

"To this I had no answer, so I bethought me perhaps my nose could tell what my sense of touch could not. When I raised her hand to my lips I made a most careful examination of it, and also, I did smell. Trowbridge, my friend, I made sure those disfigurements were due to HCl—what you call hydrochloric acid in English.

"'*Morbleu*, but this is extraordinary,' I tell me. 'Why should one who has no need to handle acid have those burns on her skin?'

"'That are for you to answer in good time,' I reply to me. And then I temporarily forget the lady and her hands, because I am sure that Monsieur Gervaise desires to know what we say to the young children. *Eh bien*, I did do him an injustice there, but the wisest of us makes mistakes, my friend, and he gave me much reason for suspicion.

"When the little Betsy was answering my questions, she tells me that she has seen a 'white lady,' tall and with flowing robes, like an angel, come into the dormitory where she and her companions slept on many occasions, and I have ascertained from previous questions that no one enters those sleeping quarters after the lights are out unless there is specific need for a visit. What was I to think? Had the little one dreamed it, or has she seen this so mysterious 'white lady' on her midnight visits? It is hard to say where recollection stops and romance begins in children's tales, my friend, as you well know, but the little Betsy was most sure the 'white lady' had come only on those nights when her little companions vanished.

"Here we had something from which to reason, though the morsel of fact was small. However, when I talk further with the child, she informed me it was Mère Martin who had warned her against us, saying we would surely cut her tongue with a knife if she talked to us. This, again, was worthy of thought. But Monsieur Gervaise had been smelling at the door while we were interrogating the children, and he had also disapproved of our seeing them alone. My suspicion of him would not die easily, my friend; I was stubborn, and refused to let my mind take me where it would.

"So, as you know, when we had posted the four-footed sentry inside the children's door, I made sure we would catch a fish in our trap, and next morning I was convinced we had, for did not Gervaise wear his arm in a sling? Truly, he did.

"But at the laundry they showed me no torn pajamas of his, while I found the gowns of both Mademoiselle Bosworth and Madame Martin torn as if the dog had bitten them. More mystery. Which way should I turn, if at all?

"I find that Gervaise's window really had been broken, but that meant nothing; he might have done it himself in order to construct an alibi. Of the reason for Mademoiselle Bosworth's torn robe, I could glean no trace; but behind my brain, at the very back of my head, something was whispering at me; something I could not hear, but which I knew was of importance.

"Then, as we drove away from the home, you mentioned the acid test. My friend, those words of yours let loose the memory which cried aloud to me, but which I could not clearly understand. Of a suddenness I did recall the scene at luncheon, how Mademoiselle Bosworth declared Mère Martin ate no meat for six months, and how angry Madame Martin was at the mention of it. *Parbleu*, for six months the little ones had been disappearing—for six months Madame Martin had eaten no meat, yet she was plump and well-nourished. She had the look of a meat-eater!"

"Still," I protested, "I don't see how that put you on the track."

"No?" he replied. "Remember, my friend, how we stopped to interview the druggist. Why think you we did that?"

"Hanged if I know," I confessed.

"Of course not," he agreed with a nod. "But I know. 'Suppose,' I say to me, 'someone have eaten the flesh of these poor disappeared children? What would that one do with the bones?'

"'He would undoubtedly bury or burn them,' I reply.

"'Very good, but more likely he would burn them, since buried bones may be dug up, and burned bones are only ashes; but what of the teeth? They would resist fire such as can be had in the ordinary stove, yet surely they might betray the murderer.'

"'But of course,' I admit, 'but why should not the murderer reduce those teeth with acid, hydrochloric acid, for instance?'

"'Ah-ha,' I tell me, 'that is the answer. Already you have one whose hands are acid-stained without adequate explanation, also one who eats no meat at table. Find out, now, who have bought acid from some neighboring drug store, and perhaps you will have the answer to your question.'

"The Italian gentleman who keeps the pharmacy tells me that a lady of very kindly mien comes to him frequently and buys hydrochloric acid, which she calls muriatic acid, showing she are not a chemist, but knows only the commercial term for the stuff. She is a tall, large lady with white hair and kind blue eyes.

"'It is Mère Martin!' I tell me. 'She is the "white lady" of the orphanage!'

"Then I consult my memory some more and decide we shall investigate this night.

"Listen, my friend: In the Paris *Sûreté* we have the history of many remarkable cases, not only from France, but other lands as well. In the year 1849 a miscreant named Swiatek was hauled before the Austrian courts on a charge of cannibalism, and in the same year there was another somewhat similar case where a young English lady—a girl of much refinement and careful education and nurture—was the defendant. Neither of these was naturally fierce nor bloodthirsty, yet their crimes were undoubted. In the case of the beggar, we have a transcription of his confession. He did say in part: When first driven by dire hunger to eat of human flesh he became, as the first horrid morsel passed his lips, as it were a ravening wolf. He did rend and tear the flesh and growl in his throat like a brute beast the while. From that time forth he could stomach no other meat, nor could he abide the sight or smell of it. Beef, pork or mutton filled him with revulsion. And had not Madame Martin exhibited much the same symptoms at table? Truly.

"Things of a strange nature sometimes occur, my friend. The mind of man is something of which we know but little, no matter how learnedly we prate. Why does one man love to watch a snake creep, while another goes into ecstasies of terror at sight of a reptile? Why do some people hate the sight of a cat, while others fear a tiny, harmless mouse as though he were the devil's brother-in-law? None can say, yet these things are. So, I think it is with crime.

"This Madame Martin was not naturally cruel. Though she killed and ate her charges, you will recall how she bound the little Betsy with silk and did it in such a way as not to injure her, or even to make her uncomfortable. That meant mercy? By no means, my friend. Myself, I have seen peasant women in my own land weep upon and fondle the rabbit they were about to kill for *déjeuner*. They did love and pity the poor little beast, which was to die, but *que voulez vous?* One must eat.

"Some thought like this, I doubt not, was in Madame Martin's mind as she committed murder. Somewhere in her nature was a thing we cannot understand; a thing which made her crave the flesh of her kind for food, and she answered the call of that craving even as the taker of drugs is helpless against his vice.

"*Tiens,* I am convinced that if we searched her house we should have the explanation of the children's disappearance, and you yourself witnessed what we saw. It was well she took the poison when she did. Death, or incarceration in a madhouse, would have been her portion had she lived, and"—he shrugged his shoulders—"the world is better off without her."

"U'm, I see how you worked it out," I replied, "but will Mr. Richards be satisfied? We've accounted for one of the children, because we found part of her skeleton in the fire, but can we swear the rest disappeared in the same manner? Richards will want a statistical table of facts before he parts with three thousand dollars, I imagine."

"*Parbleu,* will he, indeed?" de Grandin answered, something like his usual elfish grin spreading across his face. "What think you would be the result were we to notify the authorities of the true facts leading up to Madame Martin's suicide? Would not the newspapers make much of it? *Cordieu,* I shall say they would, and the home for orphans over which Monsieur Richards presides so pompously would receive what you call 'the black eye.' *Morbleu,* my friend, the very black eye, indeed! No, no; me, I think Monsieur Richards will gladly pay us the reward, nor haggle over terms.

"Meanwhile, we are at home once more. Come, let us drink the cognac."

"Drink cognac?" I answered. "Why, in heaven's name?"

"*Parbleu,* we shall imbibe a toast to the magnificent three thousand dollars Monsieur Richards pays us tomorrow morning!"

THE TERRIBLE OLD MAN

H.P. LOVECRAFT

I t was the design of Angelo Ricci and Joe Czanek and Manuel Silva to call on the Terrible Old Man. This old man dwells all alone in a very ancient house on Water Street near the sea and is reputed to be both exceedingly rich and exceedingly feeble, which forms a situation very attractive to men of the profession of Messrs. Ricci, Czanek, and Silva, for that profession was nothing less dignified than robbery.

The inhabitants of Kingsport say and think many things about the Terrible Old Man which generally keep him safe from the attention of gentlemen like Mr. Ricci and his colleagues, despite the almost certain fact that he hides a fortune of indefinite magnitude somewhere about his musty and venerable abode. He is, in truth, a very strange person, believed to have been a captain of East India clipper ships in his day; so old that no one can remember when he was young, and so taciturn that few know his real name. Among the gnarled trees in the front yard of his aged and neglected place he maintains a strange collection of large stones, oddly grouped and painted so that they resemble the idols in some obscure Eastern temple. This collection frightens away most of the small boys who love to taunt the Terrible Old Man about his long white hair and beard, or to break the small-paned windows of his dwelling with wicked missiles; but there are other things which frighten the older and more curious folk who sometimes steal up to the house to peer in through the dusty panes. These folk say that on a table in a bare room on the ground floor are many peculiar bottles, in each a small piece of lead suspended pendulum-wise from a string. And they say that the Terrible Old Man talks to these bottles, addressing them by such names as Jack, Scar-Face, Long Tom, Spanish Joe, Peters, and Mate Ellis, and that whenever he speaks to a bottle the little lead pendulum within makes certain definite vibrations as if in answer. Those who have watched the tall, lean, Terrible Old Man in these peculiar conversations, do not watch him again. But Angelo Ricci and Joe Czanek and Manuel Silva were not of Kingsport blood; they were of that new and heterogeneous alien stock which lies outside the charmed circle of New England life and traditions, and they saw in the Terrible Old Man merely a tottering, almost helpless greybeard, who could not walk without the aid of his knotted cane, and whose thin, weak hands shook pitifully. They were really quite sorry in their way for the lonely, unpopular old fellow, whom everybody shunned, and at whom all the dogs barked singularly. But business is business, and to a robber whose soul is in his profession, there is a lure and a challenge about a very old and very feeble man who has no account at the bank, and who pays for his few necessities at the village store with Spanish gold and silver minted two centuries ago.

Messrs. Ricci, Czanek, and Silva selected the night of April 11th for their call. Mr. Ricci and Mr. Silva were to interview the poor old gentleman, whilst Mr. Czanek waited for them and their presumable metallic burden with a covered motorcar in Ship Street, by the gate in the tall rear wall of their host's grounds. Desire to avoid needless explanations in case of unexpected police intrusions prompted these plans for a quiet and unostentatious departure.

As prearranged, the three adventurers started out separately in order to prevent any evil-minded suspicions afterward. Messrs. Ricci and Silva met in Water Street by the old man's front gate, and although they did not like the way the moon shone down upon the painted stones through the budding branches of the gnarled trees,

they had more important things to think about than mere idle superstition. They feared it might be unpleasant work making the Terrible
Old Man loquacious concerning his hoarded gold and silver, for aged
sea captains are notably stubborn and perverse. Still, he was very old
and very feeble, and there were two visitors. Messrs. Ricci and Silva
were experienced in the art of making unwilling persons voluble, and
the screams of a weak and exceptionally venerable man can be easily
muffled. So, they moved up to the one lighted window and heard the
Terrible Old Man talking childishly to his bottles with pendulums.
Then they donned masks and knocked politely at the weather-stained
oaken door.

———

Waiting seemed very long to Mr. Czanek as he fidgeted restlessly in the
covered motorcar by the Terrible Old Man's back gate in Ship Street.
He was more than ordinarily tender-hearted, and he did not like the
hideous screams he had heard in the ancient house just after the hour
appointed for the deed. Had he not told his colleagues to be as gentle
as possible with the pathetic old sea-captain? Very nervously he
watched that narrow oaken gate in the high and ivy-clad stone wall.
Frequently, he consulted his watch and wondered at the delay. Had
the old man died before revealing where his treasure was hidden, and
had a thorough search become necessary? Mr. Czanek did not like to
wait so long in the dark in such a place. Then he sensed a soft tread or
tapping on the walk inside the gate, heard a gentle fumbling at the
rusty latch, and saw the narrow, heavy door swing inward. And in the
pallid glow of the single dim streetlamp, he strained his eyes to see
what his colleagues had brought out of that sinister house which
loomed so close behind. But when he looked, he did not see what he
had expected; for his colleagues were not there at all, but only the
Terrible Old Man leaning quietly on his knotted cane and smiling
hideously. Mr. Czanek had never before noticed the colour of that
man's eyes; now he saw that they were yellow.

Little things make considerable excitement in little towns, which is the reason that Kingsport people talked all that spring and summer about the three unidentifiable bodies, horribly slashed as with many cutlasses, and horribly mangled as by the tread of many cruel boot-heels, which the tide washed in. And some people even spoke of things as trivial as the deserted motorcar found in Ship Street, or certain especially inhuman cries, probably of a stray animal or migratory bird, heard in the night by wakeful citizens. But in this idle village gossip the Terrible Old Man took no interest at all. He was by nature reserved, and when one is aged and feeble one's reserve is doubly strong. Besides, so ancient a sea captain must have witnessed scores of things much more stirring in the far-off days of his unremembered youth.

THE WOMAN OF
THE WOOD
A. MERRITT

McKay sat on the balcony of the little inn that squatted like a brown gnome among the pines that clothed the eastern shore of the lake.

It was a small and lonely lake high up on the Vosges; and yet the word 'lonely' is not just the one to tag its spirit; rather was it aloof, withdrawn. The mountains came down on every side, making a vast tree-lined bowl that seemed filled, when McKay first saw it, with a still wine of peace.

McKay had worn the wings with honor in the World War. And as a bird loves the trees, so did McKay love them. They were to him not merely trunks and roots, branches and leaves; they were personalities. He was acutely aware of character differences even among the same species—that pine was jolly and benevolent; that one austere, monkish; there stood a swaggering bravo and there a sage wrapped in green meditation; that birch was a wanton—the one beside her virginal, still a dream.

The war had sapped McKay, nerve, brain, and soul. Through all the years that had passed the wound had kept open. But now, as he slid his car down the side of the great green bowl, he felt its peace reach out to him; caress and quiet him; promise him healing. He seemed to drift like a falling leaf through the cathedralic woods; to be cradled by the hands of the trees.

McKay had stopped at the little gnome of the inn; and there he had lingered, day after day, week after week.

The trees had nursed him; soft whisperings of the leaves, slow chant of the needled pines, had first deadened, then driven from him the re-echoing clamor of the war and its sorrow. The open wound of his spirit had closed under their healing; had closed and become scars; and then even the scars had been covered and buried, as the scars on Earth's breast are covered and buried beneath the falling leaves of autumn. The trees had laid healing hands upon his eyes. He had sucked strength from the green breasts of the hills.

As that strength flowed back to him, McKay grew aware that the place was—troubled; that there was ferment of fear within it.

It was as though the trees had waited until he himself had become whole before they made their own unrest known to him. But now they were trying to tell him something; there was a shrillness as of apprehension, of anger, in the whispering of the leaves, the needled chanting of the pines.

And it was this that had kept McKay at the inn—a definite consciousness of appeal. He strained his ears to catch words in the rustling branches, words that trembled on the brink of his human understanding.

Never did they cross that brink.

Gradually he had focused himself, so he believed, to the point of the valley's unease.

On all the shores of the lake there were but two dwellings. One was the inn, and around the inn the trees clustered protectively; confidingly; friendly. It was as though they had not only accepted it but had made it part of themselves.

Not so was it of the other habitation. Once it had been the hunting lodge of long-dead lords; now it was half-ruined, forlorn. It lay across the lake almost exactly opposite the inn and back upon the slope a half-mile from the shore. Once there had been fat fields around it and a fair orchard.

The forest had marched down upon fields and lodge. Here and there scattered pines and poplars stood like soldiers guarding some outpost; scouting parties of saplings lurked among the gaunt, broken fruit trees. But the forest had not had its way unchecked; ragged stumps showed where those who dwelt in the old house had cut down the invaders; blackened patches showed where they had fired the woods.

Here was the center of the conflict. Here the green folk of the forest were both menaced and menacing at war.

The lodge was a fortress beleaguered by the trees, a fortress whose garrison sallied forth with ax and torch to take their toll of their besiegers.

Yet McKay sensed a slow, inexorable pressing on of the forest; he saw it as an army ever filling the gaps in its enclosing ranks, shooting its seeds into the cleared places, sending its roots out to sap them; and armed always with a crushing patience. He had the impression of constant regard, of watchfulness, as though night and day the forest kept myriads of eyes upon the lodge, inexorably, not to be swerved from its purpose. He had spoken of this impression to the innkeeper and his wife, and they had looked at him, oddly.

"Old Polleau does not love the trees, no," the old man had said. "No, nor do his two sons. They do not love the trees—and very certainly the trees do not love them."

———

Between the lodge and the shore, marching down to the verge of the lake was a singularly beautiful little coppice of silver birches and firs. This coppice stretched for perhaps a quarter of a mile; it was not more than a hundred feet or two in depth, and not alone the beauty of its trees but their curious grouping vividly aroused McKay's interest. At each end were a dozen or more of the glistening, needled firs, not clustered but spread out as though in open marching order; at widely spaced intervals along its other two sides paced single firs. The birches, slender and delicate, grew within the guard of these sturdier trees, yet not so thickly as to crowd one another.

To McKay the silver birches were for all the world like some gay caravan of lovely demoiselles under the protection of debonair knights. With that odd other sense of his he saw the birches as delectable damsels, merry and laughing—the pines as lovers, troubadours in green-needled mail. And when the winds blew and the crests of the trees bent under them, it was as though dainty demoiselles picked up fluttering, leafy skirts, bent leafy hoods and danced while the knights of the firs drew closer round them, locked arms and danced with them to the roaring horns of the winds. At such times he almost heard sweet laughter from the birches, shoutings from the firs.

Of all the trees in that place McKay loved best this little wood. He had rowed across and rested in its shade, had dreamed there and, dreaming, had heard again echoes of the sweet elfin laughter. Eyes closed, he had heard mysterious whisperings and the sound of dancing feet light as falling leaves; had taken dream-draft of that gayety which was the soul of the little wood.

Two days ago, he had seen Polleau and his two sons. McKay had lain dreaming in the coppice all that afternoon. As dusk began to fall, he had reluctantly arisen and began to row back to the inn. When he had been a few hundred feet from shore three men had come out from the trees and had stood watching him—three grim powerful men taller than the average French peasant.

He had called a friendly greeting to them, but they had not answered it; had stood there, scowling. Then as he bent again to his oars, one of the sons had raised a hatchet and had driven it savagely into the trunk of a dim birch. McKay thought he heard a thin, wailing cry from the stricken tree, a sigh from all the little wood.

He had felt as though the keen edge had bitten into his own flesh.

"Stop that!" he had cried. "Stop it, damn you!"

For answer Polleau's son had struck again—and never had McKay seen hate etched so deep as on his face as he struck. Cursing, a killing rage in his heart, McKay had swung the boat around, raced back to shore. He had heard the hatchet strike again and again and, close now to shore, had heard a crackling and over it once more the thin, high wailing. He had turned to look.

The birch was tottering, was falling. Close beside it grew one of the firs, and, as the smaller tree crashed over, it dropped upon this fir like a fainting maid into the arms of her lover. And as it lay and trembled there, one of the branches of the other tree slipped from under it, whipped out and smote the hatchet-wielder a crushing blow upon the head, sending him to earth.

It had been, of course, only the chance blow of a bough, bent by pressure of the fallen trunk and then released as that had slipped down. Of course—yet there had been such suggestion of conscious action in the branch's recoil, so much of bitter anger in it; so much, in truth, had it been like a purposeful blow that McKay felt an eerie prickling of his scalp; his heart had missed its beat.

For a moment Polleau and the standing son had stared at the sturdy fir with the silvery birch lying upon its green breast. Folded in and shielded by its needled boughs as though—again the swift impression came to McKay—as though it were a wounded maid stretched on breast, in arms, of knightly lover. For a long moment father and son had stared.

Then, still wordless but with that same bitter hatred in both their faces, they had stooped and picked up the other and, with his arms around the neck of each, had borne him limply.

———

McKay, sitting on the balcony of the inn that morning, went over and over that scene; realized more and more clearly the human aspect of fallen birch and clasping fir, and the conscious deliberateness of the latter's blow. During the two days that had elapsed since then, he had felt the unease of the trees increase, their whispering appeal become more urgent.

What were they trying to tell him? What did they want him to do?

Troubled, he stared across the lake, trying to pierce the mists that hung over it and hid the opposite shore. And suddenly it seemed that he heard the coppice calling him, felt it pull the point of his attention toward it irresistibly, as the lodestone swings and holds the compass needle.

The coppice called him; it bade him come.

McKay obeyed the command; he arose and walked down to the boat landing; he stepped into his skiff and began to row across the lake. As his oars touched the water his trouble fell from him. In its place flowed peace and a curious exaltation.

The mists were thick upon the lake. There was no breath of wind, yet the mists billowed and drifted, shook and curtained under the touch of unfelt airy hands.

They were alive—the mists; they formed themselves into fantastic palaces past whose opalescent facades he flew; they built themselves into hills and valleys and circled plains whose floors were rippling silk. Tiny rainbows gleamed out among them, and upon the water prismatic patches shone and spread like spilled wine of opals. He had the illusion of vast distances—the hillocks of mist were real mountains, the valleys between them were not illusory. He was a colossus cleaving through some elfin world. A trout broke, and it was like Leviathan leaping from the fathomless deep. Around the arc of the fish's body rainbows interlaced and then dissolved into rain of softly gleaming gems—diamonds in dance with sapphires, flame-hearted rubies, pearls with shimmering souls of rose. The fish vanished, diving cleanly without sound; the jeweled bows vanished with it; a tiny irised whirlpool swirled for an instant where trout and flashing arcs had been.

Nowhere was there sound. He let his oars drop and leaned forward, drifting. In the silence, before him and around him, he felt opening the gateways of an unknown world.

And suddenly he heard the sound of voices, many voices; faint at first and murmurous. Louder they became, swiftly; women's voices sweet and lilting and mingled with them the deeper tones of men.

Voices that lifted and fell in a wild, gay chanting through whose *joyesse* ran undertones both of sorrow and of anger—as though faery weavers threaded through silk spun of sunbeams, somber strands dipped in the black of graves, and crimson strands stained in the red of wrathful sunsets.

He drifted on, scarce daring to breathe lest even that faint sound break the elfin song. Closer it rang and clearer; and now he became aware that the speed of his boat was increasing, that it was no longer drifting, as though the little waves on each side were pushing him ahead with soft and noiseless palms. His boat grounded, and as its keel rustled along over the smooth pebbles of the beach the song ceased.

McKay half arose and peered before him. The mists were thicker here but he could see the outlines of the coppice. It was like looking at it through many curtains of fine gauze, and its trees seemed shifting, ethereal, unreal. And moving among the trees were figures that threaded among the boles and flitted round them in rhythmic measures, like the shadows of leafy boughs swaying to some cadenced wind.

He stepped ashore. The mists dropped behind him, shutting off all sight of lake; and as they dropped McKay lost all sense of strangeness, all feeling of having entered some unfamiliar world. Rather was it as though he had returned to one he had once known well and that had been long lost to him.

The rhythmic flittings had ceased; there was now no movement as there was no sound among the trees—yet he felt the little wood full of watchful life. McKay tried to speak; there was a spell of silence on his mouth.

"You called me. I have come to listen to you—to help you if I can."

The words formed within his mind but utter them he could not. Over and over, he tried desperately; the words seemed to die on his lips.

A pillar of mist whirled forward and halted, eddying half an arm's length away. Suddenly out of it peered a woman's face, eyes level with his own. A woman's face—yes; but McKay, staring into those strange eyes probing his, knew that, woman's though it seemed, it was that of no woman of human breed. They were without pupils, the irises deer-large and of the soft green of deep forest dells; within them sparkled tiny star points of light like motes in a moonbeam. The eyes were wide and set far apart beneath a broad, low brow over which was piled braid upon braid of hair of palest gold, braids that seemed spun of shining ashes of gold. The nose was small and straight, the mouth scarlet and exquisite. The face was oval, tapering to a delicately pointed chin.

Beautiful was that face, but its beauty was an alien one; unearthly. For long moments the strange eyes thrust their gaze deep into his. Then out of the mist were thrust two slender white arms, the hands long, the fingers tapering. The tapering fingers touched his ears.

"He shall hear," whispered the red lips.

Immediately from all about him a cry arose; in it was the whispering and rustling of the leaves beneath the breath of the winds; the shrilling of the harp strings of the boughs; the laughter of hidden brooks; the shoutings of waters flinging themselves down into deep and rocky pools—the voices of the forest made articulate.

"He shall hear!" they cried.

The long white fingers rested on his lips, and their touch was cool as bark of birch on cheek after some long upward climb through forest; cool and subtly sweet.

"He shall speak," whispered the scarlet lips of the wood woman.

"He shall speak!" answered the wood voices again, as though in litany.

"He shall see," whispered the woman, and the cool fingers touched his eyes.

"He shall see!" echoed the wood voices.

———

The mists that had hidden the coppice from McKay wavered, thinned, and were gone. In their place was a limpid, translucent, palely green *aether*, faintly luminous—as though he stood within some clear wan emerald. His feet pressed a golden moss spangled with tiny starry bluets. Fully revealed before him was the woman of the strange eyes and the face of unearthly beauty. He dwelt for a moment upon the slender shoulders, the firm, small, tip-tilted breasts, the willow litheness of her body. From neck to knees a smock covered her, sheer and silken and delicate as spun cobwebs; through it her body gleamed as though fire of the young spring moon ran in her

He looked beyond her. There upon the golden moss were other women like her, many of them; they stared at him with the same wide-set green eyes in which danced the sparkling moonbeam motes; like her they were crowned with glistening, pallidly golden hair; like hers, too, were their oval faces with the pointed chins and perilous alien beauty. Only where she stared at him gravely, measuring him, weighing him—there were those of these her sisters whose eyes were mocking; and those whose eyes called to him with a weirdly tingling allure, their mouths athirst; those whose eyes looked upon him with curiosity alone; those whose great eyes pleaded with him, prayed to him.

Within that pellucid, greenly luminous *aether* McKay was abruptly aware that the trees of the coppice still had a place. Only now they were spectral indeed. They were like white shadows cast athwart a glaucous screen; trunk and bough, twig and leaf they arose around him and they were as though etched in air by phantom craftsmen— thin and unsubstantial; they were ghost-trees, rooted in another space.

He was aware that there were men among the women; men whose eyes were set wide apart as were theirs, as strange and pupilless as were theirs, but with irises of brown and blue; men with pointed chins and oval faces, broad-shouldered and clad in kirtles of darkest green; swarthy-skinned men, muscular and strong, with that same lithe grace of the women—and like them of a beauty that was alien and elfin.

McKay heard a little wailing cry. He turned. Close beside him lay a girl clasped in the arms of one of the swarthy, green-clad men. She lay upon his breast. His eyes were filled with a black flame of wrath, and hers were misted, anguished. For an instant McKay had a glimpse of the birch that old Polleau's son had sent crashing down into the boughs of the fir. He saw birch and fir as immaterial outlines around this man and this girl. For an instant girl and man and birch and fir seemed to be one and the same.

The scarlet-lipped woman touched his shoulder.

"She withers," sighed the woman, and in her voice, McKay heard a faint rustling as of mournful leaves. "Now is it not pitiful that she withers—our sister who was so young, so slender and so lovely?"

McKay looked again at the girl. The white skin seemed shrunken; the moon radiance that gleamed through the bodies of the others was still in hers but dim and pallid; her slim arms hung listlessly; her body drooped. Her mouth was wan and parched; her long and misted green eyes dull. The palely golden hair was lusterless, and dry. He looked on a slow death—a withering death.

"May the arm that struck her down wither!" said the green-clad man who held her, and in his voice, McKay heard a savage strumming as of winter winds through bleak boughs: "May his heart wither and the sun blast him! May the rain and the waters deny him and the winds scourge him!"

"I thirst," whispered the girl.

There was a stirring among the watching women. One came forward holding a chalice that was like thin leaves turned to green crystal. She paused beside the trunk of one of the spectral trees, reached up and drew down to her a branch. A slim girl with half-frightened, half-resentful eyes glided to her side and threw her arms around the ghostly bole. The woman cut the branch deep with what seemed an arrow-shaped flake of jade and held her chalice under it. From the cut a faintly opalescent liquid dripped into the cup. When it was filled the woman beside McKay stepped forward and pressed her own long hands around the bleeding branch. She stepped away and McKay saw that the stream had ceased to flow. She touched the trembling girl and unclasped her arms.

"It is healed," said the woman gently. "And it was your turn, little sister. The wound is healed. Soon you will have forgotten."

The woman with the chalice knelt and set it to the wan, dry lips of her who was—withering. She drank of it, thirstily, to the last drop. The misty eyes cleared; they sparkled; the lips that had been so parched and pale grew red, the white body gleamed as though the waning light within it had been fed with new.

"Sing, sisters," the girl cried, shrilly. "Dance for me, sisters!"

Again, burst out that chant McKay had heard as he had floated through the mists upon the lake. Now, as then, despite his opened ears, he could distinguish no words, but clearly he understood its mingled themes—the joy of spring's awakening, rebirth, with green life streaming singing up through every bough, swelling the buds, burgeoning with tender leaves the branches; the dance of the trees in the scented winds of spring; the drums of the jubilant rain on leafy hoods; passion of summer sun pouring its golden flood down upon the trees; the moon passing with stately steps and slow, and green hands reaching up to her and drawing from her breast milk of silver fire; riot of wild gay winds with their mad pipings and strummings; soft interlacing of boughs; the kiss of amorous leaves—all these and more, much more that McKay could not understand since they dealt with hidden, secret things for which man has no images, were in that chanting.

And all these and more were in the rhythms of the dancing of those strange, green-eyed women and brown-skinned men; something incredibly ancient, yet young as the speeding moment; something of a world before and beyond man.

McKay listened; McKay watched, lost in wonder; his own world more than half forgotten.

The woman beside him touched his arm. She pointed to the girl.

"Yet she withers," she said. "And not all our life, if we poured it through her lips, could save her."

He saw that the red was draining slowly from the girl's lips; that the luminous life-tides were waning. The eyes that had been so bright were misting and growing dull once more. Suddenly a great pity and a great rage shook him. He knelt beside her, took her hands in his.

"Take them away! Take away your hands! They burn me!" she moaned.

"He tries to help you," whispered the green-clad man, gently. But he reached over and drew McKay's hands away.

"Not so can you help her or us," said the woman.

"What can I do?" McKay arose, looked helplessly from one to the other. "What can I do to help you?"

The chanting died; the dance stopped. A silence fell, and he felt upon him the eyes of all these strange people. They were tense ... waiting. The woman took his hands. Their touch was cool and sent a strange sweetness sweeping through his veins.

"There are three men yonder," she said. "They hate us. Soon we shall all be as she is there—withering! They have sworn it, and as they have sworn so will they do. Unless—"

She paused. The moonbeam dancing motes in her eyes changed to tiny sparklings of red. They terrified him, those red sparklings.

"Three men?" In his clouded mind was dim memory of Polleau and his two strong sons. "Three men?" he repeated, stupidly. "But what are three men to you who are so many? What could three men do against those stalwart gallants of yours?"

"No," she shook her head. "No—there is nothing our—men—can do; nothing that we can do. Once, night and day, we were gay. Now we fear—night and day. They mean to destroy us. Our kin have warned us. And our kin cannot help us. Those three are masters of blade and flame. Against blade and flame we are helpless."

"Blade and flame!" echoed the others. "Against blade and flame we are helpless."

"Surely will they destroy us," murmured the woman. "We shall wither—all of us. Like her there, or burn—unless "

Suddenly she threw white arms around McKay's neck. She pressed her body close to him. Her scarlet mouth sought and found his lips and clung to them. Through all McKay's body ran swift, sweet flames, green fire of desire. His own arms went round her, crushed her to him.

"You shall not die!" he cried. "No—by God, you shall not!"

She drew back her head, looked deep into his eyes.

"They have sworn to destroy us," she said, "and soon. With blade and flame they will destroy us—those three—unless ..."

"Unless?" he asked, fiercely.

"Unless you—slay them first!" she answered.

A cold shock ran through McKay, chilling the fires of his desire. He dropped his arm from around the woman; thrust her from him. For an instant she trembled before him.

"Slay!" he heard her whisper—and she was gone.

———

The spectral trees wavered; their outlines thickened out of immateriality into substance. The green translucence darkened. He had a swift vertiginous moment as though he swung between two worlds. He closed his eyes. The dizziness passed and he opened them, looked around.

He stood on the lakeward skirts of the little coppice. There were no shadows flitting, no sign of white women nor of swarthy, green-clad men. His feet were on green moss. Gone was the soft golden carpet with its bluets. Birches and firs clustered solidly before him.

At his left was a sturdy fir in whose needled arms a broken birch tree lay withering. It was the birch that Polleau's son had so wantonly dashed down. For an instant he saw within the fir and birch the immaterial outlines of the green-clad man and the slim girl who withered! For that instant birch and fir and girl and man seemed one and the same. He stepped back, and his hands touched the smooth, cool bark of another birch that rose close at his right.

Upon his hands the touch of that bark was like—was like what? Curiously was it like the touch of the long slim hands of the woman of the scarlet lips!

McKay stood there, staring, wondering, like a man who has but half awakened from dream. And suddenly a little wind stirred the leaves of the rounded birch beside him. The leaves murmured, sighed. The wind grew stronger and the leaves whispered.

"Slay!" he heard them whisper—and again: "Slay! Help us! Slay!"

And the whisper was the voice of the woman of the scarlet lips!

Rage, swift and unreasoning, sprang up in McKay. He began to run up through the coppice, up to where he knew was the old lodge in which dwelt Polleau and his sons. And as he ran the wind blew stronger about him, and louder and louder grew the whispering of the trees.

"Slay!" they whispered. "Slay them! Save us! Slay!"

"I will slay! I will save you!" McKay, panting, hammer pulse beating in his ears, heard himself answering that ever more insistent command. And in his mind was but one desire—to clutch the throats of Polleau and his sons, to crack their necks. To stand by them then and watch them wither—wither like that slim girl in the arms of the green-clad man.

He came to the edge of the coppice and burst from it out into a flood of sunshine. For a hundred feet he ran, and then he was aware that the whispering command was stilled; that he heard no more that maddening rustling of wrathful leaves. A spell seemed to have been loosed from him; it was as though he had broken through some web of sorcery. McKay stopped, dropped upon the ground, buried his face in the grasses.

He lay there marshaling his thoughts into some order of sanity. What had he been about to do? To rush upon those three men who lived in the old lodge and—slay them! And for what? Because that unearthly, scarlet-lipped woman whose kisses he still could feel upon his mouth had bade him! Because the whispering, trees of the little wood had maddened him with that same command!

For this he had been about to kill three men!

What were that woman and her sisters and the green-clad swarthy gallants of theirs? Illusions of some waking dream—phantoms born of the hypnosis of the swirling mists through which he had rowed and floated across the lake? Such things were not uncommon. McKay knew of those who by watching the shifting clouds could create and dwell for a time with wide-open eyes within some similar land of fantasy; knew others who needed but to stare at smoothly falling water to set themselves within a world of waking dreams; there were those who could summon dreams by gazing into a ball of crystal, others who found dream life in saucers of shining ink.

Might not the moving mists have laid those same fingers of hypnosis upon his own mind—? And his love for the trees, the sense of appeal that he had felt so long, his memory of the wanton slaughter of the slim birch have all combined to paint upon his drugged consciousness the phantasms he had beheld?

McKay arose to his feet, shakily enough. He looked back at the coppice. There was no wind now; the leaves were silent, motionless. Reason with himself as he might, something deep within him stubbornly asserted the reality of his experience. At any rate, he told himself, the little wood was far too beautiful to be despoiled.

———

The old lodge was about a quarter of a mile away. A path led up to it through the ragged fields. McKay walked up the path, climbed rickety steps and paused, listening. He heard voices and knocked. The door was flung open and old Polleau stood there, peering at him through half-shut, suspicious eyes. One of the sons stood close behind him. They stared at McKay with grim, hostile faces.

He thought he heard a faint, far-off despairing whisper from the distant wood. And it was as though the pair in the doorway heard it too, for their gaze shifted from him to the coppice, and he saw hatred flicker swiftly across their grim faces. Their gaze swept back to him.

"What do you want?" demanded Polleau, curtly.

"I am a neighbor of yours, stopping at the inn—" began McKay, courteously.

"I know who you are," Polleau interrupted briskly, "but what is it that you want?"

"I find the air of this place good for me," McKay stifled a rising anger. "I am thinking of staying for a year or more until my health is fully recovered. I would like to buy some of your land and build me a lodge upon it."

"Yes, M'sieu?" There was acid politeness now in the old man's voice. "But is it permitted to ask why you do not remain at the inn? Its fare is excellent and you are well-liked there."

"I have desire to be alone," replied McKay. "I do not like people too close to me. I would have my own land, and sleep under my own roof."

"But why come to me?" asked Polleau. "There are many places upon the far side of the lake that you could secure. It is happy there, and this side is not happy, M'sieu. But tell me, what part of my land is it that you desire?"

"That little wood yonder," answered McKay, and pointed to the coppice.

"Ah! I thought so!" whispered Polleau, and between him and his son passed a look of somber understanding.

"That wood is not for sale, M'sieu," he said.

"I can afford to pay well for what I want," said McKay. "Name your price."

"It is not for sale," repeated Polleau, stolidly, "at any price."

"Oh, come," urged McKay, although his heart sank at the finality in that answer. "You have many acres and what is it but a few trees? I can afford to gratify my fancies. I will give you all the worth of your other land for it."

"You have asked what that place that you so desire is, and you have answered that it is but a few trees," said Polleau, slowly, and the tall son behind him laughed, abruptly, maliciously. "But it is more than that, M'sieu—oh, much more than that. And you know it, else why should you pay such a price as you offer? Yes, you know it—since you know also that we are ready to destroy it, and you would save it. And who told you all that, M'sieu?" he snarled.

There was such malignance, such black hatred in the face thrust suddenly close to McKay's, eyes blazing, teeth bared by uplifted lip, that involuntarily he recoiled.

"Only a few trees!" snarled old Polleau. "Then who told him what we mean to do—eh, Pierre?"

Again, the son laughed. And at that laughter McKay felt within him resurgence of his own blind hatred as he had fled through the whispering wood. He mastered himself, turned away; there was nothing he could do—now. Polleau halted him.

"M'sieu," he said, "enter. There is something I would tell you; something, too, I would show you."

He stood aside, bowing with a rough courtesy. McKay walked through the doorway. Polleau with his son followed him. He entered a large, dim room whose ceiling was spanned with smoke-blackened beams. From these beams hung onion strings and herbs and smoke-cured meats. On one side was a wide fireplace. Huddled beside it sat Polleau's other son. He glanced up as they entered and McKay saw that a bandage covered one side of his head, hiding his left eye. McKay recognized him as the one who had cut down the slim birch. The blow of the fir, he reflected with a certain satisfaction, had been no futile one.

Old Polleau strode over to that son.

"Look, M'sieu," he said, and lifted the bandage.

McKay saw, with a tremor of horror, a gaping blackened socket, red-rimmed and eyeless.

"Good God, Polleau!" he cried. "But this man needs medical attention. I know something of wounds. Let me go across the lake and bring back my kit I will attend him."

Old Polleau shook his head, although his grim face for the first time softened. He drew the bandages back in place.

"It heals," he said. "We have some skill in such things. You saw what did it. You watched from your boat as the cursed tree struck him. The eye was crushed and lay upon his cheek. I cut it away. Now he heals. We do not need your aid, M'sieu."

"Yet he ought not have cut the birch," muttered McKay, more to himself than to be heard.

"Why not?" asked old Polleau, fiercely; "since it hated him."

McKay stared at him. What did this old peasant know? The words strengthened his deep stubborn conviction that what he had seen and heard in the coppice had been actuality—no dream. And still more did Polleau's next words strengthen that conviction.

"M'sieu," he said, "you come here as ambassador—of a sort. The wood has spoken to you. Well, as ambassador I shall speak to you. Four centuries my people have lived in this place. A century we have owned this land. M'sieu, in all those years there has been no moment that the trees have not hated us—nor we the trees.

"For all those hundred years there have been hatred and battle between us and the forest. My father, M'sieu, was crushed by a tree; my elder brother crippled by another. My father's father, woodsman that he was, was lost in the forest—he came back to us with mind gone, raving of wood-women who had bewitched and mocked him, luring him into swamp and fen and tangled thicket, tormenting him. In every generation the trees have taken their toll of us—women as well as men—maiming or killing us."

"Accidents," interrupted McKay. "This is childish, Polleau. You cannot blame the trees."

"In your heart you do not believe so," said Polleau. "Listen, the feud is an ancient one. Centuries ago it began, when we were serfs, slaves of the nobles. To cook, to keep us warm in winter, they let us pick up the fagots, the dead branches and twigs that dropped from the trees. But if we cut down a tree to keep us warm, to keep our women and our children warm, yes, if we but tore down a branch—they hanged us, or threw us into dungeons to rot, or whipped us till our backs were red lattices.

"They had their broad fields, the nobles—but we must raise our food in the patches where the trees disdained to grow. And if they did thrust themselves into our poor patches, then, M'sieu, we must let them have their way—or be flogged, or be thrown into the dungeons, or be hanged.

"They pressed us in—the trees," the old man's voice grew sharp with fanatic hatred. "They stole our fields, and they took the food from the mouths of our children; they dropped their fagots to us like dole to beggars; they tempted us to warmth when the cold struck to our bones—and they bore us as fruit a-swing at the end of the foresters' ropes if we yielded to their tempting.

"Yes, M'sieu—we died of cold that they might live! Our children died of hunger that their young might find root space! They despised us—the trees! We died that they might live—and we were men!

"Then, M'sieu, came the Revolution and the freedom. Ah, M'sieu, then we took our toll! Great logs roaring in the winter cold—no more huddling over the alms of fagots. Fields where the trees had been—no more starving of our children that theirs might live. Now the trees were the slaves and we the masters.

"And the trees knew, and they hated us!

"But blow for blow, a hundred of their lives for each life of ours—we have returned their hatred. With ax and torch, we have fought them—

"The trees!" shrieked Polleau, suddenly, eyes blazing red rage, face writhing, foam at the corners of his mouth and gray hair clutched in rigid hands. "The cursed trees! Armies of the trees creeping—creeping—closer, ever closer—crushing us in! Stealing our fields as they did of old! Building their dungeon round us as they built of old the dungeons of stone! Creeping—creeping! Armies of trees! Legions of trees! The trees! The cursed trees!"

McKay listened, appalled. Here was crimson heart of hate. Madness! But what was at the root of it? Some deep inherited instinct, coming down from forefathers who had hated the forest as the symbol of their masters—forefathers whose tides of hatred had overflowed to the green life on which the nobles had laid their taboo, as one neglected child will hate the favorite on whom love and gifts are lavished? In such warped minds the crushing fall of a tree, the maiming sweep of a branch, might appear as deliberate; the natural growth of the forest seems the implacable advance of an enemy.

And yet—the blow of the fir as the cut birch fell *had* been deliberate! And there *had* been those women of the wood—!

"Patience," the standing son touched the old man's shoulder. "Patience! Soon we strike our blow."

Some of the frenzy died out of Polleau's face.

"Though we cut down a hundred," he whispered, "by the hundred they return! But one of us, when they strike—he does not return, no! They have numbers and they have—time. We are now but three, and we have little time. They watch us as we go through the forest, alert to trip, to strike, to crush!

"But, M'sieu," he turned bloodshot eyes to McKay, "we strike our blow, even as Pierre has said. We strike at that coppice that you so desire. We strike there because it is the very heart of the forest. There the secret life of the forest runs at full tide. We know—and you know! Something that, destroyed, will take the heart out of the forest—will make it know us for its masters."

"The women!" The standing son's eyes glittered, malignantly. "I have seen the women there! The fair women with the shining skins who invite—and mock and vanish before hands can seize them."

"The fair women who peer into our windows in the night—and mock us!" muttered the eyeless son.

"They shall mock no more!" shouted old Polleau. "Soon they shall lie, dying! All of them—all of them! They die!"

He caught McKay by the shoulders shook him like a child.

"Go tell them that!" he shouted. "Say to them that this very day we destroy them. Say to them it is we who will laugh when winter comes and we watch their bodies blaze in this hearth of ours and warm us! Go—tell them that!"

He spun McKay around, pushed him to the door, opened it and flung him staggering down the steps. He heard the tall son laugh; the door close. Blind with rage he rushed up the steps and hurled himself against the door. Again, the tall son laughed. McKay beat at the door with clenched fists, cursing. The three within paid no heed. Despair began to dull his rage. Could the trees help him—counsel him? He turned and walked slowly down the field path to the little wood.

———

Slowly and ever more slowly he went as he neared it. He had failed. He was a messenger bearing a warrant of death. The birches were motionless; their leaves hung listlessly. It was as though they knew he had failed. He paused at the edge of the coppice. He looked at his watch, noted with faint surprise that already it was high noon. Short shrift enough had the little wood. The work of destruction would not be long delayed.

McKay squared his shoulders and passed in between the trees. It was strangely silent in the coppice. And it was mournful. He had a sense of life brooding around him, withdrawn into itself, sorrowing. He passed through the silent, mournful wood until he reached the spot where the rounded, gleaming-barked tree stood close to the fir that held the withering birch. Still there was no sound, no movement. He laid his hands upon the cool bark of the rounded tree.

"Let me see again!" he whispered. "Let me hear! Speak to me!"

There was no answer. Again and again, he called. The coppice was silent. He wandered through it, whispering, calling. The slim birches stood, passive, with limbs and leaves adroop like listless arms and hands of captive maids awaiting in dull woe the will of conquerors. The firs seemed to crouch like hopeless men with heads in hands. His heart ached to the woe that filled the little wood, this hopeless submission of the trees.

When, he wondered, would Polleau strike? He looked at his watch again; an hour had gone by. How long would Polleau wait? He dropped to the moss, back against a smooth bole.

And suddenly it seemed to McKay that he was a madman—as mad as Polleau and his sons. Calmly, he went over the old peasant's indictment of the forest; recalled the face and eyes filled with fanatic hate. They were all mad. After all, the trees were—only trees. Polleau and his sons—so he reasoned—had transferred to them the bitter hatred their forefathers had felt for those old lords who had enslaved them; had laid upon them too all the bitterness of their own struggle to exist in this high forest land. When they struck at the trees, it was the ghosts of those forefathers striking at the nobles who had oppressed them; it was themselves striking against their own destiny. The trees were but symbols. It was the warped minds of Polleau and his sons that clothed them, in false semblance of conscious life, blindly striving to wreak vengeance against the ancient masters and the destiny that had made their lives one hard and unceasing battle against nature. The nobles were long dead, destiny can be brought to grips by no man. But the trees were here and alive. Clothed in mirage, through them the driving lust for vengeance could be sated. So much for Polleau and his sons.

And he, McKay: was it not his own deep love and sympathy for the trees that similarly had clothed them in that false semblance of conscious life? Had he not built his own mirage? The trees did not really mourn, could not suffer, could not—know. It was his own sorrow that he had transferred to them; only his own sorrow, that he felt echoing back to him from them. The trees were—only trees.

Instantly, upon the heels of that thought, as though it were an answer, he was aware that the trunk against which he leaned was trembling; that the whole coppice was trembling; that all the little leaves were shaking, tremulously.

McKay, bewildered, leaped to his feet. Reason told him that it was the wind—yet there was no wind!

And as he stood there, a sighing arose as though a mournful breeze were blowing through the trees—and again there was no wind!

Louder grew the sighing and within it now faint wailings.

"They come! They come! Farewell, sisters! Sisters—farewell!"

Clearly, he heard the mournful whispers.

————

McKay began to run through the trees to the trail that led out to the fields of the old lodge. And as he ran the wood darkened as though clear shadows gathered in it, as though vast unseen wings hovered over it. The trembling of the coppice increased; bough touched bough, clung to each other; and louder became the sorrowful crying: "Farewell, sister! Sister—farewell!"

McKay burst out into the open. Half-way between him and the lodge were Polleau and his sons. They saw him; they pointed and lifted mockingly to him their bright axes. He crouched, waiting for them to come close, all fine-spun theories gone, and rising within him that same rage which hours before had sent him out.

So crouching, he heard from the forested hills a roaring clamor.

From every quarter it came, wrathful, menacing; like the voices of legions of great trees bellowing through the horns of tempest. The clamor maddened McKay; fanned the flame of rage to white heat.

If the three men heard it, they gave no sign. They came on steadily, jeering at him, waving their blades. He ran to meet them.

"Go back!" he shouted. "Go back, Polleau! I warn you!"

"He warns us!" jeered Polleau. "He—Pierre, Jean—he warns us!"

The old peasant's arm shot out and his hand caught McKay's shoulder with a grip that pinched to the bone. The arm flexed and hurled him against the unmaimed son. The son caught him, twisted him about and whirled him headlong a dozen yards, crashing through the brush at the skirt of the wood.

McKay sprang to his feet howling like a wolf. The clamor of the forest had grown stronger.

"Kill!" it roared. "Kill!"

The unmaimed son had raised his ax. He brought it down upon the trunk of a birch, half splitting it with one blow. McKay heard a wail go up from the little wood. Before the ax could be withdrawn, he had crashed a fist in the ax-wielder's face. The head of Polleau's son rocked back; he yelped, and before McKay could strike again had wrapped strong arms around him, crushing breath from him. McKay relaxed, went limp, and the son loosened his grip. Instantly McKay slipped out of it and struck again, springing aside to avoid the rib-breaking clasp. Polleau's son was quicker than he, the long arm caught him. But as the arms tightened there was the sound of sharp splintering and the birch into which the ax had bitten toppled. It struck the ground directly behind the wrestling men. Its branches seemed to reach out and clutch at the feet of Polleau's son.

He tripped and fell backward, McKay upon him. The shock of the fall broke his grip and again McKay writhed free. Again, he was upon his feet, and again Polleau's strong son, quick as he, faced him. Twice McKay's blows found their mark beneath his heart before once more the long arms trapped him. But the grip was weaker; McKay felt that now their strength was equal.

Round and round they rocked, McKay straining to break away.

They fell, and over they rolled and over, arms and legs locked, each striving to free a hand to grip the other's throat. Around them ran Polleau and the one-eyed son, shouting encouragement to Pierre, yet neither daring to strike at McKay lest the blow miss and be taken by the other.

And all that time McKay heard the little wood shouting. Gone from it now was all mournfulness, all passive resignation. The wood was alive and raging. He saw the trees shake and bend as though torn by a tempest. Dimly he realized that the others could hear none of this, see none of it; and he wondered why this should be.

"Kill!" shouted the coppice—and ever over its tumult he was aware of the roar of the great forest.

"Kill! Kill!"

He saw two shadowy shapes—shadowy shapes of swarthy green-clad men, that pressed close to him as he rolled and fought.

"Kill!" they whispered. "Let his blood flow. Kill."

He tore a wrist free. Instantly he felt within his hand the hilt of a knife.

"Kill!" whispered the shadowy

"Kill!" shrieked the coppice.

"Kill!" roared the forest.

McKay's free arm swept up and plunged the knife into the throat of Polleau's son! He heard a choking sob; heard Polleau shriek; felt the hot blood spurt in face and over hand; smelt its salt and faintly acrid odor. The encircling arms dropped from him; he reeled to his feet.

As though the blood had been a bridge, the shadowy men leaped into materiality. One threw himself upon the man McKay had stabbed; the other hurled upon old Polleau. The maimed son turned and fled, howling with terror. A white woman sprang out from the shadow, threw herself at his feet, clutched them and brought him down. Another woman and another dropped upon him. The note of his shrieking changed from fear to agony; then died abruptly into silence.

And now McKay could see none of the trees, neither old Polleau nor his sons, for green-clad men and white women covered them!

He stood stupidly, staring at his red hands. The roar of the forest had changed to a deep triumphal chanting. The coppice was mad with joy. The trees had become thin phantoms etched in emerald translucent air as they had been when first the green sorcery had meshed him. And all around him wove and danced the slim, gleaming women of the wood.

They ringed him, their songbird—sweet and shrill; jubilant. Beyond them he saw gliding toward him the woman of the misty pillar whose kisses had poured the sweet green fire into his veins. Her arms were outstretched to him, her strange wide eyes were rapt on his, her white body gleamed with the moon radiance, her red lips were parted and smiling, a scarlet chalice filled with the promise of undreamed ecstasies. The dancing circle, chanting, broke to let her through.

Abruptly, a horror filled McKay. Not of this fair woman, not of her jubilant sisters—but of himself.

He had killed! And the wound the war had left in his soul, the wound he thought had healed, had opened.

He rushed through the broken circle, thrust the shining woman aside with his blood-stained hands and ran, weeping, toward the lake shore. The singing ceased. He heard little cries; tender, appealing little cries of pity; soft voices calling on him to stop, to return. Behind him was the sound of little racing feet, light as the fall of leaves upon the moss.

McKay ran on. The coppice lightened; the beach was before him. He heard the fair woman call him, felt the touch of her hand upon his shoulder. He did not heed her. He ran across the narrow strip of beach, thrust his boat out into the water and wading through the shallows threw himself into it.

He lay there for a moment, sobbing; then drew himself up and caught at the oars. He looked back at the shore now a score of feet away. At the edge of the coppice stood the woman, staring at him with pitying, wise eyes. Behind her clustered the white faces of her sisters, the swarthy faces of the green-clad men.

"Come back!" the woman whispered, and held out to him slender

McKay hesitated, his horror lessening in that clear, wise gaze. He half swung the boat around. But his eyes fell again upon his blood-stained hands and again the hysteria gripped him. One thought only was in his mind now—to get far away from where Polleau's son lay with his throat ripped open, to put the lake between him and that haunted shore. He dipped his oars deep, flung the boat forward. Once more the woman called to him and once again. He paid no heed. She threw out her arms in a gesture of passionate farewell. Then a mist dropped like a swift curtain between him and her and all the folk of the little wood.

McKay rowed on, desperately. After a while he slipped oars and leaning over the boat's side, he washed away the red on his hands and arms. His coat was torn and blood-stained—his shirt too. The latter he took off, wrapped it around the stone that was the boat's rude anchor and dropped it into the depths. His coat he dipped into the water, rubbing at the accusing marks. When he had lightened them all he could, he took up his oars.

His panic had gone from him. Upon its ebb came a rising tide of regret; clear before his eyes arose the vision of the shining woman, beckoning him, calling him ... he swung the boat around to return. And instantly as he did so the mists between him and the farther shore thickened; around him they lightened as though they had withdrawn to make of themselves a barrier to him, and something deep within him whispered that it was too late.

He saw that he was close to the landing of the little inn. There was no one about; and none saw him as he fastened the skiff and slipped to his room. He locked the door, started to undress. Sudden sleep swept over him like a wave; drew him helplessly down into ocean depths of sleep.

———

A knocking at his door awakened McKay, and the innkeeper's voice summoning him to dinner. Sleepily he answered, and as the old man's footsteps died away, he roused himself. His eyes fell upon his coat, dry now, and the illy erased bloodstains splotching it. Puzzled, he stared at them for a moment—then full memory clicked back into place.

He walked to the window. It was dusk. A wind was blowing and the trees were singing, all the little leaves dancing; the forest hummed its cheerful vespers. Gone was all the unease, all the inarticulate trouble and the fear. The woods were tranquil and happy.

He sought the coppice through the gathering twilight. Its demoiselles were dancing lightly in the wind, leafy hoods dipping, leafy skirts a-blow. Beside them marched their green troubadours, carefree, waving their needled arms. Gay was the little wood, gay as when its beauty had first lured him to it.

McKay hid the stained coat shrewdly in his traveling trunk, bathed and put on a fresh outfit and sauntered down to dinner. He ate excellently. Wonder now and then crossed his mind that he felt no regret, no sorrow even for the man he had killed. Half he was inclined to believe it had all been only a dream—so little of any emotion did he feel. He had even ceased to think of what discovery might mean.

His mind was quiet, he heard the forest chanting to him that there was nothing he need fear. And when he sat for a time that night upon the balcony a peace that was half an ecstasy stole in upon him from the murmuring woods and enfolded him. Cradled by it he slept dreamlessly.

McKay did not go far from the inn that day. The little wood danced gaily and beckoned him, but he paid no heed. Something whispered to wait, to keep the lake between him and it until word came of what lay or had lain there. And the peace still was on him.

Only the old innkeeper seemed to grow uneasy as the hours went by. He went often to the landing, scanning the farther shore.

"It is strange," he said at last to McKay as the sun was dipping behind the summits. "Polleau was to see me here today. He never breaks his word, or if he could not come, he would have sent one of his sons."

McKay nodded, carelessly.

"There is another thing I do not understand," went on the old man. "I have seen no smoke from the lodge all day. It is as though they were not there."

"Where could they be?" asked McKay indifferently.

"I do not know," the voice was more perturbed. "It all troubles me, M'sieu. Polleau is hard, yes; but he is my neighbor. Perhaps an accident—"

"They would let you know soon enough if there was anything wrong," McKay said.

"Perhaps, but—" the old man hesitated. "If he does not come tomorrow and again, I see no smoke, I will go to him," he ended.

McKay felt a little shock run through him—tomorrow then he would know, definitely, what it was that had happened in the little wood.

"I would if I were you," he said. "I'd not wait too long, either."

"Will you go with me, M'sieu?" asked the old man.

"No!" whispered the warning voice within McKay. "No! Do not go!"

"Sorry," he said, aloud. "But I've some writing to do. If you should need me send back your man; I'll come."

And all that night he slept, again dreamlessly, while the crooning forest cradled him.

————

The morning passed without sign from the opposite shore. An hour after noon he watched the old innkeeper and his man row across the lake. And suddenly McKay's composure was shaken, his serene certainty wavered. He unstrapped his field glasses and kept them on the pair until they had beached the boat and entered the coppice. His heart was beating uncomfortably, his hands felt hot and his lips dry. How long had they been in the wood? It must have been an hour! What were they doing there? What had they found? He looked at his watch, incredulously. Less than five minutes had passed.

Slowly the seconds ticked by. And it was all of an hour indeed before he saw them come out upon the shore and drag their boat into the water. McKay, throat curiously dry, deafening pulse within his ears, steadied himself; forced himself to stroll leisurely down to the landing.

"Everything all right?" he called as they were near. They did not answer; but as the skiff warped against the landing, they looked up at him and on their faces were stamped horror and a great wonder.

"They are dead, M'sieu," whispered the innkeeper. "Polleau and his two sons—all dead!"

McKay's heart gave a great leap, a swift faintness took him.

"Dead!" he cried. "What killed them?"

"What but the trees, M'sieu?" answered the old man, and McKay thought that his gaze dwelt upon him strangely. "The trees killed them. See—we went up the little path through the wood, and close to its end we found it blocked by fallen trees. The flies buzzed round those trees, M'sieu, so we searched there. They were under them, Polleau and his sons. A fir had fallen upon Polleau and had crushed in his chest. Another son we found beneath a fir and upturned birches. They had broken his back, and an eye had been torn out—but that was no new wound, the latter."

He paused.

"It must have been a sudden wind," said his man. "Yet I never knew of a wind such as that must have been. There were no trees down except those that lay upon them. And of those it was as though they had leaped out of the ground! Yes, as though they had leaped out of the ground upon them. Or it was as though giants had torn them out for clubs. They were not broken—their roots were bare—"

"But the other son—Polleau had two?" Try as he might, McKay could not keep the tremor out of his voice.

"Pierre," said the old man, and again McKay felt that strange quality in his gaze. "He lay beneath a fir. His throat was torn out!"

"His throat torn out!" whispered McKay. His knife! The knife that had been slipped into his hand by the shadowy shapes!

"His throat was torn out," repeated the innkeeper. "And in it still was the broken branch that had done it. A broken branch; M'sieu, pointed like a knife. It must have caught Pierre as the fir fell and ripping through his throat—been broken off as the tree crashed."

McKay stood, mind whirling in wild conjecture. "You said—a broken branch?" McKay asked through lips gone white.

"A broken branch, M'sieu." The innkeeper's eyes searched him. "It was very plain—what it was that happened. Jacques." He turned to his man, "Go up to the house."

He watched until the man shuffled out of sight.

"Yet not all is so plain, M'sieu," he spoke low to McKay, "since in Pierre's hand I found—this."

He reached into a pocket and drew out a button from which hung a strip of cloth. They had once been part of that stained coat which McKay had hidden in his trunk. And as McKay strove to speak the old man raised his hand. Button and cloth dropped from it, into the water. A wave took it and floated it away; another and another snatched it and passed it on. They watched it, silently, until it had vanished.

"Tell me nothing," said the keeper of the inn. "Polleau was a hard man and hard men were his sons. The trees hated them. The trees killed them. The—souvenir—is gone. Only M'sieu would better also—go."

———

That might McKay packed. When dawn had broken, he stood at his window, looking long at the little wood. It too was awakening, stirring sleepily—like drowsy, delicate demoiselles. He thought he could see that one slim birch that was—what?

Tree or woman? Or both?

Silently, the old landlord and his wife watched him as he swung out his car—a touch of awe, a half-fear, in their eyes. Without a word they let him go.

And as McKay swept up the road that led over the lip of the green bowl, he seemed to hear from all the forest a deep-toned, mournful chanting. It arose around him as he topped the rise in one vast whispering cloud—of farewell! And died.

Never, he knew, would that green door of enchantment be opened to him again. His fear had closed it—forever. Something had been offered to him beyond mortal experience—something that might have raised him to the level of the gods of Earth's youth. He had rejected it. And nevermore, he knew, would he cease to regret.

Bat's Belfry — by August W. Derleth

"The rock gave way, and I found myself in a vault with about a score of skeletons."

The following letter was found among the papers of the late Sir Harry Everett Barclay of Charing Cross, London.

June 10, 1925

My dear Marc,

Having received no answer to my card, I can only surmise that it did not reach you. I am writing from my summer home here on the moor, a very secluded place. I am fondling the hope that you will give me a pleasant surprise by dropping in on me soon (as you hinted you might), for this is just the kind of house that would intrigue you. It is very similar to the Baskerville home which Sir Arthur Conan Doyle describes in his *Hound of the Baskervilles*. Vague rumors have it that the place is the abode of evil spirits, which idea I promptly and emphatically pooh- poohed. You know that in the spiritual world I am but slightly interested, and that it is in wizardry that I delight. The thought that this quiet little building in the heart of England's peaceful moors should be the home of a multitude of evil spirits seems very foolish to me. However, the surroundings are exceedingly healthful and the house itself is partly an antique, which arouses my interest in archaeology. So, you see there is enough to divert my attention from these foolish rumors. Leon, my valet, is here with me and so is old Mortimer. You remember Mortimer, who always prepared such excellent bachelor dinners for us?

I have been here just twelve days, and I have explored this old house from cellar to garret. In the latter I brought to light an aged trunk, which I searched, and in which I found nine old books, several of whose title pages were torn away. One of the books, which I took to the small garret window, I finally distinguished as *Dracula* by Bram Stoker, and this I at once decided was one of the first editions of the book ever printed.

At the cessation of the first three days a typical English fog descended with a vengeance upon the moor. At the first indication of this prank of the elements, which threatened completely to obscure the beautiful weather of the past, I had hauled out all the discoveries I had made in the garret of this building. Bram Stoker's *Dracula* I have already mentioned. There is also a book on the Black Art by De Rochas. Three books, by Orfilo, Swedenborg, and Cagliostro, I have laid temporarily aside. Then there are also Strindburg's *The Inferno,* Blavatsky's *Secret Doctrine,* Poe's *Eureka*, and Flammarion's *Atmosphere.* You, my dear friend, may well imagine with what excitement these books filled me, for you know I am inclined toward sorcery. Orfilo, you know, was but a chemist and physiologist; Swedenborg and Strindburg, two who might be called mystics; Poe, whose *Eureka* did not aid me much in the path of witchcraft, nevertheless fascinated me; but the remaining five were as gold to me. Cagliostro, court magician of France; Madame Blavatsky, the priestess of Isis and of the Occult Doctrine; *Dracula*, with all its vampires; Flammarion's *Atmosphere*, with its diagnosis of the Gods of peoples; and De Rochas, of whom all I can say is to quote from August Strindburg's *The Inferno,* the following: "I do not excuse myself, and only ask the reader to remember this fact, in case he should ever feel inclined to practice magic, especially those forms of it called wizardry, or more properly witchcraft: that its reality has been placed beyond all doubt by De Rochas."

Truly, my friend, I wondered, for I had good reason to do so, what manner of man had resided here before my coming, who should be so fascinated by Poe, Orfilo, Strindburg, and De Rochas—four different types of authors. Fog or no fog, I determined to find out. There is not another dwelling near here and the nearest source of information is a village some miles away. This is rather odd, for this moor does not seem an undesirable place for a summer home. I stored the books away, and after informing my valet of my intentions to walk some miles to the village, I started out. I had not gone far, when Leon decided to accompany me, leaving Mortimer alone in the fog-surrounded house.

Leon and I established very little in the town. After a conversation with one of the grocers in the village, the only communicative person that we accosted, we found that the man who had last occupied the house was a Baronet Lohrville. It seemed that the people held the late baronet in awe, for they hesitated to speak of him. This grocer related a tale concerning the disappearance of four girls one dark night some years ago. Popular belief had and still has it that the baronet kidnaped them. This idea seems utterly ludicrous to me, for the superstitious villagers cannot substantiate their suspicions. By the way, this merchant also informed us that the Lohrville home is called the 'Bat's Belfry.' Personally, I can see no connection between the residence and the ascribed title, as I have not noticed any bats around during my sojourn here.

My meditations on this matter were rudely interrupted by Mortimer, who complained of bats in the cellar—a rather queer coincidence. He said that he continually felt them brushing against his cheeks and that he feared they would become entangled in his hair. Of course, Leon and I went down to look for them, but we could not see any of them. However, Leon stated that one struck him, which I doubt. It is just possible that sudden drafts of air may have been the cause of the delusions.

This incident, Marc, was just the forerunner of the odd things that have been occurring since then. I am about to enumerate the most important of these incidents to you, and I hope you will be able to explain them.

Three days ago, activities started in earnest. At that date Mortimer came to me and breathlessly informed me that no light could be kept in the cellar. Leon and I investigated and found that under no circumstances could a lamp or match be kept lit in the cellar, just as Mortimer had said. My only explanation of this is that it is due to the air currents in the cellar, which seem disturbed. It is true a flashlight could be kept alight, but even that seemed dimmed. I cannot attempt to explain the later fact.

Yesterday, Leon, who is a devout Catholic, took a few drops from a flask of holy water, which he continually carries with him, and descended into the cellar with the firm intention of driving out, if there were therein ensconced, any evil spirits. On the bottom of the steps I noticed, some time ago, a large stone tablet. As Leon came down the steps, a large drop of the blessed fluid fell on this tablet. The drop of water actually sizzled while Leon muttered some incantations, in the midst of which he suddenly stopped and fled precipitancy, mumbling that the cellar was incontestably the very entrance to hell, guarded by the fiend incarnate, himself! I confess to you, my dear Marc, that I was astounded at this remarkable occurrence.

Last night, while the three of us sat together in the spacious drawing room of this building, the lamp was blown out. I say 'blown out' because there is no doubt that it was, and by some superhuman agency. There was not a breath of air stirring outside, yet I, who was sitting just across from the lamp, felt a cool draft. No one else noticed this draft. It was just as if someone directly opposite me had blown forcibly at the lamp, or as if the wing of a powerful bird had passed by it.

There can be no doubt there is something radically wrong, in this house, and I am determined to find out what it is, regardless of consequences.

· · ·

(Here the letter terminates abruptly, as if it were to be completed at a later date.)

The two doctors bending over the body of Sir Harry Barclay in Lohrville Manor at last ceased their examinations.

"I cannot account for this astounding loss of blood, Dr. Mordaunt."

"Neither can I, Dr. Greene. He is so devoid of blood that some supernatural agency must have kept him alive!" He laughed lightly.

"About this loss of blood—I was figuring on internal hemorrhages as the cause, but there are absolutely no signs of anything of the sort. According to the expression of his features, which is too horrible for even me to gaze at—"

"And me."

"—he died from some terrible fear of something, or else he witnessed some horrifying scene."

"Most likely the latter."

"I think we had better pronounce death due to internal hemorrhage and apoplexy."

"I agree."

"Then we shall do so."

The physicians bent over the open book on the table. Suddenly Dr. Greene straightened up and his hand delved into his pocket and came out with a match.

"Here is a match, Dr. Mordaunt. Scratch it and apply the flame to that book and say nothing to anyone."

"It is for the best"

Excerpts from the journal of Sir Harry E. Barclay, found beside his body in Lohrville Manor on July 17, 1925.

.   .   .

June 25—Last night I had a curious nightmare, I dreamed that I met a beautiful girl in the wood around my father's castle in Lancaster. Without knowing why, we embraced, our lips meeting and remaining in that position for at least half an hour! Queer dream that! I must have had another nightmare of a different nature, although I cannot recall it; for, upon looking in the mirror, this morning, I found my face devoid of all color—rather drawn.

Later—Leon has told me that he had a similar dream, and as he is a confirmed misogynist, I cannot interpret it. Strange that it should be so parallel to mine in every way.

June 29—Mortimer came to me early this morning and said he would not stay another instant, for he had certainly seen a ghost last night. A handsome old man, he said. He seemed horrified that the old man had kissed him. He must have dreamed it. I persuaded him to stay on these grounds and solemnly told him to say nothing about it. Leon remarked that the dream had returned in every particular to him the preceding night, and that he was not feeling well. I advised him to see a doctor, but he roundly refused to do so. He said, referring to the horrible nightmare (as he termed it), that tonight he would sprinkle a few drops of holy water on himself and that (he stated) would drive away any evil influence, if there were any, connected with his dreams. Strange that he should attribute everything to evil entities!

Later—I made some inquiries today and I find that the description of the Baronet Lohrville fits to every detail the "ghost" of Mortimer's dream. I also learned that several small children disappeared from the countryside during the life of the last of the Lohrvilles. Not that they should be connected, but it seems the ignorant people ascribe their vanishing to the Baronet.

June 30—Leon claims he did not have the dream (which, by the way, revisited me last night), because of the potent effect of the holy water.

July 1—Mortimer has left. He says he cannot live in the same house with the devil. It seems he must have actually seen the ghost of old Lohrville, although Leon scoffs at the idea.

July 4—I had the same dream again last night. I felt very ill this morning but was able to dispel the feeling easily during the day. Leon has used all the holy water, but as tomorrow is Sunday, he will get some at the village parish when he attends mass.

July 5—I tried to procure the services of another chef this morning in the village, but I am all at sea. No one in the town will enter the house, not even for one hundred pounds a week, they declare! I shall be forced to get along without one or send to London.

Leon experienced a misfortune today. Riding home after mass, his holy water spilled almost all from the bottle, and later the bottle, containing the remainder of it, fell to the ground and broke. Leon, nonplussed, remarked that he would get another as soon as possible from the parish priest.

July 6—Both of us had the dream again last night. I feel rather weak, and Leon does, too. Leon went to a doctor, who asked him whether he had been cut, or severely injured so as to cause a heavy loss of blood, or if he had suffered from internal hemorrhages. Leon said no, and the doctor prescribed raw onions and some other things for Leon to eat. Leon forgot his holy water.

July 9—The dream again. Leon had a different nightmare—about an old man, who, he said, bit him. I asked him to show me where the man had bitten him in his dream, and when he loosened his collar to show me, sure enough, there were two tiny punctures on his throat. He and I are both feeling miserably weak.

July 15—Leon left me today. I am firmly convinced that he went suddenly mad, for this morning he evinced an intense desire to invade the cellar again. He said that something seemed to draw him. I did not stop him, and sometime later, as I was engrossed in a volume of Wells, he came shrieking up the cellar steps and dashed madly through the room in which I sat. I ran after him and, cornering him in his room, forcibly detained him. I asked for an explanation and all he could do was moan over and over.

"*Mon Dieu, Monsieur*, leave this accursed place at once. Leave it, *Monsieur*, I beg of you. *Le diable—le diable!*" At this he dashed away from me and ran at top speed from the house, I after him. In the road I shouted after him and all I could catch of the words wafted back to me by the wind, were: *"Lamais—le diable—Mon Dieu—tablet—Book of Thoth."* All very significant words, *"Le diable"* and *"Mon Dieu"*— "the devil" and "my God"—I paid little attention to. But Lamais was a species of female vampire known intimately to a few select sorcerers only, and the *Book of Thoth* was the Egyptian book of magic. For a few minutes I entertained the rather wild fancy that the *Book of Thoth* was ensconced somewhere in this building, and as I racked my brains for a suitable connection between "tablet" and *Book of Thoth* I at last became convinced that the book lay beneath the tablet at the foot of the cellar steps. I am going down to investigate.

July 16—I have it! *The Book of Thoth!* It was below the stone tablet as I thought. The spirits guarding it evidently did not wish me to disturb its resting place, for they roused the air currents to a semblance of a gale while I worked to get the stone away. The book is secured by a heavy lock of antique pattern.

I had the dream again last night, but in addition I could almost swear that I saw the ghosts of old Lohrville and four beautiful girls. What a coincidence! I am very weak today, hardly able to walk around. There is no doubt that this house is infested not by bats, but by vampires! Lamais! If I could only find their corpses, I would drive sharp stakes through their hearts!"

Later—I made a new and shocking discovery today. I went down to the place where the tablet lay, and another rock below the cavity wherein the *Book of Thoth* had lain gave way below me and I found myself in a vault with about a score of skeletons—all of little children! If this house is inhabited by vampires, it is only too obvious that these skeletons are those of their unfortunate victims. However, I firmly believe that there is another cavern somewhere below, wherein the bodies of the vampires are hidden.

Later—I have been looking over the book by De Rochas and I have hit upon an excellent plan to discover the bodies of the vampires! I shall use the *Book of Thoth* to summon the vampires before me and force them to reveal the hiding place for their voluptuous bodies! De Rochas says that it can be done.

Nine o'clock—As the conditions are excellent at this time, I am going to start to summon the vampires. Someone is passing and I hope he or she does not interrupt me in my work or tell anyone in the town to look in here. The book, as I mentioned before, is secured by a heavy seal, and I had trouble to loosen it. At last I succeeded in breaking it and I opened the book to find the place I need in my work of conjuring up the vampires. I found it and I am beginning my incantations. The atmosphere in the room is changing slowly and it is becoming intolerably dark. The air currents in the room are swirling angrily, and the lamp has gone out. I am confident that the vampires will appear soon.

I am correct. There are some shades materializing in the room. They are becoming more distinct ... there are five of them, four females and one male. Their features are very distinct ... They are casting covert glances in my direction ... Now they are glaring malevolently at me.

Good God! I have forgotten to place myself in a magic circle and I greatly fear the vampires will attack me! I am only too correct. They are moving in my direction. My God ...! But stay! They are halting! The old Baronet is gazing at me with his glittering eyes fiery with hate. The four female vampires smile voluptuously upon me.

Now, if ever, is my chance to break their evil spell. *Prayer!* But I cannot pray! I am forever banished from the sight of God for calling upon Satan to aid me. But even for that I cannot pray. I am hypnotized by the malefic leer disfiguring the countenance of the Baronet. There is a sinister gleam in the eyes of the four beautiful ghouls. They glide toward me, arms outstretched. Their sinuous, obnoxious forms are before me; their crimson lips curved in a diabolically triumphant smile. I cannot bear to see the soft caress of their tongues on their red lips. I am resisting with all the power of my will, but what is one mere will against an infernal horde of ghouls?

God! Their foul presence taints my very soul! The Baronet is moving forward. His mordacious propinquity casts a reviling sensation of obscenity about me. If I cannot appeal to God, I must implore Satan to grant me time to construct the magic circle.

I cannot tolerate their virulence.... I endeavored to rise but I could not do so.... I am no longer master of my own will! The vampires are leering demoniacally at me.... I am doomed to die ... and yet to live forever in the ranks of the Undead.

Their faces are approaching closer to mine and soon I shall sink into oblivion ... but anything is better than this ... to see the malignant Undead around me ... A sharp stinging sensation in my throat ... My God...! It is—

THE CURSE OF EVERARD MAUNDY

SEABURY QUINN

M*ort d'un chat!* I do not like this!" Jules de Grandin slammed the evening paper down upon the table and glared ferociously at me through the library lamplight.

"What's up now?" I asked, wondering vaguely what the cause of his latest grievance was. "Some reporter say something personal about you?"

"*Parbleu, non,* he would better not!" the little Frenchman replied, his round blue eyes flashing ominously. "Me, I would pull his nose and tweak his ears. But it is not of the reporter's insolence I speak, my friend; I do not like these suicides; there are too many of them."

"Of course there are," I conceded soothingly, "one suicide is that much too many; people have no right to—"

"Ah bah!" he cut in. "You do misapprehend me, *mon vieux.* Excuse me one moment, if you please." He rose hurriedly from his chair and left the room. A moment later I heard him rummaging about in the cellar.

In a few minutes he returned, the week's supply of discarded newspapers salvaged from the dustbin in his arms.

"Now, attend me," he ordered as he spread the sheets out before him and began scanning the columns hastily. "Here is an item from Monday's Journal:

Two Motorists Die While Driving Cars

The impulse to end their lives apparently attacked two automobile drivers on the Albemarle turnpike near Lonesome Swamp, two miles out of Harrisonville, last night. Carl Planz, thirty-one years old, of Martins Falls, took his own life by shooting himself in the head with a shotgun while seated in his automobile, which he had parked at the roadside where the pike passes nearest the swamp. His remains were identified by two letters, one addressed to his wife, the other to his father, Joseph Planz, with whom he was associated in the real estate business at Martins Falls. A check for three hundred dollars and several other papers found in his pockets completed identification. The letters, which merely declared his intention to kill himself, failed to establish any motive for the act.

Almost at the same time, and within a hundred yards of the spot where Planz's body was found by State Trooper Henry Anderson this morning, the body of Henry William Nixon, of New Rochelle, N. Y., was discovered partly sitting, partly lying on the rear seat of his automobile, an empty bottle of windshield cleaner lying on the floor beside him. It is thought this liquid, which contained a small amount of cyanide of potassium, was used to inflict death. Police Surgeon Stevens, who examined both bodies, declared that the men had been dead approximately the same length of time when brought to the station house.

"What think you of that, my friend, *hein*?" de Grandin demanded, looking up from the paper with one of his direct, challenging stares.

"Why—er—" I began, but he interrupted.

"Hear this," he commanded, taking up a second paper, "this is from the News of Tuesday:

Mother and Daughters Die in Death Pact

Police and heartbroken relatives are today trying to trace a motive for the triple suicide of Mrs. Ruby Westerfelt and her daughters, Joan and Elizabeth, who perished by leaping from the eighth floor of the Hotel Dolores, Newark, late yesterday afternoon. The women registered at the hotel under assumed names, went immediately to the room assigned them, and ten minutes later Miss Gladys Walsh, who occupied a room on the fourth floor, was startled to see a dark form hurtle past her window. A moment later a second body flashed past on its downward flight, and as Miss Walsh, horrified, rushed toward the window, a loud crash sounded outside. Looking out, Miss Walsh saw the body of a third woman partly impaled on the spikes of a balcony rail.

Miss Walsh sought to aid the woman. As she leaned from her window and reached out with a trembling arm she was greeted by a scream: "Don't try! I won't be saved; I must go with Mother and Sister!" A moment later the woman had managed to free herself from the restraining iron spikes and fell to the cement areaway four floors below.

"And here is still another account, this one from tonight's paper," he continued, unfolding the sheet which had caused his original protest:

High School Co-ed Takes Life in Attic

The family and friends of Edna May McCarty, fifteen-year-old co-ed of Harrisonville High School, are at a loss to assign a cause for her suicide early this morning. The girl had no love affairs, as far as is known, and had not failed in her examinations. On the contrary, she had passed the school's latest test with flying colors. Her mother told investigating police officials that overstudy might have temporarily unbalanced the child's mind. Miss McCarty's body was found suspended from the rafters of her father's attic by her mother this morning when the young woman did not respond to a call for breakfast and could not be found in her room on the second floor of the house. A clothesline, used to hang clothes which were dried inside the house in rainy weather, was used to form the fatal noose.

––––––

"Now then, my friend," de Grandin reseated himself and lighted a vile-smelling French cigarette, puffing furiously, till the smoke surrounded his sleek, blond head like a mephitic nimbus, "what have you to say to those reports? Am I not right? Are there not too many —*mordieu*, entirely too many—suicides in our city?"

"All of them weren't committed here," I objected practically, "and besides, there couldn't very well be any connection between them. Mrs. Westerfelt and her daughters carried out a suicide pact, it appears, but they certainly could have had no understanding with the two men and the young girl—"

"Perhaps, maybe, possibly," he agreed, nodding his head so vigorously that a little column of ash detached itself from his cigarette and dropped unnoticed on the bosom of his stiffly starched evening shirt. "You may be right, Friend Trowbridge, but then, as is so often the case, you may be entirely wrong. One thing I know: I, Jules de Grandin, shall investigate these cases myself personally. *Cordieu*, they do interest me! I shall ascertain what is the what here."

"Go ahead," I encouraged. "The investigation will keep you out of mischief," and I returned to the second chapter of Haggard's *The Wanderer's Necklace,* a book which I have read at least half a dozen times yet find as fascinating at each rereading as when I first perused its pages.

––––––

The matter of the six suicides still bothered him next morning. "Trowbridge, my friend," he asked abruptly as he disposed of his second helping of coffee and passed his cup for replenishment, "why is it that people destroy themselves?"

"Oh," I answered evasively, "different reasons, I suppose. Some are crossed in love; some meet financial reverses, and some do it while temporarily deranged."

"Yes," he agreed thoughtfully, "yet every self-murderer has a real or fancied reason for quitting the world, and there is apparently no reason why any of these six poor ones who hurled themselves into outer darkness during the past week should have done so. All, apparently, were well provided for, none of them, as far as is known, had any reason to regret the past or fear the future; yet"—he shrugged his narrow shoulders significantly—"*voilà*, they are gone!

"Another thing: At the *Faculté de Médicine Légal* and the *Sûreté* in Paris we keep most careful statistics, not only on the number, but on the manner of suicides. I do not think your Frenchman differs radically from your American when it comes to taking his life, so the figures for one nation may well be a signpost for the other. These self-inflicted deaths, they are not right. They do not follow the rules. Men prefer to hang, slash or shoot themselves; women favor drowning, poison or gas; yet here we have one of the men taking poison, one of the women hanging herself, and three of them jumping to death. *Nom d'un canard*, I am not satisfied with it!"

"H'm, neither are the unfortunate parties who killed themselves, if the theologians are to be believed," I returned.

"You speak right," he returned, then muttered dreamily to himself: "Destruction—destruction of body and imperilment of soul —*mordieu*, it is strange, it is not righteous!" He disposed of his coffee at a gulp and leaped from his chair. "I go!" he declared dramatically, turning toward the door.

"Where?"

"Where? Where should I go, if not to secure the history of these so puzzling cases? I shall not rest nor sleep nor eat until I have the string of the mystery's skein in my hands." He paused at the door, a quick, elfin smile playing across his usually stern features. "And should I return before my work is complete," he suggested, "I pray you have the excellent Nora prepare another of her so magnificent apple pies for dinner."

Forty seconds later the front door clicked shut, and from the dining room's oriel window I saw his neat little figure, trimly encased in blue chinchilla and gray worsted, pass quickly down the sidewalk, his ebony cane hammering a rapid tattoo on the stones as it kept time to the thoughts racing through his active brain.

———

"I am desolated that my capacity is exhausted," he announced that evening as he finished his third portion of deep-dish apple pie smothered in pungent rum sauce and regarded his empty plate sadly. "*Eh bien*, perhaps it is as well. Did I eat more I might not be able to think clearly, and clear thought is what I shall need this night, my friend. Come; we must be going."

"Going where?" I demanded.

"To hear the reverend and estimable Monsieur Maundy deliver his sermon."

"Who? Everard Maundy?"

"But of course, who else?"

"But—but," I stammered, looking at him incredulously, "why should we go to the tabernacle to hear this man? I can't say I'm particularly impressed with his system, and—aren't you a Catholic, de Grandin?"

"Who can say?" he replied as he lighted a cigarette and stared thoughtfully at his coffee cup. "My father was a Huguenot of the Huguenots; a several times great-grandsire of his cut his way to freedom through the Paris streets on the fateful night of August 24, 1572. My mother was convent-bred, and as pious as anyone with a sense of humor and the gift of thinking for herself could well be. One of my uncles—he for whom I am named—was like a blood brother to Darwin the magnificent, and Huxley the scarcely less magnificent, also. Me, I am"—he elevated his eyebrows and shoulders at once and pursed his lips comically—"what should a man with such a heritage be, my friend? But come, we delay, we tarry, we lose time. Let us hasten. I have a fancy to hear what this Monsieur Maundy has to say, and to observe him. See, I have here tickets for the fourth row of the hall."

Very much puzzled, but never doubting that something more than the idle wish to hear a sensational evangelist urged the little Frenchman toward the tabernacle, I rose and accompanied him.

"*Parbleu*, what a day!" he sighed as I turned my car toward the downtown section. "From coroner's office to undertakers' I have run, and from undertakers' to hospitals. I have interviewed everyone who could shed the smallest light on these strange deaths, yet I seem no further advanced than when I began. What I have found out serves only to whet my curiosity; what I have not discovered—" He spread his hands in a world-embracing gesture and lapsed into silence.

The Jachin Tabernacle, where the Rev. Everard Maundy was holding his series of non-sectarian revival meetings, was crowded to overflowing when we arrived, but our tickets passed us through the jostling crowd of half-skeptical, half-believing people who thronged the lobby, and we were soon ensconced in seats where every word the preacher uttered could be heard with ease.

Before the introductory hymn had been finished, de Grandin mumbled a wholly unintelligible excuse in my ear and disappeared up the aisle, and I settled myself in my seat to enjoy the service as best I might.

The Rev. Mr. Maundy was a tall, hatchet-faced man in early middle life, a little inclined to rant and make use of worked-over platitudes, but obviously sincere in the message he had for his congregation. From the half-cynical attitude of a regularly enrolled church member who looks on revivals with a certain disdain, I found myself taking keener and keener interest in the story of regeneration the preacher had to tell, my attention compelled not so much by his words as by the earnestness of his manner and the wonderful stage presence the man possessed. When the ushers had taken up the collection and the final hymn was sung, I was surprised to find we had been two hours in the tabernacle. If anyone had asked me, I should have said half an hour would have been nearer the time consumed by the service.

"Eh, my friend, did you find it interesting?" de Grandin asked as he joined me in the lobby and linked his arm in mine.

"Yes, very," I admitted, then, somewhat sulkily: "I thought you wanted to hear him, too—it was your idea that we came here—what made you run away?"

"I am sorry," he replied with a chuckle which belied his words, "but it was *necessaire* that I fry other fish while you listened to the reverend gentleman's discourse. Will you drive me home?"

The March wind cut shrewdly through my overcoat after the superheated atmosphere of the tabernacle, and I felt myself shivering involuntarily more than once as we drove through the quiet streets. Strangely, too, I felt rather sleepy and ill at ease. By the time we reached the wide, tree-bordered avenue before my house I was conscious of a distinctly unpleasant sensation, a constantly growing feeling of malaise, a sort of baseless, irritating uneasiness. Thoughts of years long forgotten seemed summoned to my memory without rhyme or reason. An incident of an unfair advantage I had taken of a younger boy while at public school, recollections of petty, useless lies and bits of naughtiness committed when I could not have been more than three came flooding back on my consciousness, finally an episode of my early youth which I had forgotten some forty years.

My father had brought a little stray kitten into the house, and I, with the tiny lad's unconscious cruelty, had fallen to teasing the wretched bundle of bedraggled fur, finally tossing it nearly to the ceiling to test the tale I had so often heard that a cat always lands on its feet. My experiment was the exception which demonstrated the rule, it seemed, for the poor, half-starved feline hit the hardwood floor squarely on its back, struggled feebly a moment, then yielded up its entire ninefold expectancy of life."

Long after the smart of the whipping I received in consequence had been forgotten, the memory of that unintentional murder had plagued my boyish conscience, and many were the times I had awakened at dead of night, weeping bitter repentance out upon my pillow.

Now, some forty years later, the thought of that kitten's death came back as clearly as the night the unkempt little thing thrashed out its life upon our kitchen floor. Strive as I would, I could not drive the memory from me, and it seemed as though the unwitting crime of my childhood was assuming an enormity out of all proportion to its true importance.

I shook my head and passed my hand across my brow, as a sleeper suddenly wakened does to drive away the lingering memory of an unpleasant dream, but the kitten's ghost, like Banquo's, would not down.

"What is it, Friend Trowbridge?" de Grandin asked as he eyed me shrewdly.

"Oh, nothing," I replied as I parked the car before our door and leaped to the curb, "I was just thinking."

"Ah?" he responded on a rising accent. "And of what do you think, my friend? Something unpleasant?"

"Oh, no. Nothing important enough to dignify by that term," I answered shortly and led the way to the house, keeping well ahead of him, lest he push his inquiries farther.

In this, however, I did him wrong. Tactful women and Jules de Grandin have the talent of feeling without being told when conversation is unwelcome, and besides wishing me a pleasant good night, he spoke not a word until we had gone upstairs to bed. As I was opening my door, he called down the hall, "Should you want me, remember, you have but to call."

"Humph!" I muttered ungraciously as I shut the door. "Want him? What the devil should I want him for?" And so, I pulled off my clothes and climbed into bed, the thought of the murdered kitten still with me and annoying me more by its persistence than by the faint sting of remorse it evoked.

———

How long I had slept I do not know, but I do know I was wide awake in a single second, sitting up in bed and staring through the darkened chamber with eyes which strove desperately to pierce the gloom.

Somewhere—whether far or near I could not tell—a cat had

raised its voice in a long-drawn, wailing cry, kept silence a moment, then given tongue again with increased volume.

There are few sounds more eery to hear in the dead of night than the cry of a prowling feline, and this one was of a particularly sad, almost reproachful tone.

"Confound the beast!" I exclaimed angrily, and lay back on my pillow, striving vainly to recapture my broken sleep.

Again, the wail sounded, indefinite as to location, but louder, more prolonged even, it seemed fiercer in its timbre than when I first heard it in my sleep.

I glanced toward the window with the vague thought of hurling a book or boot or other handy missile at the disturber, then held my breath in sudden affright. Staring through the aperture between the scrim curtains was the biggest, most ferocious-looking tomcat I had ever seen. Its eyes, seemingly as large as butter dishes, glared at me with the green phosphorescence of its tribe, and with an added demoniacal glow, the like of which I had never seen. Its red mouth, opened to full compass in a venomous, soundless "spit," seemed almost as large as that of a lion, and the wicked, pointed ears above its rounded face were laid back against its head, as though it were crouching for combat.

"Get out! Scat!" I called feebly, making no move toward the beast.

"S-s-s-sssh!" a hiss of incomparable fury answered me, and the creature put one heavy, padded paw tentatively over the windowsill, still regarding me with its unchanging, hateful stare.

"Get!" I repeated and stopped abruptly. Before my eyes the great beast was *growing*, increasing in size till its chest and shoulders completely blocked the window. Should it attack me I would be as helpless in its claws as a Hindoo under the paws of a Bengal tiger.

Slowly, stealthily, its cushioned feet making no sound as it set them down daintily, the monstrous creature advanced into the room, crouched on its haunches, and regarded me steadily, wickedly, malevolently.

I rose a little higher on my elbow. The great brute twitched the tip of its sable tail warningly, half lifted one of its forepaws from the floor, and set it down again, never shifting its sulfurous eyes from my face.

Inch by inch I moved my farther foot from the bed, felt the floor beneath it, and pivoted slowly in a sitting position until my other foot was free of the bedclothes. Apparently the cat did not notice my strategy, for it made no menacing move till I flexed my muscles for a leap, suddenly flung myself from the bedstead, and leaped toward the door.

With a snarl, white teeth flashing, green eyes glaring, ears laid back, the beast moved between me and the exit, and began slowly advancing on me, hate and menace in every line of its giant body.

I gave ground before it, retreating step by step and striving desperately to hold its eyes with mine, as I had heard hunters sometimes do when suddenly confronted by wild animals.

Back, back I crept, the ogre-ish visitant keeping pace with my retreat, never suffering me to increase the distance between us.

I felt the cold draft of the window on my back; the pressure of the sill against me; behind me, from the waist up, was the open night, before me the slowly advancing monster.

It was a thirty-foot drop to a cemented roadway, but death on the pavement was preferable to the slashing claws and grinding teeth of the terrible thing creeping toward me.

I threw one leg over the sill, watching constantly, lest the cat-thing leap on me before I could cheat it by dashing myself to the ground—

"Trowbridge, *mon Dieu*, Trowbridge, my friend! What is it you would do?" The frenzied hail of Jules de Grandin cut through the dark, and a flood of light from the hallway swept into the room as he flung the door violently open and raced across the room, seizing my arm in both hands and dragging me from the window.

"Look out, de Grandin!" I screamed. "The cat! It'll get you!"

"Cat?" he echoed, looking about him uncomprehendingly. "Do you say 'cat,' my friend? A cat will get me? *Mort d'un chou*, the cat which can make a mouse of Jules de Grandin is not yet whelped! Where is it, this cat of yours?"

"There! Th—" I began, then stopped, rubbing my eyes. The room was empty. Save for de Grandin and me there was nothing animate in the place.

"But it *was* here," I insisted. "I tell you, I saw it; a great, black cat, as big as a lion. It came in the window and crouched right over there, and was driving me to jump to the ground when you came—"

"*Nom d'un pore*! Do you say so?" he exclaimed, seizing my arm again and shaking me. "Tell me of this cat, my friend. I would learn more of this puss-puss who comes into Friend Trowbridge's house, grows great as a lion and drives him to his death on the stones below. Ha, I think maybe the trail of these mysterious deaths is not altogether lost! Tell me more, *mon ami;* I would know all—all!"

"Of course, it was just a bad dream," I concluded as I finished the recital of my midnight visitation, "but it seemed terribly real to me while it lasted."

"I doubt it not," he agreed with a quick, nervous nod. "And on our way from the tabernacle tonight, my friend, I noticed you were much *distrait*. Were you, perhaps, feeling ill at the time?"

"Not at all," I replied. "The truth is, I was remembering something which occurred when I was a lad four or five years old; something which had to do with a kitten I killed," and I told him the whole wretched business.

"U'm?" he commented when I had done. "You are a good man, Trowbridge, my friend. In all your life, since you attained to years of discretion, I do not believe you have done a wicked or ignoble act."

"Oh, I wouldn't say that," I returned, "we all—"

"*Parbleu*, I have said it. That kitten incident, now, is probably the single tiny skeleton in the entire closet of your existence, yet sustained thought upon it will magnify it even as the cat of your dream grew from cats' to lions' size. *Pardieu*, my friend, I am not so sure you did dream of that abomination in the shape of a cat which visited you. Suppose—" he broke off, staring intently before him, twisting first one, then the other end of his trimly waxed mustache.

"Suppose what?" I prompted.

"*Non*, we will suppose nothing tonight," he replied. "You will please go to sleep once more, my friend, and I shall remain in the room to frighten away any more dream-demons which may come to plague you. Come, let us sleep. Here I do remain." He leaped into the wide bed beside me and pulled the down comforter snugly up about his pointed chin.

———

"...and I'd like very much to have you come right over to see her, if you will," Mrs. Weaver finished. "I can't imagine whatever made her attempt such a thing—she's never shown any signs of it before."

I hung up the telephone receiver and turned to de Grandin. "Here's another suicide, or almost-suicide, for you," I told him half teasingly. "The daughter of one of my patients attempted her life by hanging in the bathroom this morning."

"*Par la tête bleu*, do you tell me so?" he exclaimed eagerly. "I go with you, *cher ami*. I see this young woman; I examine her. Perhaps I shall find some key to the riddle there. *Parbleu*, me, I itch, I burn, I am all on fire with this mystery! Certainly, there must be an answer to it; but it remains hidden like a peasant's pig when the tax collector arrives."

———

"Well, young lady, what's this I hear about you?" I demanded severely as we entered Grace Weaver's bedroom a few minutes later. "What on earth have you to die for?"

"I—I don't know what made me want to do it. Doctor," the girl replied with a wan smile. "I hadn't thought of it before—ever. But I just got to—-oh, you know, sort of brooding over things last night, and when I went into the bathroom this morning, something—something inside my head, like those ringing noises you hear when you have a head-cold, you know—seemed to be whispering, 'Go on, kill yourself; you've nothing to live for. Go on, do it!' So, I just stood on the scales and took the cord from my bathrobe and tied it over the transom, then knotted the other end about my neck. Then I kicked the scales away and"—she gave another faint smile—"I'm glad I hadn't locked the door before I did it," she admitted.

De Grandin had been staring unwinkingly at her with his curiously level glance throughout her recital. As she concluded he bent forward and asked: "This voice which you heard bidding you commit an unpardonable sin, *Mademoiselle*, did you, perhaps, recognize it?"

The girl shuddered. "No!" she replied, but a sudden paling of her face about the lips gave the lie to her word.

"Pardonnez-moi, Modemoiselle," the Frenchman returned. "I think you do not tell the truth. Now, whose voice was it, if you please?"

A sullen, stubborn look spread over the girl's features, to be replaced a moment later by the muscular spasm which preludes weeping. "It—it sounded like Fanny's," she cried, and turning her face to the pillow, fell to sobbing bitterly.

"And Fanny, who is she?" de Grandin began, but Mrs. Weaver motioned him to silence with an imploring gesture.

I prescribed a mild bromide and left the patient, wondering what mad impulse could have led a girl in the first flush of young womanhood, happily situated in the home of parents who idolized her, engaged to a fine young man, and without bodily or spiritual ill of any sort, to attempt her life. Outside, de Grandin seized the mother's arm and whispered fiercely: "Who is this Fanny, Madame Weaver? Believe me, I ask not from idle curiosity, but because I seek vital information!"

"Fanny Briggs was Grace's chum two years ago," Mrs. Weaver answered. "My husband and I never quite approved of her, for she was several years older than Grace, and had such pronounced modern ideas that we didn't think her a suitable companion for our daughter, but you know how girls are with their "crushes." The more we objected to her going with Fanny, the more she used to seek her company, and we were both at our wits' ends when the Briggs girl was drowned while swimming at Asbury Park. I hate to say it, but it was almost a positive relief to us when the news came. Grace was almost broken-hearted about it at first, but she met Charley this summer, and

I haven't heard her mention Fanny's name since her engagement until just now."

"Ah?" de Grandin tweaked the tip of his mustache meditatively. "And perhaps Mademoiselle Grace was somewhere to be reminded of Mademoiselle Fanny last night?"

"No," Mrs. Weaver replied, "she went with a crowd of young folks to hear Maundy preach. There was a big party of them at the tabernacle—I'm afraid they went more to make fun than in a religious frame of mind, but he made quite an impression on Grace, she told us."

"*Feu de Dieu!*" de Grandin exploded, twisting his mustache furiously. "Do you tell me so, *Madame*? This is of the interest. *Madame*, I salute you." He bowed formally to Mrs. Weaver, then seized me by the arm and fairly dragged me away.

"Trowbridge, my friend," he informed me as we descended the steps of the Weaver portico, "this business, it has *l'odeur du poisson*— how is it you say?—the fishy smell."

"What do you mean?" I asked.

"*Parbleu*, what should I mean except that we go to interview this Monsieur Everard Maundy immediately, right away, at once? *Mordieu*, I damn think I have the tail of this mystery in my hand and may the blight of prohibition fall upon France if I do not twist it!"

———

The Reverend Everard Maundy's rooms in the Tremont Hotel were not hard to locate, for a constant stream of visitors went to and from them.

"Have you an appointment with Mr. Maundy?" the secretary asked as we were ushered into the anteroom.

"Not we," de Grandin denied, "but if you will be so kind as to tell him that Dr. Jules de Grandin, of the Paris *Sûreté*, desires to speak with him for five small minutes, I shall be in your debt."

The young man looked doubtful, but de Grandin's steady, catlike stare never wavered, and he finally rose and took our message to his employer.

In a few minutes he returned and admitted us to the big room where the evangelist received his callers behind a wide, flat-topped desk.

"Ah, Mr. de Grandin," the exhorter began with a professionally bland smile as we entered, "you are from France, are you not, sir? What can I do to help you toward the light?"

"*Cordieu, Monsieur*," de Grandin barked, for once forgetting his courtesy and ignoring the preacher's outstretched hand, "you can do much. You can explain these so unexplainable suicides which have taken place during the past week—the time you have preached here. That is the light we do desire to see."

Maundy's face went masklike and expressionless. "Suicides? Suicides?" he echoed. "What should I know of—"

The Frenchman shrugged his narrow shoulders impatiently. "We do fence with words, *Monsieur*," he interrupted testily. "Behold the facts: Messieurs Planz and Nixon, young men with, no reason for such desperate deeds, did kill themselves by violence; Madame Wester-felt and her two daughters, who were happy in their home, as everyone thought, did hurl themselves from an hotel window; a little schoolgirl hanged herself; last night my good friend Trowbridge, who never understandingly harmed man or beast, and whose life is dedicated to the healing of the sick, did almost take his life; and this very morning a young girl, wealthy, beloved, with every reason to be happy, did almost succeed in dispatching herself.

"Now, *Monsieur le prédicateur*, the only thing this miscellaneous assortment of persons had in common is the fact that *each of them did hear you preach the night before, or the same night, they attempted self-destruction*. That is the light we seek. Explain us the mystery, if you please."

Maundy's lean, rugged face had undergone a strange transformation while the little Frenchman spoke. Gone was his smug, professional smirk, gone the forced and meaningless expression of benignity, and in their place a look of such anguish and horror as might rest on the face of one who hears his sentence of damnation read.

"Don't—don't!" he besought, covering his writing face with his hands and bowing his head upon his desk while his shoulders shook with deep, soul-racking sobs. "Oh, miserable me! My sin has found me out!"

For a moment he wrestled in spiritual anguish, then raised his stricken countenance and regarded us with tear-dimmed eyes. "I am the greatest sinner in the world," he announced sorrowfully. "There is no hope for me on earth or yet in heaven!"

De Grandin tweaked the ends of his mustache alternately as he gazed curiously at the man before us. "*Monsieur*," he replied at length, "I think you do exaggerate. There are surely greater sinners than you. But if you would shrive you of the sin which gnaws your heart, I pray you shed what light you can upon these deaths, for there may be more to follow, and who knows that I shall not be able to stop them if you will but tell me all?"

"*Mea culpa!*" Maundy exclaimed, striking his chest with his clenched fists like a Hebrew prophet of old. "In my younger days, gentlemen, before I dedicated myself to the salvaging of souls, I was a scoffer. What I could not feel or weigh or measure, I disbelieved. I mocked at all religion and sneered at all the things which others held sacred.

"One night I went to a Spiritualistic séance, intent on scoffing, and forced my young wife to accompany me. The medium was an old colored woman, wrinkled, half-blind and unbelievably ignorant, but she had something—some secret power—which was denied the rest of us. Even I, atheist and derider of the truth that I was, could see that.

"As the old woman called on the spirits of the departed, I laughed out loud, and told her it was all a fake. The woman came out of her trance and turned her deep-set, burning old eyes on me. "White man," she said, "you will feel mighty sorry for those words. I tell you the spirits can hear what you say, an' they will take their revenge on you an' yours—you, an' on them as follows you—till you wish your tongue had been cut out before you said those words this here night."

"I tried to laugh at her—to curse her for a sniveling old faker—but there was something so terrible in her wrinkled old face that the words froze on my lips, and I hurried away.

"The next night my wife—my young, lovely bride—drowned herself in the river, and I have been a marked man ever since. Wherever I go it is the same. God has seen fit to open my eyes to the light of Truth and give me words to place His message before His people, and many who come to sneer at me go away believers; but wherever throngs gather to hear me bear my testimony there are always these tragedies. Tell me, gentlemen"—he threw out his hands in a gesture of surrender—"must I forever cease to preach the message of the Lord to His people? I have told myself that these self-murders would have occurred whether I came to town or not, but—is this a judgment which pursues me forever?"

Jules de Grandin regarded him thoughtfully. "*Monsieur*," he murmured, "I fear you make the mistakes we are all too prone to make. You do saddle *le bon Dieu* with all the sins with which the face of man is blackened. What if this were no judgment of heaven, but a curse of a very different sort, *hein*?"

"You mean the devil might be striving to overthrow the effects of my work?" the other asked, a light of hope breaking over his haggard face.

"U'm, perhaps; let us take that for our working hypothesis," de Grandin replied. "At present we may not say whether it be devil or devilkin which dogs your footsteps; but at the least we are greatly indebted to you for what you have told. Go my friend, continue to preach the Truth as you conceive the Truth to be, and may the God of all peoples uphold your hands. Me, I have other work to do, but it may be scarcely less important." He bowed formally and, turning on his heel, strode quickly from the room.

———

"That's the most fantastic story I ever heard!" I declared as we entered the hotel elevator. "The idea! As if an ignorant old woman could put a curse on—"

"*Zut!*" de Grandin shut me off. "You are a most excellent physician in the State of New Jersey, Friend Trowbridge, but have you ever been in Martinique, or Haiti, or in the jungles of the Congo Belgique?"

"Of course not," I admitted, "but—"

"I have. I have seen things so strange among the *Voudois* people that you would wish to have me committed to a madhouse did I but relate them to you. However, as that Monsieur Kipling says, 'that is another story.' At the present we are pledged to the solving of another mystery. Let us go to your house. I would think, I would consider all this business-of-the-monkey. *Pardieu*, it has as many angles as a diamond cut in Amsterdam!"

———

"Tell me, Friend Trowbridge," he demanded as we concluded our evening meal, "have you perhaps among your patients some young man who has met with a great sorrow recently; someone who has sustained a loss of wife or child or parents?"

I looked at him in amazement, but the serious expression on his little heart-shaped face told me he was in earnest, not making some ill-timed jest at my expense.

"Why, yes," I responded. "There is young Alvin Spence. His wife died in childbirth last June, and the poor chap has been half beside himself ever since. Thank God I was out of town at the time and didn't have the responsibility of the case."

"Thank God, indeed," de Grandin nodded gravely. "It is not easy for us, though we do ply our trade among the dying, to tell those who remain behind of their bereavement. But this Monsieur Spence; will you call on him this evening? Will you give him a ticket to the lecture of Monsieur Maundy?"

"No!" I blazed, half rising from my chair. "I've known that boy since he was a little toddler—knew his dead wife from childhood, too; and if you're figuring on making him the subject of some experiment—"

"Softly, my friend," he besought. "There is a terrible Thing loose among us. Remember the noble martyrs of science, those so magnificent men who risked their lives that yellow fever and malaria should be no more. Was not their work a holy one? Certainly. I do but wish that this young man may attend the lecture tonight, and on my honor, I shall guard him until all danger of attempted self-murder is passed. You will do what I say?"

He was so earnest in his plea that, though I felt like an accessory before the fact in a murder, I agreed.

Meantime, his little blue eyes snapping and sparkling with the zest of the chase, de Grandin had busied himself with the telephone directory, looking up a number of addresses, culling through them, discarding some, adding others, until he had obtained a list of some five or six. "Now, *mon vieux*," he begged as I made ready to visit Alvin Spence on my treacherous errand, "I would that you convey me to the rectory of St. Benedict's Church. The priest in charge there is Irish, and the Irish have the gift of seeing things which you colder-blooded Saxons may not. I must have a confab with this good Father O'Brien before I can permit that you interview the young Monsieur Spence. *Mordieu*, me, I am a scientist; no murderer!"

I drove him past the rectory and parked my motor at the curb, waiting impatiently while he thundered at the door with the handle of his ebony walking stick. His knock was answered by a little old man in clerical garb and a face as round and ruddy as a winter apple.

De Grandin spoke hurriedly to him in a low voice, waving his hands, shaking his head, shrugging his shoulders, as was his wont when the earnestness of his argument bore him before it. The priest's round face showed first incredulity, then mild skepticism, finally absorbed interest. In a moment the pair of them had vanished inside the house, leaving me to cool my heels in the bitter March air.

———

"You were long enough," I grumbled as he emerged from the rectory.

"*Pardieu*, yes, just long enough," he agreed. "I did accomplish my purpose, and no visit is either too long or too short when you can say that. Now to the house of the good Monsieur Spence, if you will. *Mordieu*, but we shall see what we shall see this night!"

———

Six hours later de Grandin and I crouched shivering at the roadside where the winding, serpentine Albemarle Pike dips into the hollow beside the Lonesome Swamp. The wind which had been trenchant as a shrew's tongue earlier in the evening had died away, and a hard, dull bitterness of cold hung over the hills and hollows of the rolling countryside. From the wide salt marshes where the bay's tide crept up to mingle with the swamp's brackish waters twice a day there came great sheets of brumous, impenetrable vapor which shrouded the landscape and distorted commonplace objects into hideous, gigantic monstrosities.

"*Mort d'un petit bonhomme*, my friend," de Grandin commented between chattering teeth, "I do not like this place; it has an evil air. There are spots where the very earth does breathe of unholy deeds, and by the sacred name of a rooster, this is one such. Look you at this accursed fog. Is it not as if the specters of those drowned at sea were marching up the shore this night?"

"Umph!" I replied, sinking my neck lower in the collar of my ulster and silently cursing myself for a fool.

A moment's silence, then: "You are sure Monsieur Spence must come this way? There is no other road by which he can reach his home?"

"Of course not," I answered shortly. "He lives out in the new Weiss development with his mother and sister—you were there this evening—and this is the only direct motor route to the subdivision from the city."

"Ah, that is well," he replied, hitching the collar of his greatcoat higher about his ears. "You will recognize his car—surely?"

"I'll try to," I promised, "but you can't be sure of anything on a night like this. I'd not guarantee to pick out my own—there's somebody pulling up beside the road now," I interrupted myself as a roadster came to an abrupt halt and stood panting, its headlights forming vague, luminous spots in the haze.

"*Mais oui,*" he agreed, "and no one stops at this spot for any good until *It* has been conquered. Come, let us investigate." He started forward, body bent, head advanced, like a motion picture conception of an Indian on the warpath.

Half a hundred stealthy steps brought us abreast of the parked car. Its occupant was sitting back on the driving seat, his hands resting listlessly on the steering wheel, his eyes upturned, as though he saw a vision in the trailing wisps of fog before him. I needed no second glance to recognize Alvin Spence, though the rapt look upon his white, set face transfigured it almost beyond recognition. He was like a poet beholding the beatific vision of his mistress or a medieval eremite gazing through the opened portals of Paradise.

"A-a-ah!" de Grandin's whisper cut like a wire-edged knife through the silence of the fog-bound air, "do you behold it, Friend Trowbridge?"

"Wha—" I whispered back, but broke the syllable half uttered. Thin, tenuous, scarcely to be distinguished from the lazily drifting festoons of the fog itself, there was a *something* in midair before the car where Alvin Spence sat with his yearning soul looking from his eyes. I seemed to see clear through the thing, yet its outlines were plainly perceptible, and as I looked and looked again, I recognized the unmistakable features of Dorothy Spence, the young man's dead wife. Her body—if the tenuous, ethereal mass of static vapor could be called such—was bare of clothing and seemed endued with a voluptuous grace and allure the living woman had never possessed, but her face was that of the young woman who had lain in Rosedale Cemetery for three-quarters of a year. If ever living man beheld the simulacrum of the dead, we three gazed on the wraith of Dorothy Spence that moment.

"Dorothy—my beloved, my dear, my dear!" the man half whispered, half sobbed, stretching forth his hands to the spirit-woman, then falling back on the seat as the vision seemed to elude his grasp when a sudden puff of breeze stirred the fog.

We could not catch the answer he received, close as we stood, but we could see the pale, curving lips frame the single word, "Come!" and saw the transparent arms stretched out to beckon him forward.

The man half rose from his seat, then sank back, set his face in sudden resolution and plunged his hand into the pocket of his overcoat.

Beside me de Grandin had been fumbling with something in his inside pocket. As Alvin Spence drew forth his hand and the dull gleam of a polished revolver shone in the light from his dashboard lamp, the Frenchman leaped forward like a panther. "Stop him, Friend Trowbridge!" he called shrilly, and to the hovering vision:

"Avaunt, accursed one! Begone, thou exile from heaven! Away, snake-spawn!"

As he shouted, he drew a tiny pellet from his inner pocket and hurled it point-blank through the vaporous body of the specter.

Even as I seized Spence's hand and fought with him for possession of the pistol, I saw the transformation from the tail of my eye. As de Grandin's missile tore through its unsubstantial substance, the vision-woman seemed to shrink in upon herself, to become suddenly more compact, thinner, scrawny. Her rounded bosom flattened to mere folds of leatherlike skin stretched drum-tight above staring ribs, her slender graceful hands were horrid, claw-tipped talons, and the yearning, enticing face of Dorothy Spence became a mask of hideous, implacable hate, great-eyed, thin-lipped, beak-nosed—such a face as the demons of hell might show after a million years of burning in the infernal fires. A screech like the keening of all the owls in the world together split the fog-wrapped stillness of the night, and the monstrous thing before us seemed suddenly to shrivel, shrink to a mere spot of baleful, phosphorescent fire, and disappear like a snuffed-out candle's flame.

Spence saw it, too. The pistol dropped from his nerveless fingers to the car's floor with a soft thud, and his arm went limp in my grasp as he fell forward in a dead faint.

"*Parbleu*," de Grandin swore softly as he climbed into the unconscious lad's car. "Let us drive forward, Friend Trowbridge. We will take him home and administer a soporific. He must sleep, this poor one, or the memory of what we have shown him will rob him of his reason."

So, we carried Alvin Spence to his home, administered a hypnotic and left him in the care of his wondering mother with instructions to repeat the dose if he should wake.

———

It was a mile or more to the nearest bus station, and we set out at a brisk walk, our heels hitting sharply against the frosty concrete of the road.

"What in the world was it, de Grandin?" I asked as we marched in step down the darkened highway. "It was the most horrible—"

"*Parbleu*," he interrupted, "someone comes this way in a monstrous hurry!"

His remark was no exaggeration. Driven as though pursued by all the furies from pandemonium, came a light motorcar with plain black sides and a curving top. "Look out!" the driver warned as he recognized me and came to a bumping halt. "Look out, Dr. Trowbridge, it's walking! It got out and walked!"

De Grandin regarded him with an expression of comic bewilderment. "Now what is it that walks, *mon brave?*" he demanded. "*Mordieu*, you chatter like a monkey with a handful of hot chestnuts! What is it that walks, and why must we look out for it, *hein?*"

"Sile Gregory," the young man answered. "He died this mornin', an' Mr. Johnson took him to th' parlors to fix 'im up, an' sent me an' Joe Williams out with him this evenin'. I was just drivin' up to th' house, an' Joe hopped out to give me a lift with th' casket, an' old Silas *got up an' walked away!* An' Mr. Johnson embalmed 'im this mornin', I tell you!"

"*Norn, d'un chou-fleur!*" de Grandin shot back. "And where did this so remarkable demonstration take place, *mon vieux?* Also, what of the excellent Williams, your partner?"

"I don't know, an' I don't care," the other replied. "When a dead corpse I saw embalmed this mornin' gets outa its casket an' walks, I ain't gonna wait for nobody. Jump up here, if you want to go with me; I ain't gonna stay here no longer!"

"*Bien*," de Grandin acquiesced. "Go your way, my excellent one. Should we encounter your truant corpse, we will direct him to his waiting *bière.*"

The young man waited for no second invitation, but started his car down the road at a speed which would bring him into certain trouble if observed by a state trooper.

"Now, what the devil do you make of that?" I asked. "I know Johnson, the funeral director, well, and I always thought he had a pretty levelheaded crowd of boys about his place, but if that lad hasn't been drinking some powerful liquor, I'll be—"

"Not necessarily, my friend," de Grandin interrupted. "I think it not at all impossible that he tells but the sober truth. It may well be that the dead do walk this road tonight."

I shivered with something other than the night's chill as he made the matter-of-fact assertion but forbore pressing him for an explanation. There are times when ignorance is a happier portion than knowledge.

We had marched perhaps another quarter-mile in silence when de Grandin suddenly plucked my sleeve. "Have you noticed nothing, my friend?" he asked.

"What d'ye mean?" I demanded sharply, for my nerves were worn tender by the night's events.

"I am not certain, but it seems to me we are followed."

"Followed? Nonsense! *Who* would be following us?" I returned, unconsciously stressing the personal pronoun, for I had almost said, "What would follow us," and the implication raised by the impersonal form sent tiny shivers racing along my back and neck.

De Grandin cast me a quick, appraising glance, and I saw the ends of his spiked mustache lift suddenly as his lips framed a sardonic smile, but instead of answering he swung round on his heel and faced the shadows behind us.

"*Holà, Monsieur le Cadavre!*" he called sharply. "Here we are, and —*sang du diable!*—here we shall stand."

I looked at him in open-mouthed amazement, but his gaze was turned steadfastly on something half seen in the mist which lay along the road.

Next instant my heart seemed pounding through my ribs and my breath came hot and choking in my throat, for a tall, gangling man suddenly emerged from the fog and made for us at a shambling gait.

He was clothed in a long, old-fashioned double-breasted frock coat and stiffly starched shirt topped by a standing collar and white, ministerial tie. His hair was neatly, though somewhat unnaturally, arranged in a central part above a face the color and smoothness of wax, and little flecks of talcum powder still clung here and there to his eyebrows. No mistaking it! Johnson, artist that he was, had arrayed the dead farmer in the manner of all his kind for their last public appearance before relatives and friends. One look told me the horrible, incredible truth. It was the body of old Silas Gregory which stumbled toward us through the fog. Dressed, greased and powdered for its last, long rest, the thing came toward us with faltering, uncertain strides, and I noticed, with the sudden ability for minute inventory fear sometimes lends our senses, that his old, sunburned skin showed more than one brand where the formaldehyde embalming fluid had burned it.

In one long, thin hand the horrible thing grasped the helve of a farmyard ax, the other hand lay stiffly folded across the midriff as the embalmer had placed it when his professional ministrations were finished that morning.

"My God!" I cried, shrinking back toward the roadside. But de Grandin ran forward to meet the charging horror with a cry which was almost like a welcome.

"Stand clear, Friend Trowbridge," he warned, "we will fight this to a finish, I and It!" His little, round eyes were flashing with the zest of combat, his mouth was set in a straight, uncompromising line beneath the sharply waxed ends of his diminutive mustache, and his shoulders hunched forward like those of a practice wrestler before he comes to grips with his opponent.

With a quick, whipping motion, he ripped the razor-sharp blade of his sword-cane from its ebony sheath and swung the flashing steel in a whirring, circle about his head, then sank to a defensive posture, one foot advanced, one retracted, the leg bent at the knee, the triple-edged sword dancing before him like the darting tongue of an angry serpent.

The dead thing never faltered in its stride. Three feet or so from Jules de Grandin it swung the heavy, rust-encrusted ax above its shoulder and brought it downward, its dull, lack-luster eyes staring straight before it with an impassivity more terrible than any glare of hate.

"*Sa ha!*" de Grandin's blade flickered forward like a streak of storm lightning and fleshed itself to the hilt in the corpse's shoulder.

He might as well have struck his steel into a bag of meal.

The ax descended with a crushing, devastating blow.

De Grandin leaped nimbly aside, disengaging his blade and swinging it again before him, but an expression of surprise—almost of consternation—was on his face.

I felt my mouth go dry with excitement, and a queer, weak feeling hit me at the pit of the stomach. The Frenchman had driven his sword home with the skill of a practice fencer and the precision of a skilled anatomist. His blade had pierced the dead man's body at the junction of the short head of the biceps and the great pectoral muscle, at the coracoid process, inflicting a wound which should have paralyzed the arm—yet the terrible ax rose for a second blow as though de Grandin's steel had struck wide of the mark.

"Ah?" de Grandin nodded understandingly as he leaped backward, avoiding the ax-blade by the breadth of a hair. "*Bien. À la fin!*"

His defensive tactics changed instantly. Flickeringly his sword lashed forward, then came down and back with a sharp, whipping motion. The keen edge of the angular blade bit deeply into the corpse's wrist, laying bare the bone. Still the ax rose and fell and rose again.

Slash after slash de Grandin gave, his slicing cuts falling with almost mathematical precision in the same spot, shearing deeper and deeper into his dreadful opponent's wrist. At last, with a short, clucking exclamation, he drew his blade sharply back for the last time, severing the ax-hand from the arm.

The dead thing collapsed like a deflated balloon at his feet as hand and ax fell together to the cement roadway.

Quick as a mink, de Grandin thrust his left hand within his coat, drew forth a pellet similar to that with which he had transformed the counterfeit of Dorothy Spence, and hurled it straight into the upturned, ghastly-calm face of the mutilated body before him.

The dead lips did not part, for the embalmer's sutures had closed them forever that morning, but the body writhed upward from the road, and a groan which was a muted scream came from its flat chest. It twisted back and forth a moment, like a mortally stricken serpent in its death agony, then lay still.

Seizing the corpse by its grave clothes, de Grandin dragged it through the line of roadside hazel bushes to the rim of the swamp, and busied himself cutting long, straight withes from the brushwood, then disappeared again behind the tangled branches. At last:

"It is finished," he remarked, stepping back to the road. "Let us go."

"Wha—what did you do?" I faltered.

"I did the needful, my friend. *Morbleu*, we had an evil, a very evil thing imprisoned in that dead man, and I took such precautions as were necessary to fix it in its prison. A stake through the heart, a severed head, and the whole firmly thrust into the ooze of the swamp —*voilà*. It will be long before other innocent ones are induced to destroy themselves by *that*."

"But—" I began.

"*Non, non,*" he replied, half laughing. "*En avant, mon ami!* I would that we return home as quickly as possible. Much work creates much appetite, and I make small doubt that I shall consume the remainder of that so delicious apple pie which I could not eat at dinner."

———

Jules de Grandin regarded the empty plate before him with a look of comic tragedy. "May endless benisons rest upon your amiable cook, Friend Trowbridge," he pronounced, "but may the curse of heaven forever pursue the villain who manufactures the woefully inadequate pans in which she bakes her pies."

"Hang the pies, and the platemakers, too!" I burst out. "You promised to explain all this hocus-pocus, and I've been patient long enough. Stop sitting there like a glutton, wailing for more pie, and tell me about it."

"Oh, the mystery?" he replied, stifling a yawn and lighting a cigarette. "That is simple, my friend, but these so delicious pies— however, I do digress:

"When first I saw the accounts of so many strange suicides within one little week I was interested, but not greatly puzzled. People have slain themselves since the beginning of time, and yet"—he shrugged his shoulders deprecatingly—"what is it that makes the hound scent his quarry, the war-horse sniff the battle afar off? Who can tell?

"I said to me: 'There is undoubtedly more to these deaths than the newspapers have said. I shall investigate.'

"From the coroners' to the undertakers', and from the undertak- ers' to the physicians', yes, *parbleu*! and to the family residences, as well, I did go, gleaning here a bit and there a bit of information which seemed to mean nothing, but which might mean much did I but have other information to add to it.

"One thing I ascertained early: In each instance the suicides had been to hear this Reverend Maundy the night before or the same night they did away with themselves. This was perhaps insignificant; perhaps it meant much. I determined to hear this Monsieur Maundy with my own two ears; but I would not hear him too close by.

"Forgive me, my friend, for I did make of you the guinea-pig for my laboratory experiment. You I left in a forward seat while the reverend gentleman preached, me, I stayed in the rear of the hall and used my eyes as well as my ears.

"What happened that night? Why, my good, kind Friend Trowbridge, who in all his life had done no greater wrong than thoughtlessly to kill a little, so harmless kitten, did almost *seemingly* commit suicide. But I was not asleep by the switch, my friend. Not Jules de Grandin! All the way home I saw you were *distrait*, and I did fear something would happen, and I did therefore watch beside your door with my eye and ear alternately glued to the keyhole. *Parbleu*, I entered the chamber not one little second too soon, either!

"'This is truly strange,' I tell me. 'My friend hears this preacher and nearly destroys himself. Six others have heard him and have quite killed themselves. If Friend Trowbridge were haunted by the ghost of a dead kitten, why should not those others, who also undoubtedly possessed distressing memories, have been hounded to their graves by them?'

"'There is no reason why they should not,' I tell me.

"Next, morning comes the summons to attend the young Mademoiselle Weaver. She, too, have heard the preacher; she, too, have attempted her life. And what does she tell us? That she fancied the voice of her dead friend urged her to kill herself.

"'Ah, ha!' I say to me. 'This whatever-it-is which causes so much suicide may appeal by fear, or perhaps by love, or by whatever will most strongly affect thy person who dies by his own hand. We must see this Monsieur Maundy. It is perhaps possible he can tell us much.'

"As yet I can see no light—I am still in darkness—but far ahead I already see the gleam of a promise of information. When we see Monsieur Everard Maundy and he tells us of his experience at that séance so many years ago—*parbleu*, I see it all, or almost all.

"Now, what was it acted as agent for that aged sorceress' curse?"

He elevated one shoulder and looked questioningly at me.

"How should I know?" I answered.

"Correct," he nodded, "how, indeed? Beyond doubt it were a spirit of some sort; what sort we do not know. Perhaps it were the spirit of some unfortunate who had destroyed himself and was earth-bound as a consequence. There are such. And, as misery loves company in the proverb, so do these wretched ones seek to lure others to join them in their unhappy state. Or, maybe, it was an Elemental."

"A *what*?" I demanded.

"An Elemental—a Neutrarian."

"What the deuce is that?"

For answer he left the table and entered the library, returning with a small, red leather-bound volume in his hand. "You have read the works of Monsieur Rossetti?" he asked.

"Yes."

"You recall his poem, *Eden Bowers*, perhaps?"

"H'm; yes. I've read it, but I never could make anything of it."

"Quite likely," he agreed, "its meaning is most obscure, but I shall enlighten you. *Attendez-moi!*"

Thumbing through the thin pages he began reading at random:

> *It was Lilith, the wife of Adam,*
> *Not a drop of her blood was human,*
> *But she was made like a soft, sweet woman ...*

> *Lilith stood on the skirts of Eden,*
> *She was the first that thence was driven,*
> *With her was hell and with Eve was heaven ...*

> *What bright babes had Lilith and Adam,*
> *Shapes that coiled in the woods and waters.*
> *Glittering sons and radiant daughters ...*

"You see, my friend?"

"No, I'm hanged if I do."

"Very well, then, according to the rabbinical lore, before Eve was created, Adam, our first father, had a demon wife named Lilith. And by her he had many children, not human, nor yet wholly demon.

"For her sins Lilith was expelled from Eden's bowers, and Adam was given Eve to wife. With Lilith was driven out all her progeny by Adam, and Lilith and her half-man, half-demon brood declared war on Adam and Eve and their descendants forever. These descendants of Lilith and Adam have ever since roamed the earth and air, incorporeal, having no bodies like men, yet having always a hatred for flesh and blood. Because they were the first, or elder race, they are sometimes called Elementals in the ancient lore; sometimes they are called Neutrarians, because they are neither wholly men nor wholly devils. Me, I do not take sides in the controversy; I care not what they are called, but I know what I have seen. I think it is highly possible those ancient Hebrews, misinterpreting the manifestations they observed, accounted for them by their so fantastic legends. We are told these Neutrarians, or Elementals are immaterial beings. Absurd? Not necessarily. What is matter—material? Electricity, perhaps—a great system of law and order throughout the universe and all the millions of worlds extending throughout infinity.

"Very good, so far; but when we have said matter is electricity, what have we to say if asked, 'What is electricity?' Me, I think it a modification of the ether.

"'Very good,' you say; 'but what is ether?'

"*Parbleu*, I do not know. The matter—or material—of the universe is little, if anything, more than electrons flowing about in all directions. Now here, now there, the electrons coalesce and form what we call solids—rocks and trees and men and women. But may they not coalesce at a different rate of speed, or vibration, to form beings which are real, with emotions and loves and hates similar to ours, yet for the most part invisible to us, as is the air? Why not? No man can truthfully say, 'I have seen the air,' yet no one is so great a fool as to doubt its existence for that reason."

"Yes, but we can see the effects of air?" I objected. "Air in motion, for instance, becomes wind, and—"

"*Mort d'un crapaud!*" he burst out. "And have we not observed the effects of these Elementals—these Neutrarians, or whatsoever their name may be? How of the six suicides; how of that which tempted the young Mademoiselle Weaver and the young Monsieur

Spence to self-murder? How of the cat which entered your room? Did we see no effects there, *hein*?"

"But the thing we saw with young Spence, and the cat, were visible," I objected.

"But of course. When you fancied you saw the cat, you were influenced from within, even as Mademoiselle Weaver was when she heard the voice of her dead friend. What we saw with the young Spence was the shadow of his desire—the intensified love and longing for his dead wife, plus the evil entity which urged him to unpardonable sin."

"Oh, all right," I conceded. "Go on with your theory."

He stared thoughtfully at the glowing tip of his cigarette a moment, then: "It has been observed, my friend, that he who goes to a Spiritualistic séance may come away with some evil spirit attached to him—whether it be a spirit which once inhabited human form or an Elemental, it is no matter; the evil ones swarm about the lowered lights of the Spiritualistic meeting as flies congregate at the honey-pot in summer. It appears such a one fastened to Everard Maundy. His wife was its first victim, afterward those who heard him preach were attacked.

"Consider the scene at the tabernacle when Monsieur Maundy preaches: Emotion, emotion—all is emotion; reason is lulled to sleep by the power of his words; and the minds of his hearers are not on their guard against the entrance of evil spirits; they are too intent on what he is saying. Their consciousness is absent. *Pouf!* The evil one fastens firmly on some unwary person, explores his innermost mind, finds out his weakest point of defense. With you it was the kitten; with young Mademoiselle Weaver, her dead friend; with Monsieur Spence, his lost wife. Even love can be turned to evil purposes by such a one.

"These things I did consider most carefully, and then I did enlist the services of young Monsieur Spence. You saw what you saw on the lonely road this night. Appearing to him in the form of his dead beloved, this wicked one had all but persuaded him to destroy himself when we intervened.

"*Très bien.* We triumphed then; the night before I had prevented your death. The evil one was angry at me; also, it was frightened. If I continued, I would rob it of much prey, so it sought to do me harm. Me, I am ever on guard, for knowledge is power. It could not lead me to my death, and, being spirit, it could not directly attack me. It had recourse to its last resort. While the young undertaker's assistant was about to deliver the body of the old Monsieur Gregory, the spirit seized the corpse and animated it, then pursued me.

"Ha, almost, I thought, it had done for me at one time, for I forgot it was no living thing I fought and attacked it as if it could be killed. But when I found my sword could not kill that which was already dead, I did cut off its so abominable hand. I am very clever, my friend. The evil spirit reaped small profits from fighting with me."

He made the boastful admission in all seriousness, entirely unaware of its sound, for to him it was but a straightforward statement of undisputed fact. I grinned in spite of myself, then curiosity got the better of amusement. "What were those little pellets you threw at the spirit when it was luring young Spence to commit suicide, and later at the corpse of Silas Gregory?" I asked.

"Ah"—his elfish smile flickered across his lips, then disappeared as quickly as it came—"it is better you do not ask me that, *mon cher*. Let it suffice when I tell you I convinced the good *Père* O 'Brien that he should let me have what no layman is supposed to touch, that I might use the ammunition of heaven against the forces of hell."

"But how do we know this Elemental, or whatever it is, won't come back again?" I persisted.

"Little fear," he encouraged. "The resort to the dead man's body was its last desperate chance. Having elected to fight me physically, it must stand or fall by the result of the fight. Once inside the body, it could not quickly extricate itself. Half an hour, at least, must elapse before it could withdraw, and before that time had passed, I had fixed it there for all time. The stake through the heart and the severed head makes that body as harmless as any other, and the wicked spirit which animated it must remain with the flesh it sought to pervert to its own evil ends henceforth and forever."

"But—"

"Ah bah!" He dropped his cigarette end into his empty coffee cup and yawned frankly. "We do talk too much, my friend. This night's work has made me heavy with sleep. Let us take a tiny sip of cognac, that the pie may not give us unhappy dreams, and then to bed. Tomorrow is another day, and who knows what new task lies before us?"

The Tomb

H.P. Lovecraft

"Sedibus ut saltem placidis in morte quiescam." —*Virgil*

In relating the circumstances which have led to my confinement within this refuge for the demented, I am aware that my present position will create a natural doubt of the authenticity of my narrative. It is an unfortunate fact that the bulk of humanity is too limited in its mental vision to weigh with patience and intelligence those isolated phenomena, seen and felt only by a psychologically sensitive few, which lie outside its common experience. Men of broader intellect know that there is no sharp distinction betwixt the real and the unreal; that all things appear as they do only by virtue of the delicate individual physical and mental media through which we are made conscious of them; but the prosaic materialism of the majority condemns as madness the flashes of super-sight which penetrate the common veil of obvious empiricism.

My name is Jervas Dudley, and from earliest childhood I have been a dreamer and a visionary. Wealthy beyond the necessity of a commercial life, and temperamentally unfitted for the formal studies and social recreations of my acquaintances, I have dwelt ever in realms apart from the visible world, spending my youth and adolescence in ancient and little-known books, and in roaming the fields and groves of the region near my ancestral home. I do not think that what I read in these books or saw in these fields and groves was exactly what other boys read and saw there; but of this I must say little, since detailed speech would but confirm those cruel slanders upon my intellect which I sometimes overhear from the whispers of the stealthy attendants around me. It is sufficient for me to relate events without analyzing causes.

I have said that I dwelt apart from the visible world, but I have not said that I dwelt alone. This no human creature may do; for lacking the fellowship of the living, he inevitably draws upon the companionship of things that are not, or are no longer, living. Close by my home there lies a singular wooded hollow, in whose twilight deeps I spent most of my time, reading, thinking, and dreaming. Down its moss-covered slopes my first steps of infancy were taken, and around its grotesquely gnarled oak trees my first fancies of boyhood were woven. Well did I come to know the presiding dryads of those trees, and often have I watched their wild dances in the struggling beams of a waning moon—but of these things I must not now speak. I will tell only of the lone tomb in the darkest of the hillside thickets; the deserted tomb of the Hydes, an old and exalted family whose last direct descendant had been laid within its black recesses many decades before my birth.

The vault to which I refer is of ancient granite, weathered and discolored by the mists and dampness of generations. Excavated back into the hillside, the structure is visible only at the entrance. The door, a ponderous and forbidding slab of stone, hangs upon rusted iron hinges, and is fastened *ajar* in a queerly sinister way by means of heavy iron chains and padlocks, according to a gruesome fashion of half a century ago. The abode of the race whose scions are here inurned had once crowned the declivity which holds the tomb but had long since fallen victim to the flames which sprang up from a disastrous stroke of lightning. Of the midnight storm which destroyed this gloomy mansion, the older inhabitants of the region sometimes speak in hushed and uneasy voices; alluding to what they call "divine wrath" in a manner that in later years vaguely increased the always strong fascination which I felt for the forest-darkened sepulchre. One man only had perished in the fire. When the last of the Hydes was buried in this place of shade and stillness, the sad urnful of ashes had come from a distant land; to which the family had repaired when the mansion burned down. No one remains to lay flowers before the granite portal, and few care to brave the depressing shadows which seem to linger strangely about the water-worn stones.

I shall never forget the afternoon when first I stumbled upon the half-hidden house of death. It was in mid-summer, when the alchemy of Nature transmutes the sylvan landscape to one vivid and almost homogeneous mass of green, when the senses are well-nigh intoxicated with the surging seas of moist verdure and the subtly indefinable odors of the soil and the vegetation. In such surroundings the mind loses its perspective; time and space become trivial and unreal, and echoes of a forgotten prehistoric past beat insistently upon the enthralled consciousness.

All day I had been wandering through the mystic groves of the hollow; thinking thoughts I need not discuss and conversing with things I need not name. In years a child of ten, I had seen and heard many wonders unknown to the throng and was oddly aged in certain respects. When, upon forcing my way between two savage clumps of briers, I suddenly encountered the entrance of the vault, I had no knowledge of what I had discovered. The dark blocks of granite, the door so curiously ajar, and the funereal carvings above the arch, aroused in me no associations of mournful or terrible character. Of graves and tombs, I knew and imagined much, but had on account of my peculiar temperament been kept from all personal contact with churchyards and cemeteries. The strange stone house on the wood-land slope was to me, only a source of interest and speculation; and its cold, damp interior, into which I vainly peered through the aperture so tantalizingly left, contained for me no hint of death or decay. But in that instant of curiosity was born the madly unreasoning desire which has brought me to this hell of confinement. Spurred on by a voice which must have come from the hideous soul of the forest, I resolved to enter the beckoning gloom in spite of the ponderous chains which barred my passage. In the waning light of day, I alternately rattled the rusty impediments with a view to throwing wide the stone door and essayed to squeeze my slight form through the space already provided; but neither plan met with success. At first curious, I was now frantic; and when in the thickening twilight I returned to my home, I had sworn to the hundred gods of the grove that *at any cost* I would someday force an entrance to the black, chilly depths that seemed calling out to me. The physician with the iron-grey beard who comes each day to my room once told a visitor that this decision marked the beginning of a pitiful monomania; but I will leave final judgment to my readers when they shall have learnt all.

The months following my discovery were spent in futile attempts to force the complicated padlock of the slightly open vault, and in carefully guarded inquiries regarding the nature and history of the structure. With the traditionally receptive ears of the small boy, I learned much; though a habitual secretiveness caused me to tell no one of my information or my resolve. It is perhaps worth mentioning that I was not at all surprised or terrified on learning of the nature of the vault. My rather original ideas regarding life and death had caused me to associate the cold clay with the breathing body in a vague fashion; and I felt that the great and sinister family of the burned-down mansion was in some way represented within the stone space I sought to explore. Mumbled tales of the weird rites and godless revels of bygone years in the ancient hall gave to me a new and potent interest in the tomb, before whose door I would sit for hours at a time each day. Once I thrust a candle within the nearly closed entrance but could see nothing save a flight of damp stone steps leading downward. The odor of the place repelled yet bewitched me. I felt I had known it before, in a past remote beyond all recollection; beyond even my tenancy of the body I now possess.

––––––

The year after I first beheld the tomb, I stumbled upon a worm-eaten translation of Plutarch's *Lives* in the book-filled attic of my home. Reading the life of Theseus, I was much impressed by that passage telling of the great stone beneath which the boyish hero was to find his tokens of destiny whenever he should become old enough to lift its enormous weight. This legend had the effect of dispelling my keenest impatience to enter the vault, for it made me feel that the time was not yet ripe. Later, I told myself, I should grow to a strength and ingenuity which might enable me to unfasten the heavily chained door with ease; but until then I would do better by conforming to what seemed the will of Fate.

Accordingly, my watches by the dank portal became less persistent, and much of my time was spent in other though equally strange pursuits. I would sometimes rise very quietly in the night, stealing out to walk in those churchyards and places of burial from which I had been kept by my parents. What I did there I may not say, for I am not now sure of the reality of certain things; but I know that on the day after such a nocturnal ramble I would often astonish those about me with my knowledge of topics almost forgotten for many generations. It was after a night like this that I shocked the community with a queer conceit about the burial of the rich and celebrated Squire Brewster, a maker of local history who was interred in 1711, and whose slate headstone, bearing a graven skull and crossbones, was slowly crumbling to powder. In a moment of childish imagination, I vowed not only that the undertaker, Goodman Simpson, had stolen the silver-buckled shoes, silken hose, and satin small-clothes of the deceased before burial; but that the Squire himself, not fully inanimate, had turned twice in his mound-covered coffin on the day after interment.

But the idea of entering the tomb never left my thoughts; being indeed stimulated by the unexpected genealogical discovery that my own maternal ancestry possessed at least a slight link with the supposedly extinct family of the Hydes. Last of my paternal race, I was likewise the last of this older and more mysterious line. I began to feel that the tomb was *mine,* and to look forward with hot eagerness to the time when I might pass within that stone door and down those slimy stone steps in the dark. I now formed the habit of listening very intently at the slightly open portal, choosing my favorite hours of midnight stillness for the odd vigil. By the time I came of age, I had made a small clearing in the thicket before the mold-stained facade of the hillside, allowing the surrounding vegetation to encircle and overhang the space like the walls and roof of a sylvan bower. This bower was my temple, the fastened door my shrine, and here I would lie outstretched on the mossy ground, thinking strange thoughts and dreaming strange dreams.

The night of the first revelation was a sultry one. I must have fallen asleep from fatigue, for it was with a distinct sense of awakening that I heard the voices. Of those tones and accents I hesitate to speak; of their quality I will not speak; but I may say that they presented certain uncanny differences in vocabulary, pronunciation, and mode of utterance. Every shade of New England dialect, from the uncouth syllables of the Puritan colonists to the precise rhetoric of fifty years ago, seemed represented in that shadowy colloquy, though it was only later that I noticed the fact. At the time, indeed, my attention was distracted from this matter by another phenomenon; a phenomenon so fleeting that I could not take oath upon its reality. I barely fancied that as I awoke, a *light* had been hurriedly extinguished within the sunken sepulcher. I do not think I was either astounded or panic-stricken, but I know that I was greatly and permanently *changed* that night. Upon returning home I went with much directness to a rotting chest in the attic, wherein I found the key which next day unlocked with ease the barrier I had so long stormed in vain.

It was in the soft glow of late afternoon that I first entered the vault on the abandoned slope. A spell was upon me, and my heart leaped with an exultation I can but ill describe. As I closed the door behind me and descended the dripping steps by the light of my lone candle, I seemed to know the way; and though the candle sputtered with the stifling reek of the place, I felt singularly at home in the musty, charnel-house air. Looking about me, I beheld many marble slabs bearing coffins, or the remains of coffins. Some of these were sealed and intact, but others had nearly vanished, leaving the silver handles and plates isolated amidst certain curious heaps of whitish dust. Upon one plate I read the name of Sir Geoffrey Hyde, who had come from Sussex in 1640 and died here a few years later. In a conspic-uous alcove was one fairly well-preserved and untenanted casket, adorned with a single name which brought to me both a smile and a shudder. An odd impulse caused me to climb upon the broad slab, extinguish my candle, and lie down within the vacant box.

In the grey light of dawn, I staggered from the vault and locked the chain of the door behind me. I was no longer a young man, though but twenty-one winters had chilled my bodily frame. Early rising villagers who observed my homeward progress looked at me strangely and marveled at the signs of ribald revelry which they saw in one whose life was known to be sober and solitary. I did not appear before my parents till after a long and refreshing sleep.

Henceforward I haunted the tomb each night; seeing, hearing, and doing things I must never reveal. My speech, always susceptible to environmental influences, was the first thing to succumb to the change; and my suddenly acquired archaism of diction was soon remarked upon. Later a queer boldness and recklessness came into my demeanor, till I unconsciously grew to possess the bearing of a man of the world despite my lifelong seclusion. My formerly silent tongue waxed voluble with the easy grace of a Chesterfield or the godless cyni-cism of a Rochester. I displayed a peculiar erudition utterly unlike the fantastic, monkish lore over which I had poured in youth; and covered the flyleaves of my books with facile impromptu epigrams which brought up suggestions of Gay, Prior, and the sprightliest of the Augustan wits and rhymesters. One morning at breakfast I came close to disaster by declaiming in palpably liquorish accents an effusion of eighteenth-century Bacchanalian mirth; a bit of Georgian playfulness never recorded in a book, which ran something like this:

> *Come hither, my lads, with your tankards of ale,*
> *And drink to the present before it shall fail;*
> *Pile each on your platter a mountain of beef,*
> *For 'tis eating and drinking that bring us relief:*
> *So fill up your glass,*
> *For life will soon pass;*

*When you're dead ye'll ne'er drink to your king or your
lass!*

*Anacreon had a red nose, so they say;
But what's a red nose if ye're happy and gay?
Gad split me! I'd rather be red whilst I'm here,
Than white as a lily—and dead half a year!
So Betty, my miss,
Come give me a kiss;
In hell there's no innkeeper's daughter like this!*

*Young Harry, propp'd up just as straight as he's able,
Will soon lose his wig and slip under the table;
But fill up your goblets and pass 'em around—
Better under the table than under the ground!
So revel and chaff
As ye thirstily quaff:
Under six feet of dirt 'tis less easy to laugh!*

*The fiend strike me blue! I'm scarce able to walk,
And damn me if I can stand upright or talk!
Here, landlord, bid Betty to summon a chair;
I'll try home for a while, for my wife is not there!
So lend me a hand;
I'm not able to stand,
But I'm gay whilst I linger on top of the land!*

About this time, I conceived my present fear of fire and thunderstorms. Previously indifferent to such things, I had now an unspeakable horror of them; and would retire to the innermost recesses of the house whenever the heavens threatened an electrical display. A favorite haunt of mine during the day was the ruined cellar of the mansion that had burned down, and in fancy I would picture the structure as it had been in its prime. On one occasion I startled a villager by leading him confidently to a shallow sub-cellar, of whose existence I seemed to

know in spite of the fact that it had been unseen and forgotten for
many generations.

———

At last came that which I had long feared. My parents, alarmed at the
altered manner and appearance of their only son, commenced to exert
over my movements a kindly espionage which threatened to result in
disaster. I had told no one of my visits to the tomb, having guarded
my secret purpose with religious zeal since childhood; but now I was
forced to exercise care in threading the mazes of the wooded hollow,
that I might throw off a possible pursuer. My key to the vault I kept
suspended from a cord about my neck, its presence known only to
me. I never carried out of the sepulchre any of the things I came upon
whilst within its walls.

One morning as I emerged from the damp tomb and fastened the
chain of the portal with none too steady hand, I beheld in an adjacent
thicket the dreaded face of a watcher. Surely the end was near; for my
bower was discovered, and the objective of my nocturnal journeys
revealed. The man did not accost me, so I hastened home in an effort
to overhear what he might report to my careworn father. Were my
sojourns beyond the chained door about to be proclaimed to the
world? Imagine my delighted astonishment on hearing the spy inform
my parent in a cautious whisper *that I had spent the night in the bower
outside the tomb;* my sleep-filmed eyes fixed upon the crevice where the
padlocked portal stood ajar! By what miracle had the watcher been
thus deluded? I was now convinced that a supernatural agency
protected me. Made bold by this heaven-sent circumstance, I began to
resume perfect openness in going to the vault; confident that no one
could witness my entrance. For a week I tasted to the full the joys of
that charnel conviviality which I must not describe, when
the *thing* happened, and I was borne away to this accursed abode of
sorrow and monotony.

I should not have ventured out that night; for the taint of thunder
was in the clouds, and a hellish phosphorescence rose from the rank

swamp at the bottom of the hollow. The call of the dead, too, was different. Instead of the hillside tomb, it was the charred cellar on the crest of the slope whose presiding daemon beckoned to me with unseen fingers. As I emerged from an intervening grove upon the plain before the ruin, I beheld in the misty moonlight a thing I had always vaguely expected. The mansion, gone for a century, once more reared its stately height to the raptured vision; every window ablaze with the splendor of many candles. Up the long drive rolled the coaches of the Boston gentry, whilst on foot came a numerous assemblage of powdered exquisites from the neighboring mansions. With this throng I mingled, though I knew I belonged with the hosts rather than with the guests. Inside the hall were music, laughter, and wine on every hand. Several faces I recognized; though I should have known them better had they been shriveled or eaten away by death and decomposition. Amidst a wild and reckless throng, I was the wildest and most abandoned. Gay blasphemy poured in torrents from my lips, and in my shocking sallies I heeded no law of God, man, or nature.

Suddenly a peal of thunder, resonant even above the din of the swinish revelry, clave the very roof and laid a hush of fear upon the boisterous company. Red tongues of flame and searing gusts of heat engulfed the house; and the roisterers, struck with terror at the descent of a calamity which seemed to transcend the bounds of unguided Nature, fled shrieking into the night. I alone remained, riveted to my seat by a groveling fear which I had never felt before. And then a second horror took possession of my soul. Burnt alive to ashes, my body dispersed by the four winds, *I might never lie in the tomb of the Hydes!* Was not my coffin prepared for me? Had I not a right to rest till eternity amongst the descendants of Sir Geoffrey Hyde? Aye! I would claim my heritage of death, even though my soul goes seeking through the ages for another corporeal tenement to represent it on that vacant slab in the alcove of the vault. *Jervas Hyde* should never share the sad fate of Palinurus!

As the phantom of the burning house faded, I found myself screaming and struggling madly in the arms of two men, one of whom was the spy who had followed me to the tomb. Rain was pouring down in torrents, and upon the southern horizon were flashes of the lightning that had so lately passed over our heads. My father, his face lined with sorrow, stood by as I shouted my demands to be laid within the tomb; frequently admonishing my captors to treat me as gently as they could. A blackened circle on the floor of the ruined cellar told of a violent stroke from the heavens; and from this spot a group of curious villagers with lanterns were prying a small box of antique workmanship which the thunderbolt had brought to light.

Ceasing my futile and now objectless writhing, I watched the spectators as they viewed the treasure-trove, and was permitted to share in their discoveries. The box, whose fastenings were broken by the stroke which had unearthed it, contained many papers and objects of value; but I had eyes for one thing alone. It was the porcelain miniature of a young man in a smartly curled bagwig, and bore the initials "J. H." The face was such that as I gazed, I might well have been studying my mirror.

———

On the following day I was brought to this room with the barred windows, but I have been kept informed of certain things through an aged and simple-minded servitor, for whom I bore a fondness in infancy, and who like me loves the churchyard. What I have dared relate of my experiences within the vault has brought me only pitying smiles. My father, who visits me frequently, declares that at no time did I pass the chained portal, and swears that the rusted padlock had not been touched for fifty years when he examined it. He even says that all the village knew of my journeys to the tomb, and that I was often watched as I slept in the bower outside the grim facade, my half-open eyes fixed on the crevice that leads to the interior. Against these assertions I have no tangible proof to offer, since my key to the padlock was lost in the struggle on that night of horrors. The strange things of the past which I learnt during those nocturnal meetings with the dead he dismisses as the fruits of my lifelong and omnivorous browsing amongst the ancient volumes of the family library. Had it not been for my old servant Hiram, I should have by this time become quite convinced of my madness.

But Hiram, loyal to the last, has held faith in me, and has done that which impels me to make public at least a part of my story. A week ago, he burst open the lock which chains the door of the tomb perpetually ajar and descended with a lantern into the murky depths. On a slab in an alcove, he found an old but empty coffin whose tarnished plate bears the single word *"Jervas."* In that coffin and in that vault, they have promised me I shall be buried.

SALADIN'S THRONE-RUG

BY E. HOFFMANN PRICE

I would cheerfully have committed murder for that rug; but as it is ...

Morgan Revell smiled at the memory of his exceeding cleverness, and regarded the throne-rug of Saladin with that fanatic affection comprehensible only to a collector ...

The savage jest of it is that he did commit murder. Only he doesn't know it. Nor, for that matter, do I absolutely know. But, piecing it all together, and taking into account the emotions that take possession of a rug collector, I can draw but one inevitable conclusion. And that is—

But to approach the matter at all, some explaining is necessary. First of all, you who regard a rug as something to hide the nakedness of a floor must revise your conception of things. It is all very true that the machine-made atrocities of this country, as well as the precious weaves of the Orient, are indeed used as floor coverings; something on which to walk, something to give the vacuum cleaner its excuse for existing. But that is only a part of it: Oriental rugs are works of art, the peer of any of the numerous products of man's instinct to create unbelievable and imperishable beauty. And just as there are those who collect the works of ancient silversmiths, armorers, cabinetmakers, and bookbinders, so likewise are there those whose consuming passion and sole aim in life is the accumulating of antique specimens of Oriental weaving: rugs from Bokhara and silken Samarcand, from Shiraz, and Herat of the Hundred Gardens; prayer rugs, palace carpets, or the priceless fabric that graced the floor of a nomad's tent in Turkestan. Rugs are many, and their enumeration lengthy; and the study of their personality and traits is the pursuit of a lifetime. Some are prized for their beauty and matchless craftsmanship; others for their exceeding rarity; and some for the sake of all those qualities.

Once one has succumbed to the sorcery of a Bijar that covered the dirt floor of a Kurdish hovel, or a silken Kashan that hung, suspended by silver rings, on the walls of a king's palace, one is beyond redemption, or the desire of redemption. It is even as though one had become addicted to the smoke of the poppy, or to the grain of hasheesh dissolved in wine. One's house becomes a place designed for the sheltering and storing of rare rugs; though, of course, the collector himself has no moral scruples about utilizing a bit of that same shelter for himself.

One may wear last year's overcoat and have last year's shoes half-soled; but one can always raise the price, however exorbitant, of a threadbare Ladik, a battle-scarred Ghiordes, or a moth-eaten Feraghan.

Thus, though Morgan Revell was exaggerating when he smiled in a way reminiscent of a cat who has just had a pleasant *tête-à-tête* with a canary, and remarked, "I'd cheerfully have committed murder for that rug," he was well within the limits of poetic license. Not that he would actually consider going as far as rope, pistol, or poison; in fact, I think he would stop short of breaking and entering. But the fact remains that trifles cannot stand in one's way when a really rare rug is in sight. And very often a jest is the essence of truth.

Well, and that is that: either you still maintain that a rug is but something to put on the floor, or else you have grasped some conception of the fanaticism that consumes the confirmed collector of antique rugs. If the former, well and good: *de gustibus non disputandum est*. But if the latter, if you have grasped the idea, then perhaps you will understand why I crave a bit of fresh air and a change of scene whenever I catch a whiff of attar of roses, or a glimpse of a fine, hard-spun silken cord.

———

I was making one of my customary reconnaissance, prowling tours in search of the perfect rug, the wondrous prize; though what I'd have done with it is a bit beyond me, unless I'd have tacked it to the ceiling. All other space is occupied. Furthermore, I am at times heretical enough to fancy that it is better to know that the rent, due on the morrow, will be in cash available for payment to the landlord instead of being draped over a lounge, or parked on the last bit of vacant wall or floor space.

A chubby, oily little fellow from somewhere in Asia Minor, with features that combined Mephisto with Kewpie, approached and offered his services, assuring me that some rare bargains would be auctioned off that afternoon. I assured him that I was merely prowling about.

"A fine Kirman. Worth seven hundred dollars," he began, just from force of habit. "Perhaps you will bid on it? Get it for two-three hundred."

I didn't bother to tell him that I'd not use it for a bathmat; that it was a sickly-looking mess, with its flabby texture, its aniline dyes, bleached to unnatural softness, and its fearful, glassy luster gained from glycerin and hot rollers, and that it would hardly be a fit companion for a Kirman rose-rug of the old school. So, he left me to my own devices, to tear down several piles, shoulder-high, of rugs of varying quality; mainly atrocities recently woven to satisfy the ever-increasing demand for Oriental rugs: wretched rags which the auctioneer would later exhibit, glassily agleam under a powerful flood-light and describe as "Royal" Bijar, "Royal" Sarouk, or "Royal" Kashan, or "Royal" whatever travesty it was on some ancient, honorable weave.

Weariness and more weariness. I worked my way through the second pile, and with like result. An old Feraghan tempted me, but I decided that though honest and ancient, it would cost too much to have the worn spots rewoven. Nor did the third pile bring forth anything of interest. Then, poking about in a dark corner, I found behind a baled, room-sized carpet, a scrap of something which even in that dim light had the look of antiquity, the stamp of personality possessed only by one of the old guard. And it had the feel of ancient weaving.

I dragged it out. Through all its coating of dust and dirt, the unbelievable richness of the dyes, the "bald-headedness" of the back and subdued luster of the face were apparent. Then—horrible sight!—I saw that I had but a portion of a rug, between half and two-thirds of one, the remnant of something which if complete would be priceless. Judging from the fragment, the complete piece would be about five feet wide and twelve feet long, or thereabout. Some barbarian had sliced it in two, crosswise, with a clean, sweeping cut that left in this fragment about half of the medallion which had been the central design of the complete piece.

What fool would commit such a wanton infamy, such an uncalled-for blasphemy? And then I recalled that classic incident of early Moslem history, wherein one of the prophet's fanatic generals, in apportioning the loot of a Persian palace, had dismembered a gold-threaded carpet, giving each of his captains a portion, saying that it would have been unfair to let any one individual retain the entire rug; and offering the equally good reason that such a pagan vanity deserved mutilation!

Under stronger light, I saw that my instinct for a rarity had indeed been true. The weave was incredibly fine, at least six or seven hundred knots to the square inch; the pile, worn to the warp, was of silk; and the ground inside the main border, and surrounding the central medallion, was of silver bullion thread, woven tapestry-wise about the warp threads instead of being tied and clipped so as to make a nap, as is the practice when weaving with silk or wool. Here, certes, was the adornment of a palace, the gift of one prince to another!

Fortunately for my chances of buying the fragment, the silver bullion ground was so tarnished and caked with dirt that its true nature would scarcely be noticed: for if some collector with a bottomless wallet would see, recognize, and bid against my poverty, I'd surely lose out. But the chances were that even a keen observer, unless he had examined the relic closely, would pass it up as a mere scrap unworthy of consideration.

But then I had to take the auctioneer into account. If in handling that fragment, displaying it to the assembled bidders, he ever noticed that its ground was of silver thread, I'd be strictly out of luck. However, there was little chance he'd notice the pile was of silk; for it was worn to the warp; and since all ancient rugs, either of silk or wool, have a greasy, slick surface, his sense of touch might not enlighten him.

I had to buy that ancient fragment; and I had to get it without the auctioneer's realizing what was going on.

Just what device would minimize his chances of noticing the true nature of what was passing through his hands? And then came the solution.

"Boy, come here a minute!"

One of the uniformed porters approached, I gave him his instructions, also a couple of dollar bills, and the promise of as much more if the ruse worked; also the promise that I'd hunt him up and down the earth with a sawed-off shotgun if he failed me.

It was now 1:30, and the auction was to begin at 2. Prospective bidders were already taking seats before the auctioneer's rostrum. The average bargain hunter has such sublime confidence in his or her ability to pick a rug or other precious article at first glance that few bother to examine the treasures before bidding; and thus no one intruded on my final study of the fragment I had unearthed.

I contrived to decipher the inscription in the remaining half of the central medallion I'd stumbled across. And although I'm no scholar, I can in a pinch hammer out a few words of Arabic and get enough to supply at least the context of an inscription.

at the feet of my Lord I fall; I have bowed
me down seven times with breast and back;
and all that the King said to me,
well, well do I hear! Abimilki,
a servant of the King am I,
and the dust of thy two feet!

This much I could gather; the upper half of the inscription, in the missing upper half of the medallion, doubtless contained the preliminary honorifics, and perhaps even the name of the prince to whom the rug had been presented. Presented where? At Trebizond, Damascus, Ispahan, Baghdad? What king? Shah Abbas? Nadir Shah? Who had received the servile protestations of this princeling, Abimilki?

———

The opening of the daily auction broke into my reflections. I caught the eye of the porter I had bribed, and then found a seat. "Royal" Bijars and "Royal" Sarouks were extolled and lauded with all the dramatic art and perjury at the command of auctioneers hailing from the Near East. And under the floodlights, those pseudo-royal rugs did have a magnificent appearance.

"How much am I offered for this Royal Sarouk? This magnificent, lustrous carpet! It is worth a thousand dollars! Am I offered seven hundred? Seven hundred? They are getting scarcer every day! A genuine, Royal Sarouk! Do I hear five hundred? Is there no one here who really knows rugs? This is not a floor covering, this is—four hundred? Thank you. I am offered four hundred dollars. That shouldn't even buy the fringe! Will someone give me five hundred? Did I hear four fifty? Seventy-five ... Eighty? Thank you. Who offers five hundred ...?"

And thus, through the heap of rugs. Then came some Bokhara saddlebags, one at a time; then more "Royal" Bijars, and Kashans, and Kirmans. Valiantly the plump Mephisto, pleading, groaning, holding out for just one more dollar, perjured his way through the stacks beside the rostrum. And all the while the porter paraded up and down the aisle, giving the bidders a glimpse of the articles in question.

Finally, after an hour's exhorting, after the perspiration was trickling down his cheeks and glistening on his brow, after fatigue had left its marks on the chubby auctioneer, the porter handed him the fragment I had discovered.

Under that powerful light, its suave magnificence glowed forth through the coating of dust and dirt. Devil take that light! But thanks to the nap's being worn so close, the now weary auctioneer, somewhat dulled by fatigue, did not sense that he held the remains of a silken rug in his hands; nor did the silver bullion ground below the medallion betray itself. The porter had handed him the end nearest the original center, where the medallion reached from border to border, and where consequently there was no silver ground to meet his fingertips. Then, scarcely had the orator opened his harangue, the porter snatched the precious fabric and was dashing down the aisle, holding it as well knotted up as he could contrive without seeming to do so.

Noble African! Nevertheless, it was a ticklish moment.

"How much am I offered for this antique rug?" he had begun, flashing it beneath the flaring floodlight, before yielding it to the eager porter. "Yes, sir, I know it is half of a rug, but it is old and very rare. It is an antique, Tabriz."

Which proved that he'd never seen it before I'd exhumed it from that dark, dusty corner! That he'd not noticed the silver ground! Tabriz ... pure and simple improvisation on his part.

"Sixty dollars? Thank you. I am offered sixty. It is worth several hundred. A rare old Tabriz. Seventy? Thank you, madam!"

Damn that schoolteacher! What made her think it was worth seventy? Though she might be a decoy to raise the bids.

So, I came up five.

"Will anyone offer a hundred? Ninety? Give me ninety for this rare old—I am offered ninety! Will someone make it a hundred?"

I rather fancied that my ninety-five would land it.

"Ninety-five ... once ... ninety- five ... twice ..."

The porter was already thrusting another piece into the auction-eer's weary fingers.

But before the hammer could drop—

"*El hamdu li-lláh!*" gasped someone at my right. "One hundred!"

A lean foreigner with a nose like the beak of a bird of prey took the seat next to me; a Turk, perhaps, or a Kurd whom civilization had not robbed of his alert, predatory air and desert gauntness.

"And ten!" I snapped back.

"One-fifty," enunciated the newcomer.

Hell's hinges! Who was that fool? And who ever heard of an Oriental, unless he were a dealer, caring a happy hoot about the threadbare, worn fragment of an antique ring.

"And seventy-five!"

That ought to stop him. But it didn't. Not for a moment.

"Two hundred," he pronounced.

And when I raised him twenty-five, he did as much for me, and without batting an eyelash. I prayed that some angel would slip me the handle of a meat-ax, and then offered fifty more.

The auctioneer beamed and gloated and rubbed his hands and praised heaven for connoisseurs who appreciated antiques. The porter, from force of habit, once more began to deploy the precious piece to egg on the bidders, but, catching my eye, he desisted; though it could have done no harm, for that relentless heathen at my right was out for that rug. That *"El-hamdu li-lláh!"* was the incredulous gasp of one who has stumbled around a corner and met fate face to face; it would be my roll against his.

"Three-fifty!" he announced, scarcely giving the overjoyed auctioneer a chance to acknowledge my last bid.

"Five hundred!" was my last despairing effort.

And five-fifty came like the crack of doom.

The stranger rose from his seat, peeled a wad of bills from a roll that would have choked a rhinoceros, and claimed his prize. Have it delivered? Absolutely not! And when I saw the look in his eye, and the gesture with which he draped that scrap over his arm, I knew that all the wealth of the Indies could not separate him from one thread of that ancient relic.

———

I climbed to my feet and strode down the aisle, talking to myself in non-apostolic tongues. But as I reached the paving, my meditations were interrupted.

"Allow me to thank you, *effendi*"

It was the foreigner, still caressing the nap of the precious fragment he had draped over his arm.

"I owe you a great deal for having discovered this piece. Though I was almost too late."

I couldn't resist that courtly manner, that cordial good-fellowship. The bird of prey had laid aside his predatory manner and seemed really overjoyed about something; happiness, exaltation was mingled with his triumph.

"Don't thank me; thank my slim bankroll," I laughed, and swallowed the remnants of my disappointment.

"I have been hunting that piece for years," continued the stranger. "In Stamboul, Sultanabad, Tabriz ... New York ... London ... wherever rugs are sold. And now I, or rather you, have found it. I regret your disappointment. But I had to have that rug," he concluded.

"So, I noted," was my reply; though it wasn't as ill-natured as it may sound.

"If you can spare the time, I shall tell you the story. And show you the other half of the rug. You knew of course that there was another half."

This was becoming interesting.

"I suspected as much; though who, and where—"

"I am Ilderim Shirkuh bin Ayyub," announced the stranger, and bowed in response to my acknowledgment of the introduction.

Ilderim Shirkuh bin Ayyub. Very impressive. But what of it? Though there was something familiar about that resonant handle.

He led the way to a car parked at the curbing.

———

During our drive north, bin Ayyub maintained a reflective silence that gave me a bit of time for my own thoughts. And as the long, aristocratic car purred its way toward the Gold Coast, I began to sense that I had indeed fallen into something. True, I had lost the prize I had sought to capture; but had I made the grade, I'd probably have remained in ignorance of its entire significance.

A few blocks past the Edgewater Beach Hotel we drew up before an ancient, bulky mansion set back of an acre of lawn; a great house, its dignity still overshadowing its approaching decrepitude; an outlaw, a rebel that still withstood the encroachment of apartments and apartment hotels.

A man, arrayed in a striped *kuftán* and wearing a massive, spirally twisted turban, ushered us into a dimly lit salon which, though almost bare of furniture, was magnificently carpeted and tapestried with ancient, lustrous Persian rugs. Clusters of arms and armor placed at intervals along the walls gleamed icily in the dull light of several great, brazen floor lamps. It seemed almost sacrilege to tread on that magnificent palace carpet whose exquisite loveliness, framed by a border of hardwood floor, reminded me of a diamond set off by its background of onyx.

Bin Ayyub finally broke the silence he had maintained; for as we entered, he had with a gesture invited me to be seated, he himself remaining on his feet, preoccupied, regarding the precious fragment he had captured, looking at it as though all the splendor about him was cheap and tawdry in comparison to that threadbare, eroded scrap he held in his hands.

"Unintentionally—and involuntarily also—you have done me a great service," he at last began, as he seated himself. "As I told you, I am Ilderim Shirkuh bin Ayyub."

Again, he paused as if to let that impressive title sink home. And as I saw him against that background of lustrous rugs and damascened simitars and armor, I wondered whether I had been wrong in having omitted a salaam.

Bin Ayyub turned to the man and—I can in no other way describe his manner—published an order. Then, to me, "You have heard of Salah ad Din Yusuf bin Ayyub? In your language, Saladin?"

"Certainly. Who has not?"

"I am descended in direct line from Saladin; that fragment is part of the throne-rug of my ancestor, the nephew of Shirkuh of Tekrit, and sultan of Syria and Egypt. Now do you begin to see why I value that scrap?"

"Do you mean to say that that rug covered the throne of Saladin?"

"Exactly. And I shall prove it."

Even as bin Ayyub spoke, the man returned, carrying a small chest of dark wood, elaborately carved, and bound in bands of discolored metal, bluish black, like age-old silver.

"Look how the pieces match!" exulted bin Ayyub, as he took from the chest that which I saw at a glance was the other part of the relic I had discovered. The pieces did indeed match perfectly; though the last-acquired fragment was somewhat the more worn and eroded by the rough use of those who had possessed it, ignorant of its worth.

"Read, *effendi*! Surely you can read, else you would never have bid this afternoon."

But I insisted that bin Ayyub read and translate into English. I felt rather foolish about strutting my halting Arabic before this polished Oriental whose very English was better than my own.

In the name of Allah,
the Merciful, the Compassionate!
To my Lord, Salah ad Din Yusuf bin Ayyub,
the Sun of Heaven, thus hath spoken Abimilkl,
the groom of thy horse; I am the dust under the
sandals of my Lord the King; seven and seven times
at the feet of my Lord I fall; I have bowed

me down seven times with breast and back;
and all that the King said to me,
well, well do I hear I Abimilkl,
a servant of the King am I,
and the dust of thy two feet!

And here it was, threadbare and eroded by the passing of eight centuries, the throne-rug of Saladin, that great prince who elevated himself from the castle of Tekrit, in Kurdistan, to the throne of Syria and Egypt, and reigned as Defender of the Faith and Sword of Islam....

Had the auctioneer's hammer fallen just an instant earlier—

"*Alláhu akbar!*" ejaculated bin Ayyub, sensing my thoughts. "To think of how close a race it was. A second later, and I might now be bargaining with you for your prize, offering you all my possessions for that one fragment of carpet. And you would have refused ... I would go barefooted through the tall flames of *Gehennem* for what I took from you an hour ago." Then, to the man: "Saoud! Prepare some coffee!"

"I wonder," he resumed, "if you have any truly rare rugs in your collection? Like that Ispahan, for example?"

Bin Ayyub plucked from the wall what even in that dim light I recognized as an ancient Ispahan: that deep wine-red and solemn green, that classically perfect rendition of the Shah Abbas border and field were unmistakable. It was indeed an old Ispahan, that final, supreme prize of the collector; that rarest and most costly of all rugs.

I admitted that I had not attained, and probably never should attain, to such a fabulously scarce piece of weaving.

"You are wrong, quite wrong. For since I need that wall space for Saladin's throne-rug, I shall give you that Ispahan with my thanks and apologies—"

"Apologies?"

"Yes. For what I am giving you is a worthless rag compared with what I took from you this afternoon."

Such generosity is dizzying. That small, perfect Ispahan would be worth several thousand dollars even had it been ragged as a last year's bird's nest. I was stumped, stopped dead.

———

Saoud, entering with coffee, interrupted my thanks. After having served the steaming, night-black, deathly bitter beverage, the man took his post at the farther end of the salon, in front of a pair of heavy curtains that I fancied must conceal an alcove.

"In El-Káhireh it is the custom to perfume one's coffee with a tiny bit of ambergris," remarked bin Ayyub. "But I have devised a more subtle combination."

In response to the master's nod, Saoud parted the silver-embroidered curtains and caught them on the hilts of the simitars that hung at each side of the alcove. A great jar, fully as tall as the man, and gracefully curved as a Grecian amphora, glowed in the level, sunset rays like a monstrous, rosy-amber bead.

He lifted the cover of the jar: and from it rolled a wave of overwhelming sweetness, an unearthly fragrance so curiously blended that I could not pick the dominant odor. Jasmine, or the rose of Naishápúr, or all the mingled spices of Cebu and Saigon ... with undertones of sandalwood and patchouli ... A dizzying madness, a surge of intoxicating warmth and richness poured resistlessly from the glowing, pulsating, almost transparent depths of that great urn.

I wondered how Saoud could endure it at such close range. And then, drinking fully of the potent wave that swept past me, I lost all physical sensation save that of floating in a sea of torrid, confusing sweetness. And then the man replaced the cover of the jar. I fancied that he reeled ever so slightly as he withdrew from that throbbing luminous fountain of unbelievable fragrance and wondered that he did not collapse.

Bin Ayyub had apparently forgotten my presence. He sipped his coffee, and with half-closed eyes stared into the depths of the urn. The unfathomable, perfect peace which Moslems wish each other with their *"Es-Salaam Aleika"* has descended upon him: *keyf*, the placid enjoyment of wakefulness that is half sleep.

The silence, the utter repose was contagious. I found myself gazing, eyes half out of focus, at the throne-rug....

And then I sensed that eyes were staring at me from some place of concealment. I turned and caught a glimpse of a dainty armful, shapely and elegantly contoured: a girl with smoldering, saracenic eyes, pools of dusky enchantment. Just for an instant I held her level, unabashed gaze which lingered long enough to let me fully sense her imperious calm and composure. It was just a glimpse, barely enough to let me recognize the transparent, olive complexion and faintly aquiline features of a Transcaucasian, a Gurjestani, the most flawlessly lovely of all Oriental women. And then the portières closed on the vision.

What a mad afternoon! The throne-rug of Saladin ... and then the descendant of that great prince ... and that girl, with her smoldering, kohl-darkened eyes ... the familiar spirit of the urn whose Byzantine curves imprisoned that glowing, rosy-amber sea of sweetness ... wild thought! But she was small and dainty enough to have emerged from that great jar, and then vanished back into its shimmering, pulsating depths....

"The contents of that jar," began bin Ayyub, emerging from the silence, "would make a rich perfume of all the seas of the world. It would be folly to try to imagine the countless myriads of blossoms and herbs, spices and gums that are imprisoned in that essence. A drop, a thousandfold diluted, and a drop of that dilution, equally diluted, would be more potent than the strongest scents known to your *Feringhi* perfumers."

"It seems you took a fearful risk in shipping such a fragile and precious article in this country," I suggested.

"It was risky. Still, I would rather have had it shattered en route than fall into the hands of the spoilers who looted my house in Stamboul. But as luck would have it, there was a babbler among my enemies, so that I had warning. I packed my treasures, and smuggled

162 E. Hoffmann Price

them out, one at a time. And the night before the bowstring was to grace my throat, my family and I left in disguise."

Bin Ayyub paused to reflect a moment, wondering, perhaps, whether to carry on or change the subject. And then the darkness of his deep-set eyes flared fiercely.

"Do you see that cord?" He indicated a fine strand of hard-braided silk which hung from the peg that supported the simitar at the right of the alcove containing the Byzantine urn. "My enemy was so careless as to walk by moonlight the evening before a doom was to settle on my house. And as a souvenir of the promenade, I brought with me that fine, stout cord which, for all he cared, I might have left there to chafe his throat," concluded bin Ayyub, as he stroked his black mustache.

And then he showed me how the bowstring is employed; that flickering, swift gesture of his long, lean hands was gruesomely convincing. Bin Ayyub was indeed a versatile man.

"Swift and probably painless?" I volunteered.

"Yes. But if I had my choice of deaths," mused bin Ayyub, "I would elect to be drowned in a pool of that perfume, with my breath so rich with its fragrance that my senses would entirely forsake me."

A tinkle of bracelets interrupted his musings. The portières parted, and the lady from Gurjestan reappeared. In that strange atmosphere, it never occurred to me to commit the *faux pas* of rising as she entered. This was doubtless bin Ayyub's "family" and, though the United States were on the street, they had not quite penetrated to this dim salon, so that I felt it would be tactful not to seem to take any notice of the girl. Upon more intimate acquaintance with bin Ayyub, I might be presented to her, but not at present.

Bin Ayyub replied to her purring, rippling syllables, speaking some language unknown to me; and then the tapestried portières closed and hid her from sight.

"You will surely pardon me, *effendi*. Though Djénane Hanoum speaks English, she prefers her native language," he remarked, then clapped his hands to summon Saoud.

Fresh coffee was served. And then, as my cigarette smoldered to its finish, bin Ayyub rose, rolled up the precious Ispahan and again offered it to me.

"And in ten days or two weeks the throne-rug of Saladin will be spliced by skilled weavers. I would be very glad to have you return and see it after it is restored."

The clicking of the latch behind me reminded me that I was again in the city of Chicago; and the Ispahan did not let me forget that I had actually been awake the past few hours.

––––––

Whenever there has been a killing, the vultures assemble. I had marveled that Morgan Revell had not stumbled across the throne-rug of Saladin before I did. Thus, it was that I was not surprised to have him call at my apartment that very evening.

"Well ... most extraordinary, that. Where did you get it?" he demanded, as he paused in the doorway, stripping off his gloves in preparation for the inspection of the Ispahan that bin Ayyub had so generously given me. "Shades of Shah Abbas! Strike me blind, but it seems genuine. And perfect."

He then parked his bulk in my favorite chair, and poured himself a drink, and proceeded to extract the story. And naturally I was not at all averse to enlightening him; for this would about even up for his eternal boasting of the mosque carpet of Eski Shehr: a remarkable tale, but one which eventually wears on one's nerves.

"On the level now, did anyone actually make you a present of this Ispahan?" he inquired as I concluded my account of the day's doings.

"Idiot," said I, "do you think I could have bought it?"

"Well, no. But still—" His features parted in a reminiscent grin. "Perhaps you remember the mosque carpet of Eski Shehr?"

"Lay off that mosque carpet! No, I got this honestly and without any of your clever devices."

"Score one for you? But really now, old egg, don't you know, this is a most unusual tale you're telling. Quite preposterous ... quite! First of all, this bin Ayyub person is a *rara avis,* and all that, if at all. Who ever heard of one of those beggars who had any appreciation of an antique rug?"

"What about—?"

"Rot! Whoever you were going to cite is probably a dealer. It's simply preposterous, this bin Ayyub who collects ancient rugs. And that descendant of Saladin; why really, old fruit, that doesn't hold water at all."

I insisted that there were Orientals who did appreciate the beauty of the wondrous rugs which they wove.

"Quite so, quite so. But just consider," countered Revell, "that this Ispahan which you treasure as an antique was painfully new in the days when good old Shah Abbas was so partial to fine weaving and inventing new designs. That jolly prince had nothing but antiques on his hands, and he craved new ones; also new patterns. So much so that he sent artists to Italy to study design."

"But, damn it, I tell you—"

"Ah yes, surely. Nevertheless, I insist that the appreciation of antiques is an Occidental taste, and one which is jolly well artificial. Remember that little Armenian in Ashjian's showrooms and how much he felt that we were upset above the ears for preferring a thread-bare Kabistan to a new Sarouk?"

I remembered.

"Well, now go to Ashjian's and let that same lad catch you admiring a Kirman rose-rug. Hear him sigh with much ecstasy; see him caper about; get the gallons of praise he pours on the heads of those fine old eggs who really knew how to weave a rug. He knows his litany now; but he wasn't born that way."

Revell scored.

"But bin Ayyub is a cultured gentleman. I'll take you out to his house, and then you'll be convinced about it all, including his being a descendant of Saladin."

"Very well, have it your own way. You know, it really may be quite possible. Only, it's just a bit unusual, if you know what I mean," Revell finally conceded as I completed my repetition of the story and added bits of color I had omitted the first time. "Not that I doubted your word. But in all honesty, old onion, can you blame me for being a shade skeptical? When even the Shah's palace in Teheran is cluttered with gilt bric-a-brac, and modern Sultanieh rugs, and all that sort of atrocious thing. Beastly taste these beggars show. But this bin Ayyub fellow may be an exception. Though I contend that whatever the art the Orient provides is the result of instinct and not intent."

I granted most of his contentions. And then we discussed the great jar of attar, and the surpassing loveliness of bin Ayyub's "family."

"Most fascinating, really. This sounds like what people think the Orient ought to be, but never actually is. *Houris*, and incense, and all that sort of thing."

Then, just as he left: "By the way, did you ever read the quaint little tale of Aladdin's lamp?"

"Sure. What of it?"

"Nothing, really nothing at all. Merely curious, you know."

Now what had that buzzard meant by that remark? A subtle way of calling me an out-and-out romancer? Or did he mean that in getting my Ispahan I had stumbled into something, Aladdin-like?

And then I carefully examined the Ispahan. No, Revell had not palmed it and left a replica in its place. Strangely enough, he had not even tried to trade or bargain for it.

———

It was fully two weeks before I could find time to call on bin Ayyub to inspect the restoration of the throne-rug. But finally, I did contrive to find some spare time, and just to convince Revell that I had not been releasing an Arabian fantasy, I decided to take him along.

"Cheers, old bean!" greeted Revell. "I was just thinking ... But how do you like it?"

It, the throne-rug of Saladin, stared me in the face: rich, lustrous, magnificent, now that it had been cleaned, and the pieces spliced together.

"Where in—?"

Revell laughed at my amazement.

"Most amazing, what? But don't rub your eyes. It is exactly what it looks like: the rug of the justly popular Saladin. I was just thinking of asking you to translate the inscription. Couldn't remember the exact wording you gave me several nights ago."

"Devil take inscriptions! How did you get it? Unless he suddenly needed the money."

"You could have done the same thing," Revell began, as he poured himself a drink, then painstakingly selected a cigar. "Especially after I told you in so many words how to go about it."

"How come, told me how to go about it?"

This was too much for me. He'd been up to dirty work of some kind. It was unbelievable that he had purchased that rug; and I doubted that he was clever enough to have outwitted bin Ayyub. Then what? Breaking and entering? Well, not very likely.

"The last thing I said the other night was something about Aladdin's lamp. I fancy you recollect. But I was jolly well certain you'd not follow my train of thought. Well, the magician from El Moghreb paraded up and down in front of Aladdin's palace, offering to exchange old lamps for new ones. And the princess—Mrs. Aladdin— was tickled pink to take an unfair advantage of an old man's foolishness. So, she joyously swapped the greasy, tarnished old magic lamp for a nice, new one. Never occurred to Aladdin to tell the young person his wife that the rather crude old lamp was of some value. Simple, really."

"Do you mean to say—?"

"Oh, yes, quite. Exactly, in fact. Mrs. bin Ayyub greatly fancied a lovely Anatolian silk rug about the same size as the revered Saladin's throne-rug, which, by the way, she thought was a bit *passé*. Liked my silk rug; bright colors, and not at all worn, and all that sort of thing. So we swapped; and I fancy I noted a gleam of triumph or something like that in her most fascinating eyes. Charming creature, yes?"

And then I exploded.

"You ought to be shot! He'll beat the tar out of her. He'll flay her alive."

"Regrets, and all that, surely. But *caveat emptor* still holds good. She had no business messing around with the master's trinkets. After all, a bit of deceit—"

"And that girl will surely smell hell—"

"Much regret, certainly. But really, would you have me pass up such an opportunity? I'd cheerfully have committed murder for that rug. As it is—"

Revell smiled at the memory of his exceeding cleverness and gazed at the throne-rug of Saladin with that fanatic affection comprehensible only to a collector.

And that smile drove me mad. Thanks to my babbling, Revell had turned a very clever trick; and thanks also to me, that dainty girl's shoulders ... no, bin Ayyub wouldn't beat her himself; he'd have Saoud lay aside his duties of footman, pipe-bearer and coffee-grinder, and peel every inch of skin off her shoulders. The noble Turk is a man of few words and short temper when dealing with his family. All of which went to my head, seeing that it was mainly my fault for having set Revell on the trail.

"Listen, you damned coyote!"

I gripped Revell by the shoulder by way of emphasis. He blinked in amazement.

"Listen and get me straight: you're going to return that rug here and now. Bin Ayyub treated me like a gentleman. And moreover, it's my fault if that girl gets the daylights hammered out of her; my fault, and yours."

"Come now, try and act naturally," mocked Revell, who had mastered his amazement at my outburst. "I, return that rug? Absurd. Really preposterous. Why, as I said, I'd have committed—"

And then Revell stared as I leaped to the arm of a davenport, reached up, and yanked Saladin's throne-rug from its place on the wall.

"Wait a minute. This is getting a bit thick. I say—"

By this time, I was seeing red and also other colors.

"One more word out of you and I'll knock your head off! I'm taking this rug back to its owner. Get me?"

Revell is far from yellow. But somehow, I convinced him. The last glimpse I had of him, he was the color of an old saddle, and choking for breath.

"Really now, but this is a bit thick," he contrived, as I slammed the door. I missed the rest, but I am sure that for the next fifteen minutes it was a bit thick in the Revell apartment.

Throne-rug trailing over my shoulder, I hopped a taxi and proceeded to bin Ayyub's house.

———

Bin Ayyub himself admitted me. I recognized him simply because no mask could disguise those lean, aquiline features; but this which faced me was but a simulacrum of the vital personality I had met two weeks ago. His face was unshaven; his eyes were cavernous and dull, lifeless; gone was all save the shell of Saladin's descendant. The change was so startling, so dismaying, that for the moment I forgot the throne-rug I carried, rolled up under my arm.

In view of the denunciation and wrath, I expected accusations of having played a part in the trickery of Revell, this listlessness of bin Ayyub left me dazed and wondering.

"I am glad to see you, *effendi*," he murmured, as he conducted me into the salon. He had not offered to take my hat and coat; had not noticed the bundle I carried.

"The throne rug," I began, offering him the precious roll. "I regret—"

"Spare your regrets. It was my fault. I should have told Djenane Hanoum of its value."

He took the rug with a listlessness that amazed me, and, moving as one suddenly aroused from sound sleep, spread it across a couch.

"I feared—"

"That I suspected you?" interrupted bin Ayyub. "No. I knew you were not guilty. You know who is guilty; but since he must be one who has eaten your bread and salt, I cannot ask you to betray him."

Bin Ayyub seemed to forget that I was not bound by the

Moslem's belief in the sanctity of bread and salt. But now that I had returned the rug, why bother about the trickster, Revell?

"Nor have I time to hunt him," continued bin Ayyub. "I have been waiting for you to return Saladin's throne-rug. And now that that is done, I have little time for hunting him."

"But now there's no need of hunting him," I suggested. "You have your rug."

Which I fancied was a sensible answer. But the look that flitted across bin Ayyub's face and took form in his eyes told me that my remark had been the thrust of incandescent iron.

Bin Ayyub rose. I wondered if this was to terminate the interview. It seemed that he might at least have thanked me, despite my having been the cause of his annoyance.

"I have dismissed Saoud for the day. But I myself will prepare coffee. One moment, please."

The aura of unbounded misery and corroding despair remained, lingering after the portières had hidden bin Ayyub from sight. Not even the clanging of the brazen pestle wherewith he pulverized the freshly roasted coffee could infuse a trace of life into the somber magnificence of that rich salon. The order of nature had been upset: this was the house of one whose spirit had died a thousand deaths without having deprived the body of life. Not even the return of the throne-rug had aroused a sparkle of the vital, predatory spirit of that fierce Kurd whose eyes had but two weeks ago flamed exultantly as he told of the enemy who had unwisely walked by moonlight.

Bin Ayyub's entry with a tray interrupted my reflections.

One of the tiny eggshell cups was white, the other, deep blue.

"No, *effendi*, blue is the color of mourning; take the white one."

A light began to dawn on me. The color of mourning ... he had taken this tactful way of letting me know that my presence was an intrusion on his sorrow. But, if there had been a death in the family, why that flash of abysmal despair when a few moments ago I had suggested that since he once more had the throne-rug, he need not bother to hunt whoever it was that had tricked Djenane Hanoum?

"*Bismillahi!*" murmured bin Ayyub, then tasted his coffee. After a moment's silence, he continued, "I bear you no ill will for what has happened. Naturally you would speak to your friends of the Ispahan I gave you, and of the throne-rug. It was my fault; I should have told her."

Worse and worse! That rug again. Hadn't I returned it? Wasn't he sitting on it even as he spoke? Well then ...

"It was my fault. I should have told her," he repeated.

He drained his cup.

The brooding silence forbade even an attempt at making conversation. My nerves were rapidly getting on edge; and I hoped bin Ayyub would end the interview.

"I am leaving very soon, *effendi*," he finally resumed. "Saoud will pack up my goods. I have been waiting for you to return the throne-rug; and I was right in waiting. For the sake of my illustrious ancestor, I treasure it. But much has happened in the last few days. I do not care to have it in my house any longer. My brother's son in Tekrit will take it."

I could think of no appropriate comment.

"Here is the piece which was exchanged for the throne-rug. Take it with you when you leave and return it to its owner."

Which was also fair enough, though Revell deserved no such fortune after his shabby trick. The loss might be a lesson to him.

"May I ask you to be so kind as to lift the cover of the jar of attar?" requested bin Ayyub, as he set aside his empty cup.

I could see that he was momentarily becoming paler. There was not a drop of blood beneath his bronzed skin. The corners of his mouth and the muscles of his cheeks twitched perceptibly; so that his request did not seem at all out of order. Though if I myself felt as he looked, the last thing in the world I'd want would be a whiff of that overpowering perfume.

"Certainly," I replied.

Poor devil! He seemed to be having a chill, shivering noticeably. No wonder he wanted me to take Saoud's place in the ritual of the perfume jar.

As I advanced across the wondrously carpeted floor, I heard him mutter to himself, "One is at times hasty ..."

I parted the curtains that veiled the great urn of Byzantine glass, and lifted the heavy cover; then, dizzied by the overwhelming surge of sweetness, recoiled a pace.

And then I dropped the cover.

Christ in heaven! But why deny my own eyes? In the throbbing, glowing rosy-amber jar was the shapely form of Djenane Hanoum! Faintly distorted by the refraction of the curved surfaces of the urn and the attar, but nevertheless and beyond any mistake, that was the Gurjestani girl. I stared, fascinated. Then looked behind the jar, hoping ... ridiculous hope ... to find that she was standing on the other side, and that I had seen her through, and not in, the urn.

It is strange how in such a moment one notices trifles.

"La illah illa allah ... wa Muhammad rasul allahi ..." came the murmuring accents of bin Ayyub, very low, but distinct.

Even in the grip of that horribly lovely sight, I had distinctly caught the Moslem's "There is no God but Allah ..." And then, scarcely perceptible, "Djenane ..."

My movements must have been those of a mechanical toy.

As I caught the curtains on the hilts of the simitars hanging at each side of the alcove, I noted that the fine, hard-woven cord of silk was missing. And then I found myself wondering what poison the blue cup of mourning had contained.

Not until fully a minute later did it dawn on me why bin Ayyub's eyes had flamed with immeasurable despair when I had reminded him that since I had returned the throne-rug of Saladin, he had no cause to concern himself about the thief.

That awful sweetness was rolling from the uncovered jar, strangling me with its richness. I wondered how a girl in the heart of an ocean of perfume could endure its fragrance ... and whether the silken cord was chafing her throat.

Bin Ayyub's drawn features were now overlaid with a shadow of a smile.

"If it were given me to elect the manner of my death, I would choose to be drowned in that perfume ..." he had once said. So instead of covering the jar, I left Ilderim Shirkuh bin Ayyub enthroned on the rug of Saladin and facing the loveliness which he had imprisoned in attar.

Revell was still frothing when I returned and tossed his Anatolian silk rug on the floor.

"I'd have committed murder for that throne-rug," he growled. "And now—"

Someday I'm going to tie an anvil to Revell's ankles and then kick him into Lake Michigan.

The DOG-EARED GOD

by Frank Belknap Long Jr.

"Then a deluge of colored fire shot out of the creature's nose and mouth."

-1-

The Egyptians' gods are shaped like beasts, but why they represent them in this way I had rather not mention. —Herodotus

W hat do you think of it?" asked Professor Dewey.

The colossal height of the mummy case accentuated my friend's littleness. Somehow (I don't know why the image should have presented itself) I thought of the opium-haunted De Quincey walking wearily about the streets of London, a grotesque little midget in carpet slippers who carried a world within his head. Professor Dewey bore an amazing resemblance to De Quincey. His forehead was high and shrunken, and covered with wrinkles, and the skin on his lean cheeks was stretched as taut as yellow parchment. His nose could scarcely be described as Roman: it was so excessively Hebraic that a strain of Jewish blood unquestionably formed a measure of his heritage. His smile, when he did smile, was grim and lifeless; and very few people would have been attracted to him. But beneath his almost repulsive exterior the little chap had a good heart, and I found his companionship delightfully stimulating.

Professor Dewey's hobby was Egyptology, and he imported large quantities of mummies annually, and I am sorry to add, illegally. No prying customs officer ever laid his sternly official hand on one of Professor Dewey's acquisitions. No blue-eyed and impertinent government clerk ever questioned Professor Dewey as to the value of his queer and often repulsive property. The professor had made arrangements with a dozen sly and secretive skippers whose Levantine dealings were seldom above reproach, and as a result of his careful bargaining he never lost a mummy or scarab or precious stone. In the course of a single year eighty-three mummies had been successfully smuggled into his stately brownstone mansion on Riverside Drive.

We stood in Professor Dewey's mummy-room, a great hall carpeted with red velvet and lined with rather sinister black curtains. It seemed ridiculous to me that the professor should furnish this repository with the trappings of occult melodrama, but I have always been singularly incapable of fathoming my friend's amusing whims. Beneath his whimsicality and eccentricity, he was reasonably genuine, and it is unfair to expect common sense or restraint from a man of genius.

The mummy before us was unusually tall. It fairly towered in the yellowish gloom of the great room, and it bore unmistakable characteristics of great age. And it was oddly shaped—its breast swelled out curiously and its nose was gigantic. Indeed, the latter member almost protruded through the aromatic and evil-smelling wrappings. "An Egyptian Cyrano," I remarked, and permitted a grin to disturb my usually severe and solemn features (the professor often assured me that my features were severe and being a very young man, I took pardonable pride in the fact!). "How the ladies must have hated him!" I added, seeing my friend scowl.

"This is a serious matter," he said after a pause that seemed interminable. "Nothing like this has ever come out of Egypt. I—do—not—like—it!"

My friend's voice was distressingly hollow; It made me nervous, and I endeavored to quiet him. "There is nothing very unusual about this mummy," I replied. "Some very peculiar types undoubtedly existed among the Egyptians. I daresay they had their sideshows and circuses with the odd assortment of freaks that usually goes with such things. This poor fellow may have been a king's jester—it is really unfair to reproach him with his ugliness after all these years. I am sure his life was a very unhappy one."

The professor's scowl grew in volume. "You must be serious," he retorted. "This mummy is very unusual. I am not a sensationalist, my dear boy, but I may say that my enemies would give a great deal to use this thing to discredit me. We must be very wary about publishing the results of our experiments."

"Experiments?" I snatched at the word. I had a boyish and ridiculous eagerness for all varieties of research.

"I have some experiments in mind that will demand a great deal of courage. If you do not feel equal to them, I shall want you to tell me so quite frankly. But first I must warn and prepare you, and describe what we have to deal with."

The professor lit an absurdly long panetela and puffed for several moments in silence. The smoke ascended spirally and formed a curious grayish nimbus above the mummy case. The mummy stood out in the depressing gloom like a sinister avenger of the eighty-three defenseless wretches that Professor Dewey had dissected and destroyed.

When my friend spoke again his voice had acquired a small measure of calm. He spoke slowly, punctuating his sentences with an occasional cough.

"There are few myths in the treasure-house of mankind that were not originally based upon solid objective facts. I do not believe that the imagination of primitive peoples is capable of creating bogies out of thin air. We are too easily deluded by modern science and altogether too apt to scoff at the legends of gods and goddesses that have come down to us. It is absurd to believe that the Egyptians created their monstrous bestial gods from mere observation of living animals. There is something so immense, so psychically terrible about the

Egyptian gods that it is difficult to believe them simply the product of normal human imagination. They are either the imaginings of some dreamer of wild and unheard-of powers, an Edgar Poe among the Egyptians, or—"

Professor Dewey paused without stating his alternative. I presume he wanted his heresy to sink in, for he waited several moments before continuing:

"These crocodile gods, these cat-headed and bat-eared divinities are really more debased than anything to be found anywhere in the modern world. Even your most primitive of fellows would be incapable of worshiping anything so vile. And yet if we are to believe historians the Egyptians had a high degree of ethical culture. They would not fashion such horrors willingly. I have often thought—"

Again, my friend hesitated, as if ashamed to put his theory into words. My eagerness apparently reassured him.

"*I have often thought that these monsters really existed.* Why should we suppose that men are the only intelligent beings on this planet? There is so much evidence to the contrary, so very much evidence, that I feel justified in my theory. I do not think that I am a fool. My enemies" (I fear my friend suffered from a persecution complex) "would give years of their lives to overhear this conversation. But they shall only hear of the results—if the results are not too revolting."

Professor Dewey sank down on a chair as if exhausted. Beads of sweat stood out horribly on his high yellow forehead. His lips quivered.

"George," he stammered. "We must put it to the test. We must sleep here tonight. Unless, of course, you fear to sleep in the room with *that*."

"But what is *that*, really?" I asked, pointing with horror to the colossal mummy.

My friend did not answer me directly, but his words were dreadfully disturbing.

"Twenty or thirty thousand years ago the Egyptians buried their first kings. *There were strange kings in the dawn world.*"

-2-

Professor Dewey was sleeping soundly, but something made me sit up. I am not sure whether I dreamed a sound, or whether a sound had actually come from the corner of the room where the great mummy stood solemnly in its filthy wrappings. But whether the dismal noise had any basis in fact it was a profoundly disturbing thing to hear at 3 o'clock in the morning.

Perhaps you have listened to hounds baying at night across lonely moors, or perhaps you have heard in the tropics the horrid moans of small monkeys when they awake from their mindless sleep and see the stars watching them evilly. If you have heard such sounds you may have a remote idea of how vile these audibly sinister exhibitions of evil and fright seem to a normally constituted man.

The low whining that I heard (and it occasionally seemed to rise to an actual baying) did not frighten me. But had the chair that loomed unpleasantly before me out of the gloom suddenly entered into conversation with the sofa, or had the clock walked across the mantel, I should not have been more horrified.

I sat up and waited. For several moments nothing happened, but then I heard a low scratching and scraping as if something were trying to get out of the closet. Claws of some sort were indubitably at work somewhere.

"Rats!" I reflected, and I clung to the suggestion warmly. Of course, there would be rats in a house given over to unhallowed and unsavory practices. "The professor is fortunate to have rats to do the really dirty work," I mused. "They save him the bother of burning the odds and ends. It must be damnably difficult to get rid of fingernails and hair and such things, unless one burns them, and of course the rats would save him that task. The professor is really very fortunate. Dear, jolly rats!"

Then I realized the fatuousness of my reflections and passed my hand rapidly back and forth across my face. My forehead was infernally warm; I was excited, feverish. "It's probably a touch of influenza," I thought. "I should never have slept in this cold room." I recalled that I had been sneezing and coughing most of the previous after-noon. The slightest touch of fever makes me delirious—in that respect I am abnormally favored.

I pulled the blankets about my neck and turned over. I think then that I slept, but I am convinced that what I saw later had some external significance. The thing was more than a mere dream and certainly more than a hallucination. It was, I think, an actual *body of memories* projected across the room. When I saw it, I was sitting up and I heard the clock outside strike 4.

A white immensity spread before me, and for a moment its white-ness blinded me. It was like a series of projections on the silver screen. The white substance was continually changing, now thinning, now thickening, and horrid, distorted forms moved about in it. The forms were amorphous, and I could not at first distinguish them clearly. They were not altogether human. They seemed to have the bodies of men, but *the heads of animals.*

When the vision, or call it what you will, became clearer I saw that the unmentionable creatures had formed into a solid phalanx, and that they were marching solemnly before me. They carried between them some unspeakable object which they made no effort to conceal.

If the forms of the marchers were revolting, the form of the long, distorted *thing* that they carried was infernal. It was covered with hair, but I never had seen anything like it under the stars. It had a sunken bat-like face, and great, dog-shaped ears, and its yellow teeth glittered ominously in the strange, unnatural light. The thing was obviously lifeless, and its cheeks were sunken and hollow.

The watchers carried torches which they waved exultantly as if almost glad that the thing had died. I had a curious sympathy for these others, but heaven knows they were vile enough. The torches gave off a weird blue light and even, I thought, a mephitic smell; and as I watched, new ones were lit and the swaying, blasphemous procession moved forward more rapidly.

And then the chanting and intoning commenced, and the dreadful hymns for the dead swelled and reverberated in the room until I put my hands before my ears to shut out the ancient and obscene chants.

"Our master out of the skies is dead!" they wailed. "Deep, deep in the earth shall we bury our king. Long has he ruled us, and horrible the evil he did to us, but he was our king out of the skies, and we revere his memory. Horrible his black tongue that shot out fire, horrible the maidens he devoured, horrible the blood he drank, but he was a king. In the book of the dead, it is written that he shall be judged by gods, by his peers he shall be judged. He shall appear as a snake, as a reptile before his peers, but by his ears they shall know him."

Then the picture cleared terribly, and I saw that the procession trod on hot reddish sands, and a great stone effigy loomed up behind them. It was a sphinx, but a more ancient sphinx than the one we know, and its eyes glowed banefully. And in a deep and perfectly round hole dug in the sand at the statue's base they buried their king, and strewed gold dust upon him, and anointed his limbs with oil which they poured from jars of veined porphyry.

Unmentionable were the rites they performed above him, and the last words of their loathsome high priest, *who had the head of a lizard,* were lethal words, and I shivered when I realized at whom they were directed.

"For thirty centuries you shall sleep, but a little shameless creature with no hair to cover him shall drag you forth, because in his time he shall be as a god. But his evil day will not be long under the sun. He too shall return unto dust, and a very thin creature with neither legs nor eyes shall play havoc with his bones. It is written. Rest in peace and remember us who worshiped you!"

The vision grew vaguer, and the forms seemed to converge and merge into each other. Then gradually the darkness closed in, and I found myself staring with frightened eyes at Professor Dewey's monstrous acquisition. It loomed vaguely out of the blackness, and it seemed to be stirring, and squirming about.

I watched fascinated while the ancient wrappings fell away, and *two long pink hands* fumbled hectically with mildewed cerements. The hands were abnormally emaciated, and covered with thin, reddish hair.

I endeavored to rise, but the eyes of the thing watched me evilly, and ordered me to be silent. It seemed angry that I should question its spiritual supremacy. It had uncovered its eyes, but the great loathsome nose remained mercifully concealed by several layers of disintegrating wrappings. It was frightful to watch the thing's efforts to free itself. It wriggled and squirmed, and in its vileness, it resembled a great fleshy worm endeavoring to escape from some deep sewer of earth.

What followed will always remain confused in my memory. I seem to recall Professor Dewey upon his back with closed eyes, and something standing above him in the dim light like an immemorial avenger. I seem to glimpse a supremely ghastly exterior—two great ears protruding from a narrow and greenish skull, and a great nose like an elephant's trunk showing briefly in profile.

Then fire—a deluge of colored fire, which shot out of the creature's nose and mouth, fire from hell, fire from beyond Arcturus. I saw the professor's eyes open, and I saw him stare at the thing for a moment in triumph. The exultation in his face was quickly replaced by agony and despair. He threw out his arms as if endeavoring to ward off an immediate doom, and while I watched, his face shriveled and blackened.

"I was right," he shrieked. "The Egyptians did not worship men. God pity my poor soul!"

I did not stay to comfort my stricken friend. I ran shrieking from the room, and out of the house into the street. I looked up to see thick black smoke pouring from an upper window, but I turned in no alarm. I ran wildly across deserted squares and through winding alleys and finally found my way to a leering subway entrance.

I fled insanely down the stairs and climbed over the turnstile without depositing a fare. Luckily no one saw me. In a moment I was in a roaring train, my arms flung about a drunken beggar, and into his astonished ears I poured a tale that made him gasp and shake his head.

"You young 'uns always get it somewhere," he grimaced. "I wish I had your luck."

I have always found newspaper men exceedingly prosaic. The following cutting from a New York paper demonstrates my point:

A fire in the upper West Side caused a great deal of disturbance yesterday morning when police reserves from three stations fought with firemen to keep excited passers-by from entering the burning building. For two hours thirty or forty hooded men endeavored to rescue the inmates and caused a great deal of disturbance. The police were unable to explain why utter strangers should take such an interest in one poor perishing wretch, since it was later ascertained that the house was occupied by an eccentric professor and misanthrope who is suspected of bootlegging operations. Patrolman Henley, from the West 93rd Street Station, claims that one of the would-be rescuers removed his hood for a brief moment, and that his face was covered with fur, *and eaten away at the corners.* Luckily for Patrolman Henley's reputation he is known to suffer from migraine, and it is probable that what he imagined he saw had no basis in fact.

The wildly excited attempts of strangers to enter the building completely frustrated operations, and the unfortunate inmate perished. For a moment he was seen at the window, and those who were standing on the sidewalk immediately underneath declare that his hair and beard were actually on fire.

The upper portion of the building was completely destroyed. A number of curious bones were found in the room, including the skeleton of a gigantic dog. During the past week three previous fires have been reported in the neighborhood, and the police are investigating rumors of a firebug.

The CITY of SPIDERS

by H. Warner Munn

"His captor set him down, with a proud air of showing off a curiosity to an interested audience."

I t was on the 12:30 train from Athol to Boston that I met the man with the beady eyes. I mention the eyes particularly, for they were the distinctive features; it is very odd that they are all that I can remember of his appearance. Vaguely I recall that he wore a gray suit, rather light for our changeable November weather, but even that is uncertain.

It was a cut-rate day, with a slash in prices for an excursion, and the coach was well filled. He got on at Gardner, with a small crowd that hustled him down the aisle and washed him beside me, so bewildered that without bothering to ask me if the other half of my seat was taken, he plumped himself down with a relieved sigh.

"Rather cool," I thought, and without knowing it I must have spoken aloud, for he nodded brightly with a quick little snap of his head, saying, "Yes, isn't it?"

Amused at the natural mistake, I determined, since he was so friendly, to strike up an acquaintance to while away the tedium of a three-hour ride and incidentally perhaps to learn something that might be of value to me in a novel I am writing. Every man has in him one good story if it can only be dug out, but some are buried pretty deep.

I forget our first words, but we exhausted the subject of the weather rather thoroughly and were pleasantly drifting into a discussion of our fellow passengers when I noticed a movement on his sleeve.

It was one of the common barn-spiders that are so often seen festooning rafters with velvety soft hangings of dove-gray. Probably chilled by the cold wind outside, the warmth of the car had brought it out of its concealment to reconnoiter.

A spider gives me the creeps, now more than ever that I know why, but then as always, I felt a surge of revulsion, struck it off his arm and crashed it with my foot.

He was smiling oddly when I looked up. "Do you know why you did that?" he said.

"Because I hate the things!" I answered. "Always did."

"I think the word you mean is 'dislike,'" he replied, "but I can truly say that I hate them, for I know more about them in one sense than any other living man on earth today. Shall I tell you why?"

"Do!" I said, smiled a secret smile within me, and prepared to take mental notes, for I scented a story at last.

-1-
Into Unknown Country

"My name is Jabez Pentreat," he began; "my mother was English and my father a Welsh miner. They moved to this country in 1887, two years before I was born as work was scarce and living but a bare existence in the old country. Here they found it but little better, although with more ambition they might have become moderately well-to-do. When I was young, things were in a bad way for us, father worked spasmodically, while mother took in washings to tide us over hard times. We never had much money.

"I went to grade school until I was fourteen and was then obliged to leave in order that I might bring in a few dollars by my bodily labor.

Brains counted for nothing in the manufacturing town where I lived. It was one of Father's favorite sayings that 'Book-larnin' never did nobody no good!' So, you see I was up against it. Three years later I ran away from home.

"I found work in Boston in connection with a fruit-importing company, and learned something of the world, as represented by the harbor-ports of South America.

"In one of those little coast towns I met a man who was to change my life. You have heard of Sir Adlington Carewe?"

"The man who astounded the scientific world with his masterly monograph on Possibilities of the Insect World?" I asked.

"That was he," answered the man with the beady eyes. "To him I am indebted for all my knowledge. At his own expense, I finished school and entered college. At his desire, I concentrated upon botany, entomology and other kindred studies, for he hoped that I should take his place in the line of discoverers when he was gone.

"Well, I can say with pride that his pains were not wasted upon me, although he is not where he can appreciate the changes that time has wrought upon that crude roustabout that I was then.

"I understand that he is on the west coast of Africa at present, experimenting with the higher forms of apes.

"South America always fascinated me with its magnificent opportunities for studying insect life. It is a forcing-house for vegetation, and in its dank, steaming jungles, for thousands of square miles untouched by white feet, who knows what marvelous things may exist, all unknown to the outer world? I have found a few, but I have only skimmed the edges and never expect to learn much more, although I leave again in the spring.

"Have you ever paused to think of the swarming life that goes on day after day, beneath your feet, busy with its own affairs, as you with yours? Another world goes about its business of loves and hates, of living and dying, of little engineering works as important to them as a Brooklyn Bridge or a Panama Canal is to us, although one step of your foot can destroy the work of days.

"There are grass-eaters and there are carnivores that prey upon them, and others that in turn feed upon the slayers. There are cities in miniature, slaves and masters, workers, idlers, miners and aviators, and all this teeming life may be in your own back yard, unnoticed except when your wife complains because the ants persist in finding the sugar-bowl, and the flies 'just will get in somehow.'

"And remember, this life is alien to us. Although it is so similar to us in some ways, it is a world in itself, far from humans. One writer, I have read, remarks in a joking way that it may even be alien to this planet.

"Here is a thought that I would like to have you ponder. While all other insects have their appointed prey, each feeding upon one certain enemy, herbivore or plant and rarely touching other types of food (thus by the wise provisions of nature keeping down the swarming life that otherwise would overwhelm humanity), the spider feeds indiscriminately upon all!

"The spider! Dread ogre of the insect world! How he is feared! Not only by his prey, but also by man, against whom, by reason of his size, and that alone, he has but little power.

"And South America is the insect paradise. Nowhere else will you find such impenetrable morasses, such dank and steamy jungles, such unbelievable monstrosities, in both vegetable and animal kingdoms.

"But I digress. To my tale, then, and think your own thoughts. I ask for no comment or interruption.

"In search of a sable butterfly, with a coffin outlined in white upon each wing, of which only one collector has ever secured a specimen, I came at last to Ciudad Bolivar, which lies in Venezuela.

"In this town I obtained eight native Indians, who were invaluable at times and nuisances at others. We searched in that mysterious mountain land of Guayana, entering where the Caroni River empties into the Orinoco. The Caroni's waters are combed by cataracts and rapids, but are well-known for fifty miles—here the dense woods begin and man's knowledge ends, for excepting myself, I believe no white man has ever explored those forests.

"It is one of the mystery lands of Venezuela, the never-never lands where almost anything can happen and usually does. Usually, a white in that section is rather a being to be taken care of, as white men are more valuable in a gift-producing way alive than dead; but there are tribes of nomadic Indians, head-hunters by choice, that roam the dismal forests, and to them the head of a white man, shrunk to the size of an orange, is their Kohinoor or Great Mogul! Not far away live the Maquitares, a tribe of blonds, almost white, and at a greater distance, the Guaharibos, whose savagery has never allowed the head-waters of the Orinoco to be discovered.

"My Indians sometimes heard their drums growling to one another far away in the steamy tropic nights, but they came always from the north and south, never from the west toward which we were pressing. On the sixth day from the river, we heard them behind us, but still far away; and as we cooked our meals in the *tambo*, a rude shelter from the night dews, such as the rubber hunters farther south construct, sometimes we wondered why they were upon all sides but never before.

"On the ninth day we heard nothing but the ceaseless drip-drip-drip into the swampy ground and occasionally the roar of some dead forest giant crashing to earth, choked to death by parasitic vines that hid the tree from sight. That night the hunters came back empty-handed. We had not seen any animal all day, not even the usual troop of monkeys that howled down curses at us, swinging along under the forest roof, dropping fruit skins and nuts upon us and warning all life for miles that strangers were at hand.

"We made hungry camp for we traveled light, and my men were disposed to grumble because we were in unknown country and no one knew what lay before us.

"The black butterfly was given up now, but I determined to press on three days more, and then to give it up as a bad job and go back, for I already had enough specimens to repay me for my trip.

"Before I curled up in my hammock, I shook it to dislodge any insects that might be in its folds, and out dropped a large spider, the size of my hand. I smashed it with my boot and at the same time saw another. As I struck that one, screams arose from my Indians, and they dashed for the fire. One was literally covered with the vermin and dropped before he reached the light. In a moment we loaded the blaze with brush and had a bonfire that roared six-foot flames."

-2-
Prisoners of Insects

"You cannot imagine the scene that met our sight! The things covered the ground and trees all about us. A carpet of gray was moving and rustling continually back from the light, and as the flames shot higher, we could see that the twigs and branches hung low with their weight. Now and then, one would drop with a plop on the ground as the light struck and scuttle over the backs of others till it found a place to rest. My hammock was now filled with the crawling things as a saucer is heaped with berries, sickening gray creatures with jet-black eyes that glistened hungrily, and all intently watching us.

"We could hear a kind of low clicking and chittering as they opened and closed their mandibles. It seemed as though they were talking to one another while they waited for us, in a curiously knowing way, and those pinpoint eyes watched and gloated most obscenely expectant.

"The body of the dead man was just outside the circle of light, and all night a swarming heap of spiders surged over and around it, while my Indians fed the fire for their lives, and race and caste were forgotten as we huddled, massed about the fire, sweat raining from us in the terrible heat.

"Morning came at last, and as the sky began to brighten, the gray horrors grew thinner until only a few stragglers still roamed near the clean-picked skeleton; and when the sun rose, they too crept to hiding places, leaving only the white bones to tell the story of that frightful night.

"When all were gone, my Indians begged me to turn back. I refused, although my own inclinations pointed in that direction. I kept a bold face and pointed out that by going west we would avoid the savages and leave this dreaded spot behind us. My head man looked grim but said nothing. So on again! On into the jungle, fighting our way through thick tangled undergrowth, followed by dense clouds of mosquitoes and gnats, the only life we saw that day, besides ourselves.

"About noon, although we could not see the sun through the riot of vegetation, we found a small stream of clear water which abounded in small fish.

"We dined royally on fish and fruit, in the midst of a deathlike stillness. Not a leaf rustled, no birds sang, not a monkey or any other animal did we see that day, and in the same breathless hush we made our tenth and last *tambo* that evening, having covered perhaps fifteen miles during the day.

"Keeping in mind the former night, we selected a clear open space for the erecting of our shelters, brought in an immense quantity of wood and sat around the fire in that charmingly complete and unqualified democracy of man when a common danger threatens.

"Before long, just as the drums snarled faintly to the east, a little black and red creature scuttled out of the wood, bustled down to the water's edge and drank daintily. I recognized one of the most venomous of the arachnids, usually the size of a silver dollar, but this specimen was easily five inches across his scarlet-barred body. I determined to have it, and cautiously loosened my butterfly net from my pack. This breed is very timid, although its bite is so deadly, and I crept up on it with the utmost care.

"About five feet away, it saw me, and instead of darting away, it jumped in my direction. Out of pure fright, I crushed it flat, and the scenes of the night before were repeated almost identically, but now there were many of the new species mingled with the gray demons that had dragged down the bearer. It seemed as though there were concentric circles of varying types, arranged about a central point, and the nearer we approached the center, the more horrible and huge grew the individuals that composed each belt. I began to wonder what lay farther on!

"Again, we shivered around a roaring fire, speaking only in low whispers. The natives believed that our besiegers were forest devils, enraged at us for intruding into their private fastnesses.

"Several times I feared for my life that night, for dark looks were cast at me, and twice there were those who advised strongly that I should be flung out to the filthy things as a sacrifice. But they could not quite screw up their courage to that point, for they knew that I would not submit tamely, and they feared that the taste of blood might enrage the creatures into a rush which would wipe out the survivors.

"A sleepless night! A night of horror, beneath gloating, incredibly malignant eyes! A night that was a cross-section of eternity!

———

"About two hours before morning, I dozed off, being startled awake again almost instantly by yells of fright. Before me just outside the fire-light crouched a gigantic monstrosity, hairy and tremendous. Its bloated abdomen was barred with black and silver, the head almost hidden from sight by a yellow mop of fur, from which projected jet-black mandibles, furiously vibrating as it watched us through red, vicious eyes.

"Behind those eyes, I sensed a personality, keenly intelligent. I found myself waiting for the frightful thing to speak and was horrified at the thought. You cannot credit, I know, but I who saw am telling you the truth. I believed then, that fearful spider was as intelligent as you or I, in a more limited way, and I can assure you it is an absolute fact that the other hideous vermin acknowledged it as their superior!

"It stood at least a foot and a half high, and I should judge that it would have tipped the scales at about twenty pounds. It walked about the fire at a safe distance, and carefully observed us twice from all angles. Then it moved off in a westerly direction and we saw the others draw back from in front of it respectfully, leaving a broad path, down which it passed, and they closed in solidly again.

"The same actions took place as on the preceding morning. Scatteringly they vanished with the dawn, leaving a few stragglers that seemed to regret the necessity that drove them off.

"There was no question now about what we should do. Rather

than spend another such night, we would have braved a thousand savages. About 10 o'clock in the forenoon therefore we started back, but we had gone too far. Before we had gone a mile on our back-trail, we heard rustling in the bushes and crepitant pattering as of many raindrops, while sometimes we could see small gray bodies bounding along beside us.

"Still, we pressed on. The march became a trot, and the trot a wild disorderly rout. We flung away our packs, our weapons, and our clothes in a mad dash for anywhere, but away! We mounted a small knoll and looked back. A sea of gray, black, and red lapped around us, like an island almost level with the water, over which the waves threaten momentarily to break. Slowly from all sides they crept in, rising higher like the chill waters of death. We broke clubs from the trees and prepared to die.

"Then came that horror of the night, hustling on from the west, with five companions that matched it in size. The resistless torrent that was just lapping over the crest of the knoll stopped and receded. The six came closer, scrutinized us and started back down the bank, pausing about ten feet away as though we were expected to follow.

"We did! We all had the same thought at once, to kill the most hideous ones and then as many more as we could before we died. So, we ran down the slope, and the man in front of me crashed his club through the largest of the six.

"Instantly we were covered from head to foot with crawling insects, and as we rolled over and over, shrieking and howling with fear, feeling the spiders pop and squelch beneath our weight like ripe plums, an acrid nauseous stench arose.

"As we lay there, half dead with sick terror, I noticed that no more were on me, the masses had withdrawn, and one of the larger insects stood very close to my face, on each ebony mandible a drop of venom glistening. Perhaps it was our first visitor, but they all looked alike to me.

"I jumped up. The Indians lay on a red noisome carpet of crushed bodies, and we were all covered with a pulpy mess. One by one they stood up, and we discovered that not one of us had been bitten. Then the hordes opened invitingly again a westward path, and we walked down it as prisoners. The prisoners of insects!

"But one stayed behind. He was the man who had destroyed the large spider. Apparently at a signal, the mass closed in about him, cutting him off from the rest of us. He tried to run to us, as they forced us down the trail, but in an instant he was a staggering, bellowing heap of vermin, that tottered a few steps and went down. Before we were out of sight, his howls had become moans, and we knew what the end would be.

"So, with one of the great, yellow-headed brutes in the lead, one at each side of us, and two bringing up the rear, we came again to the fatal *tambo* number 10 and passed westward, following the brook, the swarms surrounding us on all sides, as thickly packed as leaves."

-3-
The Spider King

"About a mile farther on, the brook emptied into a small river. This we followed down the right-hand bank, till the middle of the afternoon, when, we struck a well-defined path, hard beaten by much travel.

"The throng of gray spiders now began to disappear, having reached their farthest boundary, the five black and silver guards still remaining, and many of the red and sable fellows. But when a short time later, the path was barred by an immense crowd of frightful monsters, similar to those that guarded us, the small spiders also returned to their own zone.

"Just as dusk was falling, we marched out of the jungle into the open, and, surrounded by hundreds of silver-barred brutes, were forced down an incline into a valley. It was bare of vegetation, and in the center stood several stone buildings clustered about a larger and more pretentious edifice. These were windowless and doorless, being entered through a trap in the flat roof. They made me think of the nests of trapdoor spiders.

"As we neared these buildings, a jaguar, or *tigre*, as the natives term it, came racing down the valley, and behind it poured a hideous mob that hid the ground from sight beneath a palpitant, undulating surface that made my skin crawl to watch. He staggered nearer as though he sought the protection of man, and I saw that his tongue hung out as he panted in the last throes of exhaustion. On the beast's back rode a large spider, which urged the poor animal on to death, and as they reached the nearest building, sank its poison into the beast's spine, and *El Tigre* dropped like a stone.

"Now we saw a forecast of our own fate. It was plain that we had been brought to this gathering place to be butchered. Meat on the hoof, less troublesome to bring than if it were dead!

"A wave of frightened animals dashed up, a chattering monkey or two, many hares, snakes that writhed in agony, half crippled by bites and dragged along by their captors, lizards that hissed with mouths wide open. The lizards were the only ones that fought.

"Then from the western valley wall, another herd poured down, a great anaconda coiling beside a cluster of peccaries closely bunched together and squealing with terror, and behind all a swarm of hunters.

"Never before had I seen so many different breeds of spiders dwelling in amity with one another, and again I had the impression that these were intelligent, reasoning beings hunting together for the good of the many.

"Now we were gathered in a cluster about the stone huts, hunters and hunted, a motley crew herded from all points of the compass over a twenty-mile radius, and the spiders set up a vast clacking of mandibles and emitted little hungry yearning cries.

"In answer, I heard thuds on the low roofs as the trapdoors fell back, and from each structure crawled a creature that dwarfed our captors into insignificance. It was a disgusting, heart-stopping sight, and our stomachs retched as we saw eight enormous spiders, each the size of a horse. But it was not their incredible size and filthiness, nor their bloated bodies which betokened an unthinkable age, that so horrified our souls! It was the look of an incredible, superhuman knowledge within their eyes, a knowledge not of this earth or era, a look as they saw us that might shine in the eyes of Lucifer, conscious of a kingdom or a world that had been gained, ruled and lost! And I knew that they looked upon us as an upstart race, born to serve, that had by a freakish accident turned the tables on our masters.

"This, I say, I read in their eyes, but my memory may be colored by the things I later *knew*.

"The monsters pounced down, selecting the choicest foods before them. One seized the carcass of a deer and bore it to the rooftop, mumbling down its juices, which would soon leave it a dry mummified husk of bones and hide. Another selected a large peccary or wild pig, and a third chose a savage lizard that killed three of the black and silver guards before it was stung into helplessness.

"A man was snatched from my side, shrieking as he was dragged to the rooftop and down into the building, his cries cut short by the shutting of the trap.

"Then one took me by the side, and I gave myself up for dead. I have read of men that have been caught by lions, clawed and bitten, but feel no pain till long after they have been rescued. So it was with me. I felt neither pain nor fear as I was borne to the roof as a mouse is carried by a cat, but only regret that I might have done so many things that now I should never live to do.

"The creature dropped me upon the stone roof and inspected my clothing, which seemed to puzzle it. Then with a talon, it felt of my skin, whose whiteness I do not doubt was unfamiliar. Daintily and with exceeding care, it sank its hollow fangs into my arm and commenced the drinking of my blood. I felt no pain, only a haze before my eyes and a giddiness as I fainted.

———

"Up from an unfathomable abyss of sleep I swam, cleaving my way to consciousness with mighty strokes. I opened my eyes and saw that I still lived.

"I was lying on the roof with the eight horrors around me. The sun was set like a jewel, upon a mountain top, nearly at the day's close. The valley was a shambles, covered with spiders gruesomely feasting.

"One seemed to be communicating with the others. He was the largest of all and appeared to be in power, so that later I dubbed him King. This was the one that had chosen me and had, curiously, not finished his meal.

"Now one at a time, each came up, placed its fangs upon my wounded arm and tasted of my blood. When all had done this, there was another silent colloquy, and finally at some mysterious signal, several of the guards in silver took me off the roof, half carrying, half dragging me to another building, into which I was dropped and the door, closed down.

"The air inside was fresh and pure, ventilated through the cracks in the rude walls. A dim light that seeped in revealed that there were no furnishings in the room except a low dais in one corner, obviously built for one of the great spiders, and a runway that slanted from the floor to the roof door. The interior was swathed in webs, so thickly hung that it seemed a tapestry. I tore down part of this, to admit more light, but the sun sank below the mountains.

"I slept a dreamless sleep, upon the dais, getting what consolation I could from the thought that tomorrow was another day, and at any rate I was seeing things that had not been seen before."

-4-
Inquisition

"I woke with a start. The light of morning poured down through the open trap, but as I was considering the advisability of climbing up the runway, a large body filled the opening and backed down like a cat descending a tree. Half-way down, the spider king reversed ends and came head-first, sliding down the polished slide, worn smooth by many great bodies.

"I stood up, dizzy with the pain of my wounded arm, which had begun to fester overnight.

"The monster approached, took my arm in his mandibles and apparently observed that it was enormously swollen, for he shifted his hold and cleaned out the wound with a talon, afterward injecting something by means of his hollow mandibles. The pain lessened and in three days the swelling was gone, and I was well on the road to recovery. After this natural antiseptic had commenced its work, my captor exuded a quantity of raw web material from one of his triple-jointed spinnerets, and placed the sticky mass upon my arm, where it dried and hardened.

"He then stared unblinking into my eyes for several minutes, and again I had the impression of a mighty intelligence in that loathsome carcass that wished to communicate with mine. Finding that I made no response, the king urged me toward the runway by shoves, and with his assistance I managed to reach the roof and looked around me.

"The day was fair. Not a living thing moved in the valley, except a few of the guards busy dragging away the skeleton of a sloth. None of my Indians were visible, but I guessed their fate. All had perished in the night, and I was the only survivor.

"The king carried me to water, his fangs gripped in my clothes, and I drank deeply, after which I was carried back to the hut, and dropped in like a sack of meal. About an hour later, the trap opened, and a live agouti dropped in, and the door fell.

"I wondered if I was supposed to eat the little rabbit-like animal, but I wasn't hungry enough for that, so I lay down upon the dais and nursed my throbbing arm, while my fellow prisoner hid under the runway and the morning dragged along to midday.

"The spider king appeared a second time and investigated my condition. When he saw that the wound was not so angrily inflamed, he eyed me gravely, with a sage air of pondering the case, for all the world like a little German doctor of my acquaintance. I almost expected to hear him say, 'Ach, dot is goot!'

"Again, he assisted me to climb the polished slide, and upon the roof I found the other monsters. My captor set me down, with a proud air of showing off a curiosity to an interested audience and squatted down where he could look into my eyes.

"I observed that the entire eight were males and wondered whether there were others in the buildings. If so, they must be frightful indeed, for the female spider is usually larger and more ferocious than her mate, and often uses him as food when other dainties run low in the larder.

"Engrossed with such thoughts, I failed to notice at first that objects around me were growing hazy and vague in outline. It was as though gauze curtains were being lowered between me and the spiders. They dimmed until I strained my eyes to see them, then another curtain descended, and the world went dark.

———

"It seemed that inside my skull the brain began to itch (I can think of no better simile), as though a light tendril of cobweb had been laid across it. Cautiously searching, the feeler groped in the convolutions of my brain, an intangible finger tickling until my skin crawled and my hair rose. Occasionally it paused with a firm pressure, and at this I saw bright flecks in the dark and heard a crackling, like an electric current leaping a spark gap. Then suddenly, connections were established, my mind and the spider's were *en rapport* and my memory was probed and read like an open book by the spider king. I felt a great loss of energy, as though my life forces were being sapped.

"Of what the king learned from me, I have a very slight knowledge. In the light of later discoveries, I suppose that he obtained very concise information about the outer world, but only fragments of scenes leaked to me through the gray fog that shrouded my brain.

"Once, I remember, I was reading in a picture-book, learning my alphabet under the guidance of an elder child. I had not seen or thought of that child before for years, but now her face with all its freckles was as clear before me as the book from which I read. Then the vision was wiped away and again the gray mist shut in. Next, I was walking the crowded streets of a city. I recognized Times Square in New York, I paused to speak to a friend that approached me; the meeting had taken place long ago, but I wonder if you can understand this? While we were conversing, I entertained the most cannibalistic thoughts. Laterally, I regretted that I had not sprung at his throat and devoured that man, and he was one of the best friends that a man has ever had. I could not conceive how I had missed such a wonderful opportunity. To roam for days in crowded cities, with wonderful food all about me and never to feast, when it could have been obtained so easily!

"Again, the fog closed. I realized that those thoughts had been not mine, but the spider king's.

"I was reading in a library, reading of people. Other people walked by me, sat beside me, brought me books. Such a wealth of delicious food—in the outer world! Come! I shall go there! Never again shall I look with jaded eye upon my neighbor. He is sweet, he is dainty, he is nutritious, there is a peculiar savor about him that no other animal possesses! To the hunting grounds then, where there is meat enough for all!

"But what do I say and think? All is a lie! There are no people, no libraries, no books. There is nothing but a vast sea of clouds, of spiraling vapors, in which I float, a being smaller than the atom! There is a sound of many singing—a low and melancholy chant. If I can understand the words, I shall be free. Hush! Let me listen closer. Now the song is nearer, a wild unearthly chant, and now the voices strengthen and now the words are clear! And now I *see* a vast concourse of people, with skins the hue of brass, and they float from out the mists, while outstretched are pleading hands, hands of men, and chubby baby hands, beautiful well-kept hands of young and lovely women, and wrinkled, sallow hands of the very old! Hands that point me out, as I float lost in eddying vapors, hands that clench in anger, hands that plead and entreat in a language of their own, while their owners sing words quite different. All the universe seems a tangled knot of hands that twist and twine! Oh God! And all the voices sing in tones of dolor and of woe:

> *"All the suns are impotent to succor us,*
> *In a vast dungeon barred with ever-shafting rain;*
> *When a silent people of spiders infamous*
> *Have come to weave their filaments upon our brain.*

"But the knotted hands and fingers, as they squirm and tangle, command with many voices: 'Avenge us! Avenge us!! Vengeance!!!' And as I swear that I will, I break through the clinging mists and find myself upon the stone roof in the city of spiders!

"With a start, I realized that the last vision had been given to me *alone*. The spider king had no inkling of my command, or of my acceptance! How did I know this? I cannot tell. I only knew with surety, that I possessed *one* secret from my jailers.

———

"It was dusk again. From the western wall began to pour the hunters, driving their prey to the slaughtering grounds. The king carried me to the hut, and dropped me in. The trap closed.

"I had spent almost six hours in a trance, and I wondered what these beings had learned in that time, besides the scraps that I had retained. I felt empty, not only physically, but mentally, as though all my cherished knowledge had been brutally stolen and nothing had been put in its place. But I ran over my memories, and I seemed normal. It was a wild and uncanny experience.

"Outside was a pandemonium of shrieks and howls. The roar of some gigantic animal boomed close to my hut and the wall trembled. The little agouti crept out from under the runway and cuddled its head in my lap. It was shivering in an agony of terror. I stroked it, and it shuddered violently but nudged closer.

"A strident clicking like locusts outside, and then again the eerie wail of a jaguar. It was filled with plaintive amazement, as though the beast could not credit what was happening to him. Ah, strike with your heavy paws, *El Tigre,* fight on, oh mighty one! The master of the jungle at last has met his master, and *El Tigre* roams the forest nevermore!

"A long hiss, and I knew that another of the valiant lizards was taking toll amongst his butchers, but there were no more hisses, so the sequel was plain.

"The dull roar of combat died away, leaving only isolated squeaks as a herd of wild pigs was brought down, somewhere in the valley. And then nothing, for when a spider dines, he does so quietly and without undue disturbance.

"A few minutes later, a large piece of meat was flung in. I did not inspect it too critically but fell to at once. It was raw, of course, but I was ravenous, and a hungry man that has not eaten for nearly three days feels a surge of appetite for almost anything that seems fit for food. True, I had not killed the agouti, but I had been so feverish with my wound and the shock of my captivity that I had then no desire for food.

"I slept upon the dais, until a beam of moonlight struck through a chink and lay across my eyes. I began to worry about my chances for escape, until I could no longer rest. I went to the opening and looked out. It was a beautiful moonlit night; the valley as far as I could see was bare. It brought a plan into my head and I tore down much of the clinging webs, until I had exposed the lower foundations of the hut. As I expected, the large boulders were filled in by small stones. I worried some of these loose, until I had opened a passageway large enough for a small man, but as I stooped to remove the last stone, the little agouti, seeing an opening to freedom, dashed past me and out upon the greensward. It had not gone ten feet from the hut, when a black and silver ghost was after it, and when it doubled to return, several more heaped themselves upon it.

"Very quietly, I replaced the stones and wedged them tight; there was no hope of escape at night for me. Well, one can always sleep if his nerves are iron, and finally I dozed off, a philosophic prisoner."

-5-
The Farther Vision

"Each morning, the spider king carried me to water, and each night I was fed. How I grew to loathe raw meat, and how I yearned for green food, milk and salt! Some nights I dreamed about salt, white mountains of it, which I walked over on snowshoes and slid down upon toboggans and skis, every once in a while reaching down and scooping up great handfuls of it which I swallowed with relish. Often, I awoke to find myself licking the palms of my hands to get what saline content I might out of the perspiration and dreaming it was salt. Even now, I season my food with salt to an extent that makes it impossible for anyone else to enjoy the meal but myself. I grew thin, but my wound healed rapidly, and I had no more visions as wild as the first one.

"The day after my abortive attempt to escape, my mind was probed again. In all the lucid intervals I remember, the only scenes I saw were of people. Cities that swarmed like hives, villages of people, and little isolated houses and cottages. How easy to storm one of those cottages, so far from any neighbor! How easy for that horde to conquer a small village and, flushed with victory, to advance upon a city, with all the spiders in the country flocking to our standard! Perhaps even to wipe the continent clean of Man, leaving this valley and establishing a rule elsewhere!

"And the night after *that* unconscious revelation, I began to suspect. I had just come from an interview with the king. As I satisfied my hunger, I tried to imagine the reasons that led him to learn of the outer world and to give me in turn glimpses of the past. For I had learned strange things, which shall be revealed in their place. Why had he sampled my blood? Had they relished the flavor, so different from the natives, and were reserving me for an especial tidbit, *or as a guide to places where more of my kind might be found?*

"Now I come to a point where I must take care not to strain your credulity to its limit, for I have things to tell that have made me a pariah in the scientific world. I am the butt for the most idiotic and asinine jokes because I have told what I saw, bald narrative, with no fancy trimming of mine to make it more acceptable.

"And this is the story of Man's rise and fall. The story of the first reasoning being upon earth, the account of his inglorious servitude and the miraculous freak that saved you and me today from being hewers of wood and drawers of water to an insect!

"I put my separate visions into short accounts as each was given to me, for each vision holds within it a fact, as each nut a kernel, and if I made a connected story of the whole, it would be more incoherent than in the original form. There are blanks but use your imagination to fill them; there may be faults of memory but there is much that tallies with the facts we know.

"Upon the third day of my imprisonment, the king held communion with me alone, the other spiders of his species remaining in their huts. Apparently having learned from me all that he wished to know or all that I could tell him, he opened a door for me to read the past.

"In all the scenes which follow, a word of explanation is necessary. I was granted to peep into the past, it is true, but there were bounds over which I might not trespass. Often the gray mists closed between me and some enthralling picture that I longed desperately to see more of. I participated, by proxy, in battles and was wounded, but never felt pain. I was present at scenes of the most frightful carnage, when the screams and groans of the dying and the howls of the victors must have produced a deafening din, but I heard no sounds.

"Is it that the mind cannot hold the memory of pain? I think so. Hark back if you will, to the time when you suffered with a sprained ankle, a broken bone, or a toothache. You remember that you suffered, but the pain in all its varying, degrees you cannot call back to say, 'At such a moment I felt *these* sensations.'

"But in regard to sounds, I believe that the sense of hearing in spiders is slight, and I doubt that these had ever possessed it at all.

"It seemed as though I was closeted within a small compartment. I watched a magic panorama that unreeled before my eyes, as a motion picture operator might observe the screen from his projection booth. Then the reel would end, the lights fade, and all my world became a whirling fog.

"These, then, are the discoveries that I made and the facts that I learned from them, as I beheld the most marvelous drama that it has ever been given a man to witness.

———

"I stood by the shore of a stagnant lake, which was covered with a thick slimy growth that undulated with oily ripples, as though some great animal moved beneath it, for there was no wind. To my right, the ground was carpeted with a lush growth of coarse vegetation over which danced a maze of insects. I saw dragonflies whose gauzy wings would measure several feet from tip to tip, whirl in mimic battle. A procession of gigantic ants near-sightedly wove their tortuous path among the thick clumps of mushrooms that studded the fern-forest like varicolored jewels embedded in dark green plush.

"Above me a dome of clouds was spread, that marched from left to right, drizzling a fine mist as they passed. No sun or moon was visible, but a soft lambent light shone through the clouds, diffused by the mist, so that the landscape was well illuminated.

"A multitude of living creatures swarmed in the skies, but as far as I could see there moved no mammalian life as we know it. A thing that I took for a vulture hovering high, dropped and became on closer inspection a huge wasp that darted down into the ferns and rose with a kicking insect in its claws, darting swiftly across the lake. All life seemed to be represented by insects!

"It seemed as though I was called, although I heard no sound. I turned, to behold a like scene to that I had been watching. A stone pier projected out above the slimy liquid. From this platform a path wound into the shrubbery. This I expectantly watched, waiting for the one who had signaled to come in sight. Presently the ferns swayed, and a huge bulk lumbered down to the pier.

"It was an immense spider, similar in size to the king, but it was a dull brown and hairless, its skin as thick and tough as sole-leather and oozing moisture. I was not surprised by the sight, for I had expected this, and I knew with the calm acceptance of the most amazing facts that we meet only in dreams, that I was also a spider, or at least looking through the eyes of one for a time.

"I understood, or rather my control understood (for this took place long, long ago), that I was to follow, and we two started along the path. Once we stopped to allow an army of ants, similar to driver ants, to cross our route. We were unseen by them, so that they passed on devouring everything that lay before them and leaving a wide swath of desolation, bare of any living thing. A short time after this, we came on a wide plain that hummed with activity. Spiders of all types were there, hustling to and fro, herding beasts before them in small bands, toward a large stockade that was built of stone. One of these bands had stopped, and a hubbub was taking place. As we neared this commotion, I saw that these beasts were sometimes standing erect and sometimes upon all fours, and coming closer still, I beheld that their skins were white and that they were men!

"Men, I say, but not as men are now. Their faces were dull and stupid, their bodies were grossly fat, and like sheep they crowded together for mutual protection. A very few were thin and wiry, more energetic than the others and more daring. These few were leaving their own bands and were clustering about the scene of trouble, only to be forced back by a guard of small spiders like the black and silver fellows, but these guards were almost hairless, having only the yellow crest of fur that denoted their rank. There were many of the rulers, packed into a knot which disintegrated as I came up, and I saw that the center of the disturbance was a man.

"Quickly the situation was explained to me, and I gathered that the slave had killed a spider. At my order, he was seized; and we returned to the lake, followed by most of the spiders and all of the men.

"He was forced to walk out upon the stone pier, and as he did so the surface of the liquid began to eddy fiercely. He came nearer and the slime rose and lapped the surface of the pier. Then he turned to run back, but already the mucilaginous liquid had him thickly by the feet. Slowly it crawled up his knees, his thighs and chest, while his mouth gasped wide for air, or with a cry that I could not hear. Then the sticky slime retreated into the lake and with it went the slave.

"Thus, were offenders against the spider's law punished for an abject lesson to the rest!

"The mob trooped back into the forest and as I marched, I pondered upon my surroundings. This was clearly a younger world than mine.

"An inner voice began to explain that this was a past unthinkably remote, a period of time when the equator and the temperate zones were still in a state of flux, when the equator was one roaring belt of volcanoes that belched lava and ashes into the hissing seas that rose in steam to obscure half the world in clouds. Countless eons would yet elapse before Atlantis and its sister-continent, Mu, would be raised from the oceans to breed a civilization upon each and then to sink again, the one beneath the blue waters of the Pacific and the other in the ocean which bears its name!

"But while the rest of the world was unfit for life, at the tropical polar countries the earth was cool enough to support vegetation in abundance, and where vegetation is, creatures will be found to live upon it.

"Here, as the different species commenced the race for supremacy, the insects forged ahead. The spiders, being the most intelligent and, save man, the most savage, had become the dominant reasoning beings of the globe. Man, arising later, was bred for food, and his spirit broken. But now and again one rose and struck back with the results I had seen.

"The voice died away and as I marched, I thought that it was something, after all, that a man dared to rebel. At any rate he was not fully conquered, and at this thought, it seemed as though I had learned my lesson from the episode, the misty clouds lowered and shrouded me in gray, and with a great roaring in my ears I passed from that era.

———

"I stood upon a mountain that overlooked a dreadful chasm. A fierce gale was sweeping along the heights and there were no clouds in the sky. Around me were grouped several of the rulers, shivering in the wind, their hides but little protection against the cold. The air was no longer warm and sticky, and I knew that we were seeking a warmer climate.

"To my left, at the foot of the mountain, there was a plain that was swarming with the beast-men, all converging toward the ravine, with a multitude of spiders herding them on.

"Thus far, we had come unhindered on our march from the cooling pole, but a mountain range across our path had barred our progress until we had discovered a way to pass through. On the other side of the range dwelt a nation of men that had never known the spiders' rule, tall and slim and of noble aspect. A budding civilization that we obliterated from existence. This nation was formed of many small cities, built of stone and wood, and walled in for protection against the beasts and other men, more savage than beasts as they are at this day. They probably had some commerce with one another, some trade, some slight banding together against a common foe, but we spiders learned little of their life, for we smashed that nation and fed upon its people. But I anticipate.

"There was fighting in the chasm. A small troop of brass-hued men armed with spears and slings were bitterly contesting the advance of our armies. The pass was glutted with bodies forced on by the pressure of the masses behind, who in turn were forced on by the spiders. Timid and weak as were our slaves, by their very numbers they were a power to reckon with, and though they feared the men that held the pass, they dreaded the spiders more. Gradually they were winning through.

"From our height we could see that the brass-faced defenders were striking weaker blows. They were whittling away the head of the column still, but for every man that fell, two sprang into his place. There were dead in that crowd that had been slain at the beginning of the battle and were standing erect in the press, heads idiotically lolling from side to side, unable to fall!

"We moved along the mountainside, keeping the fighting beneath us. The ravine began to widen, and our enemy had a greater front to cover, giving our beast men an advantage which they speedily took.

"Now came a hungry horde of spiders that swooping past me down the mountain, flung themselves upon the weary defenders of the pass, and over their bodies the beast-men rushed in mad scramble from the monsters that crowded them on.

"My band followed down the mountain wall and came finally to the new land of promise. Beyond the entrance to the pass, a walled city stood, gates barred and parapets manned with warriors that pelted our masses with stones and sleeting flights of arrows.

"But while the clumsy slaves scattered on the plain, we spiders with grim resolve sealed the walls, which offered no barrier to our taloned limbs. The brass-hued men fought bravely, but we mastered them, and the city was ours.

"About a mile away, another city was beleaguered, and as the spiders rose along the wall, smoke began to rise from the huts within, in ever-increasing abundance. The people in despair had fired their homes, in sad preference for the fiery death to the worse fate that awaited them. The grass-thatched roofs made a roaring hell of the city, and the spiders were driven back.

"Now farther upon the plain, another pillar of smoke began to rise, and then a third, until all the cities had followed the example set by their brave countrymen, and as a nation the brass-hued race perished in the ruins of their homes.

"So it was that sorrow crossed the mountains, and there was weeping and wailing in the land.

————

"I stood again before the spider king, through whose memory I had searched the past, as through mine he had explored the present. The blood began to circulate through my numbed limbs, prickling like a thousand needles. I felt as though I had traveled far.

"My guards carried me to the dungeon, dropped in a shoulder of venison and left me alone. I fell upon the raw meat, wolfing it down in great mouthfuls, and as I ravenously satisfied my hunger, I tried to imagine the reasons that led the king to learn of the outer world and to give me, in turn, glimpses of the past.

"Clearly, this was his method of relating his people's history, but why trouble himself at all? Why not slay me as he had the natives? I could only decide that I was being reserved for a guide to the outer world! They had relished the taste of my blood!

"On pondering over the visions, I recognized the chant of the brass-hued people to be a quotation from one of the poems of Baudelaire, but in the age when those beings fought the spiders, unthinkable periods of time would yet elapse before men began to dream of rhyme. I eventually reached the conclusion that if I *had* seen a vision and made a promise, the impression that the pleading voices had desired to convey to me struck a chord in my subconscious mind that nearly equaled that eerie verse, so that in semi-stupor I fancied they chanted in the words of the French poet. I still believe that my theory is correct, but I wonder often what they really *did* say? The vision was so very real!

"I decided that each episode took place in the life of a different spider, and by the clearness of each vision, it would seem to indicate that the spider king recalled the incidents in his various reincarnations, or that lacking the written word to preserve history, this race had developed the ability of storing facts in their brain cells that were passed from one generation to another as physical attributes sometimes are with men.

"In all of these glimpses, I saw as a spider; I thought as a spider; I looked upon men as beasts of burden, created for the well-being of the spider people, an unclean miserable race, but necessary for our slaves.

"Thus, they lifted themselves to a dangerous pinnacle, upon a foundation of sand, by depending so much upon a lower race of beings for their own existence. History is full of such errors. For look you! Your slave revolts or dies, with nothing to lose and all to gain, and if he succeeds—where are the rulers then? If he fails, progress has stopped or has been delayed, but it is the overlords that bear the expense, not the slaves. They can but die, and a dead or crippled slave is not of much value!

"Steadily after the smashing of this polar race, the breed deteriorated, civilization came to a halt for ages and began to retrogress. This was the true Dark Age for mankind, the faint dim remembrance of which has persisted in the myth of the Garden of Eden and the driving forth of Adam and Eve, a primeval people, into the wilderness. All that saved the world today from being ruled by spiders, is the unknown cataclysm that caused the first Ice Age, when the world grew cold and the glaciers ground down from the North. The spiders died in the cold, being a tropical race, and only those that could adapt themselves to the changing conditions, growing warm coats of hair and becoming smaller and more lively, continued to exist.

"Perhaps you can imagine the antiquity of this period of change when you realize that all fossil spiders or those preserved in amber that have yet been found are the same size as those we know today!

"As they became smaller, some of the larger types persisted as freaks—still the rulers, but gradually losing their hold on man. Here then follows the story of the Great Migration."

-6-

Before The Cavemen

"I was allowed to rest a day, without seeing the king, and the next morning I was brought forth and commenced the last series of visions, the first scene apparently taking place many years after the taking of the city.

"A slash of purple light cleft the vapory haze and it rolled back before me, as a curtain rises at a play. I was on the roof of the central tower in the city, the sun beating down with but little warmth. It had lost a third of its former size and brilliance.

"The spider through whose eyes I looked moved nearer to the edge and stood staring out over the city. The roofs were covered with snow, a bank of heavy clouds was gathering to the left of the observatory, and the scene was dismal in the extreme. The palm trees that originally had appeared at the taking of the city were gone and in their places were gnarled, stunted willows, whose bare limbs clattered like a skeleton's arms in the wind.

"Below, a procession was forming. A new breed of spiders had arisen. Half the size of the conquerors, they were covered thickly with hair. Their faces, which were turned toward my tower as though in expectancy, portrayed the savageness of fiends. Scattered thinly amongst the multitude were larger spiders of the ancient type, either throwbacks or survivals of the original rulers.

"Here and there sat bands of men, low-browed, hairy and brutalized. To such had the human race retrogressed! There were beasts of burden (and these also were men) that tottered beneath their loads of coarse vegetation intended for their own sustenance on the march. For this was an emigration to seek a warmer climate, and the city was being deserted.

"Climbing up the sheer wall came a large spider, as large as myself, that stood beside me in silent communion of minds. I gathered the impression that all was ready, and they waited only for me. I followed my friend into the street. My control shivered and I knew it was bitter cold. We took places at the head of the column and commenced the hegira. At the city gates we stopped and looked back for the last time.

"The clouds covered the sky, the city was drab and deserted; we must have been the last or nearly the last, expedition to leave. A white flake floated by my eyes, the pinnacles of the tower were dull as lead: I swung into my stride, the slaves lurched on.

"Man and his Master were on the march! And over all the snow was gently falling.

———

"It was night. Over my head the stars gleamed resplendent. Countless eons had passed, for the sky showed familiar forms. The pole star was the one we have always known, but in a former vision it had not been Polaris!

"I was some form of sentry, for I was walking a regular beat around a natural valley, accompanied by a troop of guards. All along my path slept the great spiders, who still wielded the whip of power.

"In the valley were penned a savage tribe of men, short, hairy and bandy-legged, whose language was composed mainly of signs and horrid grimaces.

"I knew that our control was slipping, for it was against these that

I guarded my comrades' sleep. The day before, the slaves had arisen and fled to the forests, many escaping from the horde of small spiders, that rulers had perished in the fight and had pursued them. Several of them decided to move again.

"This was the last watch. Soon the horizon flushed ruddy with the rising sun and the business of the day began.

"From the thickets came all that were left of the gigantic spiders. We allowed the guard to release the slaves, and after they had gathered their possessions we traveled along the sandy shore. The spiders kept to the rear as the men shambled along, heads swinging from side to side as they peered viciously for signs of game in the sand. Ice floes drifted in the billows, grinding against the cliffs that we were nearing.

"Suddenly the men sniffed like dogs as they caught a scent, and we saw great tracks in the sand. They started off in a wide circle that finally led us to the foot of a tremendous glacier, where our game turned to face us. It was a hairy mammoth, his tusks curving like hoops, the points a little below the eyes.

"The men surged about him throwing spears and stones, and a multitude of small spiders swarmed over him until the great beast was a heap of vermin and his sides ran blood. Like a falling mountain he crashed to earth, raining spiders that leaped for safety, and we rulers, careful as usual of ourselves, advanced to the feast.

"As from a distance we watched the smaller spiders feasting, and the slaves resting near the glacier cliff on the thin strip of beach that separated them from the sea, suddenly a lump of ice dropped, splintering, from the sky, and following with quick descent came others! Then between us and the men roared an avalanche of ice boulders, raising a barrier unclimbable.

"We dashed, scattering, to the land, and behind us the beach was black with spiders, pouring a mighty river, racing for life before the advancing glacier, grinding the rocks to powder beneath it as a fissure rent it along a mile-long front!

"And as we looked back, we saw that long quiet torrent of ice in motion at last, for as a shot or a whoop is sufficient to start an avalanche of snow in menacing charge and men frown upon one who whistles or sings beneath a snowy slope of the Alps, so the titanic thud of the mammoth's fall, the earth-shaking crash of his sudden death, had startled the glacier into a nervous leap. And now, separated from the parent body of ice, the mighty cliff towered toppling toward the sea and moved, ponderously staggering like a drunken world, crowding the slaves and pounding thinner the ribbon.

"The men panted, so far behind us as we gained the outside rim, that they were cut off. Madly they tore back and forth along the ever-narrowing beach, some swimming in the icy water, some falling upon their spears in superstitious dread of the devils of the sea, whose fins cut the waves as they feasted on the bodies of our slaves. Then the glacier moved inevitably on, entered the water, and the face thundered down with a splash that sent a wave lapping against our feet.

"Titanic icebergs floated in the tossing sea, monuments to the last of our slaves, that marked the resting place of the remnants of the brass-hued race.

"No more slaves! No more civilization for the spiders! Hereafter we would hunt our own food, fight our own battles, build our own shelters, becoming more savage and more tiny with the years, until we were tolerated parasites in the palaces of men! Our destiny was that we should clear the filth and pests from the homes of an upstart, minor, inferior race of men, but still that time was far in the future.

"Then followed many snapshots of the past, so that I followed in quick glimpses the fate of that wandering, deteriorating band of spiders whose ancestors had conquered a world.

"Driven by the ever-advancing cold, they traveled south, deserted always by bands that stayed behind while the main body kept on. Always it was the smallest that lagged behind, the fiercest, the ugliest, the least intelligent! It is their progeny that spins the webs in forest, farm and field and in the end comes to inherit the proudest edifices of humanity.

"As the years were left behind us, our numbers decreased, until from millions we had become thousands, our rulers could be numbered by hundreds. From time to time we met other bands, some with slaves, but most without. Often, we fought with these, for the years had made such differences in the species that we could no longer understand our fellow invaders. We saw brutal tribes of men, armed with stone hatchets and clubs, who gave us a wide berth. These were not the descendants of the polar race, but had evolved separately. We saw others, yet to evolve, and great apes, semi-arboreal, that were beginning to learn the possibilities that lay in the human thumb for grasping tools.

"But we passed on, our numbers dwindling ever, skirted volcanoes that thundered at us and slew many, fought through the terrible storms of that time, smashed by the pitiless hail, buried by avalanches, and at last found peace, those that were left of us, in the primeval jungles, where no glaciers could ever reach; and here we made a home. We built houses with the aid of savages that roamed where we had determined to settle and fed upon their bodies afterward. We established the rings of different species of spiders about our central community and about a hundred of our rulers, all that remained to carry on the race.

"And here in the heart of the steaming forests we dwelt, no more of our progeny being born, for our age was great, but as our numbers decreased by natural deaths and the years gave us an infernal cunning our ambition rose to the point where we had almost decided to move again. But what lay outside our home? That was the question which gave us pause. Should we again brave the crunching glaciers and the bellowing volcanoes?

"But if the glaciers had fought the volcanoes and had been destroyed, then perhaps there were men again. Not the tough and unsavory savages that our hunters sometimes brought in, but large, fat and toothsome light-colored brutes that we could again rear in herds!

"And perhaps with the new food would be found others of our race, so that with their strength and our cunning, centuries in development, we should win to undreamed-of heights, as under our crafty leadership our smaller spiders, less intelligent than their forebears, conquered for us a world!

"At the next glimpse, there were only sixty or seventy of the rulers, the males predominating; and as the years went on, this little band became less until at my last vision I opened the trap of my hut and only seven of my fellows were to be seen on their roofs, as we watched a herd of animals gathered for the evening feast, among them being brown naked men and a peculiar white-faced man, covered with a strange hide, the like of which I had never seen before, and whom I intended to dine upon!

"I, Jabez Pentreat, looked out through the eyes of the spider king and saw myself standing as I remembered I had stood, days before, as I had waited for the great spiders to pounce down from the roofs, and at this unbelievable sight, the curtain of gauze shut down and I realized I was at the end of the road! This is the only proof I have that my story is true."

-7-
The City In The Smoke

"Three days later, being fully cured of my wound, I was again brought from the prison. The spiders were waiting. The valley was acrawl with vermin, whose dry rustling filled the air with whispers. Yellow-headed guards surrounded the huts, gray devils mingled with the scarlet-barred insects, huge black leaping tarantulas were present in great numbers, but in all that crowd I saw not a single insect whose bite is not poisonous to man.

"The spider king in his silent communication made it understood to me that my life depended upon my ability to guide them to the nearest community of whites, and I consented readily. Who would not have done the same? I intended to lead them to the river and take my chances of escape there, knowing that they were as careful as cats about entering water, for although the king had promised me my life, I had but little faith in the promise.

"So, on the eighth day of my captivity we set out to the conquering of an unsuspecting continent. I walked in the center of the huge rulers' formation. About us rustled an imposing troop of guards, and for miles on each side the forest was filled with our myrmidons, scattered far and wide.

"How I feasted on fruit, that day! As we passed the small brook at *tambo* number 10, I caught some small fish and ate them raw, and no epicure ever tasted anything more delicious than that meal was to me. The drums growled again that night, as I lay in the midst of the lightly sleeping horde that quivered angrily at my slightest movement.

"It took me, urged on by the spiders, only seven days to cover the distance that I had taken ten to accomplish coming in.

"Toward night we began to hear the roar of the Caroni River as it struggled through a *raudal*, or rapid, on its way to the Orinoco.

"Suddenly, about a mile ahead, there burst out a pandemonium of frightful screams that I recognized as humans voicing inhuman terror. The great brutes scuttled on faster, so that I was hard put to keep my place. Clouds of smoke rolled up ahead of us from a campfire, and presently we broke out of the forest and saw the flames. A tribe of ugly natives were trapped by the river, where they had made camp in a clearing, building their fire on a sandy spot. Around them, the tall reed-like grass, shoulder-high to a tall man, waved and shuddered and bent low with the rush of the spider army.

"The men had been surrounded and held until the arrival of the king, and as we came up, I recognized their paint and tribal marks to be those of the Guaharibo Indians, savage men who slay for the love of murder and who had roved from their home near the upper reaches of the Orinoco, searching for heads and loot.

"Many heads hung in the smoke, partly cured—and several of them were white! At this sight, something turned to steel with me, and had it been possible to save them, I would not if I could.

"I said to the king, 'These are the first.' He understood my meaning if not my words and gave the signal for the attack.

"A great wave of spiders broke over the savages, clicking their battle cry, leaping from one to another, darting through the smoke. Seized with the madness of slaughter, the spider king and his fellows, to whom this was a joy they had probably been long without, charged with the rest.

"In a second, I was forgotten and absolutely alone! Dazed by the marvel of it, I was yet not too blind to seize my opportunity. Quickly, yet with the utmost care, I crept toward the river where the log canoes were drawn up on the shore and pushed all off but one. Still the battle raged.

"As I put one foot inside the canoe, something gave me pause. Again, I heard the despairing, pleading cries of the brass-faced people and saw those writhing hands that swore me to vengeance. Stealthily I crawled back to the fire, gathered an armful of resinous, light wood, and with a burning brand trailing behind me set the grass aflame as I ran to the canoe.

"I paddled upstream to where the forest joined the clearing and beached the canoe. The wind was blowing strongly downstream. With my torch, I lit stick after stick and hurled the flaming wood far out into the field. Then I drifted down and held my position in midstream and waited.

"The battle was almost to its inevitable end. The fire that I had first lit was burning stubbornly into the teeth of the wind, and now, fanned to fury, a fifteen-foot wall of flame came down with a whirring roar to meet it!

"The fighting stopped. Man and spider, both were doomed, and from both sides the fire closed in. I yelled in joy, howling crazy, broken curses. Strange how much it looked like a great city in the smoke, with flaming, sputtering sheets of fire that lapped its phantom walls! From that whirlwind of sparks came a vast sound of frying! I heard a bursting mutter like gigantic kernels of corn popping in an enormous pan. A wave of sooty smoke, redolent of burned flesh, rolled out over the river and set me blind and coughing. As I wiped my streaming eyes, a horrid thing staggered from the flames, little spikes of fire shooting from its fat and bloated body! Although his hair was burned away and his mandibles were gone, I recognized the spider king. He lurched nearer and I saw that he was blind, just as his charred legs snapped with his weight and he subsided into the river.

"The water boiled and hissed when he struck it. Once he rose, lashing feebly, and I beheld that his body was swarming with little fish that rent and tore pieces of flesh away. These were the savage little piranhas, the miniature fresh-water sharks that give short shrift to anything that falls within a school of them. Again, he came to the surface, the water frothed a bloody foam and then the last of the monster sank, in tatters, into the Caroni!

"Not many of the others escaped. After the fire had swept into the forest, I saw that the ground was black with charred bodies that lay in tumbled heaps around the skeletons of the Guaharibos. By easy stages, I made my way to civilization, bearing a stupendous tale to my friends.

"I told them my story and said in substance, 'While you have been wasting your time for hundreds of years, searching, back through the ages; with pick and shovel scrabbling in the dust of forgotten empires; with arduous sifting of myths and legends to find some small fact; with titanic efforts of geological, biological and philological research to bring the past nearer, the link that could tell you all you wish to know—is hunting flies in the rafters of your own houses! Apply yourselves therefore to the means of wresting this secret from it, for you can learn both of this and other lands more than by your explorations.'

"They laughed as I expected they would," he concluded bitterly.

———

As he finished, we were passing into Waltham and we began locating our luggage, for we had only a few more miles to travel. Then as the train neared Boston, he resumed at the original cause of our discussion upon the word "hate" of uncertain usage.

"So, while you feel repulsion," he began, "and a sickened disgust at the sight of a spider, it is because the hereditary, subconscious memory *knows* that these creatures were once your lords in another existence and it commands you to obliterate this loathsome, alien life from another age. When you crushed that barn spider under your foot, you unconsciously took revenge for uncounted eras of oppression, which has made such a mark on the human brain that forever and ever most men will sicken at the sight of a spider.

"You are repelled without understanding the reason for your

dislike, but I—I *hate* them, for I know *what* they are—a fact which no other man alive is certain of.

"All spiders that I come in contact with now are attracted to me. I enter a room, for instance: there is not the sign of a web about, my hostess would swear that the house is spotless, but if there is a spider it feels my presence somehow, and before I leave, I may find one perched upon my shoe, or near me, steadily gazing with its beady black eyes.

"I hate them, but I have not the fear, which you mistakenly call hatred. I am going to search for Carewe and *we* will search for that polar country where the brass-hued men lived, and may even find a frozen or fossil spider that will prove that I did not lie to my fellow scientists. But until that day, I tell my story to no more scoffers, nor should I have told you if I had not wished to see how a layman received the theory that all my contemporaries have rejected."

"What, Boston so soon?" he ejaculated as we pulled into the North Station. "I hope I have not bored you."

"Indeed, you have not, Mr. Pentreat," I answered, with a smile. "I wish you good fortune in your search." And I extended my hand.

"Thank you, I shall need it," he said gruffly, and wringing my hand, he stepped into the crowd and I saw my last of the man with the beady eyes.

———

I shall, not include this in my novel, nor shall I change his version of affairs. It is an amazing theory at least, and if it were proved, it would cause havoc to cherished opinions, but if he goes to find his lost city in the North, he goes alone—for I read that Sir Adlington Carewe has disappeared into the jungles of Africa's West Coast, and as his experiments dealt with great apes and lunatics, I do not think he will be back.

Well, you have read the story. I give you fair warning that I don't believe it myself. His eyes were just a wee bit *too* bright!

THE CATS OF ULTHAR

H.P. LOVECRAFT

It is said that in Ulthar, which lies beyond the river Skai, no man may kill a cat; and this I can verily believe as I gaze upon him who sitteth purring before the fire. For the cat is cryptic, and close to strange things which men cannot see. He is the soul of antique Ægyptus, and bearer of tales from forgotten cities in Meroë and Ophir. He is the kin of the jungle's lords, and heir to the secrets of hoary and sinister Africa. The Sphinx is his cousin, and he speaks her language; but he is more ancient than the Sphinx and remembers that which she hath forgotten.

In Ulthar, before ever the burgesses forbade the killing of cats, there dwelt an old cotter and his wife who delighted to trap and slay the cats of their neighbours. Why they did this I know not; save that many hate the voice of the cat in the night and take it ill that cats should run stealthily about yards and gardens at twilight. But whatever the reason, this old man and woman took pleasure in trapping and slaying every cat which came near to their hovel; and from some of the sounds heard after dark, many villagers fancied that the manner of slaying was exceedingly peculiar. But the villagers did not discuss such things with the old man and his wife; because of the habitual expression on the withered faces of the two, and because their cottage was so small and so darkly hidden under spreading oaks at the back of a neglected yard. In truth, much as the owners of cats hated these odd folk, they feared them more; and instead of berating them as brutal assassins, merely took care that no cherished pet or mouser should stray toward the remote hovel under the dark trees. When through some unavoidable oversight a cat was missed, and sounds heard after dark, the loser would lament impotently; or console himself by thanking Fate that it was not one of his children who had thus vanished. For the people of Ulthar were simple and knew not whence it is all cats first came.

One day a caravan of strange wanderers from the South entered the narrow, cobbled streets of Ulthar. Dark wanderers they were, and unlike the other roving folk who passed through the village twice every year. In the marketplace they told fortunes for silver and bought gay beads from the merchants. What was the land of these wanderers none could tell; but it was seen that they were given to strange prayers, and that they had painted on the sides of their wagons, strange figures with human bodies and the heads of cats, hawks, rams, and lions. And the leader of the caravan wore a headdress with two horns and a curious disc betwixt the horns.

There was in this singular caravan a little boy with no father or mother, but only a tiny black kitten to cherish. The plague had not been kind to him, yet had left him this small furry thing to mitigate his sorrow; and when one is very young, one can find great relief in the lively antics of a black kitten. So the boy, whom the dark people called Menes smiled more often than he wept as he sat playing with his graceful kitten on the steps of an oddly painted wagon.

On the third morning of the wanderers' stay in Ulthar, Menes could not find his kitten; and as he sobbed aloud in the market-place certain villagers told him of the old man and his wife, and of sounds heard in the night. And when he heard these things his sobbing gave place to meditation, and finally to prayer. He stretched out his arms toward the sun and prayed in a tongue no villager could understand; though indeed the villagers did not try very hard to understand, since their attention was mostly taken up by the sky and the odd shapes the clouds were assuming. It was very peculiar, but as the little boy uttered his petition there seemed to form overhead the shadowy, nebulous figures of exotic things; of hybrid creatures crowned with horn-flanked discs. Nature is full of such illusions to impress the imaginative.

That night the wanderers left Ulthar and were never seen again. And the householders were troubled when they noticed that in all the village there was not a cat to be found. From each hearth the familiar cat had vanished; cats large and small, black, grey, striped, yellow, and white. Old Kranon, the burgomaster, swore that the dark folk had taken the cats away in revenge for the killing of Menes' kitten; and cursed the caravan and the little boy. But Nith, the lean notary, declared that the old cotter and his wife were more likely persons to suspect; for their hatred of cats was notorious and increasingly bold. Still, no one durst complain to the sinister couple; even when little Atal, the innkeeper's son, vowed that he had at twilight seen all the cats of Ulthar in that accursed yard under the trees, pacing very slowly and solemnly in a circle around the cottage, two abreast, as if in performance of some unheard of rite of beasts. The villagers did not know how much to believe from so small a boy; and though they feared that the evil pair had charmed the cats to their death, they preferred not to chide the old cotter till they met him outside his dark and repellent yard.

So Ulthar went to sleep in vain anger, and when the people awaked at dawn—behold! Every cat was back at his accustomed hearth! Large and small, black, grey, striped, yellow, and white, none was missing. Very sleek and fat did the cats appear, and sonorous with purring content. The citizens talked with one another of the affair and marveled not a little. Old Kranon again insisted that it was the dark folk who had taken them, since cats did not return alive from the cottage of the ancient man and his wife. But all agreed on one thing: that the refusal of all the cats to eat their portions of meat or drink their saucers of milk was exceedingly curious. And for two whole days the sleek, lazy cats of Ulthar would touch no food, but only doze by the fire or in the sun.

It was fully a week before the villagers noticed that no lights were
appearing at dusk in the windows of the cottage under the trees. Then
the lean Nith remarked that no one had seen the old man or his wife
since the night the cats were away. In another week the burgomaster
decided to overcome his fears and call at the strangely silent dwelling
as a matter of duty, though in so doing he was careful to take with him
Shang the blacksmith and Thul the cutter of stone as witnesses. And
when they had broken down the frail door, they found only this: two
cleanly picked human skeletons on the earthen floor, and a number of
singular beetles crawling in the shadowy corners.

There was subsequently much talk among the burgesses of
Ulthar. Zath, the coroner, disputed at length with Nith, the lean
notary; and Kranon and Shang and Thul were overwhelmed with
questions. Even little Atal, the innkeeper's son, was closely questioned
and given a sweetmeat as reward. They talked of the old cotter and his
wife, of the caravan of dark wanderers, of small Menes and his black
kitten, of the prayer of Menes and of the sky during that prayer, of the
doings of the cats on the night the caravan left, and of what was later
found in the cottage under the dark trees in the repellent yard.

And in the end the burgesses passed that remarkable law which is
told of by traders in Hatheg and discussed by travelers in Nir; namely,
that in Ulthar no man may kill a cat.

BACK to the BEAST

by
MANLY
WADE
WELLMAN

(From the Smith City Mirror, June 26, 1927)

Police are searching today for Dr. J. E. Lawlor, well-known physician and scientist, following a report from his secretary, James Brock, that he had disappeared from his home at 2100 Van Ness Avenue.

According to Brock, Dr. Lawlor locked himself into his private laboratory twelve days ago, ordering his servants not to disturb him, and to send food down by means of a dumbwaiter. As he had followed this plan several times before while working on experiments, Brock complied with his request. The time set was ten days and when there had been no response from the laboratory during the two days following the elapse of this period, Brock feared some accident and, with the help of Georges Dmitri, Dr. Lawlor's cook, and Emil Bonner, his chauffeur, he forced the door this morning and found that the doctor was gone.

A weird angle is added to the incident by the dead body of a large ape which Brock found in a corner of the disordered laboratory. Although Dr. Lawlor was known to be interested in natural history and to have conducted several experiments with animals recently, Brock stated that he was sure the ape was not in the laboratory when it was closed twelve days ago. The table was covered with papers, which have been turned over to the police.

Brock, Dmitri and Bonner are held for questioning by Chief of Police John Walton.

Dr. Lawlor has no immediate family. A brother, Stanley Lawlor, of Topeka, Kansas, has been notified.

(From the Smith City Mirror, June 28, 1927)

Attempts to determine the species of the ape found dead in the laboratory of Dr. J. E. Lawlor, who disappeared last Saturday, were unsuccessful when Professor F. W. Baylor, head of the natural science department of the state university, said today that he had never seen such a creature before.

"There are eight kinds of anthropoid apes known to science," said Professor Baylor, "but this ape belongs to none of them. It has some of the characteristics of several but resembles no single kind greatly. It is either a freak or of a species unknown until now."

Professor Baylor has ordered the animal embalmed and intends to send it to fellow-students of natural history in Chicago.

(From the Smith City Mirror, June 29, 1927)

James Brock, private secretary of Dr. J. E. Lawlor, 2100 Van Ness Avenue, was placed under arrest today to face charges of kidnaping and possibly murder of his employer last Saturday.

The arrest took place following the reading of papers purporting to be a journal of an experiment performed by the doctor, which Brock turned over to the police upon his employer's disappearance.

Brock had been held for questioning but was given his liberty Saturday.

The contents of the journal were not made public, but Chief John Walton described them as "preposterous and unbelievable, a forgery by Brock to cover a very evident crime."

(Extracts from the papers given to police by James Brock as the journal of Dr. James Everett Lawlor)

June 15—All is in readiness for my experiment—the final step in my great work that will afford scientists a true glimpse of how man appeared in the dim past. The narrow persons who refuse to believe in evolution will be forced to see the truth, for we will confront them, not with theories, but with proofs.

I have material now that would fill a great book—notes telling how I first discovered the combination of elements that induces deterioration and of my experiments with it, first on the lowest forms of life, then on more complex animals, with surprising and enlightening results. Years have been consumed in this study, but soon they will be paid for when I reveal what I have learned.

The elements for the two serums, products of nearly a lifetime of labor and observation, are at hand. One serum is the deteriorator, which when properly mingled and administered will make vital changes in the organs and tissues of an animal, changes which finally result in giving it the appearance of its ancestors untold ages ago. This change can be arrested by the administration of the counter-agent, which will restore the transformed creature to its former condition.

I do not suppose that any person less determined or less scientific in mind than I would dare perform this experiment upon himself; but after all, it is as safe as such a thing can be. I have studied its effects and powers too much and too long to go wrong now, and I know that I shall not be mentally incapable of handling it. The change is physiological, not psychological. Foretelling the course of the whole process is a mere matter of rationalization.

As I plan it, I will let the deteriorator work in my blood for five days, then the counter-agent for five days, to make sure that the effects of the experiment are completely dissipated. Thus, I expect to see in my mirror what my ancestors were like five thousand centuries ago, and then return to the body and semblance of Dr. Lawlor, all within two weeks at the least.

I have locked my door for ten days. Brock, a sound, sensible fellow who obeys my orders without questioning, will see to it that I am undisturbed. And after this private experiment, I shall present my findings to my fellow-scientists as the proof of their theories. Who can say that my name shall not be numbered with those of the great evolutionists?

June 16—For twenty-four hours I have had the serum in my blood. With what care I compounded it and injected it into the vein of my arm, you may well imagine. The effects were noticeable at once. My blood flowed faster and for a few moments I felt strangely light-headed, as if I had been drinking. This latter feeling passed away, and I perspired freely but felt no unpleasant sensations. Throughout the day I have taken notes on the progress of the experiment, and tonight my mirror shows me that it is a success.

The change in my appearance has not been so great as I expected, but it is very evident. I am florid and ruddy where I have generally been pale. I am far more robust and all over my body my hair has grown out, especially on the breast and shoulders and outsides of the arms—a strange condition for me, always smooth-skinned and of late years partly bald. I never felt better physically in my life, and I look, not the fine-drawn and slender scientist, but a full-bodied, really splendid savage.

In excess of well-being and in joy at the certain fulfilment of my expectations, I danced and leaped up and down this evening. Then, a little ashamed of myself, I sat down to write.

. . .

June 17—The effects of the serum are more pronounced today. Where yesterday I was but a primitive man, still decidedly human, I am today a man with a pronounced bestial look. My forehead has receded, my jaw is heavy, with sharp-pointed teeth. The change works in me every moment; I can feel it in my flesh and bones. Among other things, I am positively shaggy. The hair makes my clothes a discomfort and I have left them completely off.

I am never weary of watching my body as it changes almost before my very eyes. It is especially interesting to see how springy and flexible my joints have become, and how my feet have a tendency to turn their palms inward. This is because of the great toe, which is beginning to stand out from the others like a thumb; excellent proof that our ancestors were tree-dwellers and could get a grip with their feet.

June 18—When I awoke on my cot this morning, my first glance was toward the mirror. It was unable to recognize myself, unable to recognize even the thing I had been last night. In the broad, coarse face, with flat nose, splay nostrils, little beady eyes under beetling brows, wide mouth and brutal jaws, in the hairy, hulking body, there was no reminder of what had once been Dr. Lawlor. Some scholars would be frightened at the speed and effectiveness with which the serum has worked, but I can think of nothing save the triumph to science.

I am stooped considerably and stand unsteadily on my legs; not that they are not strong, but the tendency of my feet to turn inward has increased, so that I walk for the most part on the outer edges. Their prehensile powers are developed, too, and they can pick up objects quite easily.

It is also interesting to note that my mental processes have not changed one whit—I can think as clearly and as deeply as ever. As I predicted, the serum does not affect the brain tissues; or, if it does, it does not keep them from functioning properly.

I have been hungry all day. The food Brock sent to me was not sufficient, especially as regards meat, and I must send up a note with the empty dishes for him to increase the amount.

. . .

June 19—This part of the experiment will stop tomorrow, for I shall then mix and administer the counter-agent.

Tonight, I see myself to be an eerie creature, half beast, half man. I am hard put to it to walk without supporting myself on the table and the backs of the chairs. So must our ancestors have looked when they swung down from the trees to achieve their first adventures on the ground and to conquer the world.

These five days, what with the many notes I have taken, will provide a fitting climax for the scientific book that I contemplate. How it will astound the world! What honors and distinctions may descend upon me! Fame is mine, certainly; fortune if I wish it, may follow.

So good night and good-bye, my primitive self, yonder in the mirror. Tomorrow I shall commence the journey back to the appearance of Dr. Lawlor, that I may immortalize you in all your fascinating grotesqueness.

June 20—How could I—oh, how could I not provide against this? With all the machinery of my experimentation evidently flawless, I must forget a single item—an item maddeningly simple, maddeningly obvious, and yet a thing that has proved my undoing.

Let me remain sane for a moment and marshal the incidents as they occurred. There is not much to tell. This morning I went to my shelf of chemicals for the ingredients to compound into the counter-acting serum. My hands, which of course had become clumsy and primitive, seemed to have trouble in picking up the little vials, but this did not worry me as I began the combining of my materials. Two of them I mixed in a graduated glass and then reached for a pipette to administer the third.

But my unsteady manipulation did not allow the proper proportion to flow in. I released a drop too much, and though there was a corresponding effervescence, I could see that the mixture was a failure.

I poured it out and tried again, with the same result. With growing uneasiness, I made a third attempt, and again my clumsy hands failed me.

Too late, I realized that the mingling of the elements in the proper proportions and manner had been a task that required all the delicacy of a skilled chemist. My hands, no longer the deft, steady hands of Dr. Lawlor, were those of a sub-human creature, and as such not equal to the feat!

Horrible, horrible! I moaned aloud when I realized what had happened and what would follow. Without the counter-agent I could not neutralize, or even halt, the progress of the deteriorator. Down I must go, back along the road up which the human race has struggled for untold centuries!

Again and again, I desperately tried to mix the dose, until I had used up all my materials. Once or twice, I thought that I had approximated the proper mingling, but when I injected it, there was no effect.

I sit here tonight, a rung farther toward the beast from whence we sprang, instead of on the road back toward man. Like one lowered into a well, I see above me a circle of light growing smaller and dimmer as I descend into darkness and horror! What shall I do?

[From this point forward, the journal is written in an almost unintelligible scrawl.]

June 24—For three days I have not written. I have not slept and have eaten only when the pangs of hunger roused me from my half-trance of misery. Horror has closed over my head like water.

At first, I searched frantically for more materials for the counter-agent, literally wrecking my laboratory, but to no avail. I had used it all in trying to mix the saving dose three days ago.

Today was to have been the last day of my experiment. Perhaps the servants will force the lock if I do not come out. And then?

I could never make them understand. I have no more power of speech than any other beast, for a beast I have surely become. I cannot bear to look in the mirror, for I see only a dark, hairy form, hunched over the table, a pencil clutched in its paw. And that is I, James Lawlor! What wonder that I border on the edge of insanity?

Let whoever reads these words take warning from my plight. Do not meddle with the scheme of things as nature has planned—delve not into her mysterious past. I have done that, and it was my complete and dreadful undoing. If it had not come in this way it would have come in another, I do not doubt for a moment.

June 25—Morning. I have not budged from the chair where I sat to write last evening. I heard Brock's voice outside the door, asking me if I was coming out. I dared not make a sound in reply, and he went away.

Is existence bearable in such a condition? Even now, the sliding back into lower and lower form continues. It will not be long before I am no longer even the ape-thing I appear. Perhaps the serum will carry me back through the ages until I am the slimy sea-crawler from which all life had its beginning. Oh, God!

And as if in answer to that name, comes the memory of what still remains in a drawer of my table. Arsenic—not an easy death, but a quick one. So shall I die, for if ever a creature was justified in taking its own life, that creature is myself.

I will leave this journal as an account of what has happened, and as a warning to others. The formulas for my serums and all that pertains to them I will destroy. Never shall another scientist meet with my fate if I can order it otherwise. There, the papers are flaming in the grate. Now for the arsenic—so much, in a glass of water—farewell!

[Here the journal ends.]

A Suitor from the Shades
by Greye La Spina

"No—no—no!" she screamed, and sank back unconscious into the arms of her father.

-1-

C heck." Father Rooney chuckled deep in his throat and lifted his hand from the knight that had just made an unexpected foray among his opponent's pieces.

The old doctor leaned over the board to study the situation carefully. "It does look as though you had me," he admitted unwillingly. "Well, next time you may not have such good luck."

"Luck?" queried the priest softly, a whimsical smile curving his lips.

"Poor papa! You are always beating him, Father," reproached a soft voice from the other end of the room.

The floor lamp illuminated a narrow circle about the chess players and but dimly disclosed a little figure that pressed against the curtain at the open window as though to escape observation from without as well as from within. Against the wall behind her the polished surface of a pair of crutches caught the light in long lines. It was characteristic of Clare that she should put unpleasant things behind her.

The face she turned occasionally toward the chess players disclosed singular beauty, even in the softly diffused light of the big lamp. One saw dark, sensitive eyes and felt the tenderness of the habitual gentle smile that made her expression so attractive. Her low forehead was shaded by light brown hair that fell over her small ears and was knotted loosely at the nape of a slender neck. But Clare's real beauty lay in the spirituality that beamed from her eyes.

There was a brilliant moon. Clare, gazing out into the garden, thought she had never seen it as strange as it seemed that night. It was a mysterious dreamland, not the garden she knew. It was full of unexpected patches of light that changed shape imperceptibly as the moon swam upward across the sky, and against these light spots, outlining them abruptly, were massively upreared structures of ebony-black shadow. The garden she thought she knew so well was like an unknown, entirely new country and one that, oddly enough, seemed to hold a dark threat in those ominous shadows that crept upon and engulfed the moonlit spots that relieved its blackness.

A slow shudder crept over the slight figure of the lame girl, who leaned back instinctively against the curtain and toward the soft and homely light of the tall lamp beneath which sat her father and his old friend at their game of chess. Still her gaze was held by the garden in its new aspect.

Out of the black shadows a figure advanced into a moonlit space, and like some goddess of the night lifted slim arms to her sister queen floating in her cloud chariot overhead. Out upon the hush of the night floated the rich notes Clare so adored. "Ah," she murmured with a kind of relief in her voice, "Margaret is going to sing."

The song was Ned Wentworth's *Ode to the Queen of Night*. It was the favorite lyric in Ned's last musical comedy, then crowding one of New York's best theaters night after night, incidentally filling Ned's pockets with gold. Clare closed her eyes that the velvet tones might have their full effect upon her entranced senses.

At the other end of the room, the chess players stopped their game to listen, the chess board carefully balanced across their old knees. Father Rooney characteristically lifted his kindly eyes heavenward, although his physical gaze was limited by the low ceiling; the old doctor's eyes went straight to the great portrait that hung over the divan, the portrait of his dead wife.

For Clare the evil spell lying upon the garden was broken. The strange enchantment with its vague threat passed away at the thrill of that dear voice. As the tones died away on a lingering high note, she turned her face upon her sister and opened her eyes. Margaret was apparently all alone in the still night and the lonely garden. The chess players had resumed their game; the lame girl could hear their occasional low murmurs.

"Where can Ned be?" she questioned as she gazed.

Ned Wentworth had been standing in the black shadow of a great walnut tree, watching the throbbing of Margaret's full throat as her rich notes poured out their benediction upon the still night air. His heart expanded so painfully that it seemed it must burst; her beauty actually hurt him. He looked hungrily at the great coils of heavy auburn hair, gleaming with gold under the magical light of the autumn moon; he saw as if for the first time the healthy pallor of her clear skin thrown into relief as she lifted her face upward in her invocation to the Queen of Night; he followed the line of the fine throat that swept into and was absorbed by the noble curve of her bust; and he clenched his fists with his effort to control himself—he felt that he could no longer refrain from telling her how madly he loved her.

He stepped impulsively toward her as the last gorgeous notes quivered upon the cool silence and died softly away. She paused, hands still outstretched as she had stood while singing, lost in the maze of emotion that had suddenly swept over her at Ned's impulsive movement. Rich scarlet began to mount in her cheeks until they blazed hotly under the tranquil light of the cold Lady of Night. Into the broad sweep of moonlight beside her stepped her lover, his gray eyes almost black with the intensity of his feeling; he did not speak, nor did she. It appeared to them that they had both been waiting for this very moment all their lives.

Margaret was quite motionless, her head very high, dark eyes on his face steadily, gravely, as if the wonder and richness of her emotion were too great to be carried off lightly. Ned took another step forward, a movement that brought her still outstretched arms to his shoulders, upon which her light palms dropped tenderly.

"Margie! Then it is true? You love me?"

He swept her into his embrace; her arms met about his neck and he felt her hands caressing his hair. Sudden self-consciousness fell upon them and they drew back into the shade of the walnut lest they be observed from the house.

-2-

With such careless haste that the chessmen were tossed hither and thither, Father Rooney sprang from his chair and across the room.

"What ails our little girl?" cried the old priest, deeply disturbed.

Dr. Sloane got out of his chair with more difficulty; sciatica had made a semi-invalid of him for months. He joined the other man who leaned over Clare. The blond head lay on outstretched arms across the windowsill. So motionless was she that for a terrible moment her father felt the clutching fear which his love for the daughter so like his dead wife made more terrible.

The priest held a listening ear against the girl's side. "She lives, old friend. Her heart is beating—but sluggishly. Let me carry her to the divan, where she will be more comfortable. It is only a fainting spell."

Father Rooney knew well the name of the fear that was lifting a grisly head in his friend's breast, and his heart ached for the old doctor, who followed him haltingly and painfully as he carried the limp little form across the room and disposed it on the broad divan. Sitting beside her, the priest began to stroke Clare's hands softly, while her father held a bottle of salts under her nose.

The lame girl stirred feebly. Then suddenly she broke out into hysterical sobbing, so heart-racking and so pitiful that tears rose to the eyes of the old priest who had seen so much, heard so much, of human suffering, that one felt he must have grown hardened by it.

Now, however, he sat stroking a limp, cold hand, and hot tears slowly formed in his eyes and dropped upon it.

He loved Clare as though she had been his own child. Hers was a rare soul that knew and appreciated the lofty truths in his church just as she recognized and loved the same unchangeable truths that formed the foundation of the faith of her fathers. For so young a girl (she was only nineteen) Clare possessed a lucidity of thought and a fairness of judgment that made her especially interesting to the good priest, who secretly believed her one of God's favored souls.

"She has never been like this before," worried Dr. Sloane, wrinkled brow troubled. "Clare, dear! Clare! It's Dad calling you, dear. Clare!"

The girl's sobbing increased in intensity. Her body began to writhe on the divan as if in sharp agony. The priest in Father Rooney lifted an attentive ear to the undertones of this sobbing that somehow fell strangely upon that clerical ear; he felt intuitively that here was a matter of soul trouble, not a mere hysterical weakness on Clare's part, and he was deeply disturbed.

Suddenly he looked up sharply and threw a searching glance about the room. His eye met that of Dr. Sloane, who had also looked about quickly.

"I would have sworn that there was someone else in the room just now," said the doctor in a puzzled tone, as he met his friend's gaze. "Didn't you feel it, yourself?"

The expression of the priest's face was troubled. "A very unpleasant someone, if you care for my opinion," he declared dryly. "I presume it was the effect on us of our poor little Clare's hysterics," he offered, but without conclusiveness.

Clare had become quiet and lay very still. At last, her dark eyes opened heavily, and she searched the solicitous faces of the two men contritely. "Sorry I made such a fuss," she murmured. "It wasn't like me, was it? I—I don't know what happened to me. It—it wasn't like a heart attack. It was as if something from outside had robbed me of all my strength, in an unguarded moment." She paused, her lips parted as if to say more, then closed firmly.

Father Rooney's brow wrinkled ever so slightly; a half-puzzled expression that had rested on his face a moment past, returned. He looked gravely at the delicate beauty of the face on the divan cushion. Her last words—and her silence—had disturbed him far more than he cared to admit to himself; for some strange reason they seemed ominous. It was with an effort that he threw off his depression to meet the two radiant faces that now looked in at the door.

"Father, Ned and I—What's the matter? Is anything the matter with Clare?" Margaret sprang from the encircling arm of her lover to kneel at the side of the divan. The shadow that always lay, though ever so lightly, upon her younger sister, was a dread shadow and its gloom now drew fringes of trailing darkness across the bliss of her new happiness.

"It's quite nothing, Margie darling. Don't be frightened. Anyway, I'm all right now," Clare hastened to reassure her.

Then with characteristic self-forgetfulness—and none but the wise old priest knew how generous was her spirit at that moment—Clare put out her hand to Ned.

"You and Margie—love each other? How beautiful! Forgive me if I cry. I'm just glad you're both so happy." She turned her face against the pillow and began to cry softly. So different was it from her previous hysterical weeping that the priest drew a small, half-smothered sigh of relief. He rose, touching with kindly benediction the soft hair.

"Good night, Clare. Good night, all. I must be on my way."

"But you haven't congratulated us yet," interrupted Margaret, springing to her feet and turning a beaming face upon him.

"May heaven send you its richest blessings, my daughter," he told her gravely. "And you, too, Mr. Wentworth." His hand went out to Ned in a hearty handshake.

Dr. Sloane had sunk into a nearby armchair, reminded painfully of his sciatica by twinges that doubled him up after his recent exertions. He waved one hand at the departing cleric.

"I really need a hankie," apologized Clare comically from the depths of her cushion. Ned whipped out one and tried to dry her eyes in big-brotherly fashion. "I can do it better," she said.

Ned suddenly threw a quick glance at the door. "Did someone come in?" he asked the doctor.

"No one."

"That's strange. I felt someone looking at me from the doorway."

"Ned, you're dreaming tonight," Margaret rallied him, laughing. "He felt eyes on him while we were in the garden."

"Then they must, have been mine," Clare said, sitting up. "I was watching Margaret while she sang."

Ned and Margaret exchanged glances; both colored and laughed, but Clare's pale face remained impassive. They exchanged glances again; Clare could not have seen that first rapture of their love, after all.

-3-

It was nearly midnight when the sisters finally retired to the room they shared together. There had been a bottle of old port opened that the healths of the young pair might be toasted. And it seemed that the hours had only been minutes, to Margaret.

"Clare darling, I've kept you up awfully late tonight," she apologized with compunction, turning a flushed, happy face to her sister. "You should have been in bed ages ago."

"This is a special night, Margie."

"Wasn't it magnificent?" Margaret's voice dropped into an almost solemn key as she stopped brushing out her wonderful auburn hair. "It seemed to—us—that there had never been such a night before."

"I thought much the same. But, Margie, did it seem to you— don't tell me I'm imagining things, please—did it seem to you that there was something strange, something almost awful, about the beauty of the garden tonight? I was really afraid of it, and I have never felt that way before. But tonight, it actually seemed that there was a presence abroad, a presence that boded no good to someone."

Margaret, her smooth forehead wrinkled, whirled about suddenly to face her sister.

"That's odd," she commented briskly. "Ned complained of the very same feeling. He declared that he felt jealous, envious eyes upon him."

Clare tumbled over into bed and turned her face from her sister. She slipped something under her pillow as she did so—it was Ned's handkerchief. In a smothered voice she said. "Margie! That was not a heart attack I had this evening."

"Clare dear, you are dreaming. If it wasn't a heart attack, what was it?"

"That is just what I would give worlds to know," answered the other girl earnestly. "Margie, there was something strange in our garden tonight, something no one could see—but it was there, nevertheless. And—I know what it was! Oh, don't turn out the light, Margie! I just can't sleep in the dark tonight."

Such unusual timidity on Clare's part made Margaret look at her sister searchingly. Then she sat on the edge of the bed and began to smooth the brown hair gently.

"And what was it you saw in the garden?" she inquired, with a touch of light humor in her tone.

"I didn't see. I just felt. But something took all my strength out of me suddenly. It was as if something else had clothed itself with my body, only my body didn't go with it into the garden; it stayed inside. But I knew—I know—all that that Other saw and did."

"Dearest, you are overwrought and tired. This glorious night has thrown a spell over you, and it has been too much for your tired little head."

"Margie!" Clare drew herself up, to a sitting posture. "Do you remember Clifford Bentley?" There was so much significance in her tone that the older girl gave her an amazed look as she replied affirmatively.

"Margie, Clifford Bentley was in the garden tonight, spying on you and Ned."

For a moment Margaret regarded her sister with a kind of terror; then she broke into a soft laugh.

"Oh, come now, Clare. That is too much to ask me to believe. Clifford Bentley has been dead many years, quite too dead, poor boy, to come wandering about our garden."

"But he was there," persisted Clare stubbornly. "I tell you, Margie, I *felt* him there. Please don't laugh. I am quite serious. Oh, why can't you understand? Don't you remember his last words to you?"

Margaret's face paled under the warm color and she stared wide-eyed at her sister.

"I remember—I was to remain true to him until death joined us; and if I did not—but Clare! How absurd! He a mere boy of fifteen and I an infant of eleven! It is so ridiculous that I can't help laughing, dearest."

"It isn't ridiculous," protested Clare unhappily but positively. "Because he may be able to cause trouble between you and Ned yet. You know, Margie, you owe your life to Clifford—and if it had not been for you, he would be alive and well."

"Clare, you are positively idiotic tonight! I must insist that you go to sleep and get rid of your morbid thoughts. Why should you try to spoil my wonderful night, the most beautiful of my life?"

———

Margaret withdrew pettishly, and a few minutes afterward Clare heard her tucking herself into her own bed, that stood on the other side of their common reading stand. Slowly the lame girl slipped down into her bed again, but her eyes did not close. Still, she was not looking at the picture which she stared at; she was looking back across the years to the time when Margaret was eleven and she was nine—and Clifford Bentley fifteen.

It was a boy-and-girl love affair—precocious, to be sure. Clifford adored the little tomboy with her mop of brilliant hair and her impulsiveness and her enchanting ways. She had let him put his seal ring upon her "engagement" finger, in return for his promise to give her a ride on his iceboat. That had been a wonderful sport! Then the tragic moment came when the thin ice broke under a too sudden turn of the skeleton craft, and both children had been thrown into the icy water by the shock. It was Clifford who first came to the surface; it was he who dived and groped under the ice for Margaret, who brought her unconscious to the surface.

When rescue came, the boy's coat was wrapped about the girl's shivering form. Both children had had pneumonia from the exposure, but it was Clifford who had not survived it. His last words to his mother had been for Margaret: "Tell her I expect her to be true to me until death joins us. If she is not true, I shall come back to remind her of her promise."

Clare, reviewing the pathetic and tragic little story, felt deep sympathy for Clifford, Clifford who had given his life for Margaret and was now forgotten. She, too, would gladly have done the same. She lay very quiet, although she did not sleep.

As she heard the library clock chime the hours once, twice, she suddenly moved the handkerchief and pressed it against her lips. As she did it she breathed out a prayer for Ned Wentworth and his happiness. Then with a little sigh, she slipped softly off to sleep.

Ned Wentworth could not sleep. He filled his pipe and settled down before the hearth where glowed the urbanite's humble apology for a wood-fire, a gas log. He had felt it impossible to write while he was fresh from the sweet influence of Margaret's presence; he wanted to think over his happiness. Also, he wanted to think over another thing—an intuition he had had of a something sinister hovering near while he had been in the garden with Margaret.

Exactly as he had told his sweetheart, he had *felt* burning, envious, malignant eyes fixed upon him from the black shadows of the garden. Even when he had taken Margaret into the lighted room, he had felt this entity near at hand. Who could it be that was trying to penetrate his objective consciousness so strangely? Who could be so bitter against the man who had won Margaret's love, except some rival? He entertained not the slightest doubt that it was an unsuccessful rival whose bitter envy he had felt. But who?

He remembered distinctly that in the moment Margaret had finished her song, turning to him with all her soul in her eyes, he had felt as though someone stood between them, someone about whose person he must pass to reach her. Who could this individual be? Who was interested in separating two young people so eminently suited to each other? Ned simply could not understand the situation, yet felt that it was a tangible situation. The fact that this unknown person was strong enough to make his unseen presence strongly felt was sufficient to give thought to the young lover. But an invisible rival could not long occupy Ned's thoughts to the exclusion of pleasanter things. He mused and smoked while the hours fled.

The clock struck one. Simultaneously, Ned Wentworth sprang, as if catapulted, out of his chair, and whirled around to face the door, in full expectancy of seeing a stranger there. The doorway was vacant; it framed nothing but empty air. The young man's eye roved the apartment with keen scrutiny. There was nothing more suspicious than a tall screen that served to hide his writing desk from the rest of the room. Upon this screen Ned's glance finally rested with curious intentness. Then he shook himself impatiently and again sat down before the hearth. The impression of a strange presence was so strong, however, that he was induced to move his chair so that he faced the screen.

For fully five minutes he sat motionless, smoking. Then he rose, went directly to the screen, whirled it aside and looked behind it. Nobody there. Furious at himself for entertaining the thought of a discarnate personality, he yet found himself considering it; he was actually angry because he had given the unknown the satisfaction of seeing him look behind the screen. When he returned to his place before the hearth, he deliberately turned his chair so that the screen was behind him.

He refilled his pipe and touched a match to it nonchalantly. Stealing insidiously into his mind came thoughts of the girl who sang his *Ode to the Queen of Night* at the performances in the Bedford Theater. She was slight and graceful, lacking Margaret's robust, fearless poise; dainty and petite, while Margaret was almost too heavy to be graceful; she was charmingly pretty and knew just how to make herself fascinating, while Margaret made not the slightest pretext at using beauty aids, such as rouge, which with her dead-white skin would be so attractive. Beatrice Randall knew how to charm and fascinate a man, Ned reflected with a slow smile; Margaret, unfortunately, was entirely without that subtle mystery, that feminine art and guile that attracts the male so positively. Beatrice would go any length to enchant an admirer; Margaret would have considered such efforts beneath her. On the whole, thought Ned, when Margaret sang his *Ode,* she appeared a proud and unapproachable goddess; when Beatrice sang it, she was a most approachable, enticing, and desirable woman.

Instinctively Wentworth glanced up at the mantel shelf where a framed portrait of Margaret stood. As he looked, his brow contracted; a puzzled, almost startled expression flitted over his face. He put down his pipe. Incredulous, indignant, remorseful, he reached for the photograph and carried it to his lips.

"Three hours engaged," he said, and whistled. "Three hours engaged—and beginning to criticize Margaret! Comparing her with another woman who isn't fit to tie her shoes. "What on earth has got into me?"

Then he remembered the entrance of that sinister presence a few minutes ago. Furious indignation swept over him as he began to realize what had taken place; the thing was intolerable. A gust of futile anger shook him.... Someone with a deep interest in Margaret Sloane was attempting telepathically to turn his mind from her, and toward some other woman. He put Margaret's portrait on the table beside him and clenched his fists as he faced about toward the empty room.

Aloud he exclaimed: "Whoever you are that is trying to separate Margaret and me, you cannot prevail. We love each other! You may as well be off, my invisible rival, for I am on my guard now." He laughed grimly but shamefacedly at his spoken words. They seemed absurd, addressed to thin air, but he had the feeling that whatever or whoever it was that had entered his room and had actually succeeded for a few minutes in swaying his thoughts, this personality would understand —if not his words, his intentions.

He looked long at Margaret's portrait, his lips parting in a tender smile. Who could compare with her? Ah, there was never such a glorious girl; how could he have thought otherwise, even for a passing moment? To be sure, she was a bit over-independent, and a man enjoys the clinging-vine type of woman for a sweetheart. Beatrice Randall was just such a helpless little thing; with all her guile and her feminine arts, a man felt he must look after the child. How appealingly feminine she was when she sang his *Ode* in that entrancing "little girl" way of hers; no wonder it always brought down the house. Now Margaret had a way of surrounding herself with such an atmosphere of independence, of proud confidence in herself, that a man almost felt he would be entirely superfluous in her life. Now that she was engaged to be married, it would not be such a bad idea for her to cultivate a little more of the womanly attitude of helpless dependence that was so pretty in Beatrice.

Ned had been pacing back and forth. He stopped and stood stock still; the sickening realization swept over him that once more the unknown rival had entered into his secret thoughts and swung them away from Margaret. It was too much! He caught up a hat and stick and went out of the house to walk about under the stars; perhaps the presence would tire of following him about in the open. It may have been so; it may also have been that the unknown had done all he cared to do for one night. After a brisk hour's walk, Ned found his mind cleared of its cobwebs, and he went home, to sleep soundly.

-5-

With daylight, Ned's recollections of his uncanny experience faded as dreams in one's first waking moments; he remembered only that he had unaccountably given more thought to the prima donna in his musical comedy than he had ever given that damsel before, or ever would again, he told himself.

Ostensibly to inquire about Clare, but in reality, to assure himself of his happiness, he telephoned Margaret early.

"Clare's all right. But she's worrying herself sick over an utterly ridiculous fancy, an absurd thing she declares took place last night."

"What was that?" Ned's voice was vaguely troubled.

"Some kind of ghostly visitor who she insists visited us last night. Dad is encouraging her; yes, he is. He declares that he and Father Rooney felt the presence of an outsider in the room last night when Clare had that fainting spell. For my own part, I felt nothing. I consider the whole subject too utterly absurd for discussion."

"Not as ridiculous as it may seem at first glance, dear," Ned replied hesitantly, a sudden flood of memory rushing upon him, carrying conviction with it. "I had a rather strange experience last night, myself." Even as he said it, he hoped Margaret would not insist upon details; how would it sound in her ears that he had spent hours thinking about some other woman when he had just engaged himself to her?

"What happened, Ned?"

"Really, the thing was so intangible that it would be extremely difficult to put it into words," hedged Wentworth desperately. "Perhaps when I see you, I can explain better than I can over the telephone now."

This excuse appearing reasonable, Margaret did not insist further, much to Ned's relief. But the girl was far more troubled after this conversation than she cared to admit to herself. She fidgeted about the house, wishing it were evening; in the evening Father Rooney would surely be over to inquire about her sister, and she wanted to hear from his own lips if he had felt any supernatural experience the night before.

Margaret scoffed at the ridiculous idea that a boy of fifteen should come back from the dead to keep her from marrying another man, even granted that the boy had attained manhood in another world in the meantime. Her keen sense of humor and her abounding good health combined to restrain her thoughts from wild surmises; she merely wondered if some contagion of diseased thought had fastened upon the others of her immediate circle, leaving her untouched. This seemed far more probable to her, than that the veil separating the visible and invisible worlds could have been lifted to permit the entrance into her life of a long-dead boy sweetheart.

She did not have to wait until evening to see the old priest. About 3 o'clock she saw him entering the garden. He stopped to speak with Clare, who was basking in the sunshine.

"Cobwebs brushed away?" he asked the lame girl, pointedly.

She colored but met his eyes bravely. "Oh, yes, Father."

He looked keenly at her slightly clouded face. "Perhaps there is something I can do for you, my child?"

"I'm afraid you would be the last one to help me," she laughed ruefully. "I want to find out the name and address of a good psychic. I must talk with someone who understands—supernatural things. There is an influence abroad that bodes evil to Ned—and to my sister," she added hastily, lowering her eyes before the kindly scrutiny of the priest.

"I wish I could help you, Clare." He paused a moment, considering. "If you were only a Catholic, my child," he added regretfully.

"But it isn't religious help that I want, Father. What I need is something that I don't believe you could give me. If I only knew what to do!"

"Can't you leave it in higher hands than those of a mere mortal, my daughter? If you can do that with your whole heart, the problem will be solved for you. You believe that, do you not?"

She nodded slowly and thoughtfully. The old man passed a caressing hand over her brown locks, sighed, and went up the path with knit brow.

Margaret, impatiently waiting for him, was standing at the top of the porch steps.

"Ned called up this morning, Father," she said abruptly. "He persists in saying that he had an uncanny experience last night. My sister says the same, and Dad. Father Rooney, do you believe that a man can come back from the dead, in these days?"

"Why 'in these days?'" he inquired whimsically. "These days differ in no way from other days, Margaret; they are all a part of eternity."

"But do you?"

"What difference would it make, Margaret, what *I* believe? In the olden days, did not someone ask that same question? It is in Holy Writ, Margaret."

"You are evading my question, Father," the girl cried with an impatient shake of her head.

"What do *you* think, Margaret?" asked the old priest mildly.

"I don't know what to think. Clare says it is true. Ned—why, I actually believe he would agree with her, Dad too. Tell me, did you feel someone in the room with us last night, someone we couldn't see?"

Her question was sufficiently pointed this time for Father Rooney to get the drift of her inquiry; he smiled.

"My child, a priest becomes very intuitive, and senses presences good and evil that other people do not ordinarily feel. It is his study, his ardent prayers, his meditations alone, that make him more sensitive. And a man who employs his brain in creative work, as does Mr. Wentworth, is also liable to psychic impressions. Your dear father— why, he is a physician, and a good physician must be intuitive. While as for our little Clare—ah, her physical disability has kept her very near the Unseen; you can trust her intuitions, Margaret."

"How about me?" scornfully.

"You are far less liable to such delicate impressions because you are in robust health; your employments are active physical employments; your outlook upon life is—well, my child; largely material. There," and he raised a hand to still her quick protest, "you have not yet had a sorrow, my child. When you have suffered disillusion, disappointment, grief—then perhaps you will find yourself closer than now, to the veil that hides the Unseen."

"In other words, Father, the rest of you felt that there was a spook in the room, but for me that spook didn't exist?"

"Something like that, Margaret; something like that. I don't know but that you are better off than we are, in that respect. It is not always a pleasant thing to have these other entities thrust themselves upon one's notice without invitation."

"Well," with a slightly scornful laugh, "when I see a spirit, I shall believe that they exist and return to earth, but I fear I shall never be convinced by my own good eyes."

Little did Margaret dream as she spoke so skeptically under what circumstances her own good eyes were to teach her the frailness of the veil that separates the material and the spiritual worlds!

Father Rooney shook one finger at the young girl in half-playful admonition.

"I wish there were some way to help my little Clare," he murmured to himself as he went on into the house. "She is too suscep-tible to psychic influences. May our Lady watch over her," he finished softly and earnestly.

-6-

"Why, there comes Mrs. Campbell across the road. I wonder what she wants?" Margaret went slowly down the path to meet the visitor, stopping at Clare's side to drop her gentle hands on the lame girl's drooping shoulders.

The woman who came briskly up the bricked path was short and rather heavily built without being actually stout. Her graying hair was pulled back tightly from her round face and drawn into a "figure eight" at the nape of the neck. Although her face had not the slightest trace of actual beauty, her features were pre-possessing; there was about her that atmosphere of homely and agreeable motherliness that warms the heart. She wore a starched white linen shirtwaist and a pepper-and-salt tailored skirt, to the black belt of which was hooked a chatelaine bag of black leather. Stout black shoes completed her utili-tarian, rather than handsome, clothes.

As she approached the sisters, Clare leaned forward with a kind of breathless interest, her eyes fixed upon the newcomer. A mixture of anxiety and expectation appeared on the lame girl's face.

Mrs. Campbell did not speak until she was directly up to the girls; it would have been most unlike her to have wasted her energy upon the balmy afternoon air by speaking when there was a possibility of not being heard perfectly.

"Well, Margaret and Clare, good afternoon, both of you. Clare, I came over especially to see you," she said abruptly.

Margaret laughed musically.

"Well, that is unkind of you, Mrs. Campbell," she said. "Am I to take that as a summary dismissal?"

"You can stay if you like, Margaret, but I'm thinking that you would not believe a word I'm going to say, and I don't choose to give you the chance to laugh at me, Margaret Sloane."

Clare gasped audibly. Margaret, although accustomed to her Scotch neighbor's frankness, pretended to be offended.

"Really, Mrs. Campbell, if you think me incapable of appreciating your pearls of wisdom—"

She moved off with her swinging, easy walk, leaving Clare gazing after her with troubled eyes. The lame girl was deeply disturbed, and it was not until Margaret turned to throw her half-mocking smile that she realized her sister's pique was more apparent than real.

The Scotchwoman went directly to the heart of her message.

"My dear, do you know that there was a stranger in your garden last night?"

"Then you saw him?" gasped the girl, starting involuntarily at the other's words.

"Ah, you know, then?"

"I—I felt his presence," admitted Clare.

"Well, I saw him, and I hope I don't see him again. He isn't a pleasant individual," dryly. "Do you know who he is, Clare? Spirits like that don't usually trouble human beings unless there is some powerful tie between them. Be frank with me, my dear. I may be able to help you, and I foresee that you may need help, you and Margaret, too."

Clare drew a long breath. "His name, if I'm not mistaken, is Clifford Bentley," she began. And she plunged into the forlorn little story of the childhood romance with its tragic ending. Her listener nodded understandingly.

"Do you think he intends to make any trouble for my sister?" asked the lame girl anxiously.

"I'm afraid he does, Clare. I'll tell you what I saw. He was looking over your shoulder into the garden at Margaret. Suddenly he leaned over you, and you disappeared in a cloud of luminous vapor. But the luminosity, Clare, was not that light shed from the aura of an entity that is trying to uplift itself or others; it was the murky, red-shot vapor that betrayed the presence of evil.

"Whether it is evil for you or for Margaret, matters little, for that entity has taken advantage of your physical weakness, your psychic susceptibility, your unselfish nature, and unless you can beat off his influence, you will end by becoming little better than the instrument by which that evil thing will eventually seek to make its actual physical appearance among us."

"Mrs. Campbell! You terrify me!"

"I terrify myself," said the lady, dryly. "If you only could have seen that evil atmosphere that enveloped you—" The pause was eloquent; Clare met it with understanding eyes.

"It was that I felt, then. It was that which robbed me of consciousness. Oh, dear Mrs. Campbell, you have the wonderful gift of second sight. Can't you tell me what this all means? Why has he come back?"

The Scotchwoman nodded with the half-proud, half-mortified air of one who admits something to one's detriment, which yet one cannot help but consider a merit.

"Yes, Clare, I have the second-sight. My mother had it, and my grandmother before her. It's a wonderful thing, as you say—but not such a pleasant thing, sometimes."

"Tell me what to do, won't you? I know Mr. Campbell hates to have you exercise your power—but—isn't this an exceptional occasion?" begged the lame girl.

"Clare, I'll try." She glanced cautiously at the house as she spoke, to ascertain if Margaret were in sight. "You know, I cannot promise success. It is for this that I cannot discuss the thing with your sister; Margaret is so skeptical that I would be quite uneasy in her presence, and unable to let myself go, as I must if I wish to go into a trance."

She moved closer to the girl. "Give me your two hands, my dear," she commanded gently, her voice seeming already to come from a distance. She stood perfectly stiff for a moment, while the lame girl's whole soul was watching in her eyes.

There was not the slightest suspicion in Clare's mind as to the seeress' honesty. The Sloanes had known the Campbells for more than seven years, and no one in the suburb had anything but admiration and respect for the little Scotchwoman. Douglas Campbell, while admitting his wife's gift of second sight, was stubbornly set against her use of it; he believed it a weakening and unhealthy practice even when exercised by an effort of the will. In this Laura Campbell differed from her husband, but she was too docile a wife to question his well-meant authority—at least, in public. It is a fact that when she felt herself justified, she had no hesitation in yielding to her intuitions, and in the case of the Sloane girls her friendliness for them drove her to seek them out for the purpose, for she had seen plainly that the uninvited guest of the previous night was an undesirable, and might prove a troublesome, visitor.

———

After a long moment, during which Clare felt her heart beating loudly and painfully, the Scotchwoman began to speak. Her intonation was stiff and harsh, the very opposite of her customary rapid, easy speech. The words dropped off her lips slowly, one by one, with monotonous regularity. Meantime her hands gripped those of the lame girl with a grip that made Clare wince.

"You—seek—to—learn—the—reason—for—my—presence. You —shall—know—soon—enough. Tell—Margaret—that—she—must —never—marry—Ned—Wentworth. While—you—live—I—have—

the—means—to—prevent—it—but—I—will—not—trouble—her —if—she—will—keep—her—vow—to—me."

"Oh!" Clare Sloane cried out suddenly as if in acute pain.

The seeress gave a deep sigh, shuddered from head to foot, and closed her eyes tightly. Then she released the hands she had been holding so tightly, and opened her eyes, to see the lame girl laboring for breath, her head thrown back on the cushions.

"Margaret! Margaret! Bring your sister's tablets!"

Mrs. Campbell began to stroke and beat at one of the delicate hands, while she looked anxiously toward the house. Margaret came running down the path, a glass of water in one hand and Clare's medicine in the other. She threw a reproachful look at their neighbor, as she hastily began to minister to her sister.

"What on earth did you tell Clare, to upset her like this?" asked the older girl, indignantly.

"I'm sorry, Margaret, but I can't tell you what upset her."

"You mean, you *won't* tell me," flashed the girl.

"No, I mean just what I said. She's reviving—look, the color is coming into her cheeks again."

"What did you do? Did you try any of that trance business?"

"Clare asked me to try it for her," replied the other woman quickly. "It was to help her out about something," she hesitated.

"And you mean to tell me," Margaret said scornfully, "that you don't know what you told her?"

"You're going a little too far, Margaret," rebuked the Scotchwoman, indignant in her turn. "I'm not accustomed to having my word disputed. If you knew anything at all about the nature of a trance, you would know that the medium is never aware of what is said."

"Oh, I believe you," hastily. "Clare, darling, are you feeling better now?"

Clare was breathing more naturally, and her cheeks were not as pallid as they had been a moment since. Her hands were still cold to the solicitous Margaret's touch, and the girl began chafing them. Clare, as soon as she could speak, began to beg brokenly, "Oh, can you tell me what he meant? Was it you talking? Or was it he, speaking with your lips?"

"He?" Mrs. Campbell's lips parted; she looked strangely at the lame girl. "What did I say? Tell me everything, Clare. Don't forget a single word."

Clare repeated it, to the best of her ability.

"I don't like that," said the Scotchwoman anxiously. "He means, that while you live, he can control you psychically, gathering from you the force to make himself felt unpleasantly on this plane. The alternative is," and she directed her gaze sharply and narrowly at Margaret, who colored under it resentfully, "the alternative is, that Margaret keeps her vow to him, her vow never to marry."

"In other words, Mrs. Campbell, my sister must pay for my happiness with her life, or I must pay for her life with my happiness? Excuse me," coldly, "but I think you go too far with this mysterious jargon. Come, Clare dear, the sun is sinking. Let me help you into the house."

The Scotchwoman silently assisted in drawing Clare to her feet and adjusted the crutches, while Margaret picked up the cushions upon which the lame girl had been reclining. As the sisters went slowly up the path to the house, she stood watching them, with perturbed countenance.

"It's bad. It's very, very bad. And Margaret won't believe the peril she is in. Poor Clare! I must tell Douglas of this. If it comes to the worst, he'll have to permit me to make up a circle, and Dr. Sloane will have to override Margaret's objections—for object she surely will, unless she falls into the sphere of influence of that unwelcome guest, herself. I can only watch—and pray," she whispered to herself.

-7-

Ned Wentworth was an impulsive lover. Moreover, his uncanny obsession on the night of his engagement to Margaret had weighed on his mind; he felt that the sooner they were married, the sooner the unseen rival for the girl's affections would be induced to leave the field to him. He lost no time, therefore, in urging an early marriage upon Margaret.

His plans met with Dr. Sloane's approval. The old man was relieved to see at least one of his girls happily married and provided for. In secret he grieved much for his younger daughter, whose lameness might prove a serious obstacle to her satisfactory settlement in life. He agreed that Ned and Margaret should be married very quietly early in the coming month, and that after the wedding the young pair should make an extended trip through the Southwest.

Margaret's days became an orgy of shopping expeditions. Her nights were occupied with dreams of the happy future she was going to spend with her lover. The ominous and mysterious words of Mrs. Campbell had apparently been erased from her mind. Not so with Clare; the lame girl remembered with terrible distinctness the dilemma that her sister had so tersely and indignantly stated; one of the two must pay for the other's life or happiness by sacrificing her own.

To do Margaret full justice, she would not knowingly have accepted happiness at the expense of her younger sister, but she had dismissed the words of the seeress as fantastic vaporing, unworthy of consideration. Clare, however, had been deeply impressed; she spent hours pondering on them. If her death would purchase Margaret's happiness, the lame girl was ready to surrender it. She did not put into words her secret thought, that Margaret's happiness was also the happiness of Ned Wentworth.

Time flew. Margaret's wedding was so near at hand that when Clare looked at the calendar on the wall of their room, she found but a single day remaining before the older sister would leave her home for the new life that spread with so much rich promise before her. Day by day Clare had prayed fervently for strength to resist any fresh attacks upon her psychic forces by the entity which she knew as Clifford Bentley. Once or twice Clare, now watchful and alert, had felt the certain indications of Clifford's presence; the failing of her vital powers that preceded the entrance of the spirit-lover so convincingly, if invisibly, into the material world. As yet she had been able to fight him off, and this gave her confidence in her ability to save her sister from the annoyance, if nothing more, that Clifford's influence might bring to bear upon either Margaret or Ned.

The night before the wedding Ned did not drop in as he had expected; he telephoned to Margaret that he was not feeling quite himself but would undoubtedly be all right in the morning. His words were mild in comparison to what he was experiencing. For several days he had been fighting off an obsession even worse than the mild one that had overcome him on the night of his engagement to Margaret. He had not dared be off his guard for a moment. As surely as he permitted his thoughts to wander ever so slightly, he felt them getting beyond his control, until his head would be awhirl with incoherencies and strange conjectures that tormented him cruelly.

He began to "remember" incidents that concerned Margaret, but in which he figured as a principal; incidents in which he knew at the same time that he had never taken part. One time he found himself saying aloud with persistence, "I am Clifford Bentley! I am Clifford Bentley!" until he caught himself up with what was almost terror clutching at his heart.

Intuition told him that Clifford Bentley must be the rival now making such desperate efforts to cause trouble between Margaret and himself. Ned swore that he would not give her up, no matter what the cost of keeping her might be. As his determination on this point increased, so did the insidious attacks upon his mental stronghold by the invisible rival.

The night before his wedding Ned had come to the point where he was half dead for want of sleep. His apprehensions had grown so strong that he had been keeping himself awake night after night with strong coffee, fearing to relax his guard for a single moment. That night he could hold out no longer; he was obliged to give way to sleep for a few hours; flesh and blood could stand no more.

When he waked the next day, he found to his consternation that he had overslept. It was already noon, and as the wedding was set for 3 o'clock, he had no more time than was absolutely necessary to dress and motor out to Dr. Sloane's. He paid little or no attention to a dull ache in his head, and a tingling, pricking sensation that occasionally shot through his body; if he thought of it at all, it was as the natural result of his sleeplessness for several nights, and the consequent nervous strain. Certain it is that he did not think of it as having any connection with Clifford Bentley.

The wedding was to be a very quiet one, the only outside person present being Father Rooney. Margaret was to be unattended. Had she chosen a bridesmaid, it would have been Clare, but the lame girl insisted that her crutches would have made a distressingly inharmonious appearance. The bride came into the room on her father's arm, the old doctor having managed to brace up sufficiently to go through the short ceremony of giving his daughter away.

Near the officiating clergyman, who had been placed near the window opening on the garden, stood the bridegroom. Ned also was unattended; he had decided that he was fully able to take care of Margaret's wedding ring without any outside assistance. As his bride approached, the young man turned his head toward her. A sudden horror and dismay seized upon him. As he looked, he became aware that, strangely enough, his emotions were so complex as to convince him, without a struggle, that *he was at once himself and that other*! In vain he fought against that terrible obsession; he could do nothing to drive out the triumphant rival who had entered his mind, his body. In despair he cast down his eyes, dreading lest others might read in them the strange and awful thing that had befallen him.

Margaret approached, her head bent, her eyes on the flowers she carried. The clergyman began to read from his prayerbook. Ned could feel the gentle presence of the girl he loved, as she paused beside him. When the clergyman addressed the question to Ned that would bind him to her, it seemed to him that the intruding personality was laughing at him as it whipped the replies out of his very mouth, responding with a decisive abruptness that caused the minister to send a quick glance at the brush bridegroom. Ned was praying for the ceremony to close.

The minister addressed the bride: "Wilt thou take this man to be thy wedded husband?"

Wentworth's heart pumped madly. In a moment it would be over. A silence succeeded to the clergyman's question, a silence that endured—that weighed down every heart. Ned lifted his head and sought Margaret's eyes in astonishment.

She was looking at him, horror on her amazed face. The flowers she was carrying fell tumbling at her feet from relaxed fingers. She took an instinctive step backward and put one hand behind her gropingly, as though seeking support. Still, she stared at him incredulously. The clergyman, not understanding, prompted her in an undertone. With a sharp anguish that cut the young lover's heart, her voice rang out wildly.

"No—no—no!" she screamed and sank back unconscious into the arms of her father.

-8-

Consternation on every face. Clare had dropped hers into both hands and was sobbing and praying behind that frail shield. Dr. Sloane stood, holding his fainting daughter as if he had been turned into stone and unable to move. The clergyman had closed his prayer-book and gazed in bewilderment at the fainting bride and the agonized, astounded groom.

Only Father Rooney grasped the situation even faintly. He it was who relieved the old doctor of his burden and carried Margaret to the divan. It was he who motioned everyone but the young lover from the room. He held salts to the girl's nostrils, while he questioned Ned with a single look of sympathetic inquiry.

"I don't know! That's the worst of it, I don't know," Ned groaned miserably. "Father, I haven't been quite myself since the night we became engaged. Do you suppose—she could have—felt the difference? I can imagine nothing else that would have turned her against me so suddenly and incomprehensibly."

"Do you mean, my poor boy, that you have felt that invisible presence again? That—that it has become an obsession?"

"Exactly. I have fought it for days. But last night—I had lost so much sleep," apologetically, "I could not keep awake. That was *its* chance, I suppose. This morning I have been feeling strange when I come to think of it." Hurriedly Ned recounted his experiences with the invisible rival who had taken possession of his very self that afternoon, replying to the minister's questions through the lips of the obsessed.

The old priest nodded his head wisely. "I think I understand, my son. It is a strange condition, and a difficult one. I hardly know what to advise you."

Ned stood looking down at the unconscious girl, his eyes melancholy. "I can only fight until I can go on with it no longer," he said despairingly. "But how am I to continue fighting with an invisible entity that takes advantage of me in my unguarded moments of sleep?"

"Do you feel the presence at this moment?" demanded Father Rooney.

"N-no, I think not. That is," correcting himself, "I feel that it is somewhere near, but not controlling me for the time being."

Father Rooney hastily crossed himself. "For the time being, Ned, there is nothing for you to do but to keep away from Margaret. Whatever this unknown entity is, its interest seems to be in keeping you two apart. Until you feel yourself complete master of the situation, it will be best for you to leave Margaret alone."

"I feel that strongly, but—it will be very hard, Father."

"Would you bring worse upon the woman you love?" said the priest gravely. "Believe me, my son, this matter will have to be solved by other power than yours or mine. I am persuaded, however, that your wisest course now will be to leave Margaret."

The young man bent, pressed a tender kiss upon the forehead of the girl who was to have been his wife, and went sadly from the room. Dr. Sloane and Clare were waiting for him in the hall; their anxious eyes questioned him.

"The marriage must be postponed. And Father Rooney feels that it will be wiser for me not to be here when Margaret comes out of her faint. I'll telephone later to learn how our dear girl is getting along."

Dr. Sloane patted his shoulder. "Cheer up, Ned. I think it's nothing more than the result of nervous strain. Wedding preparations have been too much for Margie. But I certainly never would have thought she'd keel over like that; she's so athletic and in such fine condition. Well, she'll be all right in a couple of days, and then we'll have you two tied up in a jiffy and off on your honeymoon."

Clare, who knew only too well what must be the root of the trouble, although she could not know the exact circumstances, dared not meet Ned's eyes, so disturbed was she. "I shall be praying for you, Ned," she whispered timidly, as she slipped away to assist the good priest in his ministrations.

Margaret revived presently and sat up, controlling herself with a strong effort. "I want to be alone, please," she said. "Clare, I don't mind you, of course." Her eyes dropped down upon her traveling gown. "I must take off these things," she said sadly.

As she rose to leave the room, her self-control gave way; tears gushed from her eyes, blinding her until she had to lean against the lame girl for guidance.

"Oh, it is cruel!" she sobbed. "What have we done to deserve this persecution? Tell Ned, Dad, that it isn't his fault, but I can't explain just now. I hope—I hope he will forgive me."

———

The girls went to their room, their tears mingling.

The day wore away. Ned telephoned in and received Margaret's message, to which she had added that it was her conviction their marriage could never take place, but that she would always love him— a message that half maddened the unhappy young man.

The sisters retired early, although there was no sleep for either of them for hours. Clare won her sister's confidence at last; Margaret confided to her the reason for the "no" that should have been "yes." Ned's obsession by the determined spirit of Clifford Bentley had been so plainly discernible by the girl that she had refused to marry him, because she felt it would not have been Ned she was marrying, but the intruding personality of that long-dead childhood sweetheart. The horror of the situation had been too much for her self-control. The bizarre idea of becoming the wife of two men in one body had forced from her that decisive, agonized negative.

Clare calmed her as best she might, both girls prayed together, and about half past 11 they fell asleep, exhausted by their emotions.

It was, as the girls ascertained afterward, shortly after midnight that Margaret awoke from troubled dreams. The room was in partial darkness. As she shook off her drowsiness, she became aware of arms about her, and a face that pressed close against her own. The thought flashed through her gratefully that her sister had been watching and praying over her; she turned her lips to meet those others that sought hers.

The kiss undeceived her; *that was no sister's kiss!*

With convulsive nervous force Margaret drew herself away from the arms that had been holding her and sat up in bed, half dazed. For an instant she imagined that the events of the afternoon had been a dream, and that it was the kiss of her young husband that had just been pressed upon her lips. And then she knew that it was no dream.

The soft light of the night lamp fell upon the face of a young man, a complete stranger, who in his turn rose from the kneeling posture he had been maintaining by the side of her bed. Although she had never seen that face as an adult face, the terrified girl knew intuitively that she was looking upon the features of Clifford Bentley, who had succeeded at last in making himself visible and tangible.

She felt her senses slipping weakly from her control. She was convinced that this would be fatal, as she had not the slightest confidence in the kindly intentions of that dead lover from the unknown world. With all her might she gripped at courage and stared that dead-alive entity squarely in the deep eyes that burned passionately upon her with a significance that froze the coursing blood in her veins; Margaret Sloane was no coward, but she had never shaken and trembled as she did that night, in the throes of an unearthly fear.

"What do you want?" she managed to whisper through dry lips.

"You!"

"Why do you come back to torment me? That was a child's silly promise—you cannot hold me to it."

"I can—and will!" The apparition, doubly terrible because of its tangibility, moved toward her.

"No—no!" She thrust out protesting hands wildly. "Don't come nearer! If you do, I shall scream! I cannot bear it!"

Clifford Bentley leaned toward her, smiling with white teeth showing between red lips, and regarding the shrinking, horrified girl meaningly. "You fear me—yet you have tasted my warm kisses," he whispered. "Do you think my rival will want you now, silly Margie?"

Margaret's brain began to whirl. Surmises too dreadful to shape into words prodded her mind sharply. She threw herself desperately from the bed, anywhere, away from that triumphantly smiling face, and began to scream.

Shriek after shriek rang through the startled house.

The figure of Clifford Bentley retired around the foot of Margaret's bed and approached that of Clare. Before the older sister's staring, incredulous eyes he leaned over the sleeping girl—and the next instant he had disappeared, like a dissipating vapor, from her sight.

-9-

The screams of his older daughter brought the doctor stumbling from his room across the hall. He entered abruptly to find Margaret on the floor in a dead faint, and Clare sitting up in bed rubbing her eyes, apparently half dazed. Inquiry failed to elicit anything further than that Margaret had had a nightmare which had so terrified her that she had sprung from bed to fall unconscious on the floor.

After she had been revived and tucked into bed again, and her father had left the girls alone, Clare made her sister tell the whole unbelievable story, while both glanced fearfully over their shoulders into the dim shadows of the room. As Margaret finished, her voice broken with sobs, her eyes wide with her unspoken fears, the lame girl exclaimed with indignation, "He is cruel, Margie, and a coward, to behave like this."

"I can't help being terribly afraid. Who can tell how far his power will carry him?" confessed the half-hysterical Margaret.

Clare was silent. She, too, was afraid. More, she was remembering with poignant emotion the last words the seeress had spoken to her. The lame girl pressed both hands tightly against her laboring heart, that beat so painfully in her bosom. Gladly she would have stilled its beating, could she have known surely that the act would purchase immunity for Margaret and happiness for Ned.

"Margie, the first thing we must do in the morning is to see Mrs. Campbell," she said at last. "She can help us if anyone can. Don't try to dissuade me, dear; you must admit that even a forlorn hope is worth snatching at, now."

Margaret had so far lost her former high spirits and self-confidence that she would have assented willingly to whatever plans Clare might have proposed. Still, she could not help questioning Mrs. Campbell's ability to find a way out of the terrible and tortuous maze in which she and Ned seemed lost.

"Do you really believe there is anything extraordinary about Laura Campbell's trances, Clare?" she asked earnestly. "I've always wondered at the loss of dignity such feigning costs her."

"She really has what they call second-sight, Margie. I've seen her myself, in trances. Not often, because Mr. Campbell hates to have her give way to them. But the day we were in the garden and I had that heart attack—you remember?—she spoke with the voice of a man, and—I knew, somehow, that it was he." Her own tones were modified as she spoke, and she glanced timorously about her.

"Well," conceded Margaret unhappily, "I suppose we ought to do everything we can—and if she is able to help us, I know Mr. Campbell will let her. But I can't help being skeptical; it all seems so foolish and childish to me. Of course, if you want me to, I'll run over and ask her if she can help us out."

"Oh, Margie, if you only would!" urged Clare earnestly.

Margaret accordingly went across the road to their Scotch neighbor's home and related to Laura Campbell the story of the "nightmare" she had had the previous night. The quiet-faced woman listened in grim silence, a non-committal expression on her round, motherly countenance. Only the continuous snapping of the catch of the chatelaine betrayed her nervousness.

"You'll have to make up a circle and hold a séance and call him," she said with finality.

"I don't see why," shrank the girl.

"You don't see why? You foolish girl, you make me lose all patience with you!"

"But—"

"'But' nothing!" snapped the Scotchwoman with asperity. "You are an ungrateful girl, Margaret Sloane. And a blindly selfish one, too, if you want my frank opinion. Your sister Clare is being slowly killed; all her vital forces are being drawn out of her by that—that male vampire—that satellite of your attractions. And you—you draw back at the only chance to make terms with him! I'm sure I don't know what you can be thinking of."

Margaret's color was running high. "I had no idea that my sister was in danger of any kind," she retorted spiritedly. "But the mere suggestion of such a thing is sufficient to make me agree to any plan, no matter how idiotic it may appear. Will you undertake to conduct a séance for us?" abruptly.

"Have someone telephone your fiancé to be at your home this evening at 8 o'clock. See that arrangements are made so that we can have the entire evening undisturbed by visitors. I will be over as soon as Mr. Campbell has gone to his lodge; it's fortunate tonight is lodge night, or you'd have to wait. My husband would not give me his permission to act as medium at your séance, so I've got to do it behind his back. And I can assure you, Margaret Sloane, that isn't a pleasant thing for me to do."

Margaret, confronted with the possibility that her neighbor might repent her offer, was transformed from scorner to suppliant. Her eyes pleaded eloquently.

"Get along with you, Margaret," snorted the Scotchwoman with feigned indignation. "Asking me to deceive my good Douglas, are you? There, there, don't worry, my dear. Laura Campbell has never yet turned her back on anyone who really needed her help. I'll be over at 8 o'clock."

Margaret did not feel up to talking directly with Ned, and begged Clare to telephone for her. Ned was in his rooms, happily, and almost out of his head with joy at hearing that a possible solution of the weird problem might be reached so soon. He promised to be at Dr. Sloane's at the appointed hour.

————

Clare was sitting on the porch that evening at about half past 7, when she saw the bowed figure of Father Rooney approaching through the dusk. He came up slowly, and seated himself on the top step, fanning himself with his broad-brimmed hat, for the day had been a hot one.

"I don't know that you'll want to stay this evening, Father," the lame girl said to him timidly. "Father won't be free to play chess with you tonight. You see, we're going to do something of which you won't approve—we're going to hold a séance, to see if we can't learn how to get out of the strange situation in which we seem to have been thrown."

Father Rooney stopped fanning himself. His hat half hid his face from the girl, as he looked sharply at her over its wide brim. There was an anxious note in his voice.

"A séance, my daughter? Is your father permitting it? Does he consider it a wise thing for—well, Clare, for you, my child? I'm speaking not only as a priest, but from the physician's standpoint."

Clare returned his grave query with a serene smile. "Oh, I don't believe it can do me any harm," she said thoughtfully. "Do you suppose anything could hurt me more than to believe that some malicious spirit is robbing me daily of strength in order to torment my poor sister? Besides, I'd rather risk a—a heart attack, Father, than continue to go through what I've been suffering for weeks."

Father Rooney sighed. Too well he knew the self-sacrifice that was the dominant note in Clare's nature.

"I cannot attend such a meeting, my child, as you know. But—I think I shall remain. I can pray for you and yours—it may well be that God sent me here for just that tonight—when you may need spiritual help more than ever in your lives before."

He rose to greet the doctor and Ned, who had been walking in the grounds.

Ned had not entered the house as yet, fearing a repetition of the terrible scene that had taken place on the ill-fated day of the wedding. For although he had been feeling himself almost entirely free from his obsession since he had kept away from Margaret, how could he know when it might return in force?

"Coming in?" he asked the priest.

"I will sit out here," observed Father Rooney. "Here I can watch the stars."

Mrs. Campbell came up the bricked path at this juncture, and the whole party, with the exception of the good priest, went indoors.

Margaret was sitting on the divan in the front room. As Ned entered, she rose to her feet and put out both hands, while tears sprang to her eyes and relied piteously down her cheeks.

"My poor Ned, can you ever forgive me?" she murmured brokenly.

"There is nothing to forgive," he whispered. "Oh, Margie, let us hope that tonight may open a way for us out of the tangle that seems to have been made of our happiness."

Mrs. Campbell interposed, with her usual briskness.

"Better for you to keep your exchanges of affection for a later moment," she said decidedly. "I sympathize with you, but every moment you are enraging yet more the entity who has proved powerful enough to have made a fine tangle of your affairs. Dr. Sloane, will you and Mr. Wentworth arrange the chairs so that we can sit in a circle?"

She busied herself with the preliminary arrangements for the seance, her every movement followed closely by the lame girl.

Clare sat apart from the rest, hands folded tightly in her lap, eyes dark with melancholy. When everything had been arranged to her satisfaction, the Scotchwoman indicated to each their places in the circle. She seated Ned at her left, Clare at her right; Dr. Sloane sat on the other side of the lame girl, and Margaret—half glad, half afraid—between lover and father.

The lights were turned out. Only a small night lamp, its tiny wick floating on the oil, stood upon the table at the other end of the room. In that flickering and barely discernible light, the faces of the sitters flashed into and out of sight at every draft of air that floated in at the garden window.

The seeress, tense and watchful, maintained her hold on Clare's hand with gentle force. She felt the lame girl sink back in her chair limply, with a kind of half-sob, half-sigh. The doctor spoke in hushed tones.

"I'm afraid Clare is fainting," he worried.

"I guarantee that she is all right for the time being," replied the psychic quickly. "She has slipped off into a trance. Do not try to waken her. It is better so. I shall direct, instead of becoming the medium myself, for Clare is to be our medium tonight. Now we shall be able to see and talk with Mr. Clifford Bentley."

Hardly had the words left her lips before Margaret, holding tightly to the hands of father and lover, gave a sharp exclamation.

Standing directly behind Clare's chair was the figure of Clifford Bentley, his white face and burning eyes fixed upon the unhappy bride with passionate intensity.

-10-

Ned spoke impulsively, half rising as he cried out, "You miserable scoundrel!" His eyes flashed angrily.

Mrs. Campbell maintained her grip on his hand and drew him down firmly. "Sit down, Mr. Wentworth. This is no time to call names." She addressed the newcomer with cold courtesy. "I see that you have anticipated our wishes. We are here tonight especially to talk with you."

"I know—I know," muttered the newcomer fiercely. "I understood that you intended to meddle, and I came before I was called, of my own accord. Otherwise, you would have had the mortification of not seeing me in spite of all your calling." He laughed shortly. "I want to save all my strength, however, to appear to Margie, my false, lovely Margie," he added insinuatingly.

"This is really too much," exclaimed Ned, trying in vain to extricate his hand from the iron hold of the psychic. "I intend to see if that fellow is solid enough to feel the weight of my fist. Let me go, please!"

The Scotchwoman's strong hand maintained its immovable grip, and she turned to shake her head warningly at him. Then she spoke again to the intruder.

"You have been taking the psychic energy from this poor little lame girl, so that you could appear materially. For shame, Clifford Bentley! No matter what your motive, do you consider that a manly thing to do? What has Clare ever done to you, that you should subject her to such treatment? Look at the poor child now, helpless, her disturbed spirit torn with agony as she sees you clothed in the psychic vitality you have stolen from her in order to destroy her sister's happiness! Does not that stir your heart with remorse and pity?"

"It is entirely up to Margaret," replied the materialized Clifford. "I loved Margie. She promised to be my wife. She let me put my ring on her finger. She is morally bound to me. Now she is betraying me, for that other—that weak fellow whose silly brain I can sway as I choose," scornfully.

"That is a lie!"

This time Ned would have torn his hand from Mrs. Campbell's had she not cried hastily, "Mr. Wentworth, beware of what you are doing! If you so much as injure a hair of his head, the harm done him will rebound—it will result in serious suffering to this little lame girl, entranced in our circle."

"It seems I find friends wherever I go," observed Clifford Bentley, with a mocking intonation that infuriated Wentworth. "Even Margie," he went on with pointed and deliberate malice, "lay in my arms last night, and returned my warm kisses with her own! She cannot deny it, can you, Margie?"

Ned, his tanned skin pallid with unutterable horror and loathing, turned wide eyes upon the face of the girl whose hand he held; her lids dropped before his accusing gaze.

"Margie!" he groaned. "It isn't true, dear?"

"It might be well, Mr. Wentworth, to refrain from questions and accusations for the time being," observed Mrs. Campbell dryly. "You should be ashamed to think evil of the woman you love. Mr. Clifford Bentley, you have been telling a lie that is half-truth, and that is the basest of lies. I must ask you now to tell the exact truth, or I shall waken Clare—you know I can do it—and after you have returned to your etheric form, I shall take certain steps that will result in your being bound down for many years as you may not care to be bound. Oh, you may smile! I assure you I can do this, much as I dislike it, and much as it may cost me. Are you going to speak?"

Somewhat sulkily, the unwelcome Clifford turned from her. "Oh, I suppose I must not refuse a lady's request, especially since it is put so persuasively," and he smiled sourly. "Very well, then—I lied about Margie. *I* kissed *her*. To be sure, she kissed me, too—but she didn't know it was I. But what does it matter, my dear lady?" he went on to Mrs. Campbell sarcastically. "If Margie won't remain true to her promise of her own free will, I shall have to see to it that she keeps her word and remains unwed. As long as Clare lives, I shall be able to get what I need to make myself not only visible, but tangible. Perhaps Margie won't like the idea of that," he finished, turning his terrible, burning eyes upon Margaret.

"As long as Clare lives?" said the seeress, very slowly and gravely. "And—when she shall have passed over—?"

"When she joins me here, I shall have a companion whom I can love. When I cannot come back anymore, I shall remain with her. She has a tender heart; she would be kind to me. I have been so lonesome here—no one knows how lonesome!"

Another voice fell clearly upon the ears of those present. All recognized it as Clare's, although it sounded far away. The words issued slowly but distinctly from the entranced girl's lips.

"Margie—Dad—Ned—I can see you and hear you, although I am not in my poor sick body. All is well with me. Don't forget that. *All is well with me here.* I am very happy. Here all is life and light. I am not lame here. I can run as Margie runs in our garden. Don't call me back! I am so happy here! I can be near you all when I please—and I feel no pain—only such a happiness as I never felt before. You won't call me back to limp on my crutches again, will you, dear ones?"

Clifford Bentley began wringing his hands with a kind of tense anguish that was terrible to behold. Now his voice rang out clearly.

"Oh, I have done wrong. I see it now. Poor little Clare! It is my fault that you will not return. I have made your earth life wretched, poor child. Forgive me, little Clare. I promise never to trouble Margie again, for your sake!"

"Poor Clifford!" How heavenly sweet were the tones of Clare's faraway voice! "You were lonely. Now I understand. And I cannot blame you, poor lonely Clifford. After all, you must not reproach yourself—I shall be happier here—I can be with my dear ones as I choose—and I shall suffer no more with a weak heart and useless feet."

The figure of the entranced girl sank lower in the chair. The psychic cried out suddenly as she felt that cold hand pulling on her own warm one.

"Turn on the lights!" she commanded, her voice agitated and alarmed. "Oh, why did I consent to this! I know what Douglas will say to me, now."

Margaret, almost holding her breath, heard a soft whisper in her ear. "Good-bye, my Margie. I shall always be near you. God bless you."

Ned, still holding his sweetheart's hand tightly in his own, felt a soft cheek brush his, and he trembled on the verge of tears. Something told him it was Clare's farewell to him.

———

Dr. Sloane fumbled for the electric switch. As he put out his hand to turn it on, the figure of Clifford Bentley dissolved into thin nothingness before the eyes of the dazed members of the circle.

The door opened softly.

Father Rooney, his old face pale and drawn, tiptoed into the room. Without a word he went to Clare's side, passing the Scotch-woman, who stood looking sadly down upon the lame girl's slight figure. Upon the white brow he made the sign of a cross reverently. Then he faced the others, a sob rising chokingly in his throat as he spoke, his eyes meeting those of the doctor pityingly.

"Her spirit passed me as I waited without. Our little Clare is with the angels."

PICKMAN'S MODEL
by
·H·P·LOVECRAFT·

"He had painted a monstrous being on that awful canvas."

You needn't think I'm crazy, Eliot—plenty of others have queerer prejudices than this. Why don't you laugh at Oliver's grandfather, who won't ride in a motor? If I don't like that damned subway, it's my own business; and we got here more quickly anyhow in the taxi. We'd have had to walk up the hill from Park Street if we'd taken the car.

I know I'm more nervous than I was when you saw me last year, but you don't need to hold a clinic over it. There's plenty of reason, God knows, and I fancy I'm lucky to be sane at all. Why the third degree? You didn't use to be so inquisitive.

Well, if you must hear it, I don't know why you shouldn't. Maybe you ought to, anyhow, for you kept writing me like a grieved parent when you heard I'd begun to cut the Art Club and keep away from Pickman. Now that he's disappeared, I go around to the club once in a while, but my nerves aren't what they were.

No, I don't know what's become of Pickman, and I don't like to guess. You might have surmised I had some inside information when I dropped him—and that's why I don't want to think where he's gone. Let the police find what they can—it won't be much, judging from the fact that they don't know yet of the old North End place he hired under the name of Peters. I'm not sure that I could find it again myself—not that I'd ever try, even in broad daylight! Yes, I do know, or am afraid I know, why he maintained it. I'm coming to that. And I think you'll understand before I'm through why I don't tell the police. They would ask me to guide them, but I couldn't go back there even if I knew the way. There was something there—and now I can't use the subway or (and you may as well have your laugh at this, too) go down into cellars anymore.

I should think you'd have known I didn't drop Pickman for the same silly reasons that fussy old women like Dr. Reid or Joe Minot or Bosworth did. Morbid art doesn't shock me, and when a man has the genius Pickman had I feel it an honor to know him, no matter what direction his work takes. Boston never had a greater painter than Richard Upton Pickman. I said it at first and I say it still, and I never swerved an inch, either, when he showed that *Ghoul Feeding*. That, you remember, was when Minot cut him.

You know, it takes profound art and profound insight into nature to turn out stuff like Pickman's. Any magazine-cover hack can splash paint around wildly and call it a nightmare or a Witches' Sabbath or a portrait of the devil, but only a great painter can make such a thing really scare or ring true. That's because only a real artist knows the actual anatomy of the terrible or the physiology of fear—the exact sort of lines and proportions that connect up with latent instincts or hereditary memories of fright, and the proper color contrasts and lighting effects to stir the dormant sense of strangeness. I don't have to tell you why a Fuseli really brings a shiver while a cheap ghost-story frontispiece merely makes us laugh. There's something those fellows catch—beyond life—that they're able to make us catch for a second. Doré had it. Sime has it. Angarola of Chicago has it. And Pickman had it as no man ever had it before or—I hope to heaven—ever will again.

Don't ask me what it is they see. You know, in ordinary art, there's all the difference in the world between the vital, breathing things drawn from nature or models and the artificial truck that commercial small fry reel off in a bare studio by rule. Well, I should say that the really weird artist has a kind of vision which makes models, or summons up what amounts to actual scenes from the spectral world he lives in. Anyhow, he manages to turn out results that differ from the pretender's mince-pie dreams in just about the same way that the life painter's results differ from the concoctions of a correspondence-school cartoonist. If I had ever seen what Pickman saw—but no! Here, let's have a drink before we get any deeper. Gad, I wouldn't be alive if I'd ever seen what that man—if he was a man—saw!

You recall that Pickman's forte was faces. I don't believe anybody since Goya could put so much of sheer hell into a set of features or a twist of expression. And before Goya you have to go back to the medi-aeval chaps who did the gargoyles and chimaeras on Notre Dame and Mont Saint-Michel. They believed all sorts of things—and maybe they saw all sorts of things, too, for the Middle Ages had some curious phases. I remember your asking Pickman yourself once, the year before you went away, wherever in thunder he got such ideas and visions. Wasn't that a nasty laugh he gave you? It was partly because of that laugh that Reid dropped him. Reid, you know, had just taken up comparative pathology, and was full of pompous "inside stuff" about the biological or evolutionary significance of this or that mental or physical symptom. He said Pickman repelled him more and more every day, and almost frightened him toward the last—that the fellow's features and expression were slowly developing in a way he didn't like; in a way that wasn't human. He had a lot of talk about diet and said Pickman must be abnormal and eccentric to the last degree. I suppose you told Reid, if you and he had any correspondence over it, that he'd let Pickman's paintings get on his nerves or harrow up his imagination. I know I told him that myself—then.

But keep in mind that I didn't drop Pickman for anything like this. On the contrary, my admiration for him kept growing; for that "Ghoul Feeding" was a tremendous achievement. As you know, the club wouldn't exhibit it, and the Museum of Fine Arts wouldn't accept it as a gift; and I can add that nobody would buy it, so Pickman had it right in his house till he went. Now his father has it in Salem— you know Pickman comes of old Salem stock and had a witch ancestor hanged in 1692.

———

I got into the habit of calling on Pickman quite often, especially after I began making notes for a monograph on weird art. Probably it was his work which put the idea into my head, and anyhow, I found him a mine of data and suggestions when I came to develop it. He showed me all the paintings and drawings he had about; including some pen-and-ink sketches that would, I verily believe, have got him kicked out of the club if many of the members had seen them. Before long I was pretty nearly a devotee and would listen for hours like a schoolboy to art theories and philosophic speculations wild enough to qualify him for the Danvers asylum. My hero-worship, coupled with the fact that people generally were commencing to have less and less to do with him, made him get very confidential with me; and one evening he hinted that if I were fairly close-mouthed and none too squeamish, he might show me something rather unusual—something a bit stronger than anything he had in the house.

"You know," he said, "there are things that won't do for Newbury Street—things that are out of place here, and that can't be conceived here, anyhow. It's my business to catch the overtones of the soul, and you won't find those in a parvenu set of artificial streets on made land. Back Bay isn't Boston—it isn't anything yet because it's had no time to pick up memories and attract local spirits. If there are any ghosts here, they're the tame ghosts of a salt marsh and a shallow cove; and I want human ghosts—the ghosts of beings highly organized enough to have looked on hell and known the meaning of what they saw.

"The place for an artist to live is the North End. If any aesthete were sincere, he'd put up with the slums for the sake of the massed traditions. God, man! Don't you realize that places like that weren't merely *made*, but actually *grew*? Generation after generation lived and felt and died there, and in days when people weren't afraid to live and feel and die. Don't you know there was a mill on Copp's Hill in 1632, and that half the present streets were laid out by 1650? I can show you houses that have stood two centuries and a half and more; houses that have witnessed what would make a modern house crumble into powder. What do moderns know of life and the forces behind it? You call the Salem witchcraft a delusion, but I'll wage my four-times-great-grandmother could have told you things. They hanged her on Gallows Hill, with Cotton Mather looking sanctimoniously on. Mather, damn him, was afraid somebody might succeed in kicking free of this accursed cage of monotony—I wish someone had laid a spell on him or sucked his blood in the night!

"I can show you a house he lived in, and I can show you another one he was afraid to enter in spite of all his fine bold talk. He knew things he didn't dare put into that stupid *Magnalia* or that puerile *Wonders of the Invisible World*. Look here, do you know the whole North End once had a set of tunnels that kept certain people in touch with each other's houses, and the burying-ground, and the sea? Let them prosecute and persecute above ground—things went on every day that they couldn't reach, and voices laughed at night that they couldn't place!

"Why, man, out of ten surviving houses built before 1700 and not moved since I'll wager that in eight, I can show you something queer in the cellar. There's hardly a month that you don't read of workmen finding bricked-up arches and wells leading nowhere in this or that old place as it comes down—you could see one near Henchman Street from the elevated last year. There were witches and what their spells summoned; pirates and what they brought in from the sea; smugglers; privateers—and I tell you, people knew how to live, and how to enlarge the bounds of life, in the old times! This wasn't the only world a bold and wise man could know—faugh! And to think of today in contrast, with such pale-pink brains that even a club of supposed artists gets shudders and convulsions if a picture goes beyond the feelings of a Beacon Street tea-table!

"The only saving grace of the present is that it's too damned stupid to question the past very closely. What do maps and records and guidebooks really tell of the North End? Bah! At a guess I'll guarantee to lead you to thirty or forty alleys and networks of alleys north of Prince Street that aren't suspected by ten living beings outside of the foreigners that swarm them. And what do they know of their meaning? No, Thurber, these ancient places are dreaming gorgeously and overflowing with wonder and terror and escapes from the commonplace, and yet there's not a living soul to understand or profit by them. Or rather, there's only one living soul—for I haven't been digging around in the past for nothing!

"See here, you're interested in this sort of thing. What if I told you that I've got another studio up there, where I can catch the night-spirit of antique horror and paint things that I couldn't even think of in Newbury Street? Naturally I don't tell those cursed old maids at the club—with Reid, damn him, whispering even as it is that I'm a sort of monster bound down the toboggan of reverse evolution. Yes, Thurber, I decided long ago that one must paint terror as well as beauty from life, so I did some exploring in places where I had reason to know terror lives.

"I've got a place that I don't believe three living Nordic men besides myself have ever seen. It isn't so very far from the elevated as distance goes, but it's centuries away as the soul goes. I took it because of the queer old brick well in the cellar—one of the sort I told you about. The shack's almost tumbling down, so that nobody else would live there, and I'd hate to tell you how little I pay for it. The windows are boarded up, but I like that all the better, since I don't want daylight for what I do. I paint in the cellar, where the inspiration is thickest, but I've other rooms furnished on the ground floor. A Sicilian owns it, and I've hired it under the name of Peters.

"Now if you're game, I'll take you there tonight. I think you'd enjoy the pictures, for as I said, I've let myself go a bit there. It's no vast tour—I sometimes do it on foot, for I don't want to attract attention with a taxi in such a place. We can take the shuttle at the South Station for Battery Street, and after that the walk isn't much."

———

Well, Eliot, there wasn't much for me to do after that harangue but to keep myself from running instead of walking for the first vacant cab we could sight. We changed to the elevated at the South Station, and at about twelve o'clock had climbed down the steps at Battery Street and struck along the old waterfront past Constitution Wharf. I didn't keep track of the cross streets and can't tell you yet which it was we turned up, but I know it wasn't Greenough Lane.

When we did turn, it was to climb through the deserted length of the oldest and dirtiest alley I ever saw in my life, with crumbling-looking gables, broken small-paned windows, and archaic chimneys that stood out half-disintegrated against the moonlit sky. I don't believe there were three houses in sight that hadn't been standing in Cotton Mather's time—certainly I glimpsed at least two with an over-hang, and once I thought I saw a peaked roofline of the almost forgotten pre-gambrel type, though antiquarians tell us there are none left in Boston.

From that alley, which had a dim light, we turned to the left into an equally silent and still narrower alley with no light at all; and in a minute made what I think was an obtuse-angled bend toward the right in the dark. Not long after this Pickman produced a flashlight and revealed an antediluvian ten-paneled door that looked damnably worm-eaten. Unlocking it, he ushered me into a barren hallway with what was once splendid dark-oak paneling—simple, of course, but thrillingly suggestive of the times of Andros and Phipps and the Witchcraft. Then he took me through a door on the left, lighted an oil lamp, and told me to make myself at home.

Now, Eliot, I'm what the man in the street would call fairly "hard-boiled," but I'll confess that what I saw on the walls of that room gave me a bad turn. They were his pictures, you know—the ones he couldn't paint or even show in Newbury Street—and he was right when he said he had "let himself go." Here—have another drink—I need one anyhow!

There's no use in my trying to tell you what they were like, because the awful, the blasphemous horror, and the unbelievable loathsomeness and moral fetor came from simple touches quite beyond the power of words to classify. There was none of the exotic technique you see in Sidney Sime, none of the trans-Saturnian landscapes and lunar fungi that Clark Ashton Smith uses to freeze the blood. The backgrounds were mostly old churchyards, deep woods, cliffs by the sea, brick tunnels, ancient, paneled rooms or simple vaults of masonry. Copp's Hill Burying Ground, which could not be many blocks away from this very house, was a favorite scene.

The madness and monstrosity lay in the figures in the foreground —for Pickman's morbid art was preeminently one of demoniac portraiture. These figures were seldom completely human, but often approached humanity in varying degree. Most of the bodies, while roughly bipedal, had a forward slumping, and a vaguely canine cast. The texture of the majority was a kind of unpleasant rubberiness. Ugh! I can see them now! Their occupations—well, don't ask me to be too precise. They were usually feeding—I won't say on what. They were sometimes shown in groups in cemeteries or underground passages, and often appeared to be in battle over their prey—or rather, their treasure-trove. And what damnable expressiveness Pickman sometimes gave the sightless faces of this charnel booty! Occasionally the things were shown leaping through open windows at night, or squatting on the chests of sleepers, worrying at their throats. One canvas showed a ring of them baying about a hanged witch on Gallows Hill, whose dead face held a close kinship to theirs.

But don't get the idea that it was all this hideous business of theme and setting which struck me faint. I'm not a three-year-old kid, and I'd seen much like this before. It was the *faces*, Eliot, those accursed *faces* that leered and slavered out of the canvas with the very breath of life! By God, man, I verily believe they *were* alive! That nauseous wizard had waked the fires of hell in pigment, and his brush had been a nightmare-spawning wand. Give me that decanter, Eliot!

There was one thing called *The Lesson*—heaven pity me, that I ever saw it! Listen—can you fancy a squatting circle of nameless dog-like things in a churchyard teaching a small child how to feed like themselves? The price of a changeling, I suppose—you know the old myth about how the weird people leave their spawn in cradles in exchange for the human babes they steal. Pickman was showing what happens to those stolen babes—how they grow up—and then I began to see a hideous relationship in the faces of the human and non-human figures. He was, in all his gradations of morbidity between the frankly non-human and the degradedly human, establishing a sardonic linkage and evolution. The dog-things were developed from mortals!

And no sooner had I wondered what he made of their own young as left with mankind in the form of changelings, than my eye caught a picture embodying that very thought. It was that of an ancient Puritan interior—a heavily beamed room with lattice windows, a settle, and clumsy seventeenth-century furniture, with the family sitting about while the father read from the Scriptures. Every face but one showed nobility and reverence, but that one reflected the mockery of the pit. It was that of a young man in years, and no doubt belonged to a supposed son of that pious father, but in essence it was the kin of the unclean things. It was their changeling—and in a spirit of supreme irony Pickman had given the features a very perceptible resemblance to his own.

By this time Pickman had lighted a lamp in an adjoining room and was politely holding open the door for me; asking me if I would care to see his "modern studies." I hadn't been able to give him much of my opinions—I was too speechless with fright and loathing—but I think he fully understood and felt highly complimented. And now I want to assure you again, Eliot, that I'm no mollycoddle to scream at anything which shows a bit of departure from the usual. I'm middle-aged and decently sophisticated, and I guess you saw enough of me in France to know I'm not easily knocked out. Remember, too, that I'd just about recovered my wind and gotten used to those frightful pictures which turned colonial New England into a kind of annex of hell. Well, in spite of all this, that next room forced a real scream out of me, and I had to clutch at the doorway to keep from keeling over. The other chamber had shown a pack of ghouls and witches overrunning the world of our forefathers, but this one brought the horror right into our own daily life!

Gad, how that man could paint! There was a study called *Subway Accident*, in which a flock of the vile things were clambering up from some unknown catacomb through a crack in the floor of the Boylston Street subway and attacking a crowd of people on the platform. Another showed a dance on Copp's Hill among the tombs with the background of today. Then there were any number of cellar views, with monsters creeping in through holes and rifts in the masonry and grinning as they squatted behind barrels or furnaces and waited for their first victim to descend the stairs.

One disgusting canvas seemed to depict a vast cross-section of Beacon Hill, with ant-like armies of the mephitic monsters squeezing themselves through burrows that honeycombed the ground. Dances in the modern cemeteries were freely pictured, and another conception somehow shocked me more than all the rest—a scene in an unknown vault, where scores of the beasts crowded about one who held a well-known Boston guidebook and was evidently reading aloud. All were pointing to a certain passage, and every face seemed so distorted with epileptic and reverberant laughter that I almost thought I heard the fiendish echoes. The title of the picture was, *Holmes, Lowell, and Longfellow Lie Buried in Mount Auburn.*

As I gradually steadied myself and got readjusted to this second room of deviltry and morbidity, I began to analyze some of the points in my sickening loathing. In the first place, I said to myself, these things repelled because of the utter inhumanity and callous cruelty they showed in Pickman. The fellow must be a relentless enemy of all mankind to take such glee in the torture of brain and flesh and the degradation of the mortal tenement. In the second place, they terrified because of their very greatness. Their art was the art that convinced—when we saw the pictures, we saw the daemons themselves and were afraid of them. And the queer part was, that Pickman got none of his power from the use of selectiveness or bizarrerie. Nothing was blurred, distorted, or conventionalized; outlines were sharp and life-like, and details were almost painfully defined. And the faces!

It was not any mere artist's interpretation that we saw; it was pandemonium itself, crystal clear in stark objectivity. That was it, by heaven! The man was not a fantasist or romanticist at all—he did not even try to give us the churning, prismatic ephemera of dreams, but coldly and sardonically reflected some stable, mechanistic, and well-established horror-world which he saw fully, brilliantly, squarely, and unfalteringly. God knows what that world can have been, or where he ever glimpsed the blasphemous shapes that loped and trotted and crawled through it; but whatever the baffling source of his images, one thing was plain. Pickman was in every sense—in conception and in execution—a thorough, painstaking, and almost scientific *realist*.

———

My host was now leading the way down cellar to his actual studio, and I braced myself for some hellish effects among the unfinished canvases. As we reached the bottom of the damp stairs, he turned his flashlight to a corner of the large open space at hand, revealing the circular brick curb of what was evidently a great well in the earthen floor. We walked nearer, and I saw that it must be five feet across, with walls a good foot thick and some six inches above the ground level—solid work of the seventeenth century, or I was much mistaken. That, Pickman said, was the kind of thing he had been talking about—an aperture of the network of tunnels that used to undermine the hill. I noticed idly that it did not seem to be bricked up, and that a heavy disc of wood formed the apparent cover. Thinking of the things this well must have been connected with if Pickman's wild hints had not been mere rhetoric, I shivered slightly; then turned to follow him up a step and through a narrow door into a room of fair size, provided with a wooden floor and furnished as a studio. An acetylene gas outfit gave the light necessary for work.

The unfinished pictures on easels or propped against the walls were as ghastly as the finished ones upstairs and showed the painstaking methods of the artist. Scenes were blocked out with extreme care, and penciled guidelines told of the minute exactitude which Pickman used in getting the right perspective and proportions. The man was great—I say it even now, knowing as much as I do. A large camera on a table excited my notice, and Pickman told me that he used it in taking scenes for backgrounds, so that he might paint them from photographs in the studio instead of carting his outfit around the town for this or that view. He thought a photograph quite as good as an actual scene or model for sustained work, and declared he employed them regularly.

There was something very disturbing about the nauseous sketches and half-finished monstrosities that leered around from every side of the room, and when Pickman suddenly unveiled a huge canvas on the side away from the light I could not for my life keep back a loud scream—the second I had emitted that night. It echoed and echoed through the dim vaultings of that ancient and nitrous cellar, and I had to choke back a flood of reaction that threatened to burst out as hysterical laughter. Merciful Creator! Eliot, but I don't know how much was real, and how much was feverish fancy. It doesn't seem to me that earth can hold a dream like that!

It was a colossal and nameless blasphemy with glaring red eyes, and it held in bony claws a thing that had been a man, gnawing at the head as a child nibbles at a stick of candy. Its position was a kind of crouch, and as one looked one felt that at any moment it might drop its present prey and seek a juicier morsel. But damn it all, it wasn't even the fiendish subject that made it such an immortal fountainhead of all panic—not that, nor the dog face with its pointed ears, blood-shot eyes, flat nose, and drooling lips. It wasn't the scaly claws nor the mold-caked body nor the half-hooved feet—none of these, though any one of them might well have driven an excitable man to madness.

It was the technique, Eliot—the cursed, the impious, the unnatural technique! As I am a living being, I never elsewhere saw the actual breath of life so fused into a canvas. The monster was there—it glared and gnawed and gnawed and glared—and I knew that only a suspension of nature's laws could ever let a man paint a thing like that without a model—without some glimpse of the nether world which no mortal unsold to the Fiend has ever had.

Pinned with a thumbtack to a vacant part of the canvas was a piece of paper now badly curled up—probably, I thought, a photograph from which Pickman meant to paint a background as hideous as the nightmare it was to enhance. I reached out to uncurl and look at it, when suddenly I saw Pickman start as if shot. He had been listening with peculiar intensity ever since my shocked scream had waked unaccustomed echoes in the dark cellar, and now he seemed struck with a fright which, though not comparable to my own, had in it more of the physical than of the spiritual. He drew a revolver and motioned me to silence, then stepped out into the main cellar and closed the door behind him.

I think I was paralyzed for an instant. Imitating Pickman's listening, I fancied I heard a faint scurrying sound somewhere, and a series of squeals or bleats in a direction I couldn't determine. I thought of huge rats and shuddered. Then there came a subdued sort of clatter which somehow set me all in gooseflesh—a furtive, groping kind of clatter, though I can't attempt to convey what I mean in words. It was like heavy wood falling on stone or brick—wood on brick—what did that make me think of?

It came again, and louder. There was a vibration as if the wood had fallen farther than it had fallen before. After that followed a sharp grating noise, a shouted gibberish from Pickman, and the deafening discharge of all six chambers of a revolver, fired spectacularly as a lion-tamer might fire in the air for effect. A muffled squeal or squawk, and a thud. Then more wood and brick grating, a pause, and the opening of the door—at which I'll confess I started violently. Pickman reappeared with his smoking weapon, cursing the bloated rats that infested the ancient well.

"The deuce knows what they eat, Thurber," he grinned, "for those archaic tunnels touched graveyard and witch-den and sea-coast. But whatever it is, they must have run short, for they were devilish anxious to get out. Your yelling stirred them up, I fancy. Better be cautious in these old places—our rodent friends are the one drawback, though I sometimes think they're a positive asset by way of atmosphere and color."

———

Well, Eliot, that was the end of the night's adventure. Pickman had promised to show me the place, and heaven knows he had done it. He led me out of that tangle of alleys in another direction, it seems, for when we sighted a lamp post we were in a half-familiar street with monotonous rows of mingled tenement blocks and old houses. Charter Street, it turned out to be, but I was too flustered to notice just where we hit it. We were too late for the elevated and walked back downtown through Hanover Street. I remember that walk. We switched from Tremont up Beacon, and Pickman left me at the corner of Joy, where I turned off. I never spoke to him again.

Why did I drop him? Don't be impatient. Wait till I ring for coffee. We've had enough of the other stuff, but I for one need something. No—it wasn't the paintings I saw in that place; though I'll swear they were enough to get him ostracized in nine-tenths of the homes and clubs of Boston, and I guess you won't wonder now why I have to steer clear of subways and cellars. It was—something I found in my coat the next morning. You know, the curled-up paper tacked to that frightful canvas in the cellar; the thing I thought was a photograph of some scene he meant to use as a background for that monster. That last scare had come while I was reaching to uncurl it, and it seems I had vacantly crumpled it into my pocket. But here's the coffee—take it black, Eliot, if you're wise.

Yes, that paper was the reason I dropped Pickman; Richard Upton Pickman, the greatest artist I have ever known—and the foulest being that ever leaped the bounds of life into the pits of myth and madness. Eliot—old Reid was right. He wasn't strictly human. Either he was born in strange shadow, or he'd found a way to unlock the forbidden gate. It's all the same now, for he's gone—back into the fabulous darkness he loved to haunt. Here, let's have the chandelier going.

Don't ask me to explain or even conjecture about what I burned. Don't ask me, either, what lay behind that mole-like scrambling Pickman was so keen to pass off as rats. There are secrets, you know, which might have come down from old Salem times, and Cotton Mather tells even stranger things. You know how damned life-like Pickman's paintings were—how we all wondered where he got those faces.

Well—that paper wasn't a photograph of any background, after all. What it showed was simply the monstrous being he was painting on that awful canvas. It was the model he was using—and its background was merely the wall of the cellar studio in minute detail. But by God, Eliot, *it was a photograph from life.*

The Atomic Conquerors

Edmund Hamilton

-1-

Looking back, one is struck with wonder that we know as much of the story as we do; that we comprehend as fully as we do the nature of the strange doom that rushed out onto humanity from a lonely hill in southern Scotland. Had it not been for one small thing, the casual curiosity of a young student, that appalling invasion would remain to this day quite unexplained. A trifle, certainly, that passing interest of a rather commonplace young man, but except for that interest, and what it led to, we would understand nothing of the vast drama that was played around and above us.

Not that our ignorance or knowledge could have affected the outcome of that drama! Beside the tremendous forces that rose and fought and crashed, mankind was but a mass of tiny, frightened pigmies, running about beneath battling giants. Yet one remembers that it was one of those same pigmies, it was a single embittered, insane man who loosed all of that ancient terror upon us and caused an age-old cosmic feud to flare out in dreadful war, universe struggling with universe in titanic combat, immense, unthinkable....

The story, as we know it, begins on that sultry afternoon in

August when young Ernest Hunter came into the village of Leadanfoot and dismounted wearily from his battered bicycle. A day of
pedaling over the Scotch hills had made him regret, somewhat, his
decision to visit Glasgow on his holiday trip. One of the numberless
students who swarm over the English highways each summer, on
cycles and afoot, he began to think that this side-trip over the border
was, after all, a mistake.

But once inside the dark, cool little inn, with a mug of foaming
cider at hand, these doubts fled and the world again seemed a very
pleasant place. This Hunter, lengthy and stooping of figure, with a
thin, humorous face, was a social type, and looked about now for
possible company. Except for himself there was no one in the long,
low room but the two men who stood near the open door, the stocky,
aproned innkeeper and a white-whiskered, wrinkled old man with
whom he was conversing. His cider finished, Hunter rose and lounged
toward them, catching a few words of their talk.

"Thunder? No!" the innkeeper was exclaiming. "Who ever heard
thunder like that?"

The other was nodding his agreement when their conversation
was broken into by Hunter's friendly voice.

"Thunderstorm here lately?" he asked. "I came through a bad one
down at Carlisle, Wednesday. A messy sort of thing. Lightning fired a
house there."

The host contemplated him doubtfully before replying.

"It was not a thunderstorm we spoke of," he told him. "There was
a queer thing here—I don't just know—McAndrews here heard it,
and so did I."

He paused, but Hunter was interested, and questioning him
further, found that the subject of discussion was a series of strange
detonations that had been heard throughout the village on the night
before, a succession of deep-toned, rumbling explosions that seemed
to come from the group of hills west of Leadanfoot. All in the village
had heard the sounds, and most had set it down as distant thunder,
but the innkeeper quite evidently disagreed.

"Like no thunder you ever heard," he assured Hunter. "Boom—boom—boom—boom—boom! Regular, like a big cannon firing. I've heard enough thunder in my time, and this sound was not like it, not like it at all. Eh, McAndrews?"

The wrinkled oldster sagely nodded agreement.

"Maybe it was blasting you heard," Hunter suggested. "Some farmer up there doing something of that kind, perhaps?"

For a moment the innkeeper contemplated him with that fine scorn with which the rural native regards a stranger ignorant of local geography. "Farmer up there!" he repeated, in the tone with which one would reject an unworthy statement. "Why, there's not a house through all those hills. Too steep they are, and wild. I doubt if a single soul has lived there for the last ten years."

The aged McAndrews removed his pipe from his mouth to voice dissent. "How about the scienteefic chappies?" he asked.

"Well, except for them," conceded the host, somewhat discomfited, while the older man replaced the pipe and regarded him with stern gravity. Possibly to cover up his mistake, he went rapidly on with explanations for Hunter's benefit.

"Two science professors they are, that have a cabin on one of the hills. For near a year they've been there, studying the glassy forts, I hear. I never saw them, myself, for they get everything they need over at Dykirk."

A term in his speech caught Hunter's interest. "The glassy forts?" he repeated, interrogatively.

"There's some piles of old stone ruins on some of the hilltops around here," the innkeeper explained. "Some of them have parts of stones all melted into glass. Lightning did it, I suppose. Around here we call them the glassy forts, and it's them that these men are working with, digging and such."

"Oh, I see," said Hunter. More slowly, he continued, "Do you know, I'd like to see some of them if it wouldn't take too long. Do you suppose I could, in a day?"

"Well, you can if you're a good climber," his host informed him.

"Lowder Hill is the nearest to here, and they say there's such ruins on top of it. It's not so steep, either. There's another hill right next to Lowder, Kerachan Hill, but it's too high and rough to get up and down in a day, hardly. It's on Kerachan that the science men are staying, I think. You'd best try Lowder, though."

"I'll stay here tomorrow, then," Hunter told him, "and make the trip. I'm so infernally tired of pedaling that a day of tramping will be a rest."

The prospect had intrigued the young student, and before retiring for the night he acquired enough information to guide him on the next day's trip. Also, he had been furnished with a number of weird anecdotes concerning the glassy forts, which were evidently objects of local superstition.

The sun was an hour high the next morning when he left the inn, a small package of lunch in his pocket. He swung quickly through the village and tramped steadily over stony roads and rough moor toward the dark, looming bulk of the western hills, whose sides were almost completely hidden by dense forests of fir.

Hunter had been advised to climb Lowder Hill from its farther side, so on reaching it he walked in a great circle around its base, through a narrow, wooded valley that separated it from Kerachan Hill. As he passed along this valley, he was struck by its utter peace and quiet. The smaller forest creatures were frightened away by the sound of his coming, but once he glimpsed the vague dun shape of a deer slipping through the trees in the distance, and now and then startled groups of birds burst up through the trees at his approach, noisily discussing him in disparaging terms, in their flight. The busy, shouting, bellowing world seemed inconceivably remote, in that tranquil spot.

The sun swung higher and higher while he pushed his way forward. And in the world that seemed so very far, in Leadanfoot and London and New York and Peking, other men were pushing their way forward, in their particular groove in life, scheming for disks of metal and slips of paper, for the admiration of their fellows, for riches or fame or knowledge. A vast mass of tiny conspirators, each intent on his own plots, each sublimely confident of the importance of his especial business and its outcome.

And hidden in those quiet hills into which Hunter advanced was that which was to upset all of those minute conspiracies like little houses of cards, a door through which was to come a menacing terror unknown to man, so that presently, through this world, and worlds above and beyond, would run death, and confusion, and an ancient dread....

-2-

The sun was near its greatest height when Hunter came to the farther side of Lowder Hill, and the rude path that twisted up that side. He stared at it rather doubtfully, for the hill seemed very steep and the day was almost half gone. Then, with a shrug, he was about to step forward to the path when the sound of a step behind him made him wheel in surprise.

A strange figure was walking toward him, a small, middle-aged man whose clothes were dirty and torn by briars. He was hatless, and on his pink, round, spectacled face was an expression of dazed wonder. He came forward until he was within a few yards of the astonished Hunter, then stopped and regarded him mildly.

"Not Powell," he whispered, softly, confidentially. "Not—"

He ceased speaking suddenly, looked around with a certain surprise, then sank to the ground in a dead faint.

In a moment Hunter was by the man's side, applying his vague ideas of first aid. He got his pocket flask between the man's teeth, and a little brandy down his throat, which almost instantly pulled him back to consciousness. The man lay there, his eyes sweeping over Hunter's face, then asked, quite unexpectedly, "What time is it?"

On finding that it was almost noon, he straightened to a sitting position. "I'm all right now," he assured the student, motioning the latter to a seat on the ground beside him. His glance wavered about the scene, then came back to Hunter, whom he regarded intently before addressing him.

"Who you are, I don't know," he began, and as Hunter started to explain, he added, "and it doesn't matter. You've had some education, haven't you? Ah, medical student! That makes it easier—much easier."

Hunter began to think that the man was still dizzy, delirious. "Hadn't I better help you back to Leadanfoot?" he asked.

"There would not be time," the other answered, strangely. "I was going to Leadanfoot myself, for—But there, you do not know. There is time to get back, though. You and I. But first you should hear—"

He caught the doubting, half-fearful expression on the young man's face. "No, I'm not a madman," he assured him, almost gently. "But I need help, badly. Need your help."

"But help for what?" asked Hunter. "I think if you would just go back with me to the village—"

"No!" answered the other, decisively. There was a pause, in which the older man stared across the green silence of the valley with unseeing eyes. Suddenly he turned to the watching, puzzled student.

"I will put it this way," he began. "Suppose someone was planning to kill every living person in the village yonder, to wipe it out utterly, would you try to prevent it?"

At Hunter's wondering reply he continued, "Of course you would. Now go farther still. Suppose someone, something, was trying to kill every human being on Earth, to annihilate the world as we know it. Would you try to stop that, too?"

The younger man stared at him blankly. "Would you?" persisted the other.

"Why, yes—naturally," answered the student, and the older man sighed.

"It is to prevent that that I need your help," he said, quietly.

Before Hunter could comment on that startling statement the man rushed on. "I am going to tell you enough of the matter to help you understand what threatens. You will not think me a madman when you hear! We have little time here, an hour perhaps, before we must start back. But it is enough for me to tell—

"You will wish to know who I am. Marlowe is my name, and until a year ago I held a position on the staff of the Trent Museum, in London. It was there that I met Powell, some three years ago.

"Dr. Henry Powell he was, an elderly physics professor, lately retired from Cambridge. That was all he ever told me of his past, for even after we became better acquainted, he was close-mouthed about his former career. By chance I found the reason for that. A friend told me that Powell had left Cambridge under a cloud. It seems that he had been working for many months in collaboration with a fellow professor, Wooding by name, on an element-changing experiment. You know, transmute uranium into radium, or radium into lead. Modern alchemy they were attempting. After a year of work together the two had split over some disagreement, each carrying on the experiment alone. Wooding was the first of the two to publish his results, and immediately Powell claimed that his former partner in work had stolen his own results.

"There was rather a scandal over the matter, but an investigating committee ruled that Powell's charges were unproved, so he was retired from the university. I never talked with Powell on the matter, and never learned the right of it, but I could see that the thing had embittered him greatly, so that he was wont to snarl viciously at all scientific people, and in fact, nearly all people, of any kind. He grated on me considerably, sometimes, for he was like an animated bottle of acid, thin lipped, sardonic, sneering. But one thing drew us together, a common interest in archeology. In fact, that branch of knowledge was my work, at the museum, and Powell had taken it up as a sort of hobby, to occupy his restless mind, I suppose. We got acquainted through his visits to the museum and had many a talk thereafter.

"He was intensely interested in the 'vitrified forts' of Scotland, as they are called. Piles of stone ruins on some of the Scottish hills, and in a few valleys, with some of the stones melted into glass. You've heard of them? Well, it was Powell's radical theory that those glassy streaks were not made by lightning, as is commonly supposed, but by some powerful weapon or ray, striking from above. You will see what a revolution in conventional archeological thought would be the result, if he could prove that. He got to be a fanatic on the subject and spent most of his time roaming about Scotland and hunting and digging in such ruins.

"He had been off on such a trip for several weeks when he sent me an urgent wire, from a Scotch village named Dykirk. He had made a great discovery, he said, but needed my help, and offered me a handsome salary for my aid. My own interest was aroused by his message, so I procured the necessary leave from the museum and went at once, being met by Powell when I stepped off the train.

"It turned out that his discovery was on the summit of a hill some miles from Dykirk, named Kerachan Hill. He had had a little cottage, or cabin, built on the hill, and had lived in it for some weeks. It took us most of the day to get to his little home, so we stowed my luggage and waited until the next morning to inspect his discovery.

"And it was really astounding. The summit of the hill was flat, and there, with a few crumbling stone blocks scattered about, but in the center of that level expanse, was a shallow pit, newly dug, that was circular in shape and perhaps twenty feet across. At its bottom, a foot or so from the surface of the ground, lay a flat round stone, the surface of which was almost completely covered by a mass of strange characters, carven into it deeply.

"It was to decipher this inscription that Powell needed my help, for I am by way of being an expert in hieroglyphics, cuneiform writing, and such. He said that he had found this inscription beneath a protecting layer of cement of some kind, and was afire to learn its meaning, as he well might be.

"So, I settled in the little cabin and began work that very day. To my surprise, I found the inscription quite easy to decipher, for all that the characters were totally strange and unknown. Whoever had carved it had placed in it, here and there, small pictures, symbols, giving a key for its translation purposely. Within a month I had translated and arranged my translations of it, and found that the inscription told a stupendous, incredible story.

"According to it, these ruins of forts that lay scattered through Scotland had been built ages before by a race of strange folk who had invaded the Earth then. And these strangers had come, not from another planet, as one might suppose, but from a single atom in the Earth.

"This will sound incredible to you, as at first it did to me, but consider. We know that each atom of our Earth consists of a number of electrons revolving about a nucleus, and what is that but a minia-ture solar system? Just as our sun and its circling planets may be an atom in a vastly larger system, and so on infinitely, perhaps. The idea is not new, it was advanced years ago. And in this particular atom of the Earth, on its electrons, its tiny planets, dwelt a race proportionately tiny, the atomic people, I will call them. They had crowded over every one of their electron-planets and were now gradually stifling from their ever-increasing numbers.

"They had science, a strange sort of science, and now, at the time of their greatest need, one of their scientists announced a startling discovery. He had found a way by which the size of any object could be increased or decreased indefinitely, at will. And the secret of this was stunning in its very simplicity.

"We know that the universal, all-pervading ether is the base of everything. Vibrations of that ether, in a certain octave, cause light; in a different octave, radio waves; in still another, chemical rays. But what we do not know as yet, what the scientists of the atomic people had learned, is that all matter itself is but another vibration of that ether, in a different lower octave. That stone, that tree, you and I, all but different vibrations in the ether. And the atomic scientists had found that as a stone is simply an etheric vibration, by raising the frequency of vibration the stone would be made larger, by lowering that frequency it would be made smaller.

"Their method of changing that frequency was told by the inscription. They would ascertain the frequency of vibration of an object, then concentrate on its other artificial electric vibrations, much like radio waves, which would change the vibratory frequency of the object just as the rate of swing of a pendulum can be raised or lowered by a tiny force applied to it at the correct moment. Thus, these atomic people could make any object, make even themselves, large enough to dwarf their world or small enough to disappear entirely.

"It was a chance to relieve their crowding numbers and they seized it at once. Using their discovery to grow in size, they burst up from their own atom into this world, into our Earth, and found that the atom that was their universe was an atom of a simple grain of sand, on Earth. That sand-grain, though, held their world, so they built a great structure around it, in what is now Scotland, so that it would always be there as a refuge for them to flee to, in case of need. That attended to, up from the atom, out of the sand-grain, streamed their people, gigantic masses of them.

"The Earth then was savage and forbidding, but nothing daunted, they spread over its surface, began to raise their structures of stone, to shape this world to their will. It must have seemed to them that they were secure forever in this greater universe.

"But now came disaster. Certain adventurous spirits among them were not satisfied to stop in this universe. They saw the sun and its attendant planets and realized that this, our own solar system, was after all only an atom in a still greater universe. So, a number of them, using the same method of changing size, grew again until they had entered the world above this, the universe in which ours is but an atom.

"Now in that greater universe, in that super world, as I shall call it, there was civilization, a civilization of beings who had advanced far beyond the crude semi-barbarism of the people of the atom. So, when the atomic invaders entered their world, the super people knew they had come from beneath, from an atom, for they themselves had long possessed that power of changing size which the atomic people had just discovered. Although these super people promptly beat back the invaders in that first attack, time after time in the years that followed the warlike people of the atom persisted in attempting to enter the super world, which was so much fairer than either their own world or this one.

"A long while their attacks continued until finally the patience of the super people was exhausted and they gathered together all their forces to crush these atomic invaders forever. They poured down from their greater universe to this Earth, and then was a battle such as was never known before, the people of the super world and the people of the atom locked in a death-struggle, smiting with strange weapons, a colossal war raging over the shuddering Earth that reeled beneath them.

"The atomic invaders could not stand against the mighty weapons of the super people, and soon all of them not slain were fleeing in dread to their own world, that sand-grain that held their universe. They sped back to that grain and down into it, dwindling in size and vanishing, until of all their number, only their dead remained on Earth.

"And now the super people set about to seal them forever within that atom, within that sand-grain, so that never again should they break out and carry war and death through the super world. To accomplish this, they set that grain of sand within a circle of perpetual electric force, a field of strange force within which it was impossible to grow or dwindle in size, as the atomic people had done, by changing the frequency of etheric vibration. Thus, the people of the atom were locked forever within their own tiny universe.

"This accomplished, they covered the sand-grain and the forces they placed around it, setting over them a great stone, on which was written the history of what had happened, and which warned whoever might find the stone in the future never to tamper with or change what had been done, lest they loose again the atomic invaders upon the Earth and the super world alike. Having done this, the super people left the Earth to its own devices and passed up into their own greater universe.

"Came then, on Earth, the painful upward surge of changing, ascending species, the long road from anthropoid to troglodyte to modern man. The structures of the atomic people crumbled soon, until only a few remnants were left. Overall, the world it was as if their invasion had never been, nor did men dream that such people had held the Earth ages before themselves. And up in a Scottish hill, under a great stone that was covered by the drifting dirt of ages, lay a grain of sand that held war and death and terror, in a single atom of which the atomic people were prisoned for all time."

-3-

"Such was the colossal epic the inscription narrated. And it was so convincing that neither Powell nor I doubted it. But now a dispute arose between us. I believed that we should heed the warning of the inscription and not delve farther into the thing, lest we loose dread upon the world. But Powell was afire with curiosity and would not listen. So, with help, we removed the great circular stone and set it to one side. And beneath it, as it had foretold, we found the sand-grain that held the atomic world.

"Under the circular stone was a cube of the same smooth rock, some six feet square. On the upper surface of this cube was set a small plate of smooth metal, at the center of which lay the sand-grain, set in the metal. Around this metal plate, embedded within the surface of the cube, was a circle of seven little blocks that glowed steadily with a feeble purple light. In daylight the little blocks seemed merely purple in color, and it was only in darkness that their luminosity became apparent. Without doubt that circle of glowing blocks was the producer of the force mentioned in the inscription, the force that made size-changing impossible within their field, that held the atomic people prisoners in the sand-grain.

"From that day onward Powell took me less and less into his confidence. He had fitted up a small laboratory near the cabin and began working there on some problem connected with what he had found. Once or twice, he consulted me concerning the meaning of certain technical parts of the inscription, but aside from that he told me nothing of what he was doing, and I decided that I was wasting time to stay. It was on the very day that I meant to tell Powell so, and leave, that he came running toward me excitedly, with the news that his experiment had succeeded.

"And when I found the nature of that experiment I was astounded. He had been attempting to follow up the sparse details given in the inscription and rediscover the method of changing size. And he had done it! He showed me the apparatus he had worked out, a compact black case which strapped around his chest and which would cause everything within its field of action to grow or decrease in size. And standing there on the hilltop, he grew in size until he towered up a giant of a hundred feet, then dwindled until he was an inch in height, a tiny manikin.

"He was exultant, and I thought that at last he would leave the hilltop and cover the sand-grain once more. I pointed out to him what good he might accomplish in the world with that great power, but he only snarled at me and for the first time revealed his intention. He was planning to dwindle in size until he could enter that atomic world, to go down into the sand-grain, to the atomic universe.

"Short of force, I used all my efforts to prevent him, for I was aghast at such a plan. But he went on, unheeding, making his preparations for the trip. He dug out and removed the little circle of blocks around the sand-grain, then gradually began to dwindle in size until he was a tiny figure a few inches high, standing on the metal circle near the grain of sand. Smaller and smaller he became, until he vanished entirely from my sight, and I knew that he had entered the sand-grain.

"For three days I watched beside the stone cube, waiting for his return. It was toward evening of the third day that he finally came back, a tiny upright form on the metal plate that grew swiftly to the man I knew. He had come back.

"He had come back—but changed. He seemed to be filled with an immense excitement, to be spurred on by some hidden purpose. He gave small answer to my flood of questions. He had found the atomic world, had been guided down into that particular atom of the grain by 'certain signs,' a phrase which he did not explain. As to the people of the atom, he said only that there were many of them and that they were "different." More he would not tell me, and my fear, my misgivings, increased.

***

"The night of disaster rushed upon us, a week after his return. I was asleep in the cabin while Powell worked, as I thought, in the laboratory. Sometime after midnight I woke and sensed that Powell was not in the cabin. I dressed hurriedly and found that he was not in the laboratory either. Instantly I knew where he was and hurried up to the hilltop, and to the pit on that hilltop that held the stone cube and the sand-grain.

"He was standing on the edge of that pit, watching intensely, but at the sound of my approach he wheeled instantly, holding a little stone cone in his hand, the end of which glowed suddenly with dull green light.

"At the same moment I fell in a heap to the ground and lay there quite motionless, seemingly paralyzed, unable to move a muscle. And Powell laughed. He mocked and taunted me and for the first time disclosed the depth of his plans. He was going to loose once more the atomic invaders upon our world. He had gone down into their world and conspired with those in power there, promising to free them from the world where they were prisoners, to release them upon the Earth and the super world.

"First, he boasted, the atomic invaders were to strike at the world beyond this, at the super world, to stab out unexpectedly at their ancient enemies in that greater universe, crushing them by an unlooked-for attack. Then, free from any possible interference, the invading hordes would sweep over Earth; and he laughed wildly as he pictured to me the destruction of the races of man and their works, dwelling especially on the fear and terror of his (Powell's) enemies. For the first time I saw that the man was completely insane, an embittered maniac who secreted hate for all mankind as the result of his wrongs, real or fancied.

"Even while he spoke, a slight humming sound arose from the pit. The humming waxed swiftly to a loud droning, then up from the pit floated a black disk, some three feet across and swiftly growing.

Hovering a few feet above the ground, it continued to grow, and the droning became a loud booming, a tremendous rumbling thunder. Even as I stared at it, lying there, I fathomed the cause of that rolling thunder, knew that it was the sudden expansion of the disk that beat out those thick waves of sound. The disk grew until it was perhaps thirty feet across, then ceased expanding. It slid gently down toward us until it was nearly touching the ground, and I saw that it was crowded with dark shapes that pushed toward the rail to stare down at us.

"Then down from the edge came a folding metal ladder, and clambering down this ladder came three creatures, shapes grotesque and terrible, three of the atomic people.

"I had thought of them as being somewhat human, perhaps with different features or coloring, but still essentially human. But these things! They were reptilian, saurian! In height they were a little under the human standard, and their figures were even roughly human in shape, with the head carried erect, a squat, powerful body, two thick, bowed lower limbs, and two short arms, ending in cruel, curved talons. But with that rough travesty on the human shape, all resemblance ceased. To begin with, the things were completely covered with thick, hard scales, like those of a crocodile. Their heads were peaked, instead of round, with gaping, fanged mouths and small, black, glittering eyes, browless and lashless, like the eyes of a snake. They were noseless and earless, and their only sign of clothing was a queer sort of metallic armor that seemed more designed to carry their weapons than as clothing.

"Lying there motionless, regarding them with sickened horror, I saw the three advance to Powell, who greeted them with a queer gesture. One brought forth a tablet like a small slate, on which he wrote, then passed it to Powell, who studied it, then wrote in turn and handed it back. Evidently such writing was Powell's only means of communication with the things. For a few minutes they conferred in that fashion with Powell, then returned to the disk, which immediately ascended from its hovering position on the hilltop.

"As it rose it grew, spreading out swiftly in ever-expanding size, growing until it had shut off the light of all the stars for a few seconds, then seemingly breaking up into small masses, cloudily disappearing. It had become so large that it was invisible, had passed from this universe into that greater one. For a moment I wondered if its momentary eclipse of the stars would cause any stargazer to guess at what was happening, then realized that to any chance watcher of the sky it would seem only like a drifting cloud, if noticed at all.

"Again, rose the humming from the pit, many times louder, growing to an ear-splitting thunder as another force of the atomic people floated up from the pit, a great mass of tiny black circles, miniatures of the first disk that drifted up and rose at once into the air, not stopping to confer with Powell as had the first. And as that mass of disks rose above the hilltop, the familiar droning was again waxing louder as another mass of them came up.

"How many of the disks streamed up from the atom while I lay there, I cannot guess. Their number seemed infinite, but my memories are fragmentary, disjointed. I must have been unconscious for a few minutes at least, for I remember that amid the rumbling thunder of the rising disks, as I watched Powell, who was gazing triumphantly at their coming, a dizzying blackness seemed to descend on my brain, and when consciousness returned the last mass of disks was rising from the pit, vanishing like the others in the sky above.

––––––––

"Until now Powell had held me prisoner with the glowing cone, which he had placed on the ground before conferring with the atomic people, so that it held me prisoner without his attention. Now he picked it up and permitted me to re-enter the cabin, where he forced me to lie down in the bunk, then placed the cone again on the table in the room, still pointing toward me, still holding me a prisoner, powerless to move.

"Why he did not kill me outright, I cannot say. I think it was only because he desired someone, even a prostrate enemy, to whom he might boast of what he was doing, that he desired someone to know the power and the menace that he really was. It must have been so, for the next day he boasted for hours to me of what he was doing. He spoke of the great force of invaders I had seen and said that even by that time their numbers and mighty weapons would have crushed into submission the people of the super world.

"He spoke, too, of the paralyzing cone that held me prisoner, a weapon which he had brought back from the atomic world and revealed that he had another one on his person also. It was, he said, a ray that neutralized the electric messages in the nervous system, thus wiping out the commands of the brain in that system, so that while reflex actions like the breathing of the lungs and beating of the heart were unaffected, the conscious commands of the brain to the muscles were nullified, paralyzing those muscles.

"All of that day, and all through the next night, I lay in the bunk without moving a muscle, save only an hour in which he permitted me to eat. I heard him leave the cabin early the next morning, the second after the coming of the invaders, this very morning. Lying there, I listened with dull despair to the wind slamming the door of the cabin. The cone on the table was in the line of my vision and suddenly I gasped with hope, for at a particularly hard slam that cone had rolled a little way toward the table's edge. I waited breathless. Then, just as my hope was beginning to die, the door slammed to with all the wind's force behind it and the cone rolled from the table to the floor, breaking and exploding there in a flash, of intense green light.

"My first move was to search the cabin for a gun, but there was none. The cabin stood at the edge of the bare and treeless hilltop, and from its window I could see Powell's head bobbing about in the pit of the sand-grain, as he prepared for the coming of the second force of invaders. I knew that he must be imprisoned or killed at once but knew too, that he carried with him another of the paralyzing cones, so that I dared not rush him on the open hilltop. Neither could I remain in the cabin, so my only chance was to make my way to the nearest village and get help, or at least, a gun.

"So, I slipped out a rear window and got safely away without being seen by him. All of this morning it took me to get down the hill, and when I met you here, I knew I should not have time to get to a village as I had planned, but must go back and do what I could myself. And now I have told you all. Up on that hill Powell is awaiting the second invasion of those monsters from the atom, an invasion that will annihilate our world. If we can overpower him and replace the glowing blocks around the sand-grain, we shall have prevented disaster. If not—But do you believe the story? Will you help me?"

Hunter answered slowly, his brain whirling from the things he had heard. "It's so incredible," he began, "but the booming sounds you mentioned, they heard that in Leadanfoot. It seems so queer, though—" Suddenly he thrust a hand toward Marlowe. "I believe you," he told him. "I want to help."

The other gripped his hand silently, then glanced up at the sun. "We have, perhaps, four hours," he said, rising. Hunter, too, jumped to his feet, and for a moment they looked together up the dark sides of Kerachan Hill.

Presently the two men were forging steadily up that hillside. They spoke little and their faces were set, drawn. The sun was falling ever more swiftly toward the west, and always their eyes measured the distance between that descending sun and the horizon.

By the time they surmounted the first rough heights and began their progress up the thinly wooded upper half of the hill, the gray veils of twilight were already obscuring the surrounding country. Over peaks and valleys, over forests and grassy fields, lay a strange silence, ominous, foreboding. As they toiled up toward the summit through the thickening dusk, it seemed to Hunter that the whole world was silent, breathless, tensely waiting....

Complete darkness had fallen when Marlowe turned and made a cautioning gesture.

"We are very near the summit now," he told Hunter, in a whisper. "For God's sake, go quietly."

Together they crept upward, through thick underbrush and over jagged rocks, until they crouched at the edge of the smooth, grassy space that was the hill's summit. This summit was not exactly level, but sloped down from them in a slight grade, and at its center Hunter saw the black, yawning hole Marlowe had mentioned, the pit that held the sand-grain.

Marlowe was tugging at his sleeve. "Powell—down at the other edge," he whispered, excitedly.

Glancing down to that farther edge of the summit, Hunter saw there a thin, spare figure dimly outlined against the stars, the figure of a man who was gazing silently at the twinkling lights of a distant village. And over to their right, at the very edge of the bare summit, was the rough dark mass that he knew must be the small cabin. Again, Marlowe twitched his sleeve.

"We must rush him from both sides," he told Hunter. "You crawl around the right side of the summit and I will take the left, and when you get near enough, go for him. Don't give him time to get that cone out." With a whispered "good luck," he wrung Hunter's hand and began to creep stealthily around the left edge of the hilltop.

His heart pounding violently, Hunter crept forward on the right side, toward the man at the summit's edge, who still stood motionless, watching the distant lights. Hunter wondered where Marlowe was, in the darkness. By now he was crawling past the open door of the cabin, keeping close within the shadow of the little building.

From that point he could glimpse, in the starlight, the profile of the man they stalked. A strong, mad face it was, with burning eyes beneath a mass of gleaming, iron-gray hair, a face that was turned toward the south and its distant lights as though fascinated by them.

Suddenly Powell laughed, and at the unexpected sound Hunter stopped short, on hands and knees. A bitter, mocking laughter it was, that sickened the listening student. As it ceased, the man at the hill's edge raised a clenched fist and shook it at the distant lights. And his voice rang out over the silent hilltop like the note of a warning bell.

"O man, take heed!"

Even while Powell voiced that cry of hate and menace, Hunter moved forward again. And at his first movement, his knee pressed down on a small stick that broke with the sound of a pistol-shot.

Instantly Powell turned, his hand flashing down to his pocket and emerging with a small object in its grasp. As Hunter gathered himself for a swift, desperate spring, that object glowed out, a tiny circle of luminous green, and the young student sank back to the ground, deprived of all power of motion by the paralyzing cone. Powell advanced toward him, holding the cone outstretched.

"So you escaped, Marlowe," he said, and Hunter realized that in the darkness the man had mistaken him for his former prisoner. Powell was speaking on. "I think that I'll stop your interference now, for good. Not that I have any personal animus against you, I assure you, but I can't allow you to disrupt the plans I have made." As he said this, mockingly, he carefully placed the cone on a small mound of earth, so that its rays still held Hunter paralyzed. Then he straightened and was reaching for the pistol at his belt when a dark figure sprang from behind, dashing him to earth. Marlowe!

The thought beat through Hunter's brain as he lay, unable to twitch a muscle, watching the combat of those two figures that reeled about, striking, kicking, twisting. But what was that? What? That thin humming that suddenly made itself heard, that grew to a droning, to a rumbling, reverberating thunder. Out of the pit a dark shape was drifting up, a black disk that grew, grew, grew.

Boom! Boom! Boom! It grew until it had attained a diameter of thirty feet, then hovered above the pit, near the struggling men. As he glimpsed it, Marlowe cried out despairingly, and Powell's mad laughter flung up. And now was a sudden stir at the edge of the hovering disk, a flurry of movement there. Hunter darkly glimpsed shapes that crowded about the disk's edge, that peered at the struggling men. Did they mistake the two as a menace to themselves, did they fail to recognize Powell? For even as the two men reeled in battle toward the disk, a blinding shaft of blue light stabbed out from the disk's edge and struck the struggling pair. Under that ray and in its light, Hunter saw the faces of the two men change horribly, stiffen, draw, crack, and over him swept a breath of utter cold, an icy little wind that seemed to freeze his blood.

An instant he saw Powell and Marlowe thus, staggering, reeling, falling, then they had collapsed to a shapeless heap on the ground, and the blue ray, striking out past them, had touched the glowing cone on the little mound, which instantly exploded with a flash of light, releasing Hunter from its prisoning power.

The blue ray was sweeping in a circle about the hilltop now, and with sudden frantic fear he crawled through the open door of the dark cabin, crouching in a corner of it fearfully. Suddenly the ray swept up to the cabin, and beneath its touch the glass of the windows cracked instantly. An icy puff of air again swept over Hunter, in his corner, as the ray swept through the open door and hung steady for a moment.

Its blue light illumined a little metal stove opposite the door, a stove that covered instantly with a rime of frost and ice at the ray's touch. A moment the ray hung thus, steadily, doubtfully, then abruptly vanished, as though snapped out. Hunter sighed chokingly.

The humming sounds began again outside, and his fear mastered by curiosity, he crept to the cracked window. A mass of tiny black circles was rising from the pit, floating up and growing at the same time, while the first disk hung to one side, watching. The black circles rose high, expanded almost instantly to the size of the first, were joined by that first disk.

For a minute Hunter watched the disks circling above, swirling about in an eddying mass. Then three detached from those above and sank down to the hilltop, hovering close above it and sweeping it ever and again with the deadly blue ray that came and went across the cabin while he watched. The other disks, more than a score in number, grouped in a compact formation, then raced swiftly south.

The vanguard of the atomic conquerors loosed at last upon the world of man!

-5-

It is doubtful if we shall ever know the exact purpose of that first raid on the atomic invaders. That question might be solved if we knew how much information they had received from Powell regarding our Earth. As it is, we look on that first coming as an effort, not so much to destroy as to disorganize, to terrorize. Doubtless it was their plan to break up all chance of organized opposition in England by a series of swift and deadly blows, then take over the island at their leisure and make it the base of their future operations.

Whatever their intentions, they passed over all northern England without stopping, and the world first became aware of their presence when they struck with terrific force at Manchester and Liverpool, successively.

There is no clear, coherent account of their coming to Manchester. The survivors saw that hour of dread through a haze of terror, and it was long before all accounts were pieced together to make a reasonably complete story of the happenings there. One sees, through those horror-stricken tales, a terror descending without warning out of the darkness, on the unsuspecting city beneath. No doubt the streets were crowded, and theaters and show-windows ablaze, all the life and stir of early evening. Then a swift gathering of dark shapes above, the deadly blue ray flashing down on the streets, searing an icy path of death across the city.

It must have been utterly incomprehensible destruction to those below. Even now we scarcely understand the nature of that blue ray, the Cold Ray, as it is now called. We know that all things in its path acted as if under the influence of extreme, unheard-of cold, absolute zero. It was exactly as if the invaders had concentrated utter cold and hurled it forth in a single stabbing ray. Strictly speaking, of course, there is no such thing as positive cold, only absence of heat. The theory generally accepted now is that in some unexplained manner the ray had the power of instantly sucking away the heat of anything it touched.

Certain it is that the ray was a terrible weapon. Beneath it, flesh and blood froze immediately into black hard lumps, metal cracked, trees and plants shriveled instantly. It is curious to note that the action of the ray was highly localized, that it could slay one man while another man ten feet away would feel only a sudden breath of intense cold.

As it swept steadily along the streets of Manchester that night, overtaking the fleeing crowds and leaving them in shapeless heaps, it must have seemed like the very day of doom to those below. They speak of it as enduring for hours, that time that the invaders hung above the city, while in reality the disks remained over Manchester somewhat less than twenty minutes. How many were slain in that time it is impossible to guess. The city, at least, was thrown into a wild intense panic, and no doubt that was the purpose of the invaders. That accomplished, they gathered together and sped away to the west, to Liverpool.

The story of the massacre at Liverpool is almost identical with that at Manchester. There too the disks struck down with icy death at the city, but one curious feature differentiates the Liverpool account. It seems that as the Cold Ray swept around the city, it crossed, ever and again, the city's harbor and the sea outside. And for many days afterward, immense icebergs of unprecedented size ranged the English coast, born of that striking of the ocean by the blue ray.

At Manchester and Liverpool, and even as far south as Birmingham, the invaders came down without warning, striking unexpectedly, spreading death and dread, then racing away. But some time before they reached London, word of the attacks on the northern cities had been received, and men waited, ready for battle, so that it was over London that the atomic people and the forces of man clashed for the first time.

It was the assumption of the War Office in London that Manchester and Liverpool had been attacked by the airplanes of some continental power, without the formality of a declaration of war. Certainly, they did not dream of the real nature of the menace that was speeding toward them.

Presently, from all the air-stations around the city, plane after plane was spiraling up, while in a great ring around London the giant searchlights stabbed the night, sweeping the sky in search of the invaders. Even while the planes ascended and hung in a thin line high above the city, thunder was growling, low and ominous, and lightning flickering across the sky.

It was with this gathering storm that the disks raced down toward the city, never glimpsing the line of planes above. For a space of minutes, they hung motionless, surveying the shining, splendid metropolis. The streets below, temporarily deserted beneath the coming storm, were like brilliant rivers of light, connecting the lakes of luminescence that were the squares. One imagines the invaders in the disks staring down at the city in amazement, if their reptilian natures possessed the power. As they hung there, the beam of one of the questing searchlights caught them and held them, and the stabbing rays of the other lights shifted to them at once, bathing the disks in a flood of white light. Then, from high above, the airplanes drove down upon them and the battle had begun.

One can see that battle clearest, perhaps, through the eyes of a single individual, a certain young Brownell who was the pilot of a single-seater combat plane. At the first orders he had taken the air almost joyously, with the exciting thought that at last his training was to be tested in actual battle. He thrilled to the thought, as with the other planes he swooped down upon the disks.

Down he went and down, diving toward a single disk that hung at some distance from the mass of its fellows. His hands grasped the control of the plane's machine-gun, and even above the roar of the motor he heard the pup-pup-pup-pup of the gun, spraying bullets on the disk. He swept down onto that disk and over it in a great curve, passing above it at a height of a few yards. As he flashed over it, the lightning flared out blindingly above, and as he caught momentary sight of the things on the disk, his hands trembled on the controls. He had glimpsed a mass of upturned heads, scaled and peaked, with fanged and gaping mouths. For the first time he saw the creatures of dread he was fighting. As he drove up above the battle and banked and circled for another swoop, his hands were still trembling.

From below came the popping of bombs, a few of which scored hits on the disks, most of which plunged down toward the city below, misses. The roar of their detonation seemed feeble beside the crash of the thunder, which was now rumbling forth almost continuously. Away to the left of the battle, two planes collided and dropped swiftly to earth, trailing long streamers of red flames, blazing comets plunging earthward through the upper darkness.

And now, their first shock of surprise over, the invaders struck back, and the blue ray flashed up, searching out and finding the planes, whose wings shriveled and collapsed beneath its touch. Two of the disks had been forced down by lucky hits with bombs, but the others were almost unscathed, and now the planes were falling ever more rapidly beneath the Cold Ray.

Suddenly, from high above, a single plane rushed down toward the massed disks, in a dizzying nosedive. The blue ray stabbed up from a dozen disks to meet it, but it plunged on, smashed down into one of the disks, and plane and disk whirled together down to earth, the latter spilling out a mass of grotesque figures that raced it in its fall.

Brownell shouted hoarsely as he saw. From all around planes were diving down now, smashing squarely into the disks and falling with them, a deliberate heroic suicide on the part of their pilots. An immense exaltation ran through Brownell, that vast, forceful rapture of heroism that can sweep men up to titanic heights. He circled again, then dipped the plane's nose sharply and rushed down upon a single disk like a falling plummet.

Pup-pup-pup—at the last moment he clung to the gun-control. Rush of wind past him—flash of lights—a roaring in his ears—the disk was nearer, rushing swiftly up to him—nearer—nearer—crash!

Then plane and disk were tumbling down to earth together, speeding down to the brilliant streets below, crashing down near the docks, where something in the wrecked disk exploded with stunning force.

Above, the battle was all but finished. Only a few of the planes remained and the blue ray was searching these out, one by one. Presently the invaders held the air alone, nine disks remaining of the twenty or more that had begun the attack. The city below was at their mercy, but they did not heed it. Circling and forming, they massed again together, then moved away to the north, seemingly daunted by the fierce and unexpected resistance they had met. They had conquered, but at a price that disinclined them for further battle at that time.

The people in the city below waited tensely, but no more aerial wrecks whirled down upon them. And the ever-questing searchlights revealed no sign of plane or disk over the city. Through all London reigned a deathlike silence, that first moment of astounded silence before the hoarse roar of fear and rage that would roll through the city. Only the deep rumble of thunder broke the stillness.

Across the sky the lightning flared again, once, twice. Then down upon the city swept the lashing, flooding rain.

-6-

It is to young Hunter's story that one must turn again for an account of the invaders' movements after that first raid. Crouched by the window, he saw them returning from the battle, nine scarred disks returning where more than a score had gone out. For the first time it struck him that possibly the forces of man might have checked the first rush of the invaders. He wondered intensely as to that.

During all of that period of hours while the disks had been fighting and killing and terrorizing England, he had not dared to escape from the cabin, for the three guardian disks still hung very low above the hilltop, and the blue ray constantly swept about that summit, marking a path of death. The guardians were taking no chances of anyone tampering with the sand-grain, of doing harm to their own world that lay within that grain.

And now, when the defeated nine returned, he saw that his chances of escape were even less. For except for one disk that dropped down into the pit, dwindling and vanishing, these returned disks took up a position with the watchful three, hovering low over the hilltop. Now and then, one would sweep up into the sky, circle for a time, then return to its position over the summit of Kerachan.

Hunter wondered intensely what the mission of the disk that returned into the sand-grain had been. A call for aid, for reinforcements? The waiting attitude of the others seemed to indicate that.

Dawn had come, and with its gray light he moved silently about the little cabin, finding food in plenty and bolting a hasty, uncooked meal, then returning to his position of observation by the window.

All over the world that day was wonder. The news of the battle over London, of the death that smote the northern cities, had flashed out over all the Earth, bringing surprise and doubt and fear to cities far away. A wave of terror rolled over the British Isles, and already the Channel was crowded with the shipping that bore away the first great crowds of the impending exodus.

The theory of attack by a foreign power had collapsed, and as men examined the crushed, mangled bodies found in the wreckage of the disks at London, they realized that Earth was invaded by creatures wholly different from man, but superior in power. It was but natural that they should conceive these invaders as arriving from another planet, and that was the theory held by all.

In every mind was the thought that the invaders had retired only temporarily, that they would return to spread terror and death again. The disks had been discovered, hovering watchfully over Kerachan Hill, and from all the country about that hill the inhabitants poured forth, choking the roads in their frantic haste to escape from the vicinity. By evening of that day, less than twenty-four hours after the first coming of the disks, it is doubtful if a single living person with the exception of Hunter remained within ten miles of the hill.

It strikes one as curious that the invaders, during all that day, made no effort to destroy or kill in that vicinity. They simply hung above the hill, hovering and circling restlessly, waiting, as it seemed to Hunter. Waiting, he thought, for the return of the messenger who had gone back down into the atomic world.

Once only they struck, late in the day. A force of field artillery had been ordered down from Glasgow with orders to shell the hill that was evidently the base of the invaders. Men and guns and horses rattled south along the rough road, under the hot afternoon sun. High above them a black speck suddenly appeared in the blue, the shape of a watching disk that swept down to investigate. A few ineffectual rifle shots were fired as the disk sank down toward them, then there was a bolting of men into the neighboring fields and hedges, a plunging of panic-maddened horses as the dark shape loomed above. Then the frosty blue Cold Ray, springing down from the disk, leaping swiftly along the road in a trail of icy death, pursuing and exterminating the running men in the fields. A moment the disk hovered and turned, then swept swiftly back up into the blue.

No man in that battery returned to Glasgow to report its fate, and when three planes were ordered south to investigate, none returned. Thereafter no more such futile attempts were made.

That night there was utter darkness in every city in England, for strict orders were given and enforced that no spark of light should betray a city's presence to the invaders. But though in all England, Europe, America, anxious people waited through the night for news of another attack, the disks of the invaders still hovered above Kerachan Hill, waiting, waiting.

In southern England masses of aircraft collected, the combined air power of England and France, awaiting the invaders' return. And through the English roads, meeting and passing the sea-bound masses of refugees, rolled the tanks, the guns, the long brown masses of marching soldiers. Mankind was gathering itself for the struggle, but through all those masses ran an unspoken thought, an unvoiced fear. What avail were rifles and bombs against the smiting ray? Or airplanes and dirigibles against the swift and mighty disks?

On a hilltop, miles away from Kerachan, men lay hidden with powerful telescopes and radio-transmitters, ready to flash word of the invaders' movements to all the Earth. And all the Earth waited tensely for that word, wondering, hoping, fearing.

The bright morning of that day passed, the second since the first night raid of the invaders. And all through that morning no word came from the hidden watchers. Two hours of the afternoon had passed when a message finally came, short, concise. It said only, "Disks are gathering in immense force above Kerachan Hill and are evidently preparing to move."

That message, short as it was, was sufficient to cause the last stable forms of life in England to break up, melt away. Those crowds of people who had remained, hoping against hope, now fought their way madly toward the seacoast to escape, to life. Over those fleeing hordes ran a shout, a threat, a warning. "They are coming!" They called it to one another, autos racing through country villages shouted it, the mobs on the roads voiced it fearfully, soldiers resting by the wayside repeated it thoughtfully, looking toward the north. Over England, over Europe, over the whole world it ran, swiftly, terribly:

"They are coming! They are coming!"

-7-

And now the last great hour of Earth's destiny was swiftly closing down, with that massing of the invaders above the Scottish hills. Crouched beside the window of the cabin, Hunter watched them pouring up from the pit, from their atomic world, masses of tiny disks that grew with inconceivable speed to full size, that moved away and made room for the others to rise. Up, up, up, gigantic masses of the disks, countless hordes of the monsters they held, a vast force of invaders before which all human resistance would be vain, he knew.

After that night of the invaders' first attack on Earth, that night of his imprisoning in the cabin, he had watched through a day and another night and now well into this day, except for a few hours of sleep that he had snatched. Watching, waiting, fearful of the ever-present guardian disks above, like them waiting, waiting. And now this flood of the disks, this up-springing of all their mighty forces. As he gazed at them now, floating up from the pit in dark, endless masses, it seemed to him that the malignant spirit of Powell laughed again beside him.

Boom! Boom! Boom! The rumbling thunder of the expanding disks seemed to him like the sound of a mighty bell, tolling the end of the reign of man. Boom! Boom! Boom!

He glanced up, saw the hundreds of disks above spreading out in a long double line, in an irresistible formation, awaiting the others that were still rising from the pit. But as Hunter watched them circling and forming above, the sky seemed to darken suddenly, the sunlight to be cut off, to vanish. And along the line of invaders above ran a quick start, a sudden nervous shock.

Darker and darker grew the sky, until it seemed to be obscured by a mass of small dark clouds, clouds that drew together, fused, condensed. Smaller and smaller grew that mass of blackness, the sunlight pouring down around its edges. And now it was descending, dropping swiftly down toward the massed disks above, dropping down until it showed itself as not a single mass, but as several, dropping down until he saw that it was five black disks, five that raced toward the line of other disks above. Wonder filled him, and a dawning comprehension. These were disks returning from the super-world, he saw, dwindling down until they entered our own universe—but how came it that only five returned? Five, of the mighty thousands Marlowe had seen, that had attacked the super-world! Were they messengers?

He saw the five race toward the hundreds above, saw them hang with those hundreds for a space of minutes, then confusion seemed to run through the massed disks above, that were suddenly swooping back down to the hilltop. As they sank down to the summit, their numbers darkened the sky, and he saw, without understanding, a mass of their number that seemed to grow smaller, that dwindled and vanished within the pit. Another mass did likewise, and another. They were returning to their own atom! And now Hunter understood, at last.

The five were—*survivors!*

Their attack on the super-world had failed—they were in retreat —retreat from—but look! *Look!*

The sky above was again darkening, even more intensely than before. Even as the disks of the invaders dwindled and sank with frantic haste into the pit, the darkness above was compressing, contracting, resolving into a myriad of dark, long shapes, shapes that swooped swiftly down upon the disordered disks above. Long, black, fishlike hulls, utterly different from the disks of the atomic people. As they came down upon the disks, flashes of violent lightning flickered from the fish-hulls, striking disk after disk, sending them down in whirling masses of bursting flames.

It was the super-people, Hunter knew, pursuing the atomic invaders from their own greater world, where the attack of their mighty fleet of disks had failed.

From the few disks that stood to the terrible attack of the super-people, the blue Cold Ray sprang out sullenly, but at its first appearance the circling, swooping hulls vanished entirely from view. Then from all the air around the disks, flash on flash of lightning stabbed at them. The super-warriors had made themselves invisible.

In panic haste the last few disks sank down toward the pit and the lightning ceased abruptly. It was as though the desire of the attacking super-people was only to force the atomic invaders back down into their own universe. The last few disks dwindled, diminished, vanished into the pit, into the sand-grain, and the last humming sound ceased. The invaders had been swept from the Earth. Running out from the cabin, Hunter saw that the pit was empty of them, and he shouted aloud.

Abruptly the long narrow shapes of the hulls reappeared above, swooping swiftly down upon the hilltop. And with a sudden sense of nearing peril, Hunter fled down the hillside, sinking to the ground when his stiff limbs could carry him no farther. Above, the black hulls were clustered thickly around the hilltop, and the droning of a machine of some sort reached him, then a sudden sharp tapping of metal on metal.

Within a space of minutes, the hulls suddenly swung up from the summit and hovered momentarily, circling. And from one of their number, beneath the rest, swung suspended a glistening globe of shining metal, a ball some three feet in thickness. Even as the awed Hunter comprehended that the super-people had sealed the sand-grain within that shining metal sphere, from all the gathered hulls above, flash after flash of terrific lightning stabbed down toward the hilltop, with a splitting crash, and beneath Hunter the ground heaved and swayed. He staggered to his feet, glimpsed the edge of a narrow, deep abyss in the hilltop created by that blasting force, then saw the ball of metal whirling down into this abyss, holding within it the atomic world, forever. Again, flashed down the lightning, and beneath him was a gigantic rumbling, a grinding and crashing, as the abyss closed, prisoning the ball within its incalculable depths.

Hunter sank again to the ground, his brain turning dizzily. He saw vaguely the dark hulls sweeping back up toward the zenith, dimly saw one of them that swooped down close above him and hung for a moment as if in curiosity, and from the side of this a score of faces peered down at him, faces not unhuman in shape, but unhuman in the high and untroubled serenity that lay on them, faces that seemed to look down at him with a calm benevolence, an amused but kindly pity.

Then that last hull, too, drove up toward the zenith, and all gathered there, expanding, growing, darkening the skies once more, bringing twilight that deepened into blackness, a blackness that hung for a moment, then broke up, dimmed, vanished.

Standing there on the hillside, Hunter raised tremulous hands toward the sunlit sky, as if in gratitude, as if in prayer.

-8-

Sunset illumined Leadanfoot with a glory of orange and crimson light when Hunter reached the village. He walked slowly down the silent, deserted street, and sat down wearily on a bench in front of the inn. With an uncertain smile he remembered his conversation with the innkeeper and wondered where the man was now.

And, too, with a flash of sudden pity, he remembered Marlowe, and their toiling race up the hill. A kindly, honest man he had seemed, one who had probably lived a life of serene content in his quiet museum before fate dragged him into the whirlpool of cosmic war. A war that he had striven to prevent, however powerlessly. And, more somberly, Hunter thought of the other man, of Powell. Well, it was over now, and what could one say of the dead!

As it was, he thought, with those two dead, he was the only man on Earth to know what had really happened. Those others, those millions in the world outside, they would be wondering, doubtful, puzzled, yet thankful, too. Well, soon he would be getting back to that world, to tell them what he knew.

But just now he wanted to sit in the quiet, deserted village, breathing its peace after his two nights and days of nightmare fear and terror. Just now he wanted to sit and listen to little, trivial sounds, the wind that whispered in his ears, the crickets in the long grass.

ORIGINAL PUBLICATION INFORMATION

"The Peacock's Shadow" by E. Hoffman Price originally published in *Weird Tales*, November 1926.

"The White Lady of the Orphanage" by Seabury Quinn originally published in *Weird Tales*, September 1927.

"The Terrible Old Man" by H.P. Lovecraft originally published in *Weird Tales*, August 1926.

"The Woman of the Wood" by A. Merritt originally published in *Weird Tales*, August 1926.

"Bat's Belfry" by August W. Derleth originally published in *Weird Tales*, May 1926.

"The Curse of Everard Maundy" by Seabury Quinn originally published in *Weird Tales*, July 1927.

"The Tomb" by H.P. Lovecraft originally published in *Weird Tales*, January 1926.

"Saladin's Throng Rug" by E. Hoffman Price originally published in *Weird Tales*, October 1927.

"The Dog-Eared God" by Frank Belkhap Long Jr. originally published in *Weird Tales*, Nevember 1926.

"A City of Spiders" by H. Warner Munn originally published in *Weird Tales*, November 1926.

"The Cats of Ulthar" by H.P. Lovecraft originally published in *Weird Tales*, February 1926.

"Back to the Beast" by Manley Wade Wellman originally published in *Weird Tales*, November 1927.

"A Suitor from the Shades" by Greye La Spina originally published in *Weird Tales*, June 1927.

"Pickman's Model" by H.P. Lovecraft originally published in *Weird Tales*, October 1927.

"The Atomic Conquerors" by Edward Hamilton originally published in *Weird Tales*, February 1927.

About the Editors

Jonathan Maberry is a New York Times bestselling author, 5-time Bram Stoker Award-winner, 3-time Scribe Award winner, Inkpot Award winner, and comic book writer. His vampire apocalypse books, V-WARS, was a Netflix original series. He writes in multiple genres including suspense, thriller, horror, science fiction, fantasy, and mystery; for adults, teens and middle grade. His novels include the Joe Ledger thriller series, Bewilderness, Ink, Glimpse, the Pine Deep Trilogy, the Rot & Ruin series, the Dead of Night series, Mars One, Ghostwalkers: A Deadlands Novel, and many others, including his first epic fantasy, Kagen the Damned. He is the editor many anthologies including The X-Files, Aliens: Bug Hunt, Don't Turn Out the Lights, Aliens vs Predator: Ultimate Prey, Hardboiled Horror, Aliens vs Predator, Nights of the Living Dead (co-edited with George A. Romero), and others. His comics include Black Panther: DoomWar, Captain America, Pandemica, Highway to Hell, The Punisher, Bad Blood, among others. He is the president of the International Association of Media Tie-in Writers, and the editor of Weird Tales Magazine. Visit him online at www.jonathanmaberry.com

Kaye Lynne Booth lives, works, and plays in the mountains of Colorado. As a multi-genre author and founder of WordCrafter Writing Enterprises she has compiled and edited anthologies and collections of short fiction and poetry, as well as editing novels, self-help, and spiritual books. Kaye holds an M.F.A. in Creative Writing and is currently seeking an M.A. in Publishing. She was a judge for the

2020 Western Writers of America book awards and currently serves on the editorial team for Western Colorado University and WordFire Press for the *Gilded Glass* anthology.

IF YOU LIKED...

If you liked *Weird Tales Best of the Early Years: 1926–1927,* you might also enjoy:

Weird Tales Best of the Early Years: 1923–1925
Edited by Jonathan Maberry & Justin Criado

The Cthulhu Stories of Robert E. Howard
Edited by M. Scott Lee

War of the Worlds: Global Dispatches
Edited by Kevin J. Anderson

WordFire Classics

The Lost World
The Poison Belt
by A. Conan Doyle

The Wolf Leader
by Alexandre Dumas

The Cthulhu Stories of Robert E. Howard
by Robert E. Howard

The Detective Stories of Edgar Allan Poe
by Edgar Allan Poe

The Jewel of Seven Stars (Annotated)
by Bram Stoker

From the Earth to the Moon and Around the Moon
by Jules Verne

The Complete War of the Worlds
The War in the Air
Kipps: The Story of a Simple Man
The Sleeper Awakes and Men Like Gods
by H.G. Wells

Mother of Frankenstein: Maria: or, The Wrongs of Woman &
Memoirs of the Author of A Vindication of the Rights of Woman
by Mary Wollstonecraft

We: The 100th Anniversary Edition
by Yevgeny Zamyatin

One Stormy Night : A Story Challenge That Created the Gothic Horror
Genre
by Lord Byron, Dr. John William Polidori, and Mary Shelley

HOLIDAY CLASSICS
The Ghost of Christmas Always
by Charles Dickens & Kevin J. Anderson

The Santa Claus Stories
by L. Frank Baum

Our list of other WordFire Press authors and titles is always growing.
To find out more and to shop our selection of titles, visit us at:
wordfirepress.com

Milton Keynes UK
Ingram Content Group UK Ltd.
UKHW041100290923
429627UK00004B/351